Dear Glen

We hope that you enjoy
the magical, wonderful world
of The Enchanted Culture
of Oceania !

Pixie Carlisle
and
R. Marion Troy

The Enchanted Cottage of Oceania

An American Fairytale

A Novel

by R. Marion Troy and Pixie Carlisle

authorHOUSE®

AuthorHouse™
1663 Liberty Drive
Bloomington, IN 47403
www.authorhouse.com
Phone: 1-800-839-8640

Published by AuthorHouse 1/31/2012

ISBN: 978-1-4670-8157-3 (e)
ISBN: 978-1-4670-8158-0 (hc)
ISBN: 978-1-4670-8159-7 (sc)

Library of Congress Control Number: 2011919824

Any people depicted in stock imagery provided by Thinkstock are models, and such images are being used for illustrative purposes only. Certain stock imagery © Thinkstock.

This book is printed on acid-free paper.

Because of the dynamic nature of the Internet, any web addresses or links contained in this book may have changed since publication and may no longer be valid. The views expressed in this work are solely those of the author and do not necessarily reflect the views of the publisher, and the publisher hereby disclaims any responsibility for them.

ACKNOWLEDGEMENTS

This book acknowledges our friend, Serena Medor, who was the source of inspiration for Harper and Leigh, and to Tabitha Samantha Elizabeth ("Tubby Tibby"), our beloved cat, who passed away during the writing of the book, but will live on (and be loved) forever by Harper, Leigh, R. Marion Troy, and Pixie Carlisle. We also appreciate all the readers who have taken the time to give us feedback and comments on the book, particularly Alix, Farah, and Serena Medor, Jonathan Spence, Eva Johnson, Debra Goode, Artis Hampshire-Cowan, Cosette Ryan, Lori Forman, Jacquie Roberts, Michele Williams, Professor Demetrius Venable, Professor Karen Telis, Dr. Tameka Phillips, TiyiMcCorvey, Allison Mitchell, Kyndal Wilson, Lauren Deberry, Claire Cornell, and Pamela Gomez Upegui. To KeiWana and KeiAnna Beckett who found our wonderful illustrator, Nicole Brown. To the Scott and Troy families who have supported our dreams and fancies; and to Ronald Scott, a big brother who taught a little sister how to read when she was only three years old, thereby creating two generations of storytellers who appreciate reading and telling good old-fashioned "tall tales!" A very big THANK YOU from R. Marion Troy and Pixie Carlisle!

The Authors
December 2011

In Memory

This book is lovingly dedicated to Ernest Carlyle Ricks III (1956-1989), our own personal hero who believed that all things are possible, *especially* Enchanted Cottages.

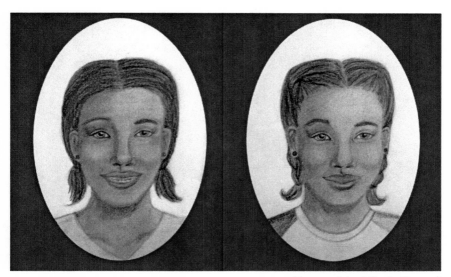

(Artwork by Nicole Brown)

"It's double the giggles & double the grins &

double the trouble if you're blessed with twins!"

— *Anonymous*

PROLOGUE

The steps that led down to the basement were made of unremarkable wood, unpainted and unvarnished. Each step was managed with great care as the pair tried to balance their heavy load. One walked down the steps backwards, chin raised over the box, facing forward, feet carefully feeling their way down, trying desperately to maintain a sense of equilibrium between mind, arms, legs, hands, and back. Although the effort was uncomfortable and unnerving, protecting the thick black box, heavy with its sacred contents, was the first order of business and nothing else mattered. At all costs they had to ensure that it was safe from harm and scrutiny.

A small dim light to the right of the bottom landing revealed a storage apparatus whose wooden slats produced cubbies that were far too narrow to safely contain the box. Reaching the bottom, the box was placed delicately on the slab, gray floor near the storage unit. Buoyed by their success, the pair removed the contents of the box to store the twenty crystal cylinders on their sides, two-by-two, for a total of four in each narrow cubbie. Once completed with that task, they counted the cubbies and discovered room for eighty more cylinders -- a finding that elicited a uniform sigh of contentment at the prospect of such a large cache. The delicious promise of at least eighty more souls being put in secret storage to be used at their disposal was almost more than they could bear in silence.

Settling for a couple of hushed high-fives, the two breathed heavily - IN-OUT-IN-OUT! - as if they had just finished a daring bit of athletics or completed a difficult and torturous Latin conjugation. Theirs was a monumental feat and they were disappointed by the fact that no one else could share their elation. No one else could know what they were doing. No one. They had done their Blood Oath to seal that vow.

As they made their way back up the same uncertain steps towards light and childish laughter, they contemplated the happy thought that soon they would have a total of one hundred innocent souls ensnared for their villainous purposes. And no one would ever suspect them – who would dare? This meant there would be absolutely no escape for the first twenty unfortunate victims. If things went off as planned, none for the next eighty either!

They grinned. In the semi-darkness, the two fourteen-year-olds' braces gleamed like expensive silver bracelets. Life was better than just good. It was, to borrow a phrase from their French tutor, Madame Geneva, 'simply grand'!

Chapter One:
HARPER: Loose Teeth

My name is Harper Leigh Reynolds. I am nearly fifteen years old (if you count the fact that I have only eight months until my birthday). Next year, I plan to have a birthday party so my birthday has obliged by falling on a Friday. How perfect can that be? Friday, June 6th. Of course this date means I'm a so-called out-of-control Gemini. But that's okay because I have company. My identical twin sister, Leigh Harper Reynolds, was born on the same day, but I guess that makes sense, right? Wednesday, June 6, 2000. Our mother, Lydia Winchester Reynolds did not believe in rhyming twin names and refused to call us 'Terri' and 'Sherri' or 'Missy' and 'Sissy' or any other foolish sounding names that remind people of cocker spaniels or French poodles. We Thank God for that. She decided to just flip the names around and guess which one we were on any given day or whatever mood she happened to be in. We look like her. Cinnamon complexions and black licorice eyes shaped like almonds. People say our mother is beautiful and I guess that means that when we outgrow the braces, our too-long arms and elbows, that we won't look half-bad either.

I'm really looking forward to that.

I guess you could say that I am the more serious twin. I believe in hard work while Leigh believes almost exclusively in the maxim that 'those who can -- don't; and those who should, shall.' I guess in her nutty head that means something profound, but my second best-friend and love of my life, Jeremy Fletcher, thinks she's just stuck-up and makes it a point to tell her that often. Which IS often because he's over here nearly every day which is perfectly okay by me, less so by Leigh, and not at all by our nosy neighbor, Miss Pringle. Anyone named after chips should be careful how they tread – at least I would think so. They could get...well...*crushed.*

Right now Jeremy is spread out on my floor, doing push-ups and reading his chemistry book upside down, his long blond hair pulled back into a short ponytail. He says that studying this way gives him motivation. I say it makes him even hotter. He's already on three varsity teams AND is president of the Chess Club. And I've already written my name as Mrs. Jeremy Fletcher in every color marker and in every notebook I've owned since we started dating. Exactly 526 days, 6 hours, and 3 minutes.

"HARPER!!"

That bellow is my mom. She never comes in the house with a simple hug or smile like the fake people you see on T.V. She comes in like a crazy person and things go downhill from there.

"HARPER LEIGH REYNOLDS!"

That means I left something on the stairs. Probably my sweater or some other inoffensive article of clothing that she has turned into something positively demonic. You would think that after running that wretched school of hers, The Enchanted College of Oceania, or Eco, as it is fondly called by the Echoes (the overly creative, frantic, native inhabitants of the school), that all her energy would be used up. Depleted.

Wrong. She actually gets charged up when she gets home.

"Coming!" I yell this back in the hopes it would forestall her entrance into my room.

I don't know if I mentioned that my mother likes Jeremy even less than Miss Pringle, but she does and she lets it show.

Our eyes meet and then hers drop to the floor where Jeremy, oblivious to anything but his count and his sweat, continues to pump his arms and heave off the floor in glorious rhythm.

Mother rolls her eyes.

"Jeremy. I'm sure you have a better way to study than that. Harper. My room."

I jump off the bed and hurry after my mother like a baby duckling, hoping that I look as cute as I did when I was three. My mother is like most mothers and is addicted to our baby pictures. And whenever I'm in trouble, I try as hard as I can to waddle and grin like a toddler. Leigh says it makes me look even more pathetically ridiculous than usual.

"LEIGH!"

Uh-oh. Both of us? All the cute tricks in the world won't help us now. She hardly ever yells at us in tandem. Says it's like screaming at the sisters from *The Shining*.

Leigh tumbles out of her room, yawning. Of course she was asleep. Or, as she puts it, she was recycling her energy for more important occasions than me and what she calls "my unfortunately challenged life."

Please.

Leigh looks at me and I shrug.

"There's no way those stupid Echoes found those containers this fast," she whispers to me in a rush as we make our way to our mother's palatial suite. "They're not that bright and they're all scared of the basement down there."

I sigh, wondering if our little adventure has been discovered. If so, we're toast.

We tap lightly on the door and let ourselves in.

"Is that idiotic boy still here?," Mother whispers, her eyes more like slits than usual.

I nod.

"Then close my door."

Chapter Two:
Leigh: Mirror, Mirror

Mother's room is exactly how I want my bedroom to look one day. It's my dream-come-true room. It has window seats for our cat, Tabitha Samantha Elizabeth – we call her Tibby for short, and a ginormous chaise lounge that is absolute perfection when you're sick and want to be cuddled. Adorable bay windows on one side and a castle-like round at the other. Wow. It's just like being in a Hans Christian Andersen fairytale. It has everything except a fire-breathing dragon and handsome prince. Although there is Jeremy...he's pretty cute. But he belongs to Harper, right? So, I'm not sure that counts for much as far as I go.

Until recently, my love-life had consisted of dramatic online poems from a boy I met in a TeenVillage chat room. His poems always ended with what he called Conversations with God. Deep. He told me he was thinking of becoming a priest and at fifteen he was ready to commit his life to two things other than God. Me and Batman. He let it slip the other day that he used to watch the original Batman show when he was little. He went on and on about it. Sent his avatar with tears spouting out at the memory of a particular episode of the Caped Crusader with Cat Woman. In other words, he wasn't remembering watching re-runs on the Family Channel like the rest of my friends. He was reliving the memory of how he had experienced the real thing – like in the 1960s? I online searched the show just to be sure of the time zone and did some quick math. Poem Boy was definitely more like fifty than fifteen. EEK! He was an Old Man.

Disappointed but determined to not become a dating-an-online-stranger-and-about-to-be-stabbed-to-death-in-a-park statistic, I changed my avatar and my user name after that piece of vital information and stayed out of TeenVillage. After I dropped Old Man, my girlfriend, Lacy, told me in a huff that I'm 'too strong', 'too opinionated' and would probably end up an old maid with my cat, Tibby, in a house without windows or doors. I tried to picture how I would get into a house without windows or doors and then I remembered who I was talking to and decided it wasn't worth the visual effort. In typical Reynolds fashion, I told her what Harper would have said. SHUT UP.

Mother cleared her throat and I was back to reality. She was sitting in her favorite paisley armchair, studying us as if we were pieces of rare art. Or a pile of manure. At any rate, she seemed intense. Her deep brown eyes were as watchful as a cat. And I didn't have to try to figure out who was the prey.

I like to pretend that because of Mother's exquisite interior design tastes - that just so happen to mimic my own - that she likes me the best. But I know better.

Most of the time, she can barely tell us apart.

"Sit down. One in one chair and one in the other."

This is her attempt to remember who was which. When we were younger, she used to put different colored ribbons in our hair, but after she figured out that we were switching them, she gave up.

We were four.

Mother faces us, her expression more grim than usual.

"I think you need to tell me what's going on."

I think I will faint. Fall right out. Onto the floor. I wonder fleetingly if fourteen-year-olds have heart attacks.

"What do you mean, Mommy?" That was Harper, trying to look and sound three.

Mother glares at her. I mean, really. Harper has yet to figure out that Mother does not fall for on-cue cuteness. But that never seems to deter Harper. She just keeps trying. She is nothing if not persistent.

"I mean THIS!!"

Mother is waving a piece of paper that has our school logo on it.

Anything coming from the Academy of the Sacred Names, addressed to our Mother, is not good.

I blink, struggling to figure out what Harper has done wrong – beyond our little joint adventure. Nine times out of ten, this is a purely Harper Problem. Something that should be prosecuted in a court of law, but is usually dismissed by the Sacred Names' Mother Superior Katherine Dominguez as grounds for two weeks of detention and an additional thirty days of service to the Sacred Names community – washing floors, running errands for the nuns, and free babysitting services for the lay teachers. In other words, slave labor. That place should really be renamed: Academy of the Sacred Names Penal Colony.

"It says that the two of you – the TWO of YOU –" Mother always repeats anything involving the two of us twice – as if we each need to hear the same thing separately, " — have been accused of taking items from the chemistry lab without permission. Is that true?"

Unfortunately, it was. How else were we supposed to contain our abducted souls? Put them in sandwich bags? Crystal cylinders seemed so much more logical – and for me - ascetically pleasing.

I could hear Harper's brain working. Not a good sign.

"Mother?" I raise my hand as if I were in class.

Mother glares at me and nods.

"I think there's been a misunderstanding. Harper and I are

working on an experiment. I think Dr. Krass simply forgot that our science fair project was so...involved. So sophisticated."

Mother allows the paper to rest on her knees while she bores holes in our faces.

"And what precisely does this project entail?"

Harper jumps in. Against my better judgment, she talks.

"It's TOP SECRET. No one must know. Mommy, please?!"

Mother tilts her head, studying Harper with that intense look she usually reserves for certain members of our father's family – down to the tight smile and uplifted eyebrow.

"Including me?" was her only comment which I consider a good thing given Harper's utterly foolish outburst.

I watch Harper giggle and squirm. I could tell she thought she was being delightfully cute again. I couldn't stand another second of ridiculous – pathetically ridiculous - toddler-like behavior.

"Mother, we would rather not discuss our scientific pursuits – even with you – our financial benefactress." I was on a roll and knew she'd appreciate recognition of her hefty commitment to our private school education. "Because we feel that it would compromise the nature of our project and the integrity of our commitment to produce something that will one day be considered completely revolutionary. We are on the verge of a scientific breakthrough – a discovery of monumental importance!"

Mother smiles at this. I could tell she appreciated the elevated use of language. If we had to plead our case, she liked the fact that it was done using good vocabulary.

"I'll have a talk with Dr. Krass tomorrow. We'll see what can be worked out."

That meant that Dr. Krass would back off. I pictured him in his spectacles and ill-fitting chemistry lab coat that hung on his almost skeletal frame like a white shroud basking in our mother's beauty and glowing, confident smile. No one said 'no' to Mother – or at least, hardly ever – when she wanted a 'yes.' And, if nothing else, she wanted us to stretch our minds, our imaginations. And she would fight to see that we had that chance – something she considered our birthright.

Good for her. Little did she know how much we were stretching.

"Okay, girls. You may go."

We rise in unison and watch her fond expression change to one of mild rebuke. She has told us repeatedly that twin behavior could be unnerving at times and that we should try harder to act independently to appear less – well - *sinister.* The fact that we look like mirror images was bad enough as far as she was concerned, but to act as one person with one body and mind was incomprehensible.

12

As we walk out, I turn to wave jauntily, glad to end the conversation ahead of the game.

"Harper. Leigh."

I had celebrated too soon. I should have kept my hand down.

"Whatever it is that you're doing - just don't blow us up, okay? I rather like this old house. And the people in it."

I grin. Mother is funny. And sometimes very sweet.

"We do, too, Mother. Not to worry."

We close the door behind us and lean against it for support. Harper slides to the floor, sucking in air.

My problem wasn't breathing, it was thinking. What were we going to do now? We need those extra containers, but with Dr. Krass on our heels, it will be impossible to borrow more without explanation.

"We simply must find more containers, Harp. The question is where?"

I knew I was whispering to myself. Harper was practically incoherent. She could only shake her head from side to side. Too spent from the recent Inquisition with Mother to say anything more. I sit down beside her, putting her hand into mine. Understanding, like only a twin can, everything she is feeling without a need for words.

Chapter Three:
ECO

The Enchanted College of Oceania, or Eco, as it is fondly called, was built on a hill overlooking the Atlantic. It was the restored mansion of a local family of rather dubious distinction. Once owned by the then-distinguished J. Lawrence Winthrop family, it was a house that most would agree was quite beautiful. But those same people would also agree that it had never been what one would call a real home. Legend (and supporting police documents) had it that upon returning home early from a European business trip back in the spring of 1920, Mr. J. Lawrence Winthrop had had the unfortunate experience of catching Mrs. J.L. Winthrop in the arms of the family chauffeur. Neither one was near the family car at the time, Mrs. Winthrop was in perfect health and not at all prone to fainting spells, so no plausible explanation beyond what was obvious could be provided. Not one to resort to polite conversation and negotiation (the Winthrops had made a fortune on selling firearms and for being particularly ferocious in the War Between the States), the Man of the House went promptly into his study, returned with a pistol, and shot both his wife and his driver quite dead before turning the gun on himself.

It had caused a great scandal in the small town of Oceania, Maryland but after an embarrassingly short period of time, people forgot. Only thirty miles away from the nation's capital, Oceania was too close to Washington, D.C. and the more dramatic scandals of congressmen and their wives to worry about a rather pedestrian crime involving a spurned husband and his wayward wife and chauffeur. The spectacles in the District of Columbia always drowned out the tinny clamor of local Oceania gossip – even the Winthrop scandal. The local Oceania News only ran the story for a week, but to its credit, the News did have a few pictures of all three parties (in happier times) and even one shadowy photograph of the crime scene itself. But, even the most morbid fascination for Eloise and J.L faded after less than a month. After all, it was far more interesting to see the mighty fall on Capitol Hill than in a house on some obscure hill in Oceania.

No one would have remembered that the event had even occurred at all until Lydia Winchester Reynolds, and her husband, Manchester "Chester" Stuart Reynolds had decided twelve years ago to excavate the ruins of the once-lovely Winthrop estate and turn it into a school for Children and Young People with Exceptional Abilities. It was to be a training ground for children of eclectic ages and abilities in which the youngest pupil was just four and the oldest was a robust twenty-two.

The application process had been simplified by the strict requirements of the school. Each candidate had to prove that they were, in some fashion, quite different from their peers in their resident schools or universities. These differences did not have to be obvious, but they did have to be proven. Children did not have to demonstrate their distinctions in-person necessarily, but it was encouraged for everyone to showcase their exceptional abilities in video or other types of creative multimedia devices and to send them as attachments to their written applications. Considered quite extraordinary, this multimedia library, a compilation of all accepted applications, was to be preserved for its potential utility as a future recruitment tool. Incoming students signed waivers regarding its uses and Eco retained sole and exclusive rights over the properties. The applications were maintained in a sealed vault in a secret place because the information was considered to be proprietary and confidential.

With a booming number of applications – nearly three thousand! – Chester and Lydia were quite pleased regarding their joint venture and felt that everything was going along according to plan. The first six days were a lovely combination of grade-bonding activities and museum and theater trips into D.C. It was on the seventh day that

that the Sightings started and things started to go NOT According To Plan.

First, a Sighting of Eloise Winthrop, wearing a blood-stained gown was seen on the east wing stairs as students were making their way to and from classes. At first, everyone assumed that Lydia and Chester (the students all called the Reynolds by their first names in the manner of most progressive schools) had hired an actress to depict the history of the house. Creative and fitting for Eco. The Echoes were very much appreciative until the so-called actress portraying Eloise let out a blood-curdling shriek and raised her arm to attack the nearest student. The fact that the Eloise before them glowed a type of sickening yellow-white-blue color was frightening enough, but when the apparition's cold grasp settled on the arm of an unlucky student, it was simply too much. Her touch sent a frigid cold right through to the bone of the young boy, who promptly threw up his breakfast and fainted, tumbling down the long staircase to the bottom landing. There was generalized panic as the younger children who had seen what had happened were desperate to get away. Shrieking "Don't touch ME! Don't touch ME!," they ran like rats before fire. The children who had not witnessed anything at all were even more terrified as their imaginations ran wild with what *could* have happened. They were, oddly enough, even more frantic than the others to flee. Hysteria gripped Eco like a noose around a horse thief's neck and Chester had been forced to dash to the Tower at the top of the house and ring the emergency bell to calm things down.

Much to his delight, the emergency drills over the last several days worked. Everyone pushed their way out onto the massive front yard and stood at attention by class grade as they had been trained. One of the college-aged boys had the decency to carry the young victim out in his arms to the grassy area, and hold him, like a limp and stricken calf, as they awaited instructions from the Tower.

Chester had been masterful. On a loud speaker, he had confidently explained the meaning of the ghost, the facts about spiritual awakenings, and the knowledge that he and Lydia had Everything Under Control and There Was No Need to Worry. He asked everyone to file back in quietly to their classes and to not pay any attention at all to the appearance of Eloise Winthrop, or any other Winthrops for that matter.

Those instructions were obeyed without hesitation from most of the student population. Seven-year-old Jamie Putnam, the actual (and only) victim of Eloise's touch, was carried to safety and was made to lay down with a cloth over his face in the nursery for the remainder of the day. His reward was a large banana shake – his favorite - and a soothing story that had nothing but good things in it. No witches or evil fairies. Just kindly giants and adventurous boys who always came out on top. No matter what.

The incident was almost forgotten by all, with the exception of one child, twelve-year-old Finch Coakley Stevens. He was unconvinced that Eloise was harmless and had made up his mind in as much time as it had taken Eloise to appear that he would get to the bottom of her so-called spiritual awakening. He would figure out how to make sure she – and any others like her – stayed asleep. Permanently. His father was a Southern Methodist minister from Georgia, who had drilled the Scriptures in the boy's head from the Old and New Testaments until Finch was a walking-talking Bible – from Genesis to Revelation he could tell you chapter, verse, and meaning from various perspectives and in a variety of languages (King James, NIV, Reformed, Jewish Orthodox, Hebrew, Greek, and Latin). Drawing upon his impressive knowledge of the Old and the New Testaments, young Finch had figured out what must be done and was more than prepared. He had decided that he, and he alone, would exorcise that hellish woman from Eco. And he was ready, like King David, to do it with just a slingshot of faith if necessary.

While the red-headed Finch perched quietly in his room, waiting for his opportunity, fortifying himself with the bread of knowledge contained in his many Bibles, the Reynolds rejoiced in the fact that all seemed to return to normal at Eco. Their happiness was shattered less than a week later when the second, and even more startling, Sighting occurred.

It was in the afternoon of the tenth day of the school's opening – three days after Eloise's unsightly appearance. Finch Coakely Stevens had been troubled. His nightly prayers did not seem to be working as planned. He had hoped that Eloise would be driven out on a spear of fire, cast down into the depths of hell and that he, Finch Coakley Stevens, would stand at the pinnacle of her descent reciting from Psalm 23 in a steady, calm, authoritative voice. And then, he would move on to his next favorite Psalm. Psalm 37.

Nothing of the sort occurred.

It was at three o'clock when the afternoon snack bell chimed that the Sighting took place. It was in the lunchroom and it was more of a spectacle than anyone could have possibly imagined.

Kara Linson, an adorable six-year-old girl with braids, skin like chocolate cashmere, and hazel eyes was sipping her juice carefully (as was her habit) when she looked up and saw the man. At first, she smiled. Why not? He wasn't particularly bad to look at and she was taught to be polite to strangers. But then her tummy started to hurt because she didn't like the look on the man's face and it made her nervous. He looked...anxious and fidgety. Like someone who needs to go to the bathroom.

"Your name is Kara, right?"

Kara looked around the room, wondering if any of her classmates could see what she was seeing. Everyone was laughing and chatting carelessly. One boy was forcing milk from his nose while his friends looked on laughing hilariously.

"Bobby?" Kara's voice sounded small in her ears. "Do you see this man?" Six-year-old Bobby was sitting right next to her. He kept laughing, a sure indication that he had not heard a word Kara was saying.

"Bobby can't see me. But you can, Kara. I'm talking to you. It's not nice to not speak to people when they are speaking to you."

Kara spotted the figure of Eloise on the opposite side of the room. She appeared to be trying to water the plants, without a watering can, her blood-soaked gown trailing behind her. Kara saw the man stiffen like a hunting dog on point after spotting quarry. He reached in his pocket, pulled out a gun and –

Kara screamed. It was a piercing shriek that ripped her out of the bubble in which J.L. Winthrop had encased her, back to her own time and space. The shriek of a girl so afraid that speech failed her and the only form of communication was as primitive as nature.

Finch figured out before the others what was happening.

"Kara!" he commanded. "Point them out!"

Kara pointed to the far wall, covering her ears to shelter them from the sound of a pistol being fired over and over and over. Hate roared from the gun, riding side-saddle on the phantom bullets.

Finch rushed over to the wall, pulled out a vial of holy water and began to spray it, like perfume, all over the wall. Screaming out verses from the Bible, shrieking in Latin, the horrified cafeteria watched as the wall turned blood-red.

"Stop it!"

That was Lydia, who had entered the room, unnoticed by the frightened students.

Finch turned to the headmistress.

"But I can do this! Please, Lydia!" He was red-faced, panting.

Lydia took the vial from the boy's hand and placed it on the floor. She settled her hands on Finch's shoulders.

"Leave it to us, Finch. Chester and I will handle things from here. Okay?"

The boy nodded. His head was held down, and he was fighting back tears of humiliation.

Lydia embraced him quickly and then released him at the urgent sound of the Tower bell.

Everyone raced outside except for Lydia, who broke with protocol and ran upstairs to the Tower. She wanted to talk to Chester and find out what more they could do to free themselves of the warring Winthrops. She had a sinking feeling in the pit of her stomach that something was terribly wrong. She sniffed the stench of Evil and quickened her pace. The Tower was empty. There was only the bell itself and the rope swinging back and forth, back and forth. Silent and alone.

Manchester Stuart Reynolds had vanished and no one, not Lydia, not the twins, or any other family members, has had the good fortune of seeing him since.

※

On occasion, Lydia visits the Tower, looking for clues. But twelve years later, she has turned up nothing. No note. No article of clothing. No explanation. No sign of hope.

To Lydia's knowledge, the Winthrops have never appeared again and there have been no more Sightings of them at Eco.

But the ongoing search for Chester has continued. To Lydia's credit, she tries to do it quietly, so Harper and Leigh will not worry too much. She wants them to have as normal a childhood as possible – play, laugh, learn, and grow to be normal girls. She wants that so much for them that she often hides deep within herself from them so they can never realize the depths of her despair. Her somber, almost professorial exterior, is a façade for the racing emotions she feels on any given day, but she strikes a balance between sanity and insanity for their sakes. Dinner still has to be prepared, bills paid, and laundry washed.

But what Lydia doesn't know is that the twins are well-aware of their Mother's heartbreak. Their mother's solitary quest to find Chester is now being conducted by other concerned Reynolds family members.

Harper Leigh. Leigh Harper.

Like their mother, they are determined to find their father and they are resolutely driven to do it by whatever means necessary. Right or wrong. Good or bad. Evil or Just. They are doing this not so much for themselves – they were less than three years old when Chester disappeared and can just barely remember him - they are doing this for their mother, Lydia.

But, from my point of view, it really doesn't matter why they are doing it, or for whom.

My job, my only job, is to STOP THEM.

Chapter Four:
Window Dressing

The Academy of the Sacred Names is a puzzle-work of add-on buildings and gardens that were built rather hastily after World War II in recognition that the growing population of Catholic and other well-to-do girls of Oceania needed somewhere to strain their intellects, and the patience of teachers, beyond the local public school. Never intended to service more than one hundred students in any given year, the buildings were originally of modest size and the design of the main teaching hall was a reflection of that objective. It had a chapel with stained glass windows, a modern upright piano for Mass and private lessons, and pews with standard prayer benches. It had a severe but quiet beauty that seemed in keeping with its purpose – to train and educate young girls to become good wives, mothers, and community stewards. There was no expectation that Sacred Names graduates would aspire to more than that. Girls with loftier ambitions were sent to schools in Washington, D.C., New York, or Boston. Neither Sacred Names nor Oceania encouraged female empowerment beyond the traditional confines of Home and Family.

Ten years after the school's creation, sentimental alumni whose young husbands had perished in the Korean War, started a fund called the Sacred Names War Widows Building Endowment. Bereft too soon of happiness, and filled with misdirected purpose, these young war widows had pooled their rather significant war pensions together to proudly produce a circular driveway for the more worldly nuns who were able to drive their cars into the marketplace of Oceania to purchase goods for the Community. This invention allowed the nuns the opportunity to transport heavy purchases to the front of the school rather than down by the stables as had been the unhappy custom.

After another decade passed, and borrowing on the earlier generation of Korean War benefactors, Vietnam era widows brought the school even more technological advances. A gazebo was added for charm and the never used stables were converted to art studios. Lighting was installed to make the galleries even more appealing to budding, but mediocre Sacred Names' artistic talent, who were able to enjoy the generosity of alumnae whose own hopes of youthful happiness had been obliterated in places with strange and exotic southeast Asian names like Phnom Penh and Ha Long. Photographs of the generations of young war widows adorn the walls of the art center and are sized according to largesse. An oil painting of the flaccid, unattractive face of the biggest donor (whose late husband's family donated a half million dollars in his name), a Mrs. Dudley Alistair Pendergrast (a widow at twenty-two from the Korean War), peers down haughtily upon girls as they enter the center. 'Miss Dud' is the disrespectful appellation most often used to refer to the painting, as in "Meet me by Miss Dud" as shorthand for "Meet me at the entrance to the art center." The nuns pretend not to hear the nomenclature used for one of the school's most generous donors, and the girls try to be careful, but youthful exuberance usually gets the better of them and there has been more than one occasion where girls are overheard excitedly directing others to "Meet at Dud's after lunch!"

Despite its rather awkward history and haphazard architecture, the Academy of the Sacred Names is still sometimes a lovely place to see.

But, depending on one's point of view, not necessarily a lovely place to learn.

"Harper Reynolds? I am assuming that it is Harper and not Leigh today?"

I play with the thought of becoming Leigh for a moment. She is hardly ever on detention – a place where I seem to have taken up semi-permanent residence, but I figure that given the class (art) and the teacher (Sister Mary Ellen), I'm safe being who I am for now.

"It's Harper, Sister."

Sister Mary Ellen is one of those nuns who would look like a nun even in a mini-skirt and knee-high boots. It was that strange look in her eyes. Some people call it other-worldly. I say spooky. Like she's looking at you, but her mind is already in heaven polishing halos, dusting off harps, or whatever it is that nuns do when they get there.

"I was hoping you could tell us why this particular painting is not from the Botticelli era."

SHE was hoping?

I squint at the painting on the screen, wondering why we cared at all about knowing who painted stuff we would never in life hang on our walls? Even if I live to be a thousand years old, most of this stuff will NEVER EVER be in my house. The faces are pale and hostile, the eyes are screaming scary, and the clothes and hairstyles are positively hideous. Like something I would never wear - not even for Halloween.

Not to mention that some of these same people, who seem to be glaring back at me – correction – ARE glaring back at me, are now encased in crystal containers in the bowels of Eco.

"Because it comes from the 18th century?," I venture. Sister Mary

Ellen usually cuts me some slack. If I don't know something she doesn't just look at me with her lip curled, like Sister Margaret Anna. Or hold her breath like Sister Virginia. She just smiles and gives that far-away look like she's receiving guidance from Someone Else and then nods.

I'm not disappointed. She smiles at me and nods.

"Thanks for the effort, Harper. But, that's not right. Who here knows the answer?"

A lot of hands go up. Of course. People without hot boyfriends and captured souls in the bottoms of their Mother's school house have time to study dead people's art. I would be able to answer that question, too, if I hadn't had to help Jeremy memorize equations for his chem exam and listen to Leigh agonize over "WHAT TO DO?! WHAT TO DO?!" until two o'clock in the morning, when her vocal cords finally gave way and she conked out in my room. I mean, really. I, too, would know the differences between Botticelli and Leonardo Dicaprio – I mean da Vinci – if this was the comparison between a supernova and a black hole. Astronomy, not art, is my thing . A note is tossed at me from some unknown source, landing on my desk like a small sigh. I open it.

I HATE YOU.

I don't have to guess who this is. Not even for a second. I cross out the period and scribble four letters to add to the violent, unoriginal thought.

I HATE YOU BACK is how it now reads. I fold it over and toss it in the general direction of Meredith Ford. A girl as ugly, and as rich, as Miss Dud.

Meredith's hand shoots up.

"Sister Mary Ellen!," her bright blue eyes are like azure firecrackers. "Harper is throwing things at me!"

Sister Mary Ellen smiles patiently, once again receiving distant, far-away Instructions.

"I believe," she says evenly, but with a small pointed smile, "that Harper was returning something to you?"

Score another point in heaven for Sister Mary Ellen. And between you and me, she deserves more than cleaning duty Up There. I mean, if I have a say. Let somebody else fold the towels.

Meredith puts her hand down and just clenches her teeth. I can practically feel her molars grinding from where I sit.

"Class, I will be giving a quiz on this next week, so I would appreciate if everyone (she looks directly at me) would pay attention to my lecture today. Mary, please turn on the lights. We have work to do."

Sister Mary Ellen turns her back to us and I take this opportunity to hold up three fingers (my pointer, middle, and ring fingers) and mouth for Meredith to 'read between the lines.'

My friends, the few that I have, snicker.

Meredith scribbles something quickly on the note she had tossed to me, unfolds it and holds it out infront of her face for all to see:

I HATE YOU BACK MORE!

"So did you see anymore interesting faces?"

Leigh has a nerve. It was bad enough that I had to sit for ninety minutes in that art room filled with some of the faces of people whose souls I had stolen, but she wants to know if I've found NEW ones!

"No. I did not."

My sister rolls her eyes at me as if to say that I'm a slackard. A do-nothing slouch. But I want to ask her just who stole those first twenty souls and made it possible for Project C (Project Chester) to even happen? It certainly wasn't Miss Talky-Talky Until Two a.m. It was me. Harper Leigh. Miss Ready Reynolds.

Please. Me. All by my lonesome.

"I am not in the mood to fight with those people right now!" I hiss back to her, exhausted at even the thought of repeating what I had done just a few days ago.

"Fine."

Leigh flounces away as if my refusal to do her bidding has wrecked her appetite and she can't sit for another minute in my disappointing presence to finish her lunch.

I happen to know better. I polish off her tuna sandwich. She hates tuna and has already eaten her dessert. I can only tolerate tuna myself (I mean we are identical in most things), but when I'm hungry I eat everything in front of me that's not currently going into someone else's mouth. If it's on their fork or spoon, they're safe. Otherwise – watch out.

Mother calls it our Growth Spurt. I guess she's right. We've shot up two inches in as many months.

Another note lands right in the middle of my chocolate pudding.

I open it. Knowing the source and guessing at the venom.

I'm right on both counts.

GO BACK TO AFRICA.

I laugh out loud. I cross that out and scribble something of my own.

This time, I get up and hand carry it over to Meredith, whose mouth falls open in fear. I can see the chocolate pudding on her tongue and dark smudges on the corners of her thin lips. The overall affect only makes her look even more ugly and gross, but I maintain my composure.

I hold out my hand for her to take the note. After a few seconds, she snatches it from my palm and opens it. Her face turns the color of the tomato soup she has on her tray and she jumps up from the table and runs out of the cafeteria, pulling her cell phone out of her pocket as she escapes.

I watch, amused.

"What on earth did you write, Harper?," her best friend, and unfortunate look-alike, Suzie Baker, demands imperiously.

"Ask *her*." I turn on my heel and return to devour my lunch, feeling as satisfied as I am satiated from the double meals.

I applaud myself, remembering what I wrote but wondering if it would get me into more trouble than it was worth. I had pictures of Sister Mary Ellen in my head as I had written it. I'm not sure if that argument would save me, but it was at least an honest start.

In scrawling letters, I had written:

I'M YOUR SISTER. ASK OUR FATHER.

I knew that I meant it the way Sister Mary Ellen, and the other nuns who taught us theology, had always said to us. We are all Sisters in Christ and we all share Our Heavenly Father, but I know how Meredith who watches soap operas and the re-runs of soap operas will take it. Her feeble brain will think it means that I am her real sister from some illicit affair her father had with a - cover your eyes! - Black Woman. Which meant that she will inherit *two* illicit African

American sisters – and identical twins at that! Of course it had been too much for her fragile nerves. Just the thought of something that she would consider as perverse as all of that had been enough to send her into hysterics. Good!

I laugh quietly. This was a small, but important victory. In this most recent skirmish, I was without question, the champion. Ooh-la-la!

But my joy, like most things in my life, is short-lived. I know that I will need to hold on to my quick sense of humor (and better still – quicker feet) because as I see Sister Virginia barreling towards me with a triumphant and smirking Meredith at her flank, I fully comprehend that neither Sister nor student is headed my way with the intention to provide me with hugs or kisses. To borrow from Leigh: This was Definitely Not Good.

What a bowl of jelly beans!

Chapter Five:
Jeremy Fletcher and the House of Cards

Mrs. Penelope Fletcher has flowing strawberry-blonde hair that clings to her slender waist like a fairy in a story book. Although her eyes are a shining emerald green, they are as tightly shuttered as the tower window at the top of Eco. As hard as you try to see in, you find that she can only see out. No one has ever been able to plumb the depths of those marble green eyes and people have long stopped trying. Rumor has it that her piercing stare, if fixated on someone in particular for too long, is sometimes enough to send that unfortunate individual into a type of panic attack. So people have learned over the years to not look directly at her. Like an eclipse, she is given only surreptitious, nervous glances. No one but Jeremy has ever been able to reach deeper than the surface of her expressions and even he is starting to get less and less lucky in seeing the true Penelope as he gets older, more worldly, and grown-up. His mother seems to be drifting further and further out of everyone's reach, operating in an orbit all her own.

She is a tallish woman – nearly five-foot-ten, and not what you would call approachable. There was that distance in her eyes, her manner, and her tone. You felt that you had her undivided attention if you were amusing, but otherwise you, and everything around you, were a bore and not to be seriously regarded for very long. She was known for just walking away - even when people were in the middle of a sentence or a syllable.

Upon meeting Mrs. Fletcher for the first time, Harper had called her Out Loud (and not in her head where it was probably better suited) a NITWIT and Jeremy had nervously, with stricken eyes, asked Harper what she had meant by that rather inflammatory remark. Harper had calmly explained in typical Harper fashion that "NIT meant someone who looked like a Nun-In-Training and WIT meant With-Interesting-Talents – making his mother a NITWIT. A Nun-in-Training-With-Interesting-Talents. Duh."

Penelope had burst into tinkling laughter, something Jeremy had not heard since he was ten, a full four years ago. He had beamed, utterly delighted over the unexpected transformation of his mother and her acceptance of the girl he adored.

"Do come back anytime, dear," she had offered to Harper, who was nonplussed by the outburst (as she was so accustomed to strange behavior in her own home – not to mention at Eco). "You are too amusing! Nothing like Jerry's other friends. Besides," she had said this over her shoulder, giving them both a meaningful look as she made her way out of the room, "If the two of you do marry one day, I must say that I've always thought that mixed-race children are simply the most lovely of all!"

Penelope had trailed off, her long green dress sweeping against her delicate, ballerina-thin ankles, its hem swirling about her feet like the crusted top of a pistachio-flavored ice cream cone.

Jeremy knew in that moment, as he had always known, that one day, Harper Leigh Reynolds would be his wife. No matter what it took, he would make that happen.

That crystal clear intention was openly declared (at least in his mind) two years ago at that meeting with his mother and Harper. And now at sixteen, Jeremy thought it was time for his father (who did not wear long dresses, give hypnotic stares, and twirl elegantly around the house) to accept Harper as his intended once and for all.

Unlike his wife, Mr. Graydon Fletcher had both feet on the ground and his alternating navy blue, black, or gray pin-striped suits were indicative of that. He did not find Harper particularly amusing. He thought she was attractive enough for a child with a crazy mother, but he had a "Problem with anyone associated with that oddly named, God-awful school." Even after a decade of harboring a grudge against the school, the City Council, and the family known as Reynolds, Graydon refused to completely surrender his belief that "Eco should be demolished."

Ten years ago (long before he ever laid eyes on Harper Leigh), he had offered this sentiment at the City Council meeting (of which he was, at least at that time, its chairman). He had urged the Council to take the action of eradicating Eco from Oceania, but before he could recite his argument, he was drowned out by Eco supporters and stalwarts who showed up in mass protest, waving banners, petitions, wearing Birkenstocks (most of whom displayed bare feet in sore need of a proper pedicure), screaming what he felt to be insane obscenities at him:

"Book Murderer! Building killer! School assassin!"

WHAT??!!! BOOK murderer? Graydon's head was spinning.

This rambunctious disruption to the normally orderly City Council session over a bizarre academic institution, and even stranger family (the Reynolds), had created more fuss than when prominent financier, J. L. Winthrop had shot his wife, Eloise in cold blood in front of their house – the very same place that was now the subject of this most recent inquiry. The Oceania News reporter, half-asleep in his reserved council chair marked MEDIA woke up with a start and started taking rapid notes and a few pictures, for good measure, to post in the next day's paper.

Graydon was furious.

Six-year-old Jeremy had watched his normally stoic father shrink before the massive verbal onslaught.

"Hitler! Genghis Khan! NAPOLEON!"

The insults buzzed about Graydon's ears like angry hornets. No Oceania police came forward to prevent or stop the barrage of loud, angry protests. Other council members looked at Graydon in horror and then to each other for comfort. Their eyes betrayed their thoughts. This chaos was all his fault. They had nothing to do with this!

One of the council members, a Charles Alexander Leeks, who had been vying for Graydon's place as chairman for the last two years, grabbed the gavel and banged it hard, hard, HARD on the wooden table.

"Come to order!," he shouted, his face bristling with emotion. "Please, good citizens of Oceania! Come to order!"

Quiet fell over the crowd, who tired of standing and out of breath from shouting, had already started to quietly fill the rows of public benches.

Graydon had felt his power slip away at the same moment as Charles Alexander hammered his way to power. Jeremy had watched as his father's face drained of all color and thought it was the only time in his young life that he had seen his father look almost... human.

There was an uneasy quiet following this show of political will and Charles Alexander Leeks used this moment to completely seize control of the situation and the City Council in one opportune swoop.

"We don't want to close Eco, do we, good people?"

"NO!" was the unified shout.

"We don't want to harm our dear friend, Lydia Reynolds, who has lost her husband and is doing her best to raise six hundred orphans. Do we?"

This was a bit much for most Oceanians to digest all at once. There was the fact that Chester Reynolds was indeed lost. Unlike most ne'er-do-well husbands, he had not run off with some fashion model, nanny, or secretary. He had vanished at the sound of the emergency bell in the Tower. Like a wisp of smoke he had completely vaporized into thin air. And it wasn't really true that the children of Eco were orphans. Most came from wealthy families from around the country and a handful were even resident on the outskirts of Oceania. There may be one or two runaways, but they were not the normal profile of Eco students, who were careful to have only one abnormal trait.

Most Oceanians were proud of Eco. Parents dropping off their unusual offspring every fall spent a lot of money in town, buying groceries, clothes, and Oceania memorabilia to take back home to share with younger or older children who had been unable (or unwilling) to make the trip. That was not an insignificant tourist investment and the shopkeepers of Oceania were delighted to see the start of each new Eco school season.

After a few seconds of digesting this faulty information, cries of protest once again populated the air with vigorous "NO! No, we don't! NO! No! NO!" And then to be absolutely sure that no one was confused as to what it was they were disclaiming, one forthright gentleman stood up and declared: "We do NOT want to close the school! WE LOVE ECO!"

This promoted a round of applause and choruses of the same:

"WE LOVE ECO! WE-LOVE-ECO! WELOVEECO!!" The three words condensed into one and there was much whooping and hollering, stomping, and shouting. Sturdy Birkenstocks joined the cacophony on the floor with flirty stilettos and sensible gentlemen's loafers. Thumperumparumpa! was the agitated sound of triumphant feet that kept time with their chants.

Satisfied that enough belligerent noise had rattled the Council chamber, Charles Alexander watched greedily as Graydon leaned back into the comfort of the chairman's chair, wondering how much more time needed to elapse before that seat was finally his own to claim. As if reading his mind, Graydon had cast a baleful eye at his rival before turning to the crowd.

"Eco is an abomination!," he had roared, no longer caring for the consequences.

The crowd had gone beserk. They rose in unison like a huge wave and Graydon conceded to the crest of their fury. Jumping down from the bench, he lunged for his terrified son, and throwing the young Jeremy over his shoulder like a bag of flour, tore out of the hall like a raging bull.

"Please come to order! People of Oceania, please settle down! Listen to ME!" Charles Alexander's plea was the last thing Graydon heard from the chamber as chairman of Oceania. He had never returned to the council chamber or City Hall. He would have moved from Oceania altogether except Penelope, speaking to him on condition that it was for "This One Time Only," said in Very Definite Terms that she and Jerry were not going anywhere but that he was free to GO. ANYWHERE HE CHOSE.

Since that awful time ten years ago, Graydon had held his ignominious Council defeat against Lydia Reynolds and everyone related to her. And that included her daughter, Harper Leigh, no matter how charming she seemed. Regardless of how smitten Jeremy was with her, he would never forgive her for her mother's sins. As far as he was concerned, Harper Reynolds was little more than a she-devil in a plaid Catholic girl's school uniform. He was surprised that she could wear it without bursting into flames.

Remembering all of this terrible past history, but resolute in his plan to marry Harper in five years, Jeremy knocked in a most determined fashion on his father's study door. He waited a few seconds for the summons to enter, but upon hearing nothing, he opened the door, peered in, and pulled back suddenly. It sounded like a cliché, but it was true. What he was seeing was simply too incredible and he couldn't – just couldn't - believe his own eyes!

Chapter Six:
Detention and Detente

The detention room walls were covered with posters and banners that represented a particular theme: "Motivation for Undisciplined Students" and "Guidance for Unruly Minds" would summarize the theme quite nicely. However, despite its best intentions the room failed to capture the imagination of any of its inmates, whose thoughts were usually wandering down the same unproductive paths that had led them, in the first place, to their shared destination.

There was a poster-sized, multicultural picture of studious children, all dressed in their Sunday best, holding heavy, dictionary-sized books under their arms. The caption read: WORK HARD, STUDY LONGER in large black letters. The children in question looked like their legs were ready to buckle under the weight of the books. In fact, the youngest child – who looked no more than five years of age, actually seemed ready to burst into tears or pass out from sheer exhaustion.

A second wall boasted a large poster board made to look like a postcard (complete with a huge fake postage stamp) from the president of the United States – the President!! The return address read: Teacher-in-Chief, White House, Washington, D.C., U.S.A and demanded students to Think Good Thoughts! Harper loved that one best. It was hilarious to consider the president, who had so many other important things to consider (border disputes with Mexico and Canada, the budget deficit, terrorism, immigration) taking the time to consider the best way to tell delinquent American students to do better in school. The last and final answer that the smartest people in Washington had decided upon was both simple and instructive: Think Good Thoughts. Harper had always reflected how it might have been more to the point if the White House had urged students to think smart thoughts. In Harper's chaotic and unpredictable world, smart seemed to usually trump good. At least from the way things had been happening of late. Better to think Smart First and Be Good (if possible) later.

But there was one last Very Special Wall – the so-called Wall of Shame – that did absolutely nothing to motivate Harper to do anything but laugh. It had a team of Sacred Names girls all dressed in cheerleader and sports uniforms, with their legs kicked up high in the air like Junior Rockettes, holding a banner that urged: READ, THINK, LEARN!!! GO TEAM!!! GO FALCONS! This was nothing more than the deliberate attempt by Sacred Names faculty to have a group of peers – the good girls – encouraging them – the wicked-bad girls - to do better, act better, BE better. In other words, be more like the high-kicking, right-thinking, clean-living girls in the poster.

That was more than just a joke. It was a source of bitter discontentment at the school. Unfortunately for the more sports-minded girls at Sacred Names, the Falcons were a collection of losing extramural teams (field hockey, lacrosse, volleyball, tennis, swimming, and basketball) – you name it, they lost at it. If a new sport were to be invented from scratch, it was more likely than not that the Falcons would lose at that, too. The detention wall poster showing the Falcons cheerleaders celebrating the more cerebral art of learning was quite an irony considering that it was placed, not in the library, but in the Academic Detention Center – a place that literally screamed out L-O-S-E-R!!! like nothing else!

However, in fairness to Sacred Names' Dean of Education (a type of wannabe provost who made it a point to remind everyone that she had graduated Magna Cum Laude and class valedictorian from Radcliffe College thirty years ago), the school had graduated ninety-nine percent of its students from the high school with another ninety-five percent of that population going straight on to colleges and universities around the country – even ones listed in *U.S. World Report* – and even girls who had taken up semi-permanent residence in the Academy of the Sacred Names Detention Center. Dean

Elizabeth Bonaventure had managed to push, squeeze, and shove nearly every unrepentant Sacred Names mind into accredited colleges through a complicated series of negotiation and strong-arm tactics usually reserved for generals and ambassadors.

The unlucky five percent who did not go on to college were, for the most part, living in disgraced single motherhood with parents or relatives, consigned to permanent oblivion and abandonment by the rest of Oceania's elite, who could not Look On Sin. And especially not Sin Living In Relative Poverty.

The door opened and the Dean and Lydia entered the room together, looking as unsatisfied as a hungry man at a Weight Watchers dinner.

"Harper, we'd like to speak to you. Please follow us back to my office, if you'd please." That was Sister Elizabeth. She said it exactly like someone waiting to start an execution. Standing by Sister Elizabeth's side, Lydia looked out at the walls, posters, and room filled with other disconsolate young faces, and made an abrupt decision.

"Harper, we're going home. Sister, please tell the headmistress that I would like to schedule an appointment with her, at her earliest convenience."

"But I thought we had AGREED—!" Sister Elizabeth alternated

between angry red and panicked white at the thought that her orders were being countermanded and justice was to be delayed.

"I've changed my mind!" Lydia drew herself up to her full height – which was a considerable six feet – and beckoned for Harper to follow her outside the room, and out of the school.

Harper followed, exhilarated, hoping against hope that this meant an end forever to her internment at the Academy of the Sacred Names Penal Colony! But judging from the look on her mother's face, it was only a respite. And probably a very short one at that as Lydia looked like she had more than one bone, of her own, to pick. And it was not from a chicken.

Chapter Seven:
Passing Time

Leigh has been texting me to do something constructive with my two days of 'home leave' – that's what it's being called because Mother said she would have More Than Just Me Suspended if that "inaccurate, biased, and misrepresentative" word went into my official school folder. I've only been out of Sacred Names for sixty minutes and already Leigh is passing out assignments! Personally, I wouldn't have cared about being suspended at all. I think it's pretty exciting having all this happen just for writing a few words down on a piece of paper. I feel like one of those medieval writers who was burned at the stake, or poisoned to death, for scribbling heretical ideas on fragile parchment paper or a linen handkerchief. I wonder if my little note will one day end up at the Smithsonian or Library of Congress as part of a "History of Wronged Young Women" traveling exhibit. I could be an inspiration to thousands of girls all over the country – maybe even the world!!

Driving us away from the Place of Terror (otherwise known as Sacred Names), my mother had listened to my idea, and had responded in her quietest (scariest) voice that Absolutely Nothing is a surprise these days, so why shouldn't a note like that end up behind glass as just one more indication of THINGS GONE TERRIBLY WRONG? I guess she meant I have a chance, but it's hard to tell sometimes with Mother. She says things like she's being nice and it's not until later that I catch on that she wasn't – at least not really. My gut tells me that after this altercation with the Sisters of Sacred Terror, she's plenty mad, so she's not being nice. Not about anything.

So much for the Smithsonian.

Girls at Sacred Terror have done far worse things than my note to get suspended. Like last year, Kelly Anderson hit Bebe Latham so hard in the stomach that air came out her mouth and rear at the same time! Kelly had shrieked (for everyone on the third floor to hear): "NOW have Tommy's baby, you no-good slut!" We weren't sure if Kelly got suspended for hitting Bebe, for using vulgar language, for having a boyfriend, or for not being as rich as Bebe Latham whose parents own half of Oceania. I guess it didn't matter which of the list of grievances was considered most foul because Sacred Names' 'no violence' policy covers both verbal and physical assaults and Kelly's parents were called to remove their offensive and offending child from the premises. Although no favorite of mine (Kelly was always saying snarky things about me and Jeremy and unborn children - but I guess she would have that on the brain), I still felt sorry for her as she was hauled off by her mortified parents. We all watched from the windows as Kelly got pushed by the dad and then slapped by the mom into the family's BMW SUV.

Well, at least those odds were in my favor. At this point, only one parent would be beating me. But I was furious that I was in on trumped up charges! Verbal assault. Verbal assault! Meredith claimed that my note had caused her mental distress and was an attack on her – check this out! – INDIGESTIVE SYSTEM. No wonder she got a D in honors Bio and got sent back down with the Bio-for-Dummies class. I should have known better than to bother playing around with her! It was a waste of time. Leigh says I'm too stubborn and too mischievous and that is what gets me into trouble. She's right. I should have NEVER given that stupid, stupid girl that note. I should have thought it through. But I didn't – not until after the fact. Which is how I landed in detention. Unlike Kelly, I did not hit a fellow student nor did I attempt to harm her innocent unborn fetus. My so-called verbal assault on Meredith consisted of exactly seven little words: I AM YOUR SISTER. ASK OUR FATHER.

Show me the violence! I should have saved all of Meredith's I HATE YOU notes she had thrown my way that day. She was the one instigating violent thoughts at school! I was the innocent party. I should ask Sister Mary Ellen to intervene on my behalf – if it comes to that I would!

I whispered in a rush to my friend, Katie Mitchell (as I was being escorted unceremoniously by the shoulder out of the cafeteria by Sister Virginia) to FIND LEIGH! She did the next best (lazy) thing. She texted Leigh, who called Mother right away.

When Mother arrived they fetched me from the Detention Center and placed me in a separate, smaller room – kind of like a holding cell you see on cop shows. The only things on the wall were bland landscapes and paintings of animals. Although to be perfectly honest, I was downright grateful to not see any menacing war widow eyes when my heart was already racing like an Arabian stallion and my nerves were as tangled up as knitting yarn.

I whispered my whole story to Mother and tried to explain my side of things, saying that the note that I had given to that Odious Girl used terms in their most biblical, agape-loving sense. I stressed the unfairness of Meredith's note (hurled at me from behind in class while I was trying to learn a DIFFICULT SUBJECT) versus MY forgiving and sympathetic theological note nicely handed to her at lunch. I underscored how I was the one sent to detention and threatened with suspension no matter how wrong or inhumane with nothing done to punish the true criminal. I started to sniffle and squirm until Mother gave me THAT LOOK.

She rose, tall and magnificent like an Amazonian warrior-mother, and went into see Sister Elizabeth while I was dumped back into the Detention Center.

Fifteen minutes later, she was back with a flustered Sister Elizabeth and then fifteen minutes after that, I was at Eco, reading Leigh's belligerent, demanding texts.

DO SOMETHING!!! the last one read. DO IT NOW!

I waited for Mother to attend to her important matters, surrounded by Eco teachers who were waving something in their hands and equally enthusiastic students who were jumping up and down – all serving as wonderful distractions. This gave me time and opportunity and I seized both and did what I knew we should have done even sooner than this.

I headed straight for the basement of Eco to check on our captured souls.

But this time it was all by myself.

Chapter Eight:
Spooky Little Children

I hate when Harper gets into trouble over stupid stuff when we have So Much to do! I have a Project C schedule. I wrote it all out in my day planner in different colored markers to make sure that nothing got mixed up or forgotten and then she goes and gets put on lockdown over that ignorant Meredith Ford. I mean, really! Why does Harper do the things that she does?? It's enough that now I have to try to steal more containers All By Myself without help because she's stuck at Eco, but I also have to try to steal souls, too? And then SHE gets mad because I ask her to go and check on the ones we have? That's the least she can do! I mean, really! What if Mother moved them, or NO! NO! NO! – someone who-should-be-minding-their-*own*-business-but-they're-not accidentally picked one up and dropped it! Who knows what runs through the minds of those crazy Echoes?

I try to calm down. I remember that nearly all Echoes are terrified of the basement for some unknown reason. It seemed perfectly harmless to us when we went down there – nothing spooky or scary or different. I think that since Father went lost, they make up scary stories to frighten themselves over nothing. After all, he didn't go missing from the basement, it was the Bell Tower! One is downstairs the other is upstairs! Is the whole world one big Meredith Ford?!!!

Anyway. It's probably to our advantage that the minds at Echo are as bad as they are because we can have full run of the basement without too much worry.

But I do. Worry. At least a little because there's always one person that messes everything all up. Her name is usually Harper, but sometimes it really is someone else and that's what I worry about. What to do about that.

My phone buzzes just as I'm about to raise my hand to answer a particularly difficult trig question that has everyone else stumped. Sister Karlotta looks over her glasses at me. She squints, trying to figure out which one I am. I guess the news of Harper's disgrace hasn't reached Sister Karlotta's ears just yet. Which is not necessarily good for me because Harper is usually not the one with academic gold stars. Sister Karlotta still gives those to us as if we were all still in baby school, but I like collecting them so never complain. I have so many, I give them out as special sparkly treats to the littlest Echoes when I visit Mother. Harper could have just as many stars if she wanted to because she's every bit as smart as me (we are identical), but she likes to play too much and distract herself with foolishness.

Like Jeremy Fletcher.

"Never mind, Sister. I thought I knew it, but now I think I don't."
I pull my hand down, my eyes fixated on my phone, surrendering my
gold star for the day.

Some in the class snicker, most yawn. No one likes trig and
most people find Sister Karlotta to be a big pushover so they know
it doesn't matter. They call this period, Nap Time, because if you
sleep in the back, she doesn't seem to care. Just don't snore. That, she
always says, is ill-mannered and you get a Big Red Mark in her grade
book. So sleep, don't snore. Raise your hand, get a gold star. It's really
Pavlovian in her class, but it's easy – she gives bonus points if you
tutor one of the weaker students (which is usually Meredith Ford or
one of her best friends) and that's why most of us like it.

The text reads: IN THE BASEMENT.

I almost sigh in relief. Thank God Harper is doing something
right. I had a nagging feeling all day that something was going to go
wrong and it had. Harper got into trouble. Bigger trouble than what's
usual – even for her. The fact that Mother had to practically threaten
the school with a lawsuit was Not Good and I certainly hope Harper
appreciates what Mother did on her behalf. It was pretty Mother of
Mother to do. I would expect her to do the same for me – her secret
favorite. But she probably would never have to given my reluctance
to do things that would land me in Harper-type trouble. Except for

Project C, I never do things that involve theft, lying, and kidnapping (or is it soul-napping)?

I had hoped that feeling would go away – would leave with Harper's house arrest, but it hadn't. In fact, the feeling had mushroomed, making me feel queasy, almost sick.

My stomach started to hurt worse than ever. I couldn't even blame it on the tuna at lunchtime. I had taken one bite and put it down. So, what was it?

THEY'RE SAFE. That text made me feel better.

OMG!! That text shrieked as if it were on audio.

OMG!!!

I was in a panic. Harper rarely used OMG unless it was to describe a TV show or new skateboard or maybe Jeremy, but hardly ever for anything else. That was my phrase!

WHAT?! I texted back as fast as I could, my mind blurred with panic.

THEY'RE OUT! I read the words and felt like I would faint, retch, or both.

OMG!!! HELO!

Helo? Huh? Was she trying to talk to them through my phone like something I'd seen done on T.V. on *The Twilight Zone*?

The next text solved that little mystery and added to my gastric discomfort.

HELP!!!

Now it was my turn. OMG!

I jumped up from my seat, not caring if I got a RED, GREEN, or PURPLE mark in Sister Karlotta's grade book. Harper was in trouble!

The hall was clear, but I knew that didn't mean I was safe. Sisters periodically patrol the halls, looking for girls to send to detention. If I didn't know better, I'd say they make money off those girls the way they go about it. And if I'm right, Harper has made them a small fortune.

I call her. Texting is too hard when your fingers are all jingly-jangly.

"What's going on!," I whisper loudly, heading for the bathroom.

Silence.

My knees are shaking and I really do feel like the bathroom is the right place for me to be right now. I really feel like I will throw up. And soon.

"Harp? Harp?!" This time I'm practically shouting, unconcerned for my surroundings. Even if Sister Dominguez herself were to catch me, I wouldn't care. This is HARPER in trouble! REAL trouble!

SCARY GIRL. She sent that text and I read it. Not sure what

she meant. The souls were of women. Grown, adult women. They looked like senior citizens. Practically forty.

Huh? That's what I texted back.

She must have hit the repeat button because the response came back so fast.

SCARY GIRL.

Yes, I was. I was plenty scared.

"Harper!," I spoke into the phone. "Talk to me!"

By then I was in one of the stalls and had locked the door.

"What's going on!"

"CNT TLK. THYLL HR."

Okay. She couldn't talk because she didn't want them to hear. That was fine.

"Who is the girl?" I type.

"DNT NO."

"IS SHE ALIVE?" I texted, making it easier on us both to be in the same medium, rather than having me alternate between voice and text on my phone.

"DNT NO."

"ASK HER!" I type this with my heart racing. Spooky dead girl in the basement was not an option we had ever considered. Maybe those crazy Echoes were right about the basement afterall. They DO live there. They must know more than we had thought.

"SHES ALIVE."

I almost wet on myself, I was so relieved.

"THEN WHO IS OUT?"

"DNT NO."

I was so confused and this was not helping with my stomach. Spooky live girl and escaped women souls. Not Good.

"LEAVE. LEAVE NOW." I type to Harper.

"WHT ABT SOULS?"

Good question. What should be done with them? Maybe it was like *I Dream of Jeannie* and we could put them back in their bottles if we do it exactly as before?

"HOW MANY OUT?"

"7."

"OMG!" I type back. "R THEY NICE?"

"THYR MAD."

I feel nauseous.

"TAKE GIRL AND GO UPSTAIRS. LEAVE SOULS. FIGURE IT OUT LATER. THIS IS NOT GOOD!" My fingers fly over the letters on my phone. I tap out my words like Bill Bojangles dancing with Shirley Temple. Rat-a-tat-tat!

"OK. IF THEY LET ME."

I throw some paper down on the toilet and prepare to erupt. Not sure if it will come out front or back, but I feel an explosion on the way.

"GO NOW!" I type, my hands feeling numb with fear, my fingers almost paralyzed.

"CANT."

I close my eyes, grit my teeth, and do something I haven't done since we were six years old.

I twin.

I enter into Harper's mind as neatly as a knife cutting soft butter. She lets me in and the transition is effortless. Looking around, I spot the little girl who is standing in the middle of a circle of seven angry-looking women. The child looks petrified. Harper is standing off to the side, transfixed. I push her legs and arms with all my might and try to force her to break the circle. I urge her to grab the child, and run upstairs as fast as she can. I send her that picture in my mind, but she won't budge. She's as scared as the little girl.

I leave part of myself with Harper and do something I know that I shouldn't do – something that will come back to haunt me worse than any scary soul or child. But THIS IS AN EMERGENCY and involves HARPER. I send a telepathic message to Mother.

HARPER IN TROUBLE IN BASEMENT! I see where Mother is, I see her stop what she's doing, and I watch as she runs towards the basement.

I see the ghouls break the circle to close in on Harper.

HURRY, MOTHER! I scream this in her head. HURRY, PLEASE!

Mother's long legs carry her in good stead through Eco's labyrinth. It was a simple fact that she had been talking to the gardener on the other side of the estate and it was a big estate and she was no longer twenty and running wasn't what it used to be, but to her credit she was Running Hard.

The souls had taken on a shimmery flesh tone and it was plain to see that they were not pleased as each wore a scowl as deep as the fear that I was feeling. Harper seemed to be stuck in place, unable to move. So did the little girl.

Who are these people, really? I wonder. When did they get all this power? Shouldn't they be tired from being dead for so long? Whatever happened to Rest In Peace? Although I guess I have some nerve asking such a question, but right now I have to worry about Harper!

MOTHER, HURRY!

They move towards Harper like an angry white cloud. I'm afraid that if they engulf her, it will be too late. The Harper I know will be gone forever!

MOTHER!!!

I scream it so loud in my head, my head feels hoarse.

Mother runs through the music room, swoops up a child that's in her way and places him down in a motion so smooth the little boy hardly misses a beat in the song he was singing. She races towards the downstairs when one of the teachers, a Mr. Donald Kimbrook, stops her. Cutting her completely off.

"Might I have a moment, Madame?"

"NOT NOW!" Mother pushes him aside so hard, the teacher (a man twice her size – at least in weight) stumbles and must gather his balance.

"I Beg Your Pardon!" Mr. Kimbrook reproves loudly.

But, Mother doesn't hear. Flying down the steps, she reaches the basement door and tumbles down the steps three at a time to find Harper, holding the spooky little girl's hand, both looking dazed.

"Harper Leigh Elizabeth Reynolds!" Mother hugs Harper hard, and takes the little girl by the hand.

"Harper. Kara. Come with me."

I disengage from both Mother and Harper, and relieve myself with deep calming breaths and natural body functions. OMG. This has to be one of the worst days of our lives.

I know we're in trouble now. Mother used our christening name. Elizabeth. I'm Leigh Harper Elizabeth Reynolds and she is Harper Leigh Elizabeth Reynolds. And like the poor unfortunate souls we've captured, we're both D-E-A-D.

Chapter Nine:
Family Matters

Lydia looked over the ledger for the third time. Eco was more than in the black – if the pages could flap their wings, they'd be ravens. No problem – at least not with money.

The headmistress' office was decorated to look like a combination business office and lady's private chamber. As a result, it was a schizophrenic design of oak, pastels, marble, and chintz that was not exactly easy on the eye. Whenever she would host the rare faculty and staff meeting in her capacious office, the men invariably sat on whatever looked like oak or cherry wood, while the women greedily snatched the softest available sofa or armchair. Some, particularly the younger staff, would sink in ecstasy into the deep pillowy folds of one of the many luxurious Persian rugs that settled comfortably on the hardwood floor.

Lydia closed the green ledger that bore her engraved initials on its cover: LWR (Lydia Winchester Reynolds). Nothing more to be learned from the tidy rows of neatly organized Revenues and Expenses at this point. What was more important was that she had more than enough money to negotiate with Graydon Fletcher for the land she so desperately needed to purchase. She had gone to see Graydon yesterday to offer him more than a fair market price for the lands adjacent to Eco. It had been a humiliating experience – going to the home of the man who had tried so hard to remove her from Eco and Oceania, but she needed that property, making his callously triumphant rejection of her offer that much more difficult. There were Things Left To Do at Eco and as big as the estate was, there were more and more applications each year that meant she needed more land than she and Chester had ever anticipated.

Chester.

Sighing, Lydia pulled out one of the small, antique drawers of her massive bureau. She kept a miniature framed picture of Chester in that drawer and every once in awhile she would take it out, kiss it, and put it back again with the promise to look for him again that day – even it was just under her desk or in the corner of one of her drawers. She recalled how Chester had remarked, at their first meeting, how oddly sweet it was that her own middle name "Winchester" held his name, too. He had teased her then – calling her "Mrs. Manchester Winchester" over and over until she had blushingly asked him to stop. "We're like Chester Chester twins!" he had announced exultantly, kissing her over her protests. He had been so delighted when a few years later real twins had decided to show up and had promptly named the first arrival after his favorite book's author, Harper Lee. But, not completely comfortable with the name despite its famous author and book (*To Kill a Mockingbird*), he had (in his own mind) "glamorized" the Lee part – thinking Harper just boyish enough for a girl. So Harper Lee became Harper Leigh, but pronounced like the original 'Lee' that rhymes with 'see.' It had been Lydia's idea to just switch the names around so that the second Reynolds offspring (who arrived 45 seconds later) would become Leigh Harper. And that was probably a good thing as he had been inclined to go with his grandmother's name which no one liked particularly: Esmeralda. Chester had positively adored her for her enchanting and fey mannerisms, but as much as he had insisted, Lydia had remained as adamant as a Republican vetoing higher taxes. Harper Leigh and Leigh Harper. So, he had been allowed to choose their christening name – Elizabeth – over no objections from anyone as everyone liked that name very much.

Lydia kissed his picture again, remembering the naming of the twins and the fun they had all had at the christening, before returning the photograph to its rightful place. This private ritual of extract (from the drawer), kiss (cold glass covering photo) and return (back to the drawer) had gone on for nearly twelve years now and Lydia was starting to despair that she would ever find Chester – no matter how hard she looked – when the phone rang, mercifully interrupting her anguish.

It was odd that the phone would ring in the middle of the day. Most parents called in the evenings or early morning to check on their interesting namesakes. Very few bothered in the middle of their busy days.

Lydia remembered her recent skirmish at Sacred Names and bristled.

It was probably Sister Dominguez. Head of the Academy of the Sacred Names.

And it was.

"Hello, Sister." Lydia was coldly polite.

Lydia listened carefully as Sister Dominguez explained the tenets of Harper's 'home leave.' Harper was to have online homework assignments and expected to write a five-paged, double-spaced essay on WHY IT IS RUDE, UNCHRISTIAN, AND INAPPROPRIATE TO IMPLY UNTRUE FACTS AND PRETEND IGNORANCE UPON DISCOVERY.

Lydia grunted loudly at that request, but said nothing. Sister Dominguez continued as if she had not heard any outburst, accustomed as she was to dealing with Harper Leigh. Harper, she had continued without batting an eye or stopping for breath, would be required to do a minimum of twenty hours Sacred Names community service that could include, but not necessarily be limited to, cleaning the art center of all dust and dirt, including paintings and the crystal chandelier (a tall stepladder would be provided); washing Sister Virginia's aging Volkswagen Beetle; and giving two hours of tutoring sessions (without the benefit of extra bonus points) to Meredith Ford in math.

Lydia was glad this conversation was taking place over the phone because her facial expression was not pleasant.

"Is that all, Sister?" she knew she sounded more abrupt than what would be considered polite, but her temper was rising.

Lydia listened as the good Sister noted that Harper's file would not reflect the word 'suspension' and the annotation of 'home leave' would even be removed after the completion of the required essay and community service.

Lydia crossed her eyes.

"Thank you, Sister," was all she said in response to that last bit of information that she knew was only offered after the threat of legal action had been made and followed-up on by a call to Sacred Names from Lydia's attorney-cousin, Ms. Barbara Coyle-Vittner.

Lydia waited for Sister Dominguez to make her polite farewell before she hung up in turn. She did not want the Sister to accuse her of hanging up on her (like rude daughter –like surly Mother she imagined the Sister would tell the rest of her flock) although the thought to do just that actually had crossed her mind at various points in their conversation.

The receiver had barely reached the console when it rang again.

She must have forgotten the forty lashes, Lydia thought uncharitably. Or the stockade. Or was it the hanging block?

"Hello? I'd like to speak to Mrs. Manchester Reynolds?"

No one called her that anymore. It was definitely a stranger.

"This is Mrs. Reynolds."

There was a pause.

"Mrs. Reynolds, my name is Miss Rosalind James and I have a package for you – a delivery of sorts – from your cousin, Barbara Coyle-Vittner, Esquire."

Really? Barbara had already done quite enough for one day – but to go through all the trouble of sending over a package?

"I'll tell the gate to allow you to enter. Someone will greet you and show you the way to me. Thank you, Miss James."

Lydia hung up the phone, wondering what her cousin was up to now. In more ways than one, the twins were just like Barbara and Lydia knew that whatever was in that package would not be ordinary. Just like Harper Leigh and Leigh Harper.

Chapter Ten:
Laurence Willoughby Lake Meridian

WHY IT IS RUDE, UNCHRISTIAN, AND INAPPROPRIATE
TO IMPLY UNTRUE FACTS AND PRETEND IGNORANCE
UPON DISCOVERY.

The words flash on my paper like neon stop lights. I resent every syllable. I was NOT rude, I was NOT unkind, and I certainly was not ignorant! Although, to her credit, Sister Dominguez did say 'PRETEND ignorance.' That soothes my wounded pride – for all of twenty seconds.

My anger returns like a hot pepper. Scowling, furious with Meredith Ford, enraged by the unfair punishment I have been leveled, I fling the paper to the floor – wanting to shred it, but didn't dare. Mother has made me write down everything I am supposed to respond to, has given me sixty minutes to complete the first draft (I've already wasted five of those minutes fuming), and I am absolutely, positively, livid!

My cell phone is flashing. I know who it is and I don't want to talk, but I know I should. Jeremy's been so worried about me. He heard about everything from that snoopy girl, Elaine Henderson from Sacred Names, who tells everybody's business all over town. They call her Brenda Starr for a reason. Leigh and I call her SBM - Stupid Big Mouth. She's hardly TMZ, and she needs to mind her own business!

"Hi, sweets."

I feel better already. Once I say that one affectionate, endearing word that's not rebuffed or ridiculed or dismissed, I feel peaceful. Almost Zen-like. I'm loved.

Jeremy was sympathetic but scolding.

"I know how much you hate that girl, Harp, but you gotta learn to control yourself. I keep telling you that for me to convince my father that we should get married in five years, you have to start acting more mature. More wife-like. Okay?"

I feel the tears start to burn. This isn't FAIR!

"SBM is spreading lies! Meredith made a big deal out of nothing! I'm being punished for nothing! You're not being fair to me! I thought you loved me!!"

I hang up.

I know it is childish, but I can't help myself. I am being forced to write a five-page essay apologizing for behavior I didn't commit, Mother is looking at me like I am some kind of criminal FOR being in trouble, FOR going down to the basement with one of her youngest students (even though it's not really my fault because after all she was there before ME for Pete's Sake and now the little girl has to stay in Eco's nursery!), FOR Leigh talking inside Mother's head (and who, may I ask, suggested that Leigh should do all that???), and even for the rain that has started to fall. Well, maybe Mother doesn't hold me responsible for the rain, but you wouldn't know it from the expression on her face.

The phone buzzes again. I look down.

Leigh.

I pick it up.

"I just hung up on Jeremy." I am miserable.

There is a second of silence.

"Call him back," is Leigh's practical suggestion, and I feel better.

"Listen, Harp. I didn't call to give TeenVillage dot-com advice. I called because I want to know how Mother is doing."

Translation: Is it safe to come home?

I sigh.

"Do you really want to know?"

More silence.

"Well," I decide to be brutally honest. "If you can find an excuse to do something after school with Polly or Lorelei or Shelby...? I'd do that. I really think you should. I would."

"And what about you?"

I shrug, knowing that even though she can't see me, we can always feel each other so well that distance usually doesn't matter.

"Well, then." She seems hesitant, but I can truthfully say that if I were anywhere but here in Eco, right now, I would stay there – wherever it was. Even if it was in Meredith Ford's house – Meredith Ford's room. And not look back. Things are not fun with Mother mad.

"I'm fine, Leigh. Honest. I don't care. I have to write a stupid apology essay for Sister, apologize to Jeremy, and keep trying to apologize to Mother – when I'm not trying to avoid her. I'm plenty busy and plenty sorry. Trust me."

Leigh laughs and I feel better. We hate to be in trouble without each other, but I know that the way Mother feels right now, Leigh will hear about it anyway - unless she joins the Marines, fights in two wars, and comes home ten years from now. That's the only way she won't hear about it.

Right after Leigh hangs up, I call Jeremy. I hate fighting with him almost as much as fighting with her.

He picks up on the first ring and won't speak to me.

For the first time in my young life, I understand why some people never get married.

"Jeremy, you picked up so talk to me."

Seconds go by.

"JEREMY!"

Nothing.

I sit there, stewing, feeling like I'm ready to explode when he finally, finally says:

"So, have you calmed down?"

I hang up. As soon as my finger releases the END button, I'm miserable all over again, but he had that coming.

This time, I walk away. From the phone, from the dejected, discarded piece of paper on the floor, from my wretched, wretched life as I know it.

I decide to go for a walk in the rain. It's mid-autumn in Oceania and it's beautiful at Eco. A breeze is blowing and the soft rain and smells from the gardens are somehow reassuring. I have on my sunshine yellow L.L. Bean rain parka that has a hood that completely covers my head so I feel nothing but dry, happy, and free.

I see a young man walking with a much older woman I don't know or recognize. I start to call out to them – to help them if they are lost - but something makes me stop. They're walking quickly under her umbrella which he is holding up as he is much, much taller than her. He looks like he's a little older than Jeremy – maybe seventeen? Possibly even a little older than that?

For some reason – Leigh would probably say a STUPID reason

– I hide. I duck behind a tree and watch as they make their way up the winding cobblestoned path to the imposing columned façade of Eco.

He is SO handsome! Tall, with a complexion like dark milk chocolate, and beautiful dark eyes. He looks like a fairytale prince.

Wow.

I decide to investigate things further. Afterall, it has been some time since I've seen someone new at Eco. Don't I, as the owner's daughter and half-heir, owe them at least a friendly 'hello?'

Mother's office door is cracked, so I peek in. The young man is now seated and it is easier to see him and watch his expressions that seem to shift from intelligent to humorous to intelligent all over again. His teeth are a perfect, sparkling white and his velvet chocolate skin is FLAWLESS.

Wow.

Again.

"Harper, why don't you come in and take off your wet jacket?" Mother says it, without looking at me, while reading a note.

Of course Mother saw me. She always sees us – even if her door had been closed she would have seen me. Leigh and I used to think she had x-ray vision. I stopped thinking that a long time ago. Now

I simply know it – like you know when you're coming down with a cold, or it's almost your moon time (that crampy time of the month), or Sister Gretchen is giving a bio quiz that you didn't prepare for. You Just Know.

I enter.

"Harper, I'd like to introduce you to Miss Rosalind James. She works with cousin Barbara. Miss James, this is my daughter, Harper Leigh."

Mother glances at the boy.

"I understand from my cousin's note that you prefer to be called 'Lance'? Fine. Lance, I'd like to introduce you to one-half of the team of Harper Leigh and Leigh Harper."

Mother gestures as she speaks. Pointing to me. Weird.

Lance grins. He actually stands up and walks over to shake my hand.

"Harper. Your jacket?" Mother watches as I drip.

Right. I take it off and hang it on one of the coat hooks Mother keeps, for that express purpose, by the door.

He continues to stand until I sit. Only then does he sit.

Wow.

"Lance is going to be staying with us for a year or so, Harper. As his godmother and now legal guardian, cousin Barbara has asked me to allow Lance to finish his schooling here at Eco. Miss James has all the papers. Barbara is in court and couldn't make the trip herself."

Okay? But where's –?

"His mother and father were killed last week in a car crash." It was as if Mother had read my thoughts. "A drunk driver. Lance was in the car, but thankfully he suffered no injuries – at least those we can see."

This is so weird. Mother is talking about Lance like he is in the next room or something.

"He has hysterical deafness, Harper. Lance is unable to hear us. The doctors say it is temporary and Barbara thought – well, that Eco being such an unusual place - that it might be good for Lance."

I could understand completely how he felt. If something like that had happened to Mother or Leigh, I would lose Hearing, Sight, Taste, Smell, Touch. All my senses would be gone. Did I add mind? I would lose my MIND.

The compassion must've shown on my face because Lance turns away from me, his face tightening. I know how he feels. It hurts worse when people hurt for you. And guys hate to cry – especially in front of girls.

"Is he going to board at Eco?" I ask Mother, still watching Lance, his gaze directed at the far wall.

"No. I've decided that under the circumstances, Lance will stay at our home. A 24-hour Eco experience might be too much for him – at least at first."

Miss James stands up. She seems anxious to leave now that her assignment is completed. Lance rises as well.

I am in heaven. Lance is like something out of King Arthur or Buckingham Palace. I mean, Jeremy is polite and everything (he covers his mouth when he sneezes or belches and he tries REALLY HARD not to fart), but this is like –

Wow.

"I will convey to Attorney Coyle-Vittner that you have accepted Laurence and that she can contact you later."

"Please do. Allow me to show you out. Harper, keep Lance company, will you?"

Mother walks out with Miss James and I am left alone with one of the most splendiferous boys I have ever met in my entire life. When Leigh gets home, she will just die. She likes etiquette and manners and chivalry more than I like skateboarding and I love skateboarding! Have the posters on my wall and bruises on my knees to prove it.

Wow. Despite this starting off as one of the worst days of our twin lives, I think things just got dramatically better!

Chapter Eleven:
Battle of the Bulge

The basement smelled damp from the recent autumn rains. No one noticed that the walls in one corner were starting to dry rot because few ventured down to Eco's most subterranean floor. It was considered OFF LIMITS! by everyone under twelve, and even the older children saw no reason to chance fate by going to a place from which a return was not promised. If someone had bothered to notice the growing decay, they would have seen a small encroachment from the outside lawn looking into the dark interior. And, if they were inclined to care about horticulture at all, they might have remarked that the soil from the tulip garden was just a teensy bit dry and in need of special care.

But as few people (other than Mr. Clyde Fielding, Eco's Building Superintendent, or Lydia) ever dared to concern themselves with the status of the basement, no one noticed the rot, the hole, or the dry soil conditions of the tulip garden. Everyone else was far too consumed by the almost one-hundred-year-old legend surrounding the Man-at-the-Bottom-of-the-Stairs to worry about such incidental matters as damp walls and dry soil.

There are always myths and implausible stories that circulate throughout an institution, particularly one as unusual as Eco, but the stories surrounding the Man-at-the-Bottom-of-the-Stairs (or MABS) were among the most notorious and well-known at Eco. The most compelling part of the MABS tale was not that there was a man at the bottom of the basement stairs, but that those who saw the man rarely came back up! Even some of the townspeople had heard about MABS, and not believing everything they heard about Eco, they uniformly chose to believe in that if nothing else. After all, MABS made perfect historical sense. No one was shocked that the ghost of Mr. J. Lawrence Winthrop haunted the basement of his one-time home. Afterall, it was a fact that he had killed his wife, her unfortunate suitor, and himself in an act of violence that still resonated throughout the town. That infamous murder-suicide had taken on a life, and persona, of its own. Vengeful Oceania men were heard telling wives that "If you aren't careful, I'll pull a J.L.W. on you!" which cautioned wives who were foolish enough to risk being perceived as unfaithful or misbehaved that their angry husbands would "justifiably" (albeit regrettably) re-enact the heinous crime of Mr. J.L. Winthrop. That threat was usually met by a cold shrug from the wife-in-question, but when followed by the husband with: "And throw you in the basement with the man himself!" there was apt to be a more animated wifely response that ended in penitent tears and promises of better, future behavior. It has been said over the years that many Oceania homes have escaped the consequences of divorce due to a well-placed, well-timed "J.L.W." threat.

Being the children of Lydia and Manchester Reynolds, Harper and Leigh were closer to the story than most. Afterall, Eco had been transformed from the Winthrop manor and often served as their second home. When they were much younger, if Lydia was too busy or too tired to return to their private residence, she would send one of the older Echoes to drive the twins from home (less than a mile away) to eat, sleep, and play at Eco. Never fearing the former Winthrop owners, Harper and Leigh had paid scant attention to the MABS legend and had written off its more frightening aspects as the foolish fancy of silly Echoes and Oceanians with too much free time and not enough imagination. In truth, Leigh had seen the man in question more than once in the large parlor room (and not the basement) that had been converted to a private study for Eco's middle school students. Both times he had been dressed rather conservatively and looked very handsome – sort of reminiscent of the actor Daniel Day Lewis in the movie their mother had so enjoyed about the early American oil business. Because he favored an actor in a film they had watched numerous times (thanks to their enamored Mother),

Leigh had lost all fear of J.L. Winthrop and had shaken her head gently when he had queried her twice: "Are you Kara?" Each time, the spectre had taken his leave, vanishing into the rose-papered wall without a trace.

Once, when Harper had chased an errant ball down the steps of the basement, Mr. Winthrop had been waiting for her, the ball suspended in mid-air, nestled in the palm of his hand. He had asked her, in the gentles of tones: "Are you Kara?" and upon her honest answer, he had vanished abruptly, the ball plummeting to the floor with a hard thud and bounce. It had not frightened nor unsettled Harper, who at six, had already seen other things at Eco far worse. Like Leigh, she had dismissed Mr. Winthrop as a kindly spirit in search of someone named Kara. Whoever that was. She had heard that his wife's name was something else altogether: Eloise. And Harper had the distinct impression (even at six) that the Kara in question was just about her age and not someone much older. What puzzled her most was that she had never heard from her mother, or anyone else, that the Winthrops had had a daughter (or any children) at all.

So who was Kara? And why was J.L. Winthrop searching for her? THAT, at least to Harper and Leigh, was a far more interesting question than why people didn't come back from the basement –

something neither twin believed, and knew (at least as far as they were concerned), to be untrue.

However, like most Echoes, for the last ten years, Leigh and Harper had taken for granted that certain parts of Eco were haunted, but had dismissed the sightings of Mr. Winthrop as no more or less harmful than recurring drought, snowstorms, or locusts at harvest. One simply endured as best as one could, and tried not to worry too much because the problem would go away eventually. That was how they regarded J. Lawrence Winthrop. A necessary inconvenience. Like unreliable plumbing.

It was the confident awareness of the limitations of Mr. J.L. Winthrop that compelled Harper to venture back down the basement stairs to see what could be done about the seven escaped souls. Unlike the Echoes, she was far less concerned about getting back up the steps than she was on devising a way down.

When my phone rings, I answer it. It is Day Two of Harper's banishment from Sacred Names and I'm forced to endure time in class, the cafeteria, and the Infamous Walk of Fame (IWF), without her. Of the three, the IWF is by far, the worse.

The Infamous Walk of Fame is the locker room at Sacred Names that is divided into subgroups – sort of like neighborhoods. There are the popular girls' lockers that are filled with teen and glamour magazines, lotions, polishes, and every cosmetic found on the best Oceania store counters and the local CVS. They share everything – including lip glosses – which is why three of them came down with a raging case of mono last year and "Sharing is NOT Caring" became the unofficial school slogan after they had to stay home in virtual isolation eighth grade summer through the first week of our ninth grade. Personally, I thought it was just rewards. The three in question are known to be particularly mean-spirited and have gone out of their way to torture Harper and me since fourth grade for no reason other than the fact that we're identical twins, prettier and smarter than they are, and our mother runs the fabulously interesting Eco.

But they returned just last week from their debilitating sick leave and are in gloriously rare form – just like Cerebus, the three-headed pit bull that guards Hades. They have newly erected a paper-mache fence with a sign that reads: AVALON: FOR THE SIX POPULAR GIRLS taped to its middle. The fence cordons off six lockers that indicate the geography of the girls in question, and defines their group status in declining order: Queen Leila, Princess Priscilla, Duchess Gordon, Countess Jaclyn, Lady Delia, and Dame Kristina. Most people get the last title somewhat confused and tend to leave off the 'e', putting an 'n' in its place, and none of us who knows better, ever corrects them.

90

To the right of the royal parade is the intellectual ghetto of Sacred Names athletes. It is variously called the "Sports Stadium" (in good years) or "The Pit" (in most years), where the twelve "star" Falcons, who despite having losing point seasons on the court and field have even less stellar grade point averages in the classroom. One might think that there would be some correlation in which a failure to do well in sports (due to sloppy and poorly executed training exercises) would translate to better grades in class (more attention to academic exercises???), but that is certainly Not The Case for the Falcon Twelve. Not at all. Those twelve girls give our pet name for them: "dumb joxe" a whole new meaning which brings me to OUR section of the Walk of Fame known as The Creep Show.

The Creep Show (so designated by the residents of Avalon) constitutes the bulk of the rest of the school. There is an overflow of books (hint: studious and purposeful learning); extra carefully folded and boxed uniform skirts and blouses (for the girls with OCD – obsessive compulsive disorder – who change at least twice a day before lunch!); and props (art and theatre girls whose colorful paints and costumes are dazzling but messy reminders of haphazard talent). Getting to our lockers (which are side-by-side and squeezed in-between smart and OCD girls) is getting to be more and more of a challenge for Harper and me, while the fairly pristine landscape of Avalon literally shimmers with clean, uncluttered, fenced-off lines.

It isn't fair.

And I am determined to do something about it.

But first I answer the phone.

"I'm back in the basement." That is Harper giving me stage directions, as if I need to think about anything beyond my own plan of strategic attack on Avalon real estate.

"Is that scary girl there?" I whisper quickly because technically you're only given three minutes to recover books and other items before returning to the classroom, and I have about sixty seconds left. The Sisters have it "all figured out" that it takes at least five minutes for most girls to steal, but I could've told them that even in the worst situations (with a nun looking right over your shoulder and holding one hand behind your back) the average Sacred Names thief could score a wallet or bank card in less than sixty seconds. But why give the Sisters more ammunition to use against me and Harper? They'll claim that we know this – not because of our rigorous Scientific Method – but because we steal. They will never believe that it's because we have teddy cams in our lockers with timers. We know all about the outrageous kleptomania that goes on because we have watched all sorts of criminal activities through our innocent teddies' eyes and timed these activities with our Tinkerbell stop watches. But can we share what we know? No, of course not. We've kept that information to ourselves, knowing how it would be perceived and received by the Cynical Sisters of Sacred Names.

We're protected anyway. Everyone at school knows that we have our lockers booby-trapped. No one tampers with our stuff. Not even Cerebus!

When Harper tells me that she's safe in the basement and she has not seen the seven women or J.L.W., I feel better. After all, she has her fight and I have my battle. As I look around at the two empty lockers whose doors hang invitingly open (lockers that just happen to be adjacent to Avalon and The Pit), I decide that Harper and I will be changing neighborhoods today and I double dare Cerebus or the rest of the Royals to do anything to stop me!

"Harp, gotta go!" I see where I am the only one around and with less than thirty seconds of free and clear time, I have to use every second to move a mountain of paper and supplies.

The Battle of the Bulge is ON!

Chapter Twelve:
Kara Jeannette Victoria Pennington

Kara loved first grade at Eco. The teachers were friendly, the children were nice, and there were always fun things to do. The first grade rooms were quite colorful and the three different classrooms fed into each other like a row of underground tunnels, separated only by high swinging saloon doors that most of the smallest children could walk under quite easily without getting pummeled from behind or in the face. Older children liked to run through the rooms, pretending to be choo-choo trains, trying to deliberately create a scenario in which the swinging doors would slap fellow classmates in the face (or better still!) on the back of the head with a SPLAT! or PLOP! (depending on the size of the head and angle of contact). It was a practice openly discouraged but universally tolerated as the fourth and fifth grade children seemed to derive so much amusement from such simple slapstick humor. And as no one had ever gotten seriously hurt, the position of most Eco teachers was to look the other way – a type of ingrained habit they had all developed as coping behavior for what was, by any account, a most unusual school.

First grade teachers (Miss Susan Kanady, Miss Julie Oliphant, and Mr. Craig Arnold) had all been specially selected by Lydia to foster and encourage the youngest Eco children's special Gifts. Lydia demanded that the tiniest Echoes be cocooned in an inclusive, nurturing environment that disallowed - and in fact punished - teasing, ridicule, or bullying of any sort. Kara appreciated the teachers' kind efforts, but despite their acceptance of each child's special talents, she still didn't much like hers (and her parents liked hers even less) which is why she had been sent to Eco from her home in faraway San Lucia, California. It was hoped, at least by Mr. and Mrs. John Alton Boardman, that their only daughter, Kara, could unlearn what came natural to her – seeing things that most people don't see and wouldn't want to see if they could see them. The problem was that Kara (even after trying as hard as she could) had still not figured out how to "unsee" anything and after the basement incident with Harper, she was getting pretty desperate to do exactly that. Unsee everything and as soon as possible!

"Kara, have you finished with your project?"

The project in question involved a sketching exercise in which Kara was to draw bunny rabbits in children's clothing. It was a timed test in which she was given five minutes or less to complete the task. Her teacher called these mini-assignments "Creative Clicks" and had instituted at least six "Creative Clicks" every day for the last eight months. Kara's most recent Click of the day was to make the bunnies as fanciful as possible without making them seem ridiculous. She wondered how clothed bunnies could be anything but ridiculous, but as she was an obedient child and wanted to please her teacher, whom she loved very much, she worked as diligently as possible to complete an assignment that was fraught with all sorts of contradictions. Kara drew a bunny in a dress with a bonnet. She even put ballet slippers on its paws so that by the time Miss Susan called on her she was actually ready and felt fairly proud – a rare emotion for her - of her accomplishment.

Standing up with unaccustomed confidence, Kara held up her picture (as was the custom when presenting shared Click activities) for everyone in the room to see.

A gasp, then a shudder went through the room. Miss Susan's face turned as white as chalk. Kara's hands started to shake because she knew that something VERY BAD was now on her paper. It was always that way. She would think good thoughts and bad things would happen. She would start to say something nice or kind and naughty or unkind words came out. Terrified, she knew that whatever sweet picture she had just finished was every bit as vanquished as her premature confidence. She flipped the page over to see the pretty pink dress defiled in blood with the bunny's tender head lying decapitated at the corpse's unsuspecting and slippered feet. To make matters worse (not that Kara felt that anything worse needed to happen), the paper started to ooze blood (and defying the laws of gravity and common decency), the blood flowed upward from the paper, to her hands, to her arms and would have traveled to her neck if Kara had not finally regained her senses and had the presence of mind to drop it from her fingers. Flinging it away as if she had been scorched, Kara and the other children watched, mesmerized, as the bunny images writhed and curled, the cut off head oozing bright, red blood that spilled out from the one-dimensional paper and onto the first grade floor. Horrified, the class scrambled to the back of the classroom, as far away from the afflicted paper as was physically possible. Kara was left, with Miss Susan, to gape in stricken terror at Kara's red-stained hands and forearms that seemed to pulsate with the same red ooze as the bunny's swollen head.

At twenty-six-years of age, Miss Susan thought that her first year at Eco had been quite an eye-opening experience of both the Unusual and Uncanny – even for a mind as young and fertile as her own. Upon accepting her teaching position, Miss Susan, like all Eco teachers, was forced to sign confidentiality agreements to ensure and maintain the privacy of the children of very wealthy Eco clients who could so easily become fodder for tabloid journalists and gossip columnists. In that contract language were stipulations regarding the consequences of leaks or contract breaches – something about how "the offending party" (meaning a Big Mouth Teacher) would be sent to Closet Nine for punishment. No one seemed to quite know what or where Closet Nine was, but something about the name and its purpose did not evoke warm feelings. Everyone agreed that it did not sound at all like a good place to be.

To remain grounded (and away from Closet Nine), Eco teachers often tried to laugh away (or outright ignore) things they saw (and tried not to see) in classrooms or even outside in Eco play areas. However, even with the best disposition and open manner, six-year-old Kara's 'talents' were even more than Miss Susan had bargained for or expected, particularly in the last six months, and she refused to simply dismiss this latest incident as an example of an Echo's special talents. It was evil, macabre, and senselessly cruel. Thankfully, the teacher's open affection for Kara overrode any unreasonable or unnatural fears or dislikes of the child (who had seemed as perplexed and frightened as everyone else), and she had acted to help the little girl without hesitation. Leading Kara by the shoulders, she pushed the trembling child to the sink at the back of the room and started scrubbing her hands and arms as hard as she could with a scrub brush and oatmeal soap.

Nothing. In fact, if anything the stains seemed to grow darker.

There was only one thing left to do and that was to go to Lydia and ask permission to take Kara to ROC (as the Room of Clocks was known) to reset the time. To go back fifteen minutes would erase this current disaster from their young lives. Miss Susan thought it through carefully. She would simply not give out a bunny assignment and she would, instead, send everyone outside to play in the waning autumn sun. The only problem with ROC is that not only is the requesting party affected by the time change, but everyone and everything at Eco – which is why Lydia herself must grant permission. Only she, as headmistress, was in the best position to consider if a fifteen minute shift in time would mean more than just a recovered parcel of minutes or the beginning of a possibly Very Bad situation.

Miss Susan pushed Kara gently forward, out of the classroom and towards Lydia's office upstairs. It was no use putting off the inevitable.

Lydia must be consulted, and consulted right away.

The basement is dark, but I am prepared. I have my little flashlight that I had begged off Jeremy last year, telling him that I needed it for a science fair project. I didn't tell him that I really wanted it to spy on a no-good girl named Bobbi, who had been spreading lies about me to my civics teacher, Mr. Farleigh. She always makes up stuff about people she doesn't like – telling stories that people are cheating (HERSELF), people are plagiarizing their work from the Internet or buying it from graduated seniors (MORE OF HERSELF), or people are stealing old tests from locked science center cabinets that are really useless because if you tug hard enough they open right up like a bottle top (HERSELF AGAIN). I mean, really. She is like one walking CRIME MACHINE. Sick of her lies, I had followed her home one day late at night (using my pen light and trusty legs), and there she was – buying old tests off last year's graduated senior, Mary Elizabeth Patterson. What a crook!

Did I threaten to tell on her?

Are you kidding? The Sisters would only send her down to Detention and then I'd have to sit with her and listen to her rag on me for two wasted hours (time better spent napping), so I did the best thing for me. It might not win me a good citizenship award, but trust me – it was better for me.

I jumped out from the tree and took her picture. BAM! Mary Elizabeth looked like she was ready to wet her pants and that stupid Bobbi just burst into tears. What a pair! I ran off, laughing all the way back home. I laughed up the porch stairs, into the house, and all the way to Leigh's room. I flung myself down on Leigh's bed, laughing like a crazy person ('not hard to do for you' is how she always puts it when I laugh like this). I am screaming laughing until I turn on the camera and remember, too late, that the battery is dead. Nothing moves, no whirring sounds, no flash. I had just taken a picture of - *nothing at all.*

Now it was MY turn to cry. And Leigh's turn to laugh.

But not this time. This time, I had the flashlight and a working camera because I want evidence of what was going on down here – proof that I can share later with Leigh so that we can figure out together what to do.

The shelving that houses the containers appears to be untouched, so it is far from clear what has happened to release the souls. No broken glass. No destruction. I hear movement.

Uh-oh.

A youngish woman steps forward. I can tell she's not completely here on Planet Earth by the way her dress seems to billow and blow, like a hidden gust of air is behind her. She's very pretty with big dark eyes and little ringlets of burnished curls the color of mahogany and just as shiny. Her skin is the color of ebony and she looks like a beautiful doll, the kind you give to older girls who won't ruin the doll's face or clothes with too much fake mothering and handling.

I really don't mean to be rude, but I shine the light right in her face. I want to SEE her and that soft light she's in fades in and out like a light bulb about to go bad.

"My name is Harper Leigh." I introduce myself, wondering for the first time who this woman is because I certainly don't recall any faces of African American women on the war widows' wall. It is extremely doubtful that the Academy of the Sacred Names had admitted African American women before 1970. Extremely doubtful.

"I'm pleased to meet you, Harper Leigh. But I know who you are and I know your sister, Leigh Harper."

Okay. I guess ghosts do have the upperhand on the latest 4-1-1. Cool. No problem. If I were a criminal like Bobbi, I'd ask her what was going to be on my chem test next week. But since I'm not (a criminal), I don't (ask). I could ask a question like "is Dr. Krass even going to give a test next week?" which is SO not like asking -

"Why did you capture the souls of the war widows?"

She asks the first question and I guess that's only fair. I was distracting myself with school stuff and she's had a long time to hang around and think of legitimate questions. It is clear from her outdated dress that she has been here quite awhile before the war widows, our parents, Eco, or anyone else except for maybe J.L.W. and Eloise.

"We have to get our dad back and we were told we need a bunch of souls to exchange for his."

The woman looks at me like Leigh sometimes looks at me. The only thing she didn't do was tilt her head.

"What makes you think that your father is dead?"

Good question.

"We don't know. He disappeared. It's been since forever. I guess you could say the souls are our insurance policy?"

The woman smiles at me.

I can tell that, like Sister Mary Ellen, she genuinely likes me.

"They're angry you know."

I shrug.

"I wasn't going to hurt them. We will just exchange them and then that's it."

A cool breeze stirs in the room. I wonder if it's The Seven gathering forces. My light (and nerve) falters a little.

"What's going on?" I ask, my voice breaking.

The lady looks at me and smiles softly.

"We're going backwards, Harper. I think we'd better say our good-byes for now."

I stare as her light starts to fade and I feel myself being pulled back upstairs to the room where I had been sitting before venturing to the basement.

"Tell me your name!" I yell into what feels like a vortex.

"My name?"

"YES!!" I have to shout as the rush of time starts to pull at me, demanding that I forsake minutes that no longer belong to me.

"Kara! My name is Kara Jeannette Victoria Pennington!"

I watch her disappear, and feel myself being pushed through a

104

small window of time and into the room where I had been writing my five-page essay on why I need to apologize to The World for my so-called bad behavior to that sneaky Meredith Ford.

As I sit there in the chair I wonder where I have heard that name before.

Kara.

And then I remember. The little girl who was in the basement with me when the seven souls had escaped, and who was every bit as scared as I had been? That little girl's name is Kara. The story I had heard from years ago about the time that J.L.W. and Eloise had appeared in Eco's cafeteria had a little girl named Kara involved. I shake my head. There are simply too many Kara girls for these to be coincidences. No one knows better than identical twins that some coincidences are not coincidences. For some strange reason Kara means something to our family and, if memory serves from my encounters with J.L., it means something to Mr. Winthrop and I am determined to get to the bottom of it. My hunch tells me that solving this mystery just might be the difference between successfully concluding Project C - getting our father back safe and in one whole piece - and giving up the search altogether.

And the one thing about the Reynolds family?

We NEVER, EVER give up!

Chapter Thirteen:
Men-at-Arms

Mother is humming. Never a good sign. It's not that she doesn't like music or she hates songs or even hates to hum, but it is a pretty good indication (ninety-nine percent of the time) that something is on her mind. And that something is usually Not Good.

At least not for me or Harper.

I glance over at Lance, who even though he can't even hear Mother humming, is grinning like the Cheshire Cat in *Alice in Wonderland* or like Harper when she's scored points against the Royals or Meredith Ford. If Lance could hear, he'd know that Harper is making plans for him and Jeremy to play basketball after dinner. She's determined to have them become best-friends. "Better for our kids," she confided last night as she cleaned spaghetti sauce from her retainer. "It'll just be a whole lot better for our kids that their fathers be friends, you know?" I had just looked at her. Not saying anything. Too scared to think. Not really sure how I felt. And feeling everything all at once.

Remembering that conversation, I watch anxiously as Lance eats his repulsive-looking thick, muscular steak. As he slashes into it, wet, red liquid gushes out the sides onto the white porcelain plate, turning my stomach, and completely ruining my appetite. At least until I look away from the gory mess and up at him.

Staring into those big, dark eyes makes me forget all about his gross culinary habits and focus on what is more important. His intelligence, sense of humor, loyalty, devotion, affection. I stop myself. Sounds more like I'm describing a King Charles Cavalier cocker spaniel than a real-life regular almost seventeen-year-old guy.

"So, Germ, you and Lance are going to play some ball after dinner, right?"

Jeremy shrugs. His blue eyes appraise Harper with just the right amount of suspicion and annoyance. She's been shoving a ball in his hands (metaphorically speaking) since he arrived at four o'clock this afternoon. That's two hours of pre-hoop coaching and he was getting a little sick of it.

"Don't ask me again, Harp."

Germ and Harp. Lance and Leigh.

This just might work.

"Don't you have football practice, Jeremy?" I ask it before thinking, realizing that I was probably right and Jeremy had skipped practice at the request of Harper to pleasepleaseplease PLAY WITH LANCE!

That explains his irritation. Jeremy loves sports almost as much as he loves Harper. And he absolutely adores *her*.

"I did."

He doesn't look at me when he says this. He looks directly, explicitly at Harper. I shove some salad in my mouth, wishing I had done that ten seconds ago and chewed rather than spoke.

Mother stops humming.

"Laurence is not going to have time for sports after dinner. I have a six-thirty appointment with Dr. Xavier Montague. We have five minutes left to eat and then leave for Lakeshore Prep."

Jeremy's eyes spit bullets at Harper and his mouth clenches into one thin line. WHAT??!! Lydia is taking Lance to HIS school, Lakeshore Prep? A place HE should have been two hours ago for football training but skipped to come with Harper to sit for two hours??! Jeremy recounts the time spent doing things he Didn't Want To Do in those one-hundred and twenty minutes. Things such as watch as Lance clumsily tried to learn American sign language from Harper (who got her information from a friend completing a Girl Scouts badge in "caring for special populations" – the same friend who is just barely literate in regular American English). Watch an hour of boring local news on close-captioned T.V. (with the sound OFF because Harper wants him to truly understand what Lance is enduring). And worst of all, eat a lousy dinner (he absolutely despises steak and loathes arugula) around his future mother-in-law, Miss Humming Bird Lydia. To suffer through All Of This only to watch as Lance gets trotted off to Prep where HE should have been two hours ago? It was simply too much!

Jeremy snatches the linen napkin from his lap and flings it to the table. Harper's face crumples and I feel sorry for her. Afterall, she is more than halfway doing this for ME, for our future, for our unborn children who will one day be best-friends (like us)! I couldn't really blame her for working her plan. Hasn't Mother always told us to "stay on your path?" Well, this is one of Harper's chosen paths and she is galloping down that trail like a wild pony, hoping to rope a very reluctant Jeremy down with her.

The reluctant colt in question stands up, glares at Lance, who seems absolutely oblivious to any of the convoluted activities orchestrated by Harper on his behalf. In fact, Lance has eyes for only one thing – his steak – and seems to have become more enraptured with each carnivorous bite.

"I gotta go. Homework." Jeremy growls.

That is really a slap in Harper's face as everyone (and that includes practically the whole town of Oceania) knows that Jeremy Fletcher prefers to do homework with Harper. Since last year, he buys an extra set of textbooks, notebooks, and pens for that express purpose.

"Germy, please!" Harper rises with him, following his angry long stride out into the hallway. "What's wrooooong?!" Harper's voice fades out of earshot as she trails Jeremy down the long corridor and out on to the lawn.

"And whatever is the matter with Mr. Fletcher today?" Mother asks, her eyes sparkling with the same mischievous humor usually observed in Harper.

"He thought he was staying to bond with Lance and now you're taking Lance to Prep and Jeremy was actually supposed to BE at Prep for football practice, but he came HERE instead because of Lance – well, really because of HARPER – and...," I stop myself, realizing that Mother is Simply Not That Interested.

To underscore that fact, she has already resumed humming.

Harper returns to the dining room, casting a bleak look in my direction before settling a disgruntled one on the indifferent Lance, who having devoured his steak, is prepared to move on to carbs. He attacks the baked potato with his fork like a sword slicing through a violent offender.

"I'm glad to see you've made some progress with Lance today." Mother is softly complimentary. "This has been a tough week for him. Harper, can you let him know that he is to come with me to Lakeshore Prep? Ask him to finish his meal as quickly as possible, please."

Harper looks at Mother and then back at Lance. I understand her dilemma completely. How on earth can she say All Of That with the limited sign language information she has been given only this afternoon by a girl who was born in Oceania, Maryland, United States of America and can still barely speak regular English? Mother is simply asking for too much!

Harper leaves the room. Mother looks at me and I am suddenly fixated on my arugula and artichoke salad.

Harper returns and more or less flings a piece of paper at Lance. He catches it neatly, reads it quickly, and smiles. It almost breaks my heart. His smile is so beautiful and Harper is so angry. I don't know if I can handle the competing emotions. I want everyone I love to be happy. At the same time.

"Well, I might agree with you that he has a bea-uuu-tiful smile, but I – I, Harper Leigh Elizabeth Reynolds -- am not happy! If anyone even cares!!" Harper announces, reading my mind and flouncing off.

Realizing that we are twinning, Mother stares at me with a definite scowl, and I realize that this evening has soured, going from Not Good to pretty bad in less time than it took Lance to clean his plate. I shudder as I remember that things can actually get worse as Harper and I have scheduled ourselves to go tonight, at midnight, to the Arts Center for a little more soul-napping.

Oh, yeah. Things can certainly get much, much worse.

Chapter Fourteen:
Lakeshore Preparatory School

It is said that boys from Lakeshore marry girls from Sacred Names. Sometimes, if the couple is lucky, they even fall in love.

Unlike the Academy of the Sacred Names that seemed to have sprawled its way to grandeur more from necessity (a growing student population) than design, Lakeshore Prep (or "Prep" as it is typically called) was constructed in the early 1900s to convey more visceral emotions: wealth, power, privilege, and exclusivity, rivaled only by an overabundance of testosterone. To ensure that Prep students retained physiques worthy of mortal gods, there was a strident focus on athletics and former Olympians (who were paid outrageous fees) served as coaches, trainers, and confidantes for those boys who were more seriously interested in pursuing sports careers into college and beyond. Unlike the losing Falcons, Prep Pirates were known all over the country for a sports prowess that had led to so many state and national championship victories that it was said a glass case in the Room Of Victory required sunglasses as the refracted sunlight was blinding off the gold and brass trophies.

To continue the Pirates sports dynasty into the next millennium, Prep generously (and strategically) provided outdoor and indoor tennis courts, equestrian facilities, indoor and outdoor Olympic sized pools, indoor and outdoor running tracks, professionally sized football and baseball fields, a golf course – in other words – Everything!

And at the center of this pagan display of physical strength and beauty was Jeremy Alexander Fletcher. Worshipped by the younger boys as a type of mythological role model and genuinely liked and admired by his peers, Jeremy tried to live up to the expectations of his teams, coaches, friends, and followers. He hated to let them down and gave his all to the trainings and the games. Unlike some of his friends, who liked to sort of ease into training, Jeremy attacked training like a Japanese ninja. He loved the feel of a ball, glove, bat, or uniform almost as much as he loved – well, HARPER. Which is why he was furious for allowing himself to be led astray today – Of All Days – during football practice before a big Saturday game!

Driving like a crazy person, he had sped over to the field to explain things to Coach Mitch Davison, but the field was bare. No loiterers, no last minute joggers, no one. Not even a note.

Jeremy was devastated.

He floored the engine of his father's vintage Aston Martin Vanquish and headed back to the Reynolds for a thorough scolding of Harper for her role in his disgrace. Going more than eighty miles per hour, he spotted the more sedate pace of Lydia's Volvo making its way across the estate to the headmaster's private residence. He remembered with a sinking feeling that Lydia was bringing Lance to meet Dr. Montague and understood that Lance was going to be more than a possible brother-in-law, he was also going to be a classmate!

Gritting his teeth, Jeremy sped off.

He'd like Lance just fine if he wasn't so handsome and if Harper didn't seem quite as absorbed in him as she was. It was 'Lance, this' and 'Lance, that' and 'Oh, isn't Lance just the most DARLING boy in the world for Leigh?' Right. For Leigh. Who's to say that Harper wasn't considering Lance for herself??? Happens all the time! Happened to his best-friend, Happy. It was just six short months ago – and with a girl, Leila, that Happy had loved since Kindergarten! Leila had pulled the wool over Happy's unsuspecting eyes and had broken his heart in the process. Jeremy recognized that his jealousy was petty and small and ridiculous, but he didn't care. Leila's unexpected disaffection frightened him and he wasn't about to be caught off guard like some rookie.

He was going to have a few words with Miss Harper Leigh Reynolds and get things straightened out once and for all. Lance might be living at the Reynold's house for now, but nothing lasts forever. And if Jeremy had his way, forever would be the shortest time ever.

🌿

Dr. Montague's office reflected the style of a man accustomed to the finer things in life. The fact that his ancestors had arrived on the ship immediately following the Mayflower was never far from his mind or his lips at Oceania dinner parties. Lest anyone feel they had "arrived" by purchasing a McMansion on the Oceania shoreline, Xavier Montague was fond of referring to his family's estates in England, France, and Spain. That usually ended most bourgeois conversations about Oceania property values, taxes, or other related issues. People were forced to turn to politics – a subject they knew even less about, but had nothing to lose in a town where politics were as bland as vanilla pudding.

Despite his rather austere upbringing (due to his Mother's fascination with all things Pilgrim), Dr. Montague was a man who enjoyed life and was pleased when Lydia Reynolds had called to tell him about her unusual charge. He was glad to hear that the young man in question had been matriculating at one of Washington, D.C.'s finest prep schools, and he thought that Lakeshore might, indeed, be happy to receive him.

Especially if young Laurence was good at sports.

He heard the chime at the door and knew that it was Lydia with the boy. He waited in his study for them to be brought in to meet him.

He was a patient man, who had waited a long time for things that most men would have long ago abandoned. Rising, Dr. Montague looked at himself in the mirror. Tall, handsome at fifty, he had been told recently that as a recent widower he was the "catch of Oceania" – not that he thought that was a particularly distinguished title – given that Oceania was – well...Oceania. However, it did matter to him that he was still attractive. It mattered quite a bit. Particularly as the object of his most passionate interest was about to enter his home, his room, and he had every hopeful expectation – his heart.

The maid opened the door as Dr. Xavier Montague opened his arms.

"Ah, Mrs. Reynolds! What a delight to have you visit Lakeshore Prepatory! Please, please DO come in! I am so very delighted to see you!"

Chapter Fifteen:
Excalibur

The doorbell chimed loudly. Lydia glanced at her clock. It read five o'clock a.m., but it actually felt like even earlier as she had not gone to bed until after midnight. Throwing on her robe, she decided to investigate. It was highly unusual for visitors to come to her private home at this time of morning. Where was the guard at the gate? Every once and again there would be mysterious drop-offs of young Echoes in the wee hours as nervous parents sought to avoid temper tantrums or tears and that was always considered acceptable. But that was in the late summer – not mid-autumn – and it was always to Eco and usually closer to one o'clock in the morning rather than five.

Having eliminated these possibilities, she wondered who on earth could it be?

Lydia made her way downstairs, turning on the light on the downstairs landing, careful not to disturb the girls or Lance. Reaching the bottom of the stairs, and peering outside through the blinds, she saw no one. Not even a shadow. The light from the porch illuminated the yard and garden in a blistering glow, and seeing nothing amiss, Lydia opened the door.

A large animal crate greeted her. It was tied with a big, red bow and an oversized card. Lydia ignored both, dropping to her knees to see what was inside.

Rising up, Lydia took a step back, puzzled.

It was a beautiful Gordon Setter puppy. Lydia knelt down again and opened the crate, watching as the black and tan puppy tumbled out at her feet. He was very young and it was plain that he had just been weaned as his milk teeth were still in evidence. Lydia picked him up, cradling him like an infant as she read the open card.

"I hope this small gesture helps young Lance to recover from his tragedy. All the best. YOURS, Xavier Montague."

The gift was from the headmaster of Lakeshore Prep. Lydia surmised that meant that Lance was accepted to Prep and could start immediately – six months before the spring semester concluded and more than enough time to get him acclimated to his classes and peers. Good, she thought with relief. Very Good.

Her second thoughts about Eco being suitable for a young man with such recent trauma had prompted her to seek out Lakeshore in the first place, and now that he had not only been accepted, but personally embraced by the school's headmaster, Lydia felt even better. Lance was better served by Prep. To her knowledge, he had no Special Gifts and his recent experiences left him emotionally fragile and unprepared for Eco's unique populations that had a great many Gifts.

Lydia set the puppy back down in the crate, locked it, and carried it into the house. Closing the door, she wondered briefly if Dr. Montague had personally delivered the dog. Dismissing that thought almost as soon as she had it, Lydia knelt down beside the crate once more and opened it, allowing the puppy to rush into her arms.

Carrying him upstairs and to her bed, she realized that this was the first time since Chester's disappearance that a dog would be in the house. Before Chester had gotten himself lost, he had owned a large Great Dane, who loved to lope after him like a miniature pony. Sir Gawain, Chester had named him for his regal, gentle bearing. The girls, being so young, had found the name difficult to pronounce, settling on "Sir Gowy" instead. Gowy had run off when Chester disappeared, and had not been seen since. There was speculation that he had left to find Chester and as devoted as he had always been to his master, Lydia did not doubt the veracity of that idea for a minute.

Lydia closed the bedroom door as a precaution. She was ready to drift off for another hour of sleep and just in case the puppy jumped off the bed and was struck by youthful wanderlust, those yearnings would be satisfied within her suite. She did not want the children disturbed. Lance had a new school to start and Harper was returning to Sacred Names to begin her dreaded community service hours.

What a Monday!

Lydia snuggled the puppy against her, pleased to see it yawn in sleepy response. Perhaps this would be easier than she had imagined, she considered drowsily as her thoughts became fused and hazy with the pleasant dream she had been having about Chester and Gowy right before her recent discovery and new family addition. It was a good omen, she reflected, before sinking deeper into sleep. A strong, sturdy puppy was a Good Thing for the family. She squeezed the puppy closer, breathing in his baby canine smells.

It was a Very Good Thing.

Leigh calls my community service days my Days of Redemption. I just call them by what they really are: free, illegal servitude. I mean, really. Where is it written that school infractions must translate into penal colony labor? I understand detention. I even get the purposes of suspension – or in my case – home leave. But community service? It's just a rip-off. A plain, old-fashioned I'm taking advantage of you and there's nothing you can do about it rip-off.

Leigh comes into my room, looking like she's swallowed sunshine. Of course she's happy. We didn't go last night to the war widows' room at midnight as planned because we decided to wait until today when I do my community service in that awful, awful room with those awful, awful EYES staring at me. PLUS Leigh doesn't have an angry boyfriend who sent her thirty hateful text messages last night that all started with: AND ANOTHER REASON WHY I'M MAD AT YOU...

What makes those messages worse is that Jeremy sent those after driving here to tell me off in person last night. I mean, really, Jeremy? Do I have to have it in writing, too?

My head hurts. Not a good way to start a Monday or any day, but especially not a Monday.

"Lance starts Prep today." Leigh sits on the edge of my bed, beaming as if she was personally responsible for his placement. Part of me is glad to see her take an interest in her future husband, but the other part of me is reeling from Jeremy's weird accusations about me and Lance, so I prefer to not talk about Lance first thing in the morning if it can be helped. Especially not this morning.

"I know, Leigh. Mother told us." I am trying to be civil, but I hear my phone vibrate and I know instinctively that it is Jeremy with message number thirty-one.

"But what you don't know is that Lance got a new puppy."

Leigh's eyes are bright as light bulbs. That part of her excitement is contagious and I sit up.

"We have a dog?!!" I LOVE dogs and Mother has refused to replace Gowy for the longest time, using some crazy superstition about how Gowy would only come back when Dad reappears – which has nothing to do with a new dog. It's just a lame excuse for not wanting to clean poop. I mean, I could understand when we were little and her not wanting to deal with the responsibilities of a dog and twins, but Leigh and I could manage one just fine now and I'm SO glad she's changed her mind and –

"WE don't have a dog. Lance has a dog."

WHAT???

"What do you mean that LANCE has a dog?"

Leigh shrugs.

"It came this morning. A puppy for Lance from Dr. Montague."

I close my eyes, refusing to get upset. I feel the burn of tears, but I push them back. Okay. Okay. But the puppy will be living here, so it will be like my dog, too...

"Mother says that the puppy will stay with Lance in his room to help him recover. He will be solely responsible for caring for it. She said that it will help him with his grief. Help him to hear and talk again."

I open my eyes. I am a selfish pig. I am a selfish, selfish pig.

Lance has lost everything – including his hearing – and I begrudge him a dog?

I should be shot.

I climb out of bed, ready to face a new day and all the new possible things that could go wrong. My phone buzzes angrily reminding me of what has already gone wrong.

I reach for the phone and Leigh meets my eyes. She crosses hers. She knows who it is, too. And why. I had told her about Jeremy's accusations.

"His name," she whispers to me as she exits my room, "is to be Excalibur! Isn't that FABULOUS?! Lance wrote it down for me to read to Mother. And we are to call him 'Cal' for short!"

Cal. I shrug. Not bad. Okay.

"So, when do I meet Cal?"

Leigh beams.

"Down in the kitchen. Soon as you're dressed. He's cute as a button, Harp. You'll fall in love with him!"

Leigh scampers off, thrilled. I feel my heart sink. To fall in love with something that will NEVER belong to me?? Followed by a Monday morning with Jeremy MAD at me does not seem like anything to get all that excited about.

At least not in Harper's Book, Chapter Three, Page Four titled

"List of Things to Be Unhappy, Downright Angry, or Uncertain About."

I mentally add Cal's name to an already long list on Page Four that includes Sacred Names (as an institution), individual nuns, girls, and sports teachers at Sacred Names. Foods like asparagus; activities like visiting hateful cousins (on both sides of the family) who tease you with venom usually reserved for pedophiles or serial killers about Eco - a place that none of them have ever even seen; and, of course, the disappearance of our father. I add Cal's name because I can already see how difficult it will be for me to not want to claim him all for myself. He sounds perfect. Unlike my life.

The phone buzzes again. This time though, I answer it. At least with Jeremy, I know what to expect. And there is some comfort in that. However small.

Chapter Sixteen:
Tri-W: War Widows Wall

The art center's War Widows' Wall was always kept dark and cold to preserve the oils and photographic images. That is the on-the-record reason the nuns give us by way of explanation for the fact that it always feels like a Sub-Zero freezer (even in July) and is as dark as King Tut's tomb. Even as stupid as they are, most Academy girls (even Meredith Ford) don't believe that story for a second. We know the real truth: that room is every bit as haunted as the creepy apartment building in *Rosemary's Baby*. There is NO WAY that eyes follow you all around a room – from any direction??? No matter how fast you walk or how quickly you turn? No Way. Im-pos-sible.

Sister Phillipa, the Honors Physics teacher, tries as hard as she can to explain it away every semester using optical illusion theory, refracted light explanations, and all kinds of hypotheses for why eyes that are CLEARLY looking toward the LEFT are suddenly PEERING AT YOU for no apparent reason from the RIGHT. However, even she cannot explain the frigid temperatures that closed blinds could NEVER produce in a room whose air is only filtered and never cooled. Even Sister Phillipa, Ms. Sacred Names' 2005 Scientist-of-the-Year can't seem to find a reason for the subhuman temperatures that force me to wear my Burberry scarf, DKNY parka, and Land's End ski gloves each time I have to come into that icy and unbearably cold room.

No reason beyond what it is.

The pictures are haunted. And the place is as spooky as a cemetery on Halloween.

I hate cleaning this room and the Sisters know it. They relish the thought of me in this room, screaming LET ME OUT! LET ME OUT! inside my head over and over like a Gregorian chant. They are every bit as evil as the eyes on the wall and I vow that when I leave the Penal Colony, I will not give them one red cent as an alumnus. Not one penny of my money will go to the continued support of Terror on Fragile Young Minds. Nada.

I am forced to work in semi-darkness to maintain the integrity and purity of the oils in those framed faces. The Sisters complain that too much light – even artificial light - will compromise their authenticity and coloring. As I dust the sturdy but elegantly contoured frames, I feel the hatred pouring out at me from every one of those women. Women who watch me from the distant far wall glare at me with snarled, hateful expressions. As the duster gently strokes the faces of paintings on which I am now working, I feel teeth reaching out to

BITE, gnash, and TEAR at me. I wonder (not for the first time this afternoon) just when Leigh plans to do her promised drop-in. I really do hope that it's sooner rather than later as my nerve is starting to give way under the angry scowls of the portraitures. Their animosity for me seems to have actually deepened along with the collective gloom of the room itself. Everything looks dark, grim, and increasingly unsettling. Not to mention the fact that the cheap little lamp that is in the corner seems to be having some difficulty. Its light flickers and wobbles like it can't make up its mind whether to stay on or turn off, and it seems quite possible that it will soon extinguish itself if a new bulb is not procured, and soon.

Not just possible. Probable. And, I am so ready to go.

The door opens and light rushes in. Leigh is all out of breath and seems cheerful, almost giddy.

"Listen, Harp. I'm taking your Lit test later today and missing mine. You can just pretend to be me for my make-up test tomorrow, okay? I'll fill you in tonight on what you should know."

I nod. I would take two chem or trig make-up tests at this point. This room was starting to really get to me.

"Have you dusted the chandelier yet?"

This was a suggestion raised by Leigh as a result of our deferred trip last night. The plan is for me to climb like Joan-in-the-Beanstalk to the tippy-top of the room on this rickety step-ladder to clean the chandelier and steal a few pieces of crystal to ensnare more war widows' souls. The fact that the ladder is as old as the widows on the wall makes this a particularly unnerving task, underscoring my feeling that this room is not just scary but downright dangerous. But as this is actually part of my stipulated community service which Mother has demanded that I follow to the letter, I really don't (just like most of my life) have a choice.

"I don't think they are going to like it, Leigh."

Leigh looks up at me.

"I know. Just do it quick."

Right. She makes it sound like the incantation is easy. It takes time saying all the words in order and using the right intonations. The first time I tried it, the war widows did not go into the cylinders at all. They floated around the room, laughing and shrieking like drunken bandits. I tried again and they turned to dust. It was on the third try that I was able to cajole them into the cylinders with little or no trouble. It wasn't until later that they figured out the ruse and got hopping mad. And they've been that way ever since.

"I'm scared." I say it as I unhook some of the delicate crystals and place them in my cushioned parka.

There. I said it. And I did it. And I meant it.

"Me, too. I'm scared, too." Leigh sounded almost apologetic.

And just as if the room agreed to make this process every bit as fearful as possible, the light goes completely out. Not a flicker to be seen. Dark, dark, darkness.

"Don't move, Harp. I'm holding the ladder."

I feel my heart race as something cold brushes my face.

"Something touched me!," I squeal, ready and anxious to get off the top of a ladder that has become a death trap in more ways than one.

"Don't move!" Leigh's voice sounds faint with fear and distance (she is more than twenty feet down), but she is resolute. "You're up really high, Harp. You can break your neck if you slip and fall."

Something else brushes past me – ostensibly trying to help me to do just that.

"They're after me, Leigh!"

I am bundled in the parka and ski gloves which I tear off to get a better grip on the ladder, as I make my way slowly down.

"Stay where you are, Harp!"

She MUST be kidding! Nearly twenty feet in the air with ghouls flapping about? In total darkness? I'm coming down! And, as fast as I can!

"Someone is standing beside me. Stay up there. Stay where you are."

Leigh's words almost cause me to wet my skirt. I mean, really. Can things get any worse? I have something after ME and now that same (or different) something is after Leigh. And this is before I say one word of the incantation! What is going on? Why couldn't they have waited until I said the special words?

The door opens wider. Light bathes us.

I don't know whether the intrusion is better or worse as I see that the visitor is none other than Sister Dominguez.

The light from the hall almost blinds us as our eyes must readjust to something other than darkness.

"It might be easier to have some light to work by, Harper. And Leigh, don't you have classes?"

I realize that this is one of the few times that Leigh and I are not going to be confused with each other because I am supposed to be the one on the ladder for purported Crimes Against Humanity. It is odd having someone address us correctly and without hesitation.

I could see the glint in Leigh's eye and knew what she was going to say before she said it.

"Leigh, get down from there," she says to me. "I need to get back up there and you need to go to class. You've taken your turn long enough! It's MY service requirement, not YOURS."

"Sure," I take the parka off and hand it to her. "It gets really cold in here. I don't know HOW you stand it."

Sister Dominguez appears uncomfortable at this declaration and changes the subject. She looks at me.

Barnes & Noble Booksellers #2314
11500 Midlothian Turnpike SP 890
Richmond, VA 23235
(804) 794-6640

STR:2314 REG:008 TRN:5943 CSHR:Bookseller S

BARNES & NOBLE MEMBER   EXP: 12/23/2012

Enchanted Cottage of Oceania: An America
  9781467081597   1
  (1 @ 23.95) Member Card 10% (2.40)
  (1 @ 21.55)   21.55

Subtotal   21.55
Sales Tax T1 (5.000%)   1.08
TOTAL   **22.63**
VISA DEBIT   **22.63**
  Card#: XXXXXXXXXXXX4411

MEMBER SAVINGS   2.40

        Thanks for shopping

                            03:07P

Return Policy

With a sales receipt or Barnes & Noble.com packing slip, a full refund in the original form of payment will be issued from any Barnes & Noble Booksellers store for returns of undamaged NOOKs, new and unread books, and unopened and undamaged music CDs, DVDs, and audio books made within 14 days of purchase from a Barnes & Noble Booksellers store or Barnes & Noble.com with the below exceptions:

A store credit for the purchase price will be issued (i) for purchases made by check less than 7 days prior to the date of return, (ii) when a gift receipt is presented within 60 days of purchase, (iii) for textbooks, or (iv) for products purchased at Barnes & Noble College bookstores that are listed for sale in the Barnes & Noble Booksellers inventory management system.

Opened music CDs/DVDs/audio books may not be returned, and can be exchanged only for the same title and only if defective. NOOKs purchased from other retailers or sellers are returnable only to the retailer or seller from which they are purchased, pursuant to such retailer's or seller's return policy. Magazines, newspapers, eBooks, digital downloads, and used books are not returnable or exchangeable. Defective NOOKs may be exchanged at the store in accordance with the applicable warranty.

Returns or exchanges will not be permitted (i) after 14 days or without receipt or (ii) for product not carried by Barnes & Noble or Barnes & Noble.com.

Policy on receipt may appear in two sections.

Glennys

Return Policy

With a sales receipt or Barnes & Noble.com packing slip, a full refund in the original form of payment will be issued from any Barnes & Noble

"What class do you have now, Leigh?"

I look right at her.

"English."

"Okay. English it is then. Leave your sister to her work." The Sister walks over to the lamp and fiddles with it. Nothing.

"I will leave the door open for light. That should be adequate. Come, Leigh. Harper must learn to accept her responsibilities with grace. Perhaps it will serve as a deterrent for future bad behavior."

It took everything in me not to shriek at Sister Dominguez, but Leigh's face commanded me to BE STILL. I could see she had a plan, but I knew that room and I knew the ladies in that room and I was NOT leaving my sister to face them alone.

"I am not leaving. Simple as that. I am staying with Harper." I say it with firmness, aware that I am getting Leigh into trouble – something rare for her, but quite ordinary for me.

"You are being disrespectful, Leigh. I expect that from your sister, but YOU?"

"I will stay with Harper, Sister Dominguez. And that is the way it will be."

Leigh is glaring at me almost as hard as Sister Dominguez and I ignore them both. I will not leave Leigh to fend for herself in that crazy, twisted room. I will not.

"Consider yourself on detention as well, Young Lady. And I am calling your mother right away!"

I watch as the Sister stalks off, furious with a surprisingly disorderly and disobedient Leigh.

Leigh covers her mouth to keep from giggling aloud. I roll my eyes and gesture for her to hand me the parka. I had to get back up the ladder and say the incantation and place the widows in the crystals before Mother arrives. And there was no question in my mind that Mother would be coming. It was bad enough having one serial delinquent, but two?

Mother was most definitely on the way.

Chapter Seventeen:
A New Catch

I close the door, knowing how upset Sister Dominguez is with me –
well, really with Harper, but who knows the truth about that except
for me? The room falls into an inky darkness that almost immediately
makes me feel like I'm suffocating. I don't know why not being able to
see makes me feel like I can't breathe, but I feel like I'm full of bottled
air and all ready to pass out. It sounds silly, but it's how I feel.

A cool breeze blows by and I know with a chill that it is not the
air filter or the wind (as all windows are sealed shut in the widows'
room), but some spirited wraith seeking vengeance on Harper and
me. I feel the presence stop and hover over me, its cold pressed like
a cloak about my shoulders.

"You ought to be ashamed." It was a whisper in my ear.

As my eyes have started to penetrate the darkness, I see that
Harper has already climbed to the top of the ladder. She seems to be
focused on grabbing a few more crystals for her task. She's muttering
something as she ascends.

"You say somethin', Harp?" That was me, hoping against hope, that it was Harper who had whispered from twenty feet up in the air into my ear.

"Not to YOU, I didn't! You're messin' me up. I gotta concentrate! I don't have time to talk to you!! Why would I do that? I gotta get this right!"

I thought so, but I just wanted to ask. Just in case.

"But you aren't ashamed, are you?" The voice persists.

I feel sick. I knew what we were getting into when we started Project C and I know that it's for a good cause, but I have to say that when you're in the dark, practically alone because let's face it – Harper is WAY UP in the air on a ladder that looks like it's a hundred years old – and a ghost comes up to you and tells you that you should be ashamed? Well, that's a good reason to feel sick. And scared. And ready to find a good old-fashioned light switch, flashlight, candle – SOMETHING, ANYTHING - that's not a broken down lamp with a burnt out light bulb. I need someone to shine some answers on what we are dealing with in that room.

"You tried to capture me, Leigh. Or I suppose I should more properly say that your pagan sister tried to capture US."

I feel my mouth fill with spit. Some people say that when they're scared, they get dry mouth. I have just the opposite problem. Just like I don't eat when I'm nervous. My stomach hurts too much. Nor do I fidget when I'm nervous. My hands and feet are like paralyzed

– numb. Who has time to twitch? It's like two totally separate worlds. The people who twitch and the people (like me) who turn to stone. We may as well not even be the same human species we're so different.

"Speaking of worlds - you took me out of my world, Leigh Harper. You took my sisters out of their worlds, too. And now we're here with you. In this world, this place. Where we don't want to be."

The cool voice purrs in my ear as calmly as if she is sharing a weather report or information on the latest fall fashions. That sweet voice does nothing to mask the sinister manner in which she is taunting me and I feel the hairs rise on my arms and neck. I also feel my feet and tongue go numb. Now I know I'm stuck. Can't talk, can't walk. I'm in real trouble.

"What's the matter, Leigh? CAT got your tongue?"

And there she is – or at least sort of is. My Tibby. Suspended in mid-air. I guess I should more properly say OUR Tibby as Harper has half a stake in her, too. But I always feel like she's more mine than Harper's. Harp loves dogs. She likes to play with them outside and run up and down the steps with them and do all the crazy, Frisbee-throwing, puddle-jumping stuff that people do with dogs. I like cats. I like the way Tibby comes to cuddle and sit with me like a big stuftie pillow, making soft, fuzzy mewing sounds. Tibby never runs with me up and down the stairs for no reason. Well, maybe one reason. When it's time to eat. The thought of something as mundane as Tabitha eating calms me. I feel like I can breathe a little better. And then I see something that makes my heart beat faster.

Oh, no! TIBBY!!!!

"We thought you'd like to see how it feels to be inconvenienced," the voice explained. "Take a closer look at your beloved little – TIBBY?"

I close my mind. Apparently, ghosts, like twins, can read private thoughts.

I want to close my eyes, but I can't. I see that the spirit is doing things to Tabitha because as I look closer I notice that my sweet little cat is doing things that she would never be able to do if she were not possessed by this creature! Her head is spinning in a rotating motion like a wheel, around and around, while the rest of her body is perfectly still. Her eyes are enormous and frightened. She doesn't make a sound, but it is plain that she is every bit as terrified as me.

I want to scream and force that horrible, WRETCHED woman to release my Tibby, but I can't make a sound. My tongue is stuck in my mouth – paralyzed with fear. I breathe quick, deep, breaths, trying to swallow the excess fluids in my mouth before I begin to drool. I close my eyes and start to pray.

"Oh, no you don't! You will not pray after being such a wicked, bad girl! YOU WILL BE PUNISHED!"

Suddenly, over the spectre's blandishments, a bright light fills the room. At the center of its sparkling comfort appears a beautiful woman whom I have never seen, but I know has to be good because Tibby is suddenly released from the spirit's spell and drops to the floor. Like most cats, she lands safely on all-fours and I kneel down as she races into my arms.

"My name," this spirit announces softly, "is Kara Jeannette Victoria Pennington, Leigh. Harper and I are already acquainted. If you ever need my help again, just call on me. Anytime. Either of you. Do you understand?"

I just nod, still unable to speak. The lady vanishes and a lovely scent of lavender lingers in the air. The light remains. Not quite as bright, but helpful to our purpose. I watch as Harper descends the ladder, her expression is as somber as my mood.

"Okay. I have ten more."

I nod, hugging Tibby close.

Harper's eyes widen.

"How did Tabitha get here?"

I can only shrug. Harper understands. She knows how I get when I am completely overwhelmed.

"Tell me later. Let's just get outta here, okay?"

As if she needs to ask twice.

Chapter Seventeen:
One Problem Too Many

We are sitting in Leigh's room trying to figure things out. Seven souls have escaped from the first round of twenty. But at least there are ten more from today's capture. You don't have to be in Honors Math to figure out that this makes for a total of thirty kidnapped souls, with only twenty-three present and accounted for. The fact that we're only three souls ahead of where we were a few days ago is not lost on us either. And given the feisty way in which at least one (if not more!) of those seven runaway spirits has been acting, if we aren't very careful, we might lose the new ones, too. I never expected all of this. I had not built in a plan for "What If They Escape?" And, as a result of my lack of foresight, those seven women are not only not ready to help us, they're out to GET us. And if that isn't bad enough, they seem to have formed some kind of unholy alliance, union, or sorority or something.

"What does The Book tell you about recapturing souls?"

I give Leigh a baleful look, unhappily aware that I am the only one of us who has read The Book.

"Have you seen that thing? It's like a gazillion pages long with no index."

Leigh looks at me as if the lack of proper cataloguing of information in The Book is MY fault!

"It must have chapters – a Table of Contents. I mean you didn't just close your eyes, open the book, and there it was!"

I stare at her without speaking.

Her eyebrows go up and she shakes her head, acknowledging the fact that this is exactly what I had done.

"Well, that means it was meant for you to find the right spell. I mean what are the odds of that happening?"

Probably great considering I got the book from Eco off a boy who looks like he could easily get a role from Central Casting for *The Hobbit* or as Spock's grandson.

"Maybe I can talk to it again."

Leigh's eyebrows go way up at this confession.

"You mean." She stopped, trying to get herself together. "You mean to say that you asked it for help?"

I nod.

"And after you asked, what happened?"

"It just opened."

Leigh stares at me.

"Those crazy Echoes. They are completely cracked! They have magic books that respond to commands?"

I shrug.

"Mother's car does that, too. It's not so weird."

Leigh makes a face.

"That's completely different. Her car is supposed to respond to voice commands. A book is not supposed to do anything but lay around and collect dust. Harp, I mean, really? You think Mother's little 'Engine Start' command is the same as you saying 'Book Open to Page Regarding How To Catch Souls?' Do you honestly think they are one and the same?"

I know they're different. SHE knows they're different and since we are in complete agreement on this, I decide it's time to move on. Besides Jeremy will be calling me any second now that BMG has had an opportunity to blab all over town that my detention was extended to four weeks instead of two because of this most recent fiasco. Every day for a month I have to go to detention after school and read essays on virtue, penance, and moral rectitude. To make it even more of a living hell, I will have to not only read but write my own reflections on what it means to be a sinner in a school that has tried so hard to make me into a more perfect Christian. I must write of my failing efforts to reach this perfection and my internal struggle to wrestle with a devil-who-is-so-obviously-in-me using Scripture, sacrifice, and prayer as redemption. I must write odes to the Sisters on their generosity of spirit, their patience, and long-suffering kindnesses that have yet (despite their best efforts) to succeed in checking my wicked and sinful inclinations.

I shake my head over the fact that I have written too many of these congratulatory tributes to these same nuns, many of whom I feel secretly worship someone whose teachings are not necessarily highlighted in red in the New Testament. My so-called "Crimes Against the Community" have varied dramatically. My very first detention in Kindergarten included an apology to my teacher, Sister Angelina; an apology to my class (who laughed through the whole thing); and a thirty minute timeout with my face to the wall. I still regard that episode as another example of Sacred Names extremism. I was standing on a toilet seat in a private stall. Who would deny that for a five-year-old a toilet seat is the perfect launch pad to the floor?!

I sigh heavily. The next detention will find me much better prepared. Like most things and most people in my life (with the exception of Jeremy who is as regimented as a drill sergeant), no one I know is fully focused. Not even Mother. Sixty percent of her mind is on us, a third on Eco, and a quarter on finding Father. Mother is like one of the mysteries you see on cable. Nothing quite ever adds up. A cold case whose answers lie in a dusty box put away on a storage shelf.

My phone buzzes.

I shake my head, looking at Leigh's laughing face.

"You'll see." I warn her, cutting my eyes. "Just wait until Lance can hear again. Just wait. You'll find out what it's like having a real boyfriend and not Poem Boy. It's a regular job!"

I carry the phone to the other side of the room, wanting to avoid Leigh's eyes that seem to cloud over, and remain angry, at just the mention of her former online suitor's name. Wow. She must have really liked Poem Boy. I drop to the floor and get comfortable. Hunkering down for my usual fifteen minute after school call with Jeremy.

"Hello?"

It isn't Jeremy. It is Joyce Tremont. She wants to talk. The only problem is that talking to Joyce takes up too much time and I have no gossip to swap. At least none that I can share.

"Listen, Joyce. Gotta go. I'm kinda on punishment again, you know?"

Of course she knows. That's the main reason she is calling. Being Falcons school newspaper editor is a big deal – at least to her. Oceania being what it is (a very small pond next to the broad cresting waves of the Atlantic), it is more likely than not that she will use this market to her advantage as she hones her bourgeoning journalistic skills. She's no Perez Hilton, but she's the next-best-thing for Oceania in terms of scoops on wannabe town celebs. Our school paper, The Falcons Crest, is really nothing more than a venue for the Royals to use as a marketing tool for their own personal victories. Photos of them appear regularly in the Crest as they win local certificates, prizes, and trophies. Over and over again. Miss Sacred Names. Miss Teen Oceania. Miss Falcon Crest. Miss Pirates Treasure (Prep's paper). Miss Lakeshore Prep. That was Queen Leila's title for the last two years. However, that is the one position that I will be lobbying for this year. After all, I am dating the most popular boy at Prep, so there's really no reason (other than my multiple detentions at my home institution) why I should lose to a girl whose dating life at Prep ended the second her boyfriend, Happy Monroe (Jeremy's best friend), discovered that she was seeing someone else. Her chances of winning Miss Prep ever again are about as likely as my chances are of putting those seven souls back into their bottles in the next sixty seconds.

Leigh comes and sits next to me on the floor. I send Joyce to voice mail.

"Houston, we have a problem," she says.

I look at her. Trying to figure out which one of our many problems she has chosen to discuss. The seven escapees? Kara Pennington? The ten new souls? The almost eighty more we need to get? The wicked woman who turned Tibby practically inside out? Tabitha is still recovering – hiding under Mother's bed.

"Poem Boy is Poem MAN and he keeps following me. And I

don't mean on the Internet. He's here. In town. I've seen him. He says he wants...wants to kiss me."

Wow. I would have never guessed all this was going on.

"What do you mean he's following you? Is he even cute?"

Leigh gets quiet.

I don't like it when she's quiet. I'd rather hear her fussing or squawking. Being herself.

"He's like fifty, Harp."

Gross.

"We need to tell Mother."

Leigh shakes her head.

"I don't want to worry her. You know she's trying to build on to Eco and she's looking for Father and she's trying as hard as she can to deal with our misbehavior. She didn't even punish us that much for what we did today. Can't you tell how distracted she is? Something's wrong with Mother. Don't tell me you can't tell."

Actually, I have noticed. And it is unnerving.

"Well, kiddo!," I break into my widest grin – it's my bluffing I'm-all-out-of-spades-but-I-will-beat-you-anyway grin.

"It's just you and me. Now do like Julie Andrews and start at the very beginning. Tell me all about Poem Man."

Chapter Eighteen:
The Search for Chester

Lydia rarely put the Volvo's windows down when she drove, particularly if she was out of Oceania. The cause for this self-imposed isolation had nothing to do with allergies or any other debilitating illnesses to speak of, as her health was never at issue. The reason why she kept her car windows tightly sealed was that she was always greatly disturbed by ambient street noise. She was uncomfortable with the level, and type, of sounds that wafted through the open air and she liked to filter those out with quiet music or meditation CDs whenever possible. Lydia had learned the hard way that if one's window is down, there is always the opportunity to overhear the random rude, ignorant, or vulgar comment that, even if not directed at her, or intended for hearing, would nevertheless find its way to her ears and offend her sensibilities. And then there were the incessant sounds of construction that were always at play in the city of Washington, whose growth spurt over the past eighteen months mirrored that of the twins.

Checking her rear-view mirror created visual dissonance for Lydia as the rows upon rows of backed-up cars were so different from the meandering and peaceful roadways of Oceania. It was almost hard for her to believe that she had once lived in Washington, D.C. And had enjoyed it so much.

Her phone rang and it went immediately through the car's hands-free sound system.

"Just making sure that you're okay and still on your way."

"I am and I am." Lydia tried to smile away her discomfort.

"Good! See you shortly. They serve breakfast until ten."

The call disconnected, leaving Lydia to her thoughts. Thoughts that ranged from cautious optimism to apprehension to downright fear.

The phone rang again. It was Leigh.

"Mother. I can't BELIEVE that you left Lance in charge of us while you run off to heaven only knows where! Lance?" Leigh dropped her voice to a conspiratorial whisper. "Mother, he's deaf."

"So why are you whispering?" Lydia tried not to laugh, but the smile was in her voice.

There was silence.

"Mother." Leigh was trying again. "We are nearly fifteen years old. We are more than capable of taking care of ourselves. It's fine that Lance is in the house, but you left him a note – a note! – telling him to watch over us! He's practically a stranger! WE should be watching HIM if anything! Harper showed the note to me. Shall I read it?"

"No, Leigh. I wrote it. Less than an hour ago. I know exactly what it says and I expect you and Harper to abide by it. Do you understand?"

"MOTHER!"

"Leigh."

The mother-daughter standoff was in full swing. There was a cacophony of sound as blaring horns and swerving cars made a deafening chorus. Lydia took a deep breath, realizing that she was back in the real world for the first time in over a decade. And it was a bit jarring to say the least.

"Gotta go, Leigh. Lots of traffic on the Interstate to D.C."

"You're in D.C.? And you didn't take us?!"

Lydia bit her lip, watching two aggressive drivers compete for a small space that had opened up in the left lane. Insanity! No one could go over 25 mph regardless of lane, so why fight?

"You're both serving detention this afternoon, Leigh. Or have your forgotten?"

Silence.

"I should be home before dinner. Have a good day at school."

No answer. Lydia sighed as she disconnected the call. She needed to pay attention to the road more than a disgruntled fourteen-year-old daughter, who was already on punishment for bad behavior. According to Sister Dominguez, Leigh was accused of talking back. Rare for Leigh, but given what had just transpired, not at all unbelievable.

What had gotten into those girls lately?, Lydia wondered, turning up an operatic arrangement of one of her favorite Mozart pieces, *The Marriage of Figaro*. They've been in more trouble than ever before. Even Harper was breaking her own record for detentions this month.

Lydia wished more than ever that Chester was around to help with these kinds of challenges. She was too much of a pushover, and she knew it. She tried to be stern, but they were such sweet girls at the core that it was hard to play the role of strict disciplinarian.

Even with Jeremy.

Lydia shifted gears, speeding up slightly to get out of the far right and into the middle lane.

Jeremy Fletcher.

There was nothing wrong with the boy. He seemed to be bright enough and was exceedingly good-looking if one is interested in young Brad Pitt-Paul Newman look-alikes, but it bothered Lydia that the young man seemed to spend such an inordinate amount of time at their house. Yes, he was an only child. At least now he was – his older sister, Ophelia, had died in a tragic accident in front of Eco a year into the school's opening. Lydia had begged – no, PLEADED – with the City Council to put a light at the corner, but they had demurred (with Graydon Fletcher as the chairman), citing financial concerns. Less than a week after her appeal, the five-year-old girl was skipping across the street in front of Eco and had stepped out suddenly into the middle of the street and had just stood there, motionless and grinning (no one could ever say why). She was hit head-on by a speeding motorbike, whose driver claimed to anyone who cared to listen (and no one did) that she wasn't there and then she was. He kept repeating that over and over as the Oceania police took him into custody. She wasn't there. And then she was. Lydia, who had been out on the front lawn tending to her newly planted tulips, had raced out into the street, and had implemented heroic rescue measures until the Oceania EMT arrived. But the wounds were too severe and nothing helped. The young girl had expired in Lydia's arms that day and the very next morning work began on the erection of traffic lights at the corner of Eco and Grand. Jeremy was not quite four at the time. No one in Oceania ever mentioned it again.

No one. It is said that it is from that day forward that Penelope Fletcher turned into a walking, talking marble statuette. Cold, beautiful, and untouchable. The only person who could reach her was her surviving child, Jeremy, and it is rumored that even he has started to lose his way with her.

Lydia shook her head, remembering that awful, awful day. IF ONLY GRAYDON HAD LISTENED. Lydia sighed heavily, trying to forget the feel of the weight of the little girl in her arms. She was a beautiful child, like a fairy. Her still plump cheeks were rosy-red and her cherubic lips, auburn hair, and violet-gray eyes, though lifeless, stared right into Lydia's own as if searching Lydia's soul, even in death.

Remembering only too vividly, Lydia shuddered and turned off the opera. Enough drama for today, she decided, shifting gears once more. No more melodramas before breakfast.

Better to stay focused on the matter at hand. The invitation to have breakfast in town signaled a rare outing for Lydia, and was something she would have ordinarily refused (given her responsibilities as mother and Eco headmistress), but the invitation also included a carefully worded note that indicated that the discussion would be one that she couldn't – wouldn't – miss. The note was very explicit. This breakfast was not intended to show-off the haute cuisine of one of Washington's toniest restaurant hotels. Its true purpose was to discuss the disappearance of her lost, and most beloved, husband, Chester Reynolds, making this one meal that Lydia was determined not to miss.

The wait staff was never far from call and Lydia marveled at how unobtrusive yet effective they were at their jobs. Her coffee cup was always replenished and her water glass filled and it seemed to happen like magic. She felt like she was back in the dining hall at Eco! It would have actually been an even more pleasant experience if it hadn't involved a subject that distracted her from enjoying the sentient charms of the Four Seasons Hotel and the sumptuous spread before them.

"You aren't eating?"

Xavier Montague seemed to watch every move she was making. She wasn't certain who was more attentive. Him or the wait staff? Maybe, she thought with an internal chuckle, she should leave a tip for them both?

"I'm rather excited about the news, Dr. Montague."

"Xavier, please. And may I call you 'Lydia'?"

Lydia felt her stomach knot into a tight cord. Men were only polite on two occasions. When they were interested in a woman. And when they were interested in a woman.

This was Not Good.

"Of course. No need for formalities, Xavier. You've been so kind to Lance – and now this?"

Xavier waved a hand of dismissal.

"The dog was merely my way of showing young Lance some

kindness after all he has been through. It must not be easy suffering through a loss of his kind. Both mother and father?"

Lydia nodded.

Xavier sighed.

"In my family, my parents didn't use the same transportation until we were all adults. It was to avoid just this kind of calamity."

Lydia shrugged. Arriving separately on family outings did not strike her as something she would want to do, but she understood its purposes.

"One never knows what will happen, Xavier."

"Exactly. One doesn't ever really know what is going to happen." Xavier bit down resolutely into a hard-boiled egg, his eyes meeting Lydia's briefly before darting back down to his plate and his manicured fingers that held the egg for him to finish.

Lydia tried to tamp down her excitement, but she was so thrilled by the prospect of hearing news about Chester that she could just barely sit still. She felt like Harper right before getting a new skateboard. Or Leigh before a spring piano recital. All tingly with anticipation.

Xavier noted her mounting enthusiasm with his own, but for very different reasons – reasons completely unrelated to Mister Reynolds. It was Madame Reynolds that had captured his attention, and he was determined to make the best of their time together at breakfast before sharing news that would take her mind away from this place. From him.

"It appears," Xavier wiped his mouth from chocolate croissant crumbs that had gathered in his moustache, "that Manchester belonged to the National Adventurers Society's Most Secret Organization. The Pelican Club."

Lydia shook her head, doubtfully.

"I don't even know what that is, Xavier." She admitted this truthfully, and with a trace of regret. It was hard to accept that Chester had mysteries and secrets that he had kept from her. But it was clear from her response that his membership in that particular club was something of which she had absolutely no knowledge. Xavier seemed to take some small comfort in knowing that Lydia and Chester had not shared everything – even once upon a time when Things Were So Wonderful. So Very Happy and Perfect. His sharp eyes missing nothing.

"Well, my dear. It is the Society's most prestigious Club. It is hard to get in – money is not the answer nor is family name. Members are given entre only by their own merits. Did your ex-husband have some extraordinary talents or training of which our little town is regretfully unaware?"

Lydia flinched at the term 'ex-husband' and the condescending manner that Xavier had assumed in discussing Chester's merits.

Lydia was determined to correct the record on those two things, if nothing else.

"Chester had a Ph.D. in genetics from MIT and was well-known and highly regarded for his cell biology work on genetic animal mutations at Howard, Hopkins, and Harvard Universities! He had made these accomplishments before we were even married – and we married well before twenty-five. My husband was a genius, Xavier. His last tested IQ was at 190 and that was on a day when he was sick with 'flu.'"

Xavier said nothing to all of this. He realized that he had gone too far in testing Lydia's continued affection for Chester and had played his hand to the point where his envy and sense of competition were too obvious. He planned to not make such juvenile mistakes again.

"Of course, my dear. One would only assume that Manchester was a wildly brilliant man to get invited into the Pelican Club. I must confess that the Society laughed at both me and my application as I tried in vain for that particular Club. I've not had the nerve to ever try again. My hat is off to him."

Lydia said nothing, but the acknowledgement of Chester's value calmed her.

"I am so sorry for you, Xavier. About Pelican."

Xavier shrugged, feigning a nonchalance he did not feel. He had deeply resented the rejection of the Pelican Club. His family was known for its achievements in the most prestigious international and national organizations and it was a slap in the face of his famous ancestors (one of whom had actually been the Founding Father of the Pelican Club back in 1792) that he, Dr. Xavier Montague, had been so outrageously dismissed.

But Manchester Reynolds – a relative nobody – had waltzed in with much fanfare and excitement. There had been such a feverish buzz over his findings and his work at a SECRET location in a small town that most members had ever heard of – at least at that time. Oceania, Maryland.

Xavier bit hard into a piece of crust. It wasn't fair.

"Did you know, Lydia?," Xavier began, buttering another piece of hot rum toast, "that Manchester disappeared exactly one week after joining the Pelican Club?"

Lydia shook her head. She couldn't have possible known that when she hadn't even known he was a member of the National Adventurers Society or that the Pelican Club even existed!

"Yes. One week. There is some significance in the first seven days of membership in that most august body, but since I was not admitted to its ranks, I would only be able to give you the spare details I've gleaned from family history. But holding you in such high esteem, Lydia, I've gone to the trouble of locating the President of the Club.

He was there when Manchester was inducted and he's here now at my invitation to dine with us."

Lydia followed Xavier's cheerful wave to see an elderly man walking towards them at a brisk clip, despite a walking stick.

"His name is Lt. Colonel Mortimer Blaine, Lydia. And I think he will provide you with some very useful information."

Lydia held her breath. Could it be true? Could this man hold the answers that she had been trying for so long to uncover?

Was it even possible?

Xavier watched her rapidly escalating emotions with some of his own. He tried to rise above his pettiness. Tried to recall some Scripture or verse that would set his restless spirit down a more righteous, and less selfish, path. But he could not get a spiritual foothold anywhere but on his own human, fleshly desires. All attempts to rein in his worldly ambitions failed before his mounting jealousy and growing passion for the woman he had secretly wanted to capture for the last twenty years. Long before his wife had taken her last breath or Lydia's Chester had disappeared.

Years and years before. But, Xavier was nothing if not patient. And he was just as determined to wait until Lydia discovered that what she had in him, Dr. Xavier Montague, was every bit as valuable and worthwhile as what she had had with Manchester Reynolds. Yes, at this moment she was eager to find her lost husband. He could not have loved and respected her if she had wavered in her commitment to her man and her marriage. Xavier understood that she couldn't have both (himself and Chester) and he was under no delusion that Chester (at this moment in time) would be the preferred choice. But, what he did know was that he would not give up. Not when he was so close to finally getting the one thing in the world he had ever wanted.

Lydia Winchester Reynolds. As his wife.

Chapter Nineteen:
Betrayal

There is nothing to do in detention except watch other people like myself squirm, fidget, and fret over five-hundred-word, unwritten essays on "How To Be a Better Sacred Names Example" or "Why It is Unladylike to Chew Gum When Speaking" or any other one of the three bazillion asinine essay titles we are forced to write in the Detention Center.

This feeling of entrapment is all new to Leigh, so like any novice examining a specimen for the first time, she finds it all to be "SO fascinating!" and "VERY interesting." Since it is also extremely unlikely that she will ever talk back to another Sister (since she didn't in the first place), I tell her to savor the moment (for what it is) and feel free to explore the hallowed walls of the Center.

"Why do they have that poster? It's perfectly ridiculous," she comments, wrinkling her nose at the Wall of Shame poster that eagerly displays high-kicking Sacred Names cheerleaders urging us to aim even higher than their kicks.

I roll my eyes.

"Too cheap to afford a Rembrandt, I guess."

My art education is paying off. She smiles.

"So, THIS is how you spend your afternoons, Harper? In HERE?" She didn't add it, but it hung in the air anyway. With THESE people?

Unquestionably the vast majority of the inhabitants are reprobates. Neither Leigh nor myself in the almost ten years of schooling at Sacred Names have ever taken one class with any of them. They're not abnormally stupid for Sacred Names, but they have developed a penchant for doing As Little As Possible and that usually (for some strange reason) irritates the heck out of the nuns. One chronic C-bird (that's what we call ourselves), named Delores, is always caught yawning and sleeping in the front of the class. I have counseled Delores numerous times on which classes are good for goofing, which classes require you to sleep without snoring, which classes will look the other way (even if you bring a pillow, blanket, AND your favorite stuftie), and which classes will throw you out if you just try to clear your throat. But in which classes does dodo bird choose to yawn, nap, and sleep? Exactly. The ones where you'd better clear your throat only when you are about to raise your hand and answer something correctly. I don't even bother to go to those classes when I'm sick. It's either that or just check right on into the Detention Center because that's where I'd be headed anyway. You get thrown out for BREATHING too hard in those classes.

Delores is a perfect little idiot, but I always take pity on her, and I help her write her essays which usually fall into one of two topical areas: "Sloth as a Weakness of the Spirit," and "Why a Lazy Girl Never Gets Married Before Forty." I didn't mean to get her into trouble with the last one, but I did list all the attributes that men find particularly attractive that have nothing whatsoever to do with sloth or snoring and it got her an extra week as a C-bird. And essay topics titled: "A Good Girl Keeps Her Mind on Jesus" and "Why Some Girls Must Marry Immediately Upon Graduation from High School."

Whatever.

Jeremy and I plan to wait until after college. For EVERYTHING.

"Harp, what's that?"

Several people look over to see where Leigh is pointing. I roll my eyes again. I feel like I'm taking her on a tour of the Smithsonian or the Museum of Modern Art when the only things in here are stupid and ordinary. These petty instruments of torture are the products of overwrought and cloistered minds is what I always say.

"It's called "The Chair." You have to sit in it if you are too disruptive in here. You know. Yelling. Not writing your essays. Throwing stuff. It's like a big girl's version of Time Out."

"But why is it red?"

"To hide the blood!"

That would be Gloria. She takes special delight in being wicked which is why she is a regular C-bird.

"Blood?"

"They beat us."

I guess it goes without saying that most of Gloria's essay topics begin with "Why Lying Is an Abomination to God" and "Why Liars End Up in a Bad Way." Whatever that last one means. That could be misinterpreted in so many different ways.

"They don't beat us and it's red to symbolize the blood that Christ shed for us sinners. That's all. A reminder that we are inmates of the Center and are Simply No Good." I explain patiently to Leigh, who is still wandering around as if she is examining a mental ward. I glare at Gloria, who sticks out her tongue. I raise a clenched fist at her and shake it. She laughs.

Not that Leigh's far off in her thinking about this being a place for those of a delicate mental balance. The Center has more than its share of kooks and I steer clear of them. It's one thing to be kind of a smart mouth like me and another altogether to be a borderline serial killer like some of these C-birds.

Sister Rosemary enters. I'm so happy that Leigh gets Sister Rosemary and not Sister Virginia or something worse. Sister Rosemary actually LIKES doing detention duty and shares stories with us about sneaking cigarettes and kissing boys when she was our age. She said one boy looked just like James Dean!

I wonder what turned her life around so abruptly. How does one leave the arms of James Dean for the arms of God? She's explained it to me a hundred times, but I gotta say that I still don't get it. I know that Jeremy has been on me like a bad itch lately because of Lance, but I would never, ever, in a million years trade him in to wear an ugly dress, no make-up, and sensible shoes. No way. I may be a tomboy, but I'm a STYLISH tomboy. Get it? I didn't just win over Jeremy with my love of all things skating! I look downright cute in a dress. And that's a quote from you-know-who!

"Okay, girls. What are we in for today?"

I like it when Sister Rosemary says that. Makes me feel like a for real convict.

"Okay," she spots me. "Theft?" She grins as she asks.

I want to raise my hand because that's true, but I can't because one of the rituals is to elocute your crime and I can hardly stand up and say that "Oh, by the way, Sister, Leigh and I have stolen thirty souls in the past few days from the widows' wall and from classic art paintings that Sister Mary Ellen has in her art books."

Not happening.

"I was disobedient."

Sister smiles.

"Too vague. What were you disobedient DOING?"

I take in a breath.

"I was supposed to be doing community service – and I was – but my sister came to help me and that was considered a violation of my sentencing of hard – and might I add – extremely dangerous labor, and my reward is time in the Center to reflect on how I have been unruly and disobedient."

I stand and bow. Sister obliges with polite claps.

Sister turns to Leigh.

"And so you are in here for being disobedient, too, Leigh?"

Leigh nods.

"And for talking back."

Rude noises sound off from all quarters after this confession.

"What, you forgot to say 'pretty please'? You have never been rude, Leigh Harper Reynolds!" This was from Jasper, a girl who would know rude when she heard it.

Leigh looks embarrassed.

Sister Rosemary looks with penetrating eyes at Leigh, who will not meet the Sister's gaze, and then she looks back at me.

"Was it really Leigh who was rude to Sister Dominguez, Harper?"

So, do the Sisters have a list of our pending grievances against the Community pre-printed and ready to hand out to the various shift wardens? Or is it simply that Sister knows us both too well to believe that Leigh would ever talk back? Jasper seems to know. And Sister is a LOT smarter than Jasper.

I shrug.

Leigh looks up.

"It was my idea, Sister."

Sister Rosemary smiles again. She and Sister Mary Ellen were robbed. I mean it. If ever two people need to reconsider occupations, they are it.

"Okay. I will give everyone thirty minutes to write on their essays and then I want a volunteer to read...," Sister Rosemary stops as the door opens. It is well past the time when most of us have been tossed in like old laundry so we're all curious to see who it will be.

OMG! I borrow Leigh's term.

Leila enters, her head held high. She looks directly at me and then at Leigh and then back again.

"I don't know which ONE of you is which ONE of you..."

I can't help snickering.

She stops and glares at me.

"But I just want you to know that I am PROUD to be in detention for what I did and I have NO REGRETS."

Sister Davida comes scurrying in and hands Sister Rosemary a piece of paper. Presumably it is Leila's warrant.

"Leila, please have a seat."

Leila tosses a look at Leigh and then sits as far away from both of us as possible. Her animosity is so palpable I can almost taste its red, angry flavor.

"Leila, you are to stand and elocute your offense to the Community."

This ought to be good. Leila, like Leigh, has never been to the Detention Center and has no idea what's in store. Elocutions are followed up by Q and A. Grueling if the girls in the room hate you. And there is not one girl in this room that does not feel particular dislike for Miss Leila Hayden Shepherd.

"I don't understand what you mean, Sister."

Unlike some of the people in the Center, Leila isn't stupid, but she is still sort of middle of the academic road. You can trust her to know the basics, but when you start getting too out of the academic suburbs and into the rougher terrain of ideas or concepts, you need to go simple. Use really basic words.

"Explain what and why you did what you did." I break it down for her.

She rolls her eyes so hard at me, I honestly think they'll get stuck.

Standing, she looks directly at Sister as if I had just vaporized.

"I am in for vandalism, Sister. And breaking and entering. And destruction of other people's private property."

I see Sister look over at me and Leigh with a worried frown.

Frankly, I am impressed. She has racked up more crimes in one day than I usually do in a month. I may have to reevaluate Leila.

"And can you explain why you did it?"

Leila pauses. I see her cut her eyes towards Leigh and me and back again.

"Some people moved their things into empty locker space next to the Royals and I had it moved back. Well, most of it anyway."

Leigh stands up. I rise with her. If anyone has to fight, it has to be me. Leigh is never good at it. I tighten my fists.

"In the move certain TEDDIES got broken and their eyes fell out. Their little windows on the world. How sad. How very sad. The spy cameras are GONE."

Gloria stands up with us. She knows how we use our teddies to help ensnare the many criminals we have at school and she likes it. It is usually the only proof she has that she has not done whatever the Royals (or whoever else) falsely accuses her of with malicious intent. Leigh and I are like her own personal security force and to have that jeopardized by someone like the simpering Leila Shepherd is almost too much for her to endure.

"WITCH! I could KILL you! WITCH!!"

I grin. Could've been worse. Could've been -

"Gloria, sit down. Sit down this second!" Sister Rosemary rarely raises her voice, but she can tell that Gloria is not into idle threats and vulgar language is seconds away.

Gloria sits, fuming.

"Give me your reasons, Leila. For dumping out the twins' things and destroying their cameras. Those things did not belong to you."

Leila looks over at us from the far side of the room, happy that her behavior has created such a ruckus, such an explosive reaction. To be perfectly honest, I don't care a hoot about the locker issue. That is Leigh's pet peeve. But I wasn't going to let anyone hurt Leigh. And that's something everyone understands. Even the Sisters.

"Everyone in their RIGHT MIND...," This is Queen Leila in her queenliest voice, glaring at us in turn. "...knows that the Royals have the spaces immediately adjacent to their lockers, Sister. Empty lockers are only empty for a short while. We have new members who want to join us and we're able to give them locker space as just one perk that goes with their membership. And since we have two new members that meant that the two usurpers must go."

Sister Rosemary shakes her head. Even she is somewhat impressed by the selfish logic of Leila's argument.

Not that I care, but just for the sake of argument, I ask:

"And what two dimwits have joined your raggedy tribe?"

Leila looks at me, and then at Leigh, and then back to me.

"I still don't know who is which and whatnot, but this I do know. The Leigh one has just lost her two best friends, Polly and Lorelei. To me."

The hateful girl actually places her hand over her chest (I refuse to call it a heart) and GRINS.

Leigh bursts into tears. And then everyone knows who is which and what is not.

Chapter Twenty:
The Missing Link

I would kill them all if I could. I especially hate those two little colored girls who run around through my house like a blustery north wind. I've seen J.L. talking to them through the years. He is always real chatty with them. Always asking them, and every other little colored girl (that's what we called African Americans in my day – it was either colored or Negro and I much preferred colored because it sounded so pretty and colorful) in my house, about some child named Kara. I try not to listen to J.L.'s voice because it frightens me all the way down to my spiritual core like a mean bolt of lightning. I run as fast as I can whenever I see him. I try to hide my shadowself before he catches me, but sometimes he's too fast and I'm just not swift enough. I still remember that terrible, awful day in the downstairs vestibule when J.L sprayed me with those hurtful metal bullets that stung just enough to remind me that I am most certainly dead, but just simply not dead enough.

It really wasn't my fault that I sucked that poor colored man into my world that day from the upstairs bell tower. He was there and then he was here. I didn't ask for him to come with me. Up until then, I hadn't seen many colored men to be perfectly honest, so I would have never voluntarily invited him here because I would have considered it to be vaguely inappropriate. I simply looked at him as I was fleeing J.L., for the thousandth time, and then suddenly the colored man was just here. Just like me. One second I was in Bobby's arms, the next second I wasn't. I was nowhere that made sense because everything around me from one side to the next looked fuzzy and awkward. I was here in my house that is no longer my home.

As I reflect back on that time before I was shot to death by the hand of my own husband, I remember how things were between J.L. and me back then. He was always gone on travel somewhere else. Unfortunately for me he's here all the time now like mold after a bad rain that needs to be purged, but when we were alive he was always away. Business travel, he had insisted, but I never quite believed that story. Call it a woman's intuition or a wife's radar, but I always suspected J.L. of hanky-panky. In London. Paris. Berlin. New York. Maybe even Oceania. The only time he bothered to take me on travel with him was the year after we married and he had business to conduct in Washington, D.C. We stayed for a weekend at the Williard Hotel that included diversions and entertainment (a play, shopping, and a very nice restaurant). My husband never even seemed to notice that, unlike that too-brief getaway, for twelve months out of each year I was here, running this house, trying to make a life for him. He thought – like most men – that I was stupid and somewhat superfluous. When he had met me at a university-sponsored social at Yale, I had appeared to be a fairly backwards girl from a small, dusty town in Genoa, Nebraska. A pretty enough girl who had been moderately trained in classical literature at a local girls' school that specialized in turning out young ladies who could speak intelligently at social functions at schools like Yale without causing themselves or their families undue embarrassment. As it turned out, he discovered that while my father was considerably well-off, my mother was several steps higher on the social ladder than his own family on either side. My mother was descendant from Boston Brahmins who had not only been ON the Mayflower, they were considered among the chief architects of the expedition itself. When she had married my father, it is said that my maternal grandfather had made my father promise to raise us correctly in that "God-forsaken, barbaric Midwest" or return our mother to him – no questions asked and all forgiven. My father (being in love with my mother) had made good on his promise to his father-in-law and my brothers and I had attended the finest schools Genoa could provide. They went on to climb the Ivys (Harvard, Yale, and Princeton), while I studied literature at Vassar. I was deliriously happy for the first time in my young life.

And then, in my second year of learning about the truth of George

Eliot (HE was actually a SHE!) and the exhilaration of discovering from painstaking research in libraries all over New England that the Holy Grail might be more metaphorical than metaphysical, I met J.L.

By our third outing, my mother was giving me long distance encouragement to abandon my dream of becoming the first female head librarian of Genoa, Nebraska in favor of a proposal from the handsome, dashing, eligible, and very rich James Lawrence Winthrop from Philadelphia, PA.

I accepted J.L.'s invitation after a six-month courtship and we were married a year later. As the only daughter, my parents spared no expense and the wedding was featured in every Society paper from the East and West coasts, and Middle America. Upon settling into marriage in Oceania, J.L. thought mistakenly that I didn't have much else to offer him except my youth (which he translated into future breeding possibilities), good family name, and a certain fragile beauty. Beyond that, I was invisible to my husband. Never mind my previously bold aspiration to become The First Female Librarian of Genoa, Nebraska. That was completely irrelevant to him and, in fact, was a matter of considerable amusement. "As if they read in Nebraska," was his comment to me when I had rebuked his contempt of the vocational dreams I had sacrificed for our marriage.

After that, my falling for our chauffeur was almost like an

inevitability of sorts – not that either the chauffeur or J.L. perceived it that way. The one (Bobby, the driver chauffeur) claimed to love me whereas the other (James Lawrence, my driven husband) claimed me as a possession – a type of Ming vase whose intrinsic beauty was to be taken for granted and never to be auctioned without permission of its owner. Neither Bobby nor J.L. seemed to understand that I had found the whole silly ordeal to be just a question of availability and convenience. This is because as men it was inconceivable to either of them that I had examined the entire matter and declared (at least to myself) that there was no future for Bobby or me, and that we should both know that as thinking adults. He was a liveried chauffeur and I was the lady of the house. The only future we had ever considered could only be regarded within that context.

As a rule, I'm very pragmatic, including where my two romantic attachments were concerned. I had only known J.L. and then Bobby before my walking entombment. I guess my fatal flaw was not understanding enough about men in general, and underestimating J.L.'s ego and patrician sense of male privilege, in particular.

And that was a deadly mistake and is the reason why I'm roaming around my own home in a filthy bloodied dress. As I watch the Lydia woman stride boldly through my house, I wonder why I can't get rid of her and all these other people and children who have taken things over and turned them into something perfectly ghastly. I know J.L.

is after me because of Bobby and I am ashamed of what I did, but I still don't think I deserve to live in a place where SORCERY is practiced! I don't think that my indiscretion should doom me to a place where people's souls are stuffed into bottles and everyone is able to go forward and backward in time at will. What have they turned my lovely home into – this evil woman, Lydia, and her demon seed twins? A haven for witches? Hell itself?

I will stop them all. Even if it costs me my very own soul!

If I can just avoid J.L. and his hateful assaults, I might be able to concentrate on how to do this and how to return the colored man who comes in and out like a twinkling night star. While I'm thinking great thoughts, I might also figure out how to throw out these morally corrupted legions of children who have taken over my house! There must be at least three hundred of them! As it is, I can only just try to figure out how to stop the terrible twins from their wicked, wicked plot to kidnap more innocent souls of young women whose only crimes were to be important enough to have their portraits on walls or in commercial art books.

I will stop those two. If I have to resort to their tactics to do it! I was raised a Presbyterian in my father's church and practiced as an Episcopalian in my husband (and mother's) church. I have a strong, unwavering belief that God solves all things if what you ARE doing is in keeping with what you are supposed to BE doing. Sometimes (like with Bobby and me) things are not properly aligned, but in the case of those two little colored girls, I know for a fact that I am supposed to Do Something!

And I will. But I am at a loss of how to do it, but I know that it must be by any means necessary!

Because time is, unfortunately, running out.

PART II:

The Enchanted Cottage of Oceania

Chapter Twenty-One:
The Four Women of Emerson Pond

Every schoolchild and adult in Oceania knows about the Enchanted Cottage and the four women who live there: Kaleidoscope, Oracle, Monocle, and Spectacle. There has always been speculation that they are sisters, but no one seems to really know who they are because they seem to have been in Oceania longer than anyone else. Legend suggests they predate the birth records kept at Oceania's City Hall which would put them all well over a hundred, but no one has the exact answer and most people have stopped trying to figure it out. It used to be a parlor game at teen birthday parties to guess at their ages – the oldest suggested age was 140 and the youngest 99, but no one knows for certain. Trying to uncover their ages is almost as bold (or ridiculous) as asking someone 'when was God born?' - that's how long those four woman have been in that house. It's agreed by everyone in Oceania that they have been there a longer time than City Hall or the Oceania Public Library – and that is a very long time indeed as those two buildings came before the Civil War. The oldest Oceanians tell the story of four very beautiful young women who were as exotic looking as Gypsies and as passionately dark as Moors. Those older citizens suggested the dusky beauties to be no more than a youthful twenty-five. According to these observers, when the women would come to town (which was not very often at all) their hair was perpetually tangled in furious, strangled black knots that reached to their knees in rowdy coal-black waves that had forsaken combs, brushes, gels, or ribbons – any form of restraint or containment. They had the shy, wild spirit of ponies frolicking on the beach, but it was said that whenever they were approached by well-intentioned townspeople the women would respond with a gentle smile to a kind word or glance. But that last sighting was so long ago that only the oldest residents in Oceania properly remember it, and from their recollection the strangest thing of all was the fact that as they walked through town, each woman's face shifted to the others' as seamlessly as thread through the eye of needle. From left to right the fleeting expressions of the women would move like quicksilver from one visage to the next. It looked like a trick of lighting, but upon closer inspection, it was plain to see that their expressions were moving like liquid lightning from one woman to the next.

At its last telling, a few years ago (at the overdone sweet sixteen party for an overwrought Jennifer Granger), the story had changed from the women were walking through town at a casual saunter to a hell-raising, barn-burning adventure in which they had arrived on smoking hot broomsticks that had set houses and terrified women's hair on fire. Depending on the gender of the person telling it, the women were either hideous mavens (from the perspective of the most frumpy Oceanian housewives) or seductive enchantresses (the view of nearly one-hundred percent of Oceanian males over the age of five).

Whether the women are as ugly as a rotted tooth or as lovely as a sunset, there is no dispute that the Enchanted Cottage sits by a small, rushing body of water that has the coloring of the finest silverplate. It is said that the water arrived WITH the cottage – something not unusual for Eco, perhaps, but considered Very Strange Indeed for other parts of Oceania. It wasn't until fifty years ago when ambitious city planners decided to call it "Silver Lake" (because of its hue) that any trouble started. That name prompted early concern and very loud clamor from Oceania residents that the waters of a lake must be high, and therefore, too dangerous for the local children. However, measurements by the City Council's resident scientist – Dr. Gregory Silverstone – a veterinarian whose closest affiliation to water was his treatment of Freddy Hanson's slightly overfed goldfish - produced evidence from City Hall's cache of topographical maps of Oceania that the highest point in that body of water was as shallow as a toddler's bath. The name was subsequently (and more accurately) changed to Emerson POND (presumably because at least one of the women carry the surname of Emerson). Everyone quieted down and seemed as satisfied as Oceanians can be over a contentious issue.

It is certain that the four women, who were always seen together (on the rare occasions that they were seen at all), were living in the house during the town debate, but no one ever saw them during this minor crisis. Never once did they participate in any of the town's meetings on the subject – a matter actually closer to them than anyone else. It would seem that they didn't really care what the NAME of the water was as long as they could use it for their own purposes and that no one in Oceania (or anywhere else) troubled them about it. Emerson Pond or Silver Lake made little difference to them. Clothes were cleaned in that water regardless of its title, and the rest of what they considered to be nonsensical discussions about its shallow depths was just more Oceanian fuss and bother as far as they were concerned. No one dared to enter even its most safe parts as it is considered (and verified by property drawings notarized in 1902) that Emerson Pond and Emerson Cottage belong exclusively to them.

No one has ever seen anyone actually washing clothes, but clothes would often blow colors of cream, pink, red, and green in the wind from an outdoors clothesline, especially in spring and summer, and the Pond would be frothy and fragrant from clean smelling detergents.

In the old days, the women seemed to come out mainly at dusk, making it almost impossible to see the dark beauty of their expressions that would shift from one face to the other. Their lithesome bodies were covered in long dark cloaks that covered every inch of their bodies from their collarbones to booted toes. On each of their left shoulders would perch one elegant and noble bird: a falcon; a hawk; a peregrine; and a nightingale. It is said by the oldest residents that the women would call out to the birds if they flew too far. From their best recollection those names were 'Midnight,' 'Sunrise,' 'Sunset,' and 'Daylight.' Unless chasing the wind, the birds would sit motionless as clay statues on their mistresses' shoulders. It was only when the wind rustled their feathers that you could tell they were alive. That and the piercing looks they would sometimes give to certain passers-by.

Given the macabre and surreal atmosphere that seemed to envelop the Emerson Four, only one person in Oceania was ever at all curious enough about them to pay them a friendly, courtesy visit. And he alone was the only one ever seen going to visit the cottage openly and without reservation.

And that someone was none other than Chester Reynolds, a man of distinguished educational pedigree and distinctive talents, who was married to a woman of equal distinction who had produced precocious twin girls whose names were mirror images like the girls themselves. People had mulled for years over the fact of "Harper Leigh and Leigh Harper" before reaching the practical conclusion that it was little wonder that Chester Reynolds would have no problem at all with the unusual names of Kaleidoscope, Spectacle, Monocle, and Oracle when his own children had such backward names!

It wasn't until years later that Molly Cartwright, aged twelve, in the sixth grade at Ocean Valley Middle School, had shed new light on both the women and their names. Against her will (and better judgment), Molly had been forced to write, and then recite, an essay regarding "The Mysteries of Oceania's Fabled Past." No one in class (or the town) had considered that Oceania was much of a mystery – much less a fable (other than Eco), but Molly (whose father was the town's only board certified opthalmologist) had announced boldly that the four women had names that were "quite mysterious INASMUCH" – Molly's favorite new word that she had picked up from her brother who had come home from his freshman semester at Dartmouth sporting a new moustache and fancy new lingo – "INASMUCH as all the women's names relate to seeing, light, and eyesight." No one, not even the teacher, disputed Molly's declaration, but no one, including the teacher, really cared. They just wanted to leave All Odd Things to the people and place called Eco and leave their part of Oceania to the nominally sane residents who wanted little to do with things that may SNATCH, GRAB, and SHAKE you in the middle of the night. The very thought of anything remotely frightening was enough to make most Oceanians immediately Think Of Something Else. To make it even easier to deal with the "Emerson Pond Issue" (as it had come to be known during the town hearings), the people had eagerly converted the names of the women to the more ordinary and less intimidating appellations of Kayla, Aura, Mona, and Spectra. From that moment on, that was the only way the women were referred to (and those references were few and far between) by Oceania residents. It was "Hi, Kayla!," "Good evening, Aura!" followed by a "SOOOO happy to see you, Mona" finished with a relieved "Have a safe walk back home, Spectra!"

But, not Chester. Whenever questioned about his visits to Emerson Pond, he had always referred to the inhabitants by their full birth names, tossing them out as carelessly as one might call out popular and acceptable names like Emma, Jane, Amy, or Rose (or for that matter: Kayla, Aura, Mona, and Spectra). Oceanians had dismissed Chester's carefree nonchalance as the expected behavior of Eco's owner. Someone who would naturally be quite accustomed to strange names and behavior of the most disturbing and unusual kind. Why would a name – no matter how bizarre – rattle the Master of Eco? They secretly wished that Chester could devise a way to transport all of Emerson Pond and its inhabitants to Eco – far away on the other side of the hill where the Enchanted College and the Enchanted Cottage could take sequential and adjacent residence. But they knew that was probably asking for too much of a favor – even from him. Chester could probably not pull off a feat as magnificent as that – not given the way he had so foolishly gotten himself lost. It was now inconceivable that the four women, the cottage, or the Pond itself would be going anywhere anytime soon.

So they learned to live with it all.

Until the day the four women came to town and decided to turn everything in Oceania quite Upside Down.

Chapter Twenty-Two:
Arena

I have never been particularly interested in sports. I'm forced to compete in some form of exercise at Sacred Names because the nuns all feel that we have to stay physically active in order to stay tired enough to keep our wayward minds focused exclusively on God, academic study and community service – in that order. It is their sincere desire to keep us from making worldly mistakes and ruining what they consider to be our spotless, unsullied reputations. What they don't know is that thirty percent of the girls at Sacred Names already have stains so bad that even bleach, acid, or confessions with the Pope inside the Vatican couldn't fade or erase. But most of us are still fairly innocent and simple-minded when it comes to People of the Opposite Sex. I can tell by their secretive smiles that our callow, romantic yearnings are amusing to the Sisters at times – they who are already brides of a Man no one will ever dare to challenge, ridicule, or question. Their dinner conversations about our juvenile crushes are probably pretty funny – at least most of the time. If I weren't suddenly part of the joke, I guess I could laugh along. But I have become the thing I have dreaded the most. The thing I swore to my faithful twitter followers – some as far away as Tokyo - that I would never become.

A teenage girl in love.

For the last two weeks – since our first kiss - all I do is think about Lance and feel weird all the time. It's a good weird, but it's weird. I feel (and this is Not Good) that I am becoming more and more like Harper.

If they had asked me, I would have told Sister Vincent and Sister Jerome that they are wasting time devising strenuous workouts that are only effective half the time and work only for those of us who don't have a Lance or Jeremy in our lives. Between rounds of running laps, jazzercise classes (to soundtracks from the *Sound of Music*, *Sister Act*, and *The Prince of Thieves*), and round robin tennis competitions, we are often pretty worn out. Just not enough to stop entirely thinking about boys.

We would have to be competing for the Olympics, Wimbledon, and the World Cup At The Same Time and On the Same Day for that to happen.

Harper cooked up this idea which actually – even for Harper - makes sense. Since Lance can't hear (at least for now), we should communicate almost exclusively by text. It has been working like a charm. He texts me all the time! I have my phone on silent in classes, but I can feel its heat when a message is coming through and I match that heat with my own passion to let him know in response to his hourly queries of "Do u miss me? R u thnkg of me?" that "Oh, yes, I do and oh, yes I am!" The most sickening thing of all? I never get sick of it. EVER. He could send those same stupid two questions over and over for the next hundred years, and I will keep texting back: "yes, I do and yes, I am" with the energy of an excited three-year-old on a sugar rush at a birthday party.

Like Harper, I have begun imagining saying those words in a white dress. "Yes, I do." IN A WHITE DRESS. LONG. With a veil!! With people behind us. Sitting on wooden benches called pews. With a man in a long, black robe and white collar facing me.

I am scaring myself. To death.

I try to snap out of it with the next lap that Sister has pushed on us as punishment for that silly Brigitte Fitzpatrick's inattention to the safety instructions on using the gymnastic horse. Why I have to run for five more minutes around the gym (when I could be texting Lance) because of her faulty listening skills seems supremely unfair to me, but I never argue with the Sisters. They always win and that one trip to the Detention Center last week with Harper was enough to keep me on the right path until graduation – which isn't for two years, but I know I can do it. Unlike Harper who has a permanent seat with her name on it in that place, I have absolutely no desire to ever see the Wall of Shame again. Really. Proud of her association with the Wall and all things detention, Harper has inked her name on a chair – claiming SPACE in that place as if it were some kind of rental unit! HARP's HIPS. That's what she labeled the chair. When I saw it, I couldn't believe it, but she admitted to it with the same level of pride as someone who has just been pronounced class valedictorian or saved a drowning infant from going down a waterfall.

Harp's Hips.

MINE.

She had gushed it out like a two-year old which isn't really that far off in how she was acting. Maybe I'm being too gracious. At least two year olds have the sense to say "no." Even when they mean "yes."

And that brings me to my latest concern. The women in the crystals. Who won't say anything to us at all. Even after we begged them to talk and even tried to summon our new friend, Kara Pennington, who wouldn't show up. Call her anytime, she said. Right.

"Leigh? Or is it Harper pretending to be Leigh? Or is it Leigh pretending to be Harper?"

At least Sister Jerome doesn't play favorites. She hates us both equally whichever one of us shows up.

I honestly don't return the sentiment (who gets all worked up over

GYM?) which is how I have studiously avoided the Wall of Shame until recently. Harper, on the other hand, who excels at sports and loathes Sister Jerome, uses every opportunity to bait and taunt the Sister, who is – to put it kindly – not exactly a walking poster board of physical strength and beauty. I would guess that more than half of Harper's detentions are a direct result of acting out in Sister Jerome's gym class.

"It's Leigh, Sister. It's Leigh Harper."

Sister Jerome heaves her massive frame from across the room and makes her way over to me. She actually waddles when she walks – something not lost on Harper who makes rude, quacking noises that garner equally rude laughter from her peers that invariably earns her more hours in detention.

"I'm a quack." That's her response when I ask her why she doesn't stop bullying Sister Jerome. "I'm a big QUAAAACK!"

This poor duck imitation would always cause Harper to fall into a helpless heap of laughter on to the floor, rolling like a cinnamon twist, holding her stomach, and belching out hysterical quacking sounds.

If I didn't love her and look exactly like her? I might just want to kill her.

Sister Jerome gets right into my face, staring hard at me as if to catch me in a lie or read my mind. I try to flash the word "Leigh" over and over in my mind, but I know that's really just a waste of time. It's not at all like she's sensitive to that sort of thing. She is probably considering this to be a preemptive strike against Harper, who usually starts things off with a low-belly, guttural quackquack.

But I'm not Harper and I do not plan to ever quack. For any reason.

"Alright, then." Sister Jerome straightens her gym uniform and puts her hands behind her back. Her eyes are still boring holes into mine. "LEIGH, could you please recite the safety rules for the use of the balance beam?"

I smile. If nothing else in my life, I am good at stuff like this. I have memorized the safety regs for every piece of equipment in the gym – for my own safety if nothing else. I don't trust either Sister Vincent or Sister Jerome to be all they need to be in a time of crisis. Sister Jerome is too mean and Sister Vincent is well...challenged. She has the spirit of a saint, the face of an angel, and the mind of a ten-year-old. She believes everything Sister Jerome says as if it is written in the Gospel and she never trusts her own instincts. Ever. Which is why I read the safety and manual instructions for good reason – I want to live.

Thank God the bell rings, signaling an end to this period. Not that I didn't know the regs, but I didn't want to have to suffer the indignity of standing in these ridiculous blue shorts discussing the safety requirements of a piece of equipment I openly fear and despise.

"Class Dismissed!"

We scatter like leaves before a November wind to the locker room.

"Germ says we need to come to the game today."

Harper is sitting next to me at lunch, something we do as sparingly as possible because of the open-mouthed stares we get whenever this happens. People know we look a lot alike, but when we actually sit together they really know we look a lot alike and it has the same effect as it always does.

Scares them. Completely out of their minds.

We even eat at the same time. Fork to mouth. Straw to lips. The whole nine yards.

Once, in second grade, a girl whose name reminds me of food gone bad – Jessica Spoiler – Spielder – Spointer – SPITLER – whatever! – told us that one of us should just DIE because we're so much alike that no one would ever notice the other was gone. It was cruel (as only the very young can be), but at the time it was a fairly true statement.

But not now. Now we are very different. And people would notice our absence.

I hope.

"What game?"

"Football. They put Lance on the Pirates team. Germ says Lance wants you to come and cheer for him or something. I told him you're against all of that –"

"What time?"

Harper looks over at me, smiling.

"So!" That was all she said, but we both knew what she was really saying. So, when was the kiss? So, when did you fall in love? So, when is the wedding date????

I hate myself. Passionately.

"We're getting picked up at 3:30 sharp, so please don't be late doing extra assignments and kiss-ups to Sister Freddy, please?"

Sister Frederica was my absolute favorite teacher in the universe. She teaches us Contemporary Poetry and is a bona fide lit genius. Not a book she hasn't read or can recite lines from without prompting. She is a combination of Einstein, Faulkner, Oprah, and Ernest Gaines.

My role model. In a habit.

"Agreed?"

Harper's nudge brings me back to reality.

"Sure. Right out front, right?"

Harper nods, her mind already on something else. A new skateboard. Jeremy's smile. How to avoid detention. Just not on me, so I, too drift. And my thoughts, unfortunately, go straight to Our Problem. Project C.

"They won't speak to us," I whisper hurriedly to Harper.

She shrugs. One of my least favorite Harper moves.

"How do we get them to speak to us? We need them!" I know my whispers are rising, but so is my panic.

"The Book. We'll simply ask The Book." Harper answers me calmly, looking sideways at me with a raised eyebrow. She says it without speaking. CALM DOWN.

Out of the corner of my eye, I spot Meredith Ford, coming in with her friends. All I can see is a big 'detention coming!' sign over their heads because I knew as surely as I share Harper's DNA that she will mix it up with that stupid, insipid girl.

"Let's go," I stand, grabbing her arm. She gives me a dirty look, spots Meredith, looks back at me, and grins.

"Aha! Someone REALLY wants to go to a Pirates game!"

Her eyes dance like fireflies in July.

I close my eyes.

Caught. And utterly, completely humiliated.

She grabs my arm in turn.

"Let's go," she whispers this into my ear, staring spiders at Meredith. "Before it's too late."

I couldn't agree more.

A loud, shrill sound jars my ears. I shake my head. And then, I wake up. I look at my digital clock and realize that this day is just starting and not on its way out to the football field at all. I check the date and it hits me that none of what I had just experienced was real. All that had supposedly transpired – Lance, Harper, me and Lance, and all the rest of my supposedly falling madly in love - was just a silly dream. I have to admit that although I am relieved, I am also maybe just a little disappointed. After all, it had felt different knowing that I had finally been kissed – not that I even saw how that had happened – but just knowing that it had happened had been nicer than I thought. Sort of like eating the last crumb of a cookie left at the bottom of the jar. You can hardly taste it, but you know it's going to be the sweetest of all because it is the last little bit and there isn't any more. Thinking I had been kissed was just like that. I sigh, stretch, yawn and yawn again, now ready to get up for school. For whatever that's worth.

Not wanting to waste another minute on what had only been a foolish dream – me and Lance in love – in love??!! – I dash into my shower. I scurry too quickly to see the woman, standing in the far corner of my room, watching me with a face and expression that would have reminded me (if I had turned in time to see her) of the woman who used to live at Eco so very long ago, and whose painting still hangs in the downstair's east corridor that is now the Music Wing. Mrs. Eloise Winthrop. Dead at age twenty-five – only about ten years older than I am now. Murdered by her raging, jealous husband, J.L.W.

But I didn't see the departed Mrs. Winthrop standing there, so I did not know that she had inconveniently decided to take up residence in our home and even more inconveniently take control of my dreams. I would probably not understand (being too young) that from her perspective, turnabout was fairplay - fitting. If I were just a little older, I might have understood that the way she probably saw it, Mother has disrupted the sanctity of Eco, her former home, turning it into a nesting place for Most Unusual (and in her mind) Unwanted Children. Her unkind gesture of dream manipulation was her small way of repaying the "favor." If I had seen her, I would realize that she plans to turn our home from a place of repose and respite into one in which the day and night dreams of Harper and me are perched as precariously in reality as Eloise's own spirit that hovers uncomfortably between heaven, earth, and hell. Even in death the tranquility of peace eludes the former mistress of the vast Winthrop estate. If

I had been just a little older, I would have seen that from Eloise's perspective, moving into our private residence was just an excuse to keep a better eye on our so-called sinister comings and goings – just an excuse because I would have known with greater certainty (had I been older) that her real reason was not to babysit us but to escape her vengeful spouse who roams Eco like a madman in search of his faithless, lovely young wife. I might have even felt sympathy for her. I would wonder how many times J.L. plans to kill his wife before he realizes that they are already both quite dead. I'd ponder over the fact that there is something in marriage vows about 'until DEATH do us part', and feel that perhaps it was time for J.L. to just let it all go as it has been well past the death part for a very long time. I'd really question whether or not J.L. had forgotten or cares about vows and oaths and things related to honor and the living?

If only I had taken the time to see her, and figure things out in a proper fashion, I think things might have gone very differently later at the football game and its aftermath - something Harper had spoken about with such urgency in my dream. But as it is, things did not go differently. And the fact that they did not, was Not Very Good news– not very good at all. For me. Harper. Jeremy.

Anyone.

Chapter Twenty-Three:
Green-Eyed MONSTERS

The ball field's stadium was swollen with Oceanians out to enjoy a good old-fashioned game of high school football in the cool fall sun. When Harper walked out onto the field with Jeremy, arm in arm, catcalls, cheers, and mixed jeers were heard. Harper did the royal wave, grinning broadly. Her scheme to become Miss Prep was fully in play. She didn't care what happened next. Even if someone threw bottles, she was going to continue to wave and smile as if her life depended on it.

Jeremy gave her a quick kiss on the cheek to louder catcalls and cries of "MORE! You missed her mouth, GERMY!" and "AWWWW! Ain't they sweet?" Jeremy, as team captain was wearing the Pirate's eyepatch which he pulled up and turned to face the crowd. His eyes searched faces and the noise subsided.

Jeremy pointed. All heads turned in that direction.

He was singling out his parents, who were both quietly and tastefully dressed in khakis, polo shirts, and navy blazers. Penelope wore a jaunty daisy behind her left ear while Graydon's more sober daisy boutonniere completed the pair's matching wardrobe. It had been years of absences by both parents to his games and Jeremy wanted to show his public appreciation and acknowledgement.

Graydon stood and saluted his son, reflecting back on his own boyhood days on Prep's field. He had never been the athlete that Jeremy was, but he had at least been able to make at least two teams: track and swimming. Feats of which he was still proud, but nothing like what he felt for his own son walking out before so many people to play a sport that he so dearly loved.

Jeremy returned the salute, lifted Harper's hand to his lips, and kissed it. More catcalls and whistles followed that show of romantic ardor.

Jeremy walked Harper to the Captain's Lady's Chair, a ceremonial chair festive in flowers and streamers that marked the significance of this particular young lady to the Pirates' Captain. This particular young lady in this year was none other than Miss Harper Leigh Reynolds, who was now more determined than ever to wear the gorgeous, bejeweled Tiffany crown bestowed on every Miss Prep each year. This chair, under Harp's Hips (now Lady Reynolds) was just the beginning of her ascent to the title of Miss Lakeshore Prep Princess!

"Prep Plays Proud!" the Prep mascot shouted as the teams lined up in formation. "GO PREP!!"

The game began like many sports games. Mildly boring and uneventful. Harper clapped enthusiastically at all the right times, but her heart was not in it. Not after receiving a text from Leigh that one of the crystals had broken. This was not something she wanted (or needed to hear) at a time when she had to seem to be enraptured over each and every move made by a Pirate. Leigh, as usual, was nowhere near Prep and couldn't have cared less about Harper's dilemma. Not when she had returned home and discovered that one of the chandelier crystals had broken. Something (or someone) kept swatting at her and it was unnerving to say the least. What did she care about a stupid game, a silly chair, or a dumb title like Miss Captain's Lady when she was at home fighting with ghosties!

Her texts pulsed like a vibrating instrument. Harper tried to pull the phone out surreptitiously and text Leigh back, but right before throwing his pass, Jeremy, the Pirate's quarterback looked over at his Lady and seeing her preoccupied, halted his throw. The crowd fell silent, but Harper never noticed, so busy was she in responding to Leigh.

"Am bzy. Lv gosts 2 me. Just w8. K?"

Harper waited for Leigh's response, and looking up, noticed that Jeremy had stopped to stare directly and purposively at her. She also noticed, all at once, how Very Quiet everything had suddenly become.

Chastened, Harper tucked away her phone, looking with remorse at Jeremy, who resumed his play, after giving her a curt, sharp nod. He passed for more yards than before and the fans went wild. He ran the next play into the end zone and scored with such athletic grace that all was forgiven by Pirates fans and Jeremy.

But not forgotten. Not by everyone.

When it seemed safe, Harper checked her text messages. Nothing more from Leigh. That was a good sign that things might have worked themselves out without a need for further involvement. That would be good because after the game she had promised to go with Jeremy and his friends to the Soda Hut right off Prep's main campus. It was a ritual that Jeremy loved and as the newly minted Captain's Lady, she could ill-afford to stand up the Captain for such an auspicious occasion.

The game finally ended as it had begun. The Pirates wiped out the Beavers – 24 to 3. Harper waited (as custom dictated) for Jeremy to escort her from the Lady's Chair and off the field. Many fans had already vacated their spots on the bleachers to reserve victory booths at the Soda Hut. Those who remained yelled out more calls for kisses and even more extreme displays of affection. Jeremy stuck a finger in the air and there was alternate laughter and jeers.

Giving Harper a kiss on the top of her head, he whispered that he had something special to show her, but it had to wait until after they had sodas with his parents.

"Your parents are coming to The Shut?" That was the popular name for The Soda Hut – The Shut.

"Just for a second. Just to say 'hi.' I asked them to come." Jeremy looked and sounded a little defensive. Harper looked up at him, crinkling her nose.

"Are they still here?"

Jeremy shook his head.

"They left thirty minutes ago to save a seat."

Harper said nothing more, a worried expression marring her earlier and prettier happiness.

"I don't think your dad likes my family, Germ."

"I know." Jeremy squeezed Harper closer, "But I do. And it's not your family I want to marry. It's YOU. I'll make him like you, okay?"

Harper nodded, not certain how certain something like that could really be.

The Soda Hut was the type of place where you had to be under thirty-five to appreciate its charms. It was loud. There were the occasional bouts of rough-housing and mock play fights between young men (mainly to show off for young women), and all the things typically associated with a certain class of youth that was shielded from the mundane requirements of life due to their protected status of privilege and wealth. The girls from Sacred Names who attended the Friday or Saturday night festivities at Shut would shed their uniforms in the one FEMALES ONLY bathroom at Prep to be properly attired in tight jean skirts, hip-hugging jeans, and cut off or skimpy blouses that showed tummies and cleavage at an alarming and distracting rate. The boys of Prep were most appreciative of the female anatomy so visibly on display and it became routine for more than one boy to be separated from a girl by Shut Management whose motto (emblazoned on all four walls) was: "We Run a Clean Establishment. No dirty floors, dirty dancing, or dirty minds. We SHUT the doors on Bad Behavior."

Parents were glad to have Ma and Pa Forrester watching over their impulsive adolescents at The Shut and that was the primary reason why permission to go to The Shut was typically granted with little or no hesitation. With each child's admittance, the Forresters cleared at least fifty dollars a head – usually more as the boys, when they weren't fighting or trying to kiss the girls, were spending a large volume of money without care or concern. Older boys, already in college, would flash their Platinum American Express cards to pay for their date's dinner and the dinners of her friends. Those young men would watch with keen interest as those coveted girls (usually considered the most attractive) would smile that much harder and brighter as the Card's silver splashed against the pale face of the check that bore the humorous command to SHUT UP (Pa Forreseter's cheeky way of demanding that students pay up after spending an almost decadent amount of money). Ma Forrester got a kick out of it, too. Telling those young scions to SHUT UP every time they paid. To use a card like that on Cajun-style fries and chicken burgers was hardly in keeping with the nobility of that Card's original design, but the effect was as powerful on the gullible women as if the young men had ordered Dom Perignon and Beluga caviar from a five-star French restaurant.

Harper entered The Shut, hoping that she looked fresh after the long, intense evening. She felt grubby and scared. Upon spotting his parents in a far, back corner, Jeremy started waving madly and Harper found herself being pushed forward through a crowd that parted like the Red Sea for Jeremy and his Lady.

Some of the men bowed and a few of Harper's friends, curtsied, giggling hysterically. Last year, it had been Leila who had been so adorned and Harper had gleefully joined in the merriment from the sidelines – a place she wished she could escape to now.

Graydon stood as Harper made her way to the booth, sliding in beside Penelope, who greeted her with a bright smile.

"You are such a darling!" Penelope squealed, hugging a surprised Harper close, squeezing her tightly. "Do you remember me?"

Harper remembered that awkward time two years ago with nothing but embarrassment, but she pushed the memory away, glad to see that all had been forgiven and chalked up to childish indiscretion.

"Yes, ma'am, I do remember."

Penelope shook her head, wagging a finger.

"You make me feel so old with that word, Harper. Call me 'Penny.' I insist!"

Graydon and Jeremy exchanged anxious looks. Jeremy knew his mother's erratic temperament and he was worried. She seemed so happy and light-hearted, but he knew that all of that could change in a split second. Unconsciously, he moved closer to Harper on the seat. If needed, he could grab her up and run out of The Shut at a moment's notice.

"Penny. I like that nickname. It's very pretty," Harper tried to salvage herself from what she had been told by Germy (on numerous occasions) had not been the absolute best way to greet her future mother-in-law at their very first meeting.

Penelope's eyes cooled.

"I remember you as having a lot more to say than that. You weren't boring. I was so looking forward to not being bored tonight!"

Penelope's tone started rising in direct proportion to Harper's anxiety.

"Mother, please!," Jeremy hissed. "You promised to be good!"

Harper sensed in the pit of her stomach that things were only going to go from bad to worse, so she decided to do something she rarely did with adults.

"Penny for your thoughts?" she asked coyly of Penelope.

Penelope looked closely at Harper. She had heard things over the years about the Gifts of Lydia and Chester's children, and she had often wondered how true those rumors were because she had an interest in uncovering some hidden thoughts of her own. Thoughts that she had never truly buried.

Penelope pulled out a penny from her purse and placed it on the table. Jeremy and Graydon exchanged another round of anxious glances.

"Harp."

Harper looked at Jeremy, giving him her most beseeching face. The one that made her look like his pet name for her that only they knew: "Kitty." Big brown eyes, pleading expression, soft skin, and cuddly look. She had it all going on - everything except whiskers and a tail.

"What can I get you folks?" It was Pa Forrester, wearing his big white apron and an extra big smile. He was fond of the twins and liked Jeremy well enough, too.

Graydon looked to his wife.

"I'll have a slice of cheese pizza and a soda." Penelope was quick, not wanting to waste a second on something as ordinary as ordering food.

"Okay on the pizza, but not okay on the soda, Mrs. Fletcher." Pa Forrester knew every single person in Oceania, whether they knew him or not. "We're called the Soda Hut for a reason. One hundred different varieties of soda. We make it fresh and do mixes, too."

Penelope considered the possibilities for a few seconds.

"A regular-type cola," she said finally. "Call me dull."

"Not you! Hardly you." Pa Forrester smiled, flirting a little with the pretty woman who rarely came into town and hadn't seemed to age a day since he had last seen her over twelve years ago. "And what about everyone else?"

Harper thought she would gag (or worse) if she ate a single crumb, but she knew that Jeremy expected her to order, so she ordered the same kind of pizza and cola to keep it simple.

"We think alike, don't we, dear?" Penelope smiled kindly.

Graydon and Jeremy ordered hurriedly, father and son aware that with Penelope in this whimsical mood things could escalate and evolve very quickly into something Not So Very Good and it was better to eat fast and Shut Up as quickly as possible.

"So, my darling dearest girl," Penelope prodded gently. "Tell me what you see."

Jeremy closed his eyes, regretting his decision to invite his parents out to sit with him on this special night that should have been shared with just him and Harper. In his car, Harper in his arms, telling Jeremy that he –

"I see Ophelia."

That announcement seemed to suck the air right out of the booth. Everyone seemed to be holding their breath. Before Penelope (whose eyes were suddenly shining with unspilled tears) could speak, the door to The Shut opened with a BANG! The back of the door hit the wall with a jarring THUMP!

In walked Kayla, Aura, Mona, and Spectacle. Their long hair was carefully coiffed and stored on top of their heads in a dazzling array of exotic styles. It was unlike anything that anyone under the age of thirty had ever seen in Oceania. Their cloaked forms that shrouded their figures suggested that more mysteries than just their hair were yet to be uncovered. Their pet birds, clutching to their shoulders, were all silent, but watchful.

Being as old as he was, Pa Forrester knew EXACTLY who they were. He saw past the cloaks and dark sunglasses, recalling how lovely each woman was in her own special and unique way. Others in the room knew OF the women of Emerson Pond, but Pa Forrester knew ABOUT them. A very big difference.

"Would you ladies like a booth?" Pa Forrester's voice sounded unnaturally loud – even in his own ears.

"Yes." That was Spectra.

"Thank you." That was Aura.

"Very much." That was Mona.

"Pa Forrester." And that was Kayla.

Pa Forrester bowed slightly.

"Please follow me."

The room watched open-mouthed as Pa Forrester calmly seated the four ladies in the booth he had been keeping on permanent reserve since most of them could remember. Now they understood who he had been saving that booth for all these years, and they wondered how Ma Forrester felt about that. Four women, no less!

There was much speculation about a great many things, but everyone was afraid to speak. Afraid to say anything at all for fear that it would cause the women to turn into salt or disappear altogether.

There was utter and complete silence as the women filed into the booth slowly, making certain their cloaks were not the cause of any one of them losing their footing along the way.

"We're ready to order." That was Kayla again.

Pa Forrester beamed.

"Great! It's so good to see you ladies here again!"

Penelope watched that scene for a few more seconds before tapping Harper's hand to return them to where they had left off.

"What about Ophelia?"

Harper's mouth went dry. Unlike her twin, who over-salivated when nervous, Harper's mouth would go as completely dry as the Saharan desert.

"She was right there and now she's gone." Harper decided that truth was best.

Penelope's eyes narrowed. That explanation sounded suspiciously like what she had heard upon Ophelia's death. Her murderer had said nearly the exact same thing!

"And just where in the world is she now –?"

"HELLO, Mr. and Mrs. Fletcher!"

Jeremy stared at Happy. It wasn't that he wasn't glad to see his best-friend, it was just that right now was not a good idea. In fact, it was a pretty Bad Idea.

"Hello, Happy!," Graydon broke into a jovial smile, the first since he had sat down.

Happy took that as an invitation and sat down, ignoring Jeremy's frantic glare.

Penelope looked crushed, but said nothing.

"I saw you in the Lady's Chair," Happy tossed out casually. "Texting someone we know?"

"Just Leigh." Harper squirmed, wishing that Happy hadn't raised a sore subject. It was obvious that Jeremy had forgiven her or else he would have never continued along this path of having dinner with his parents. He would definitely not be here with her at The Shut if he hadn't completely moved on. He would have taken her straight home and then called to tell her the two bazillion reasons why he was angry with her. And then he would have texted her about it. All night long.

"Really?" Happy followed up.

Jeremy tensed up.

"I saw Lance texting around the same time."

Harper tilted her head, looking carefully at Happy, as if seeing him for the very first time.

"I wouldn't know what Lance was doing. I was texting Leigh. My sister."

"Well, maybe the three of you were texting." Happy forced a laugh. "You know what I mean? A threesome?"

No one laughed. Graydon shifted uncomfortably in his seat, aware of Jeremy's growing impatience and feeling some of his own.

"It was good seeing you again, Hap. You and Jeremy have to shoot some hoops together again soon. Maybe I'll join you boys. We'll have our own little threesome."

Graydon's dismissal was plain as he tried to clean up Happy's bizarre and uncharacteristic comments. But Happy, for whatever his reasons, refused to budge.

"I need to talk to you about our precal class, Jeremy. It'll just take a minute."

Jeremy stared coldly at his friend, all feelings of warmth drained away in just those few minutes.

"It won't take ten seconds because I'm not going to discuss it with you. Not now. Not here." Jeremy did not raise his voice but his anger was palpable.

Happy blinked. He had never seen Jeremy that angry. Harper had seen that side of Jeremy more than she cared to remember, and she instinctively reached out for Penelope's hand, who took it wordlessly.

Graydon rose.

"See you soon, Hap. Send your parents our best."

At this, Happy rose and left, tossing a backwards, "Bye!" as he sauntered away.

Harper refused to meet Jeremy's eyes. She already knew what he was thinking. And it was Not Good.

"So, Harper," Graydon tacked on a pleasant smile, "I hear that tradition calls for the Lady of the Chair to get chaperoned by the Captain of the team for the next month to anywhere she desires. I guess you chose The Shut?"

Harper nodded, cutting her eyes over to Jeremy, who was staring out at the four women of Emerson Pond, not looking at anyone at their table.

"I like it here." Penelope announced. "Especially now that it's just us again."

Jeremy smiled softly at this. Glancing at Harper, he sent her a quick wink.

"And what does that mean, Mother?"

"Family. That's what I mean. We have family here." Penelope went directly to the point much to Jeremy's surprised delight.

Graydon said nothing. His eyes and tight smile betrayed little else.

"So about Ophelia..." Penelope started.

"She's..." Harper began.

The door banged open again, but this time there was nothing to see. A big, cold gust of wind blew in, scattering some of the teens who had been slouched by the door waiting for an empty table.

One girl screamed:

"Someone just touched me!"

Another boy shouted.

"Someone just pushed me!"

The four women of Emerson Pond rose in unison. Harper watched, fascinated, as they pointed their fingers to the door and said at the same time:

"Eloise Winthrop! James Lawrence Winthrop! Cease. Desist. STOP IT NOW! GO BACK!! GO BAAAAACK!!!"

The lights went out and girls started to shriek in fear hysterically without pausing for breath or reaching for sanity. The lights came back on and then off and then on and then off and in the midst of this almost psychedelic strobe effect, a little girl appeared.

"OPHELIA!" Penelope Fletcher shrieked and climbing over Harper, struggled to reach her daughter before Graydon or Jeremy were able to pull her back.

Penelope ran to grab at her daughter who melted like a kiss of sunshine in her arms.

This time, the lights stayed off for more than thirty seconds and when they came back up, Penelope was seen sobbing on the floor, her makeup running down her face and into the shirt of her husband, who was now cradling her like an infant.

Harper looked at Jeremy and understood for the first time what drove his rages, his sense of helplessness, and his desire to always be in control. If nothing else, maybe she could help the Fletcher family.

She and Leigh could add Ophelia to Project C and make it Project C-O.

It was worth a try. If only she could get Leigh to cooperate. Leigh wasn't that thrilled about the idea of Jeremy in their lives and the concept of letting him in on their secret and helping his family would probably not be well-received.

"Let me drive you home, Harp. We'll get some takeout along the way. Is that okay with you? I mean, it is supposed to be your choice." Jeremy fumbled for words, his distress was evident at the sight of the chaos left in the wake of what was supposed to have been a family victory dinner and the bestowal (infront of his father) of a diamond Tiffany friendship ring on the finger of the girl he planned to marry.

Harper nodded, her appetite completely obliterated for the first time in recent memory.

"Let's just go to my house, Germ. Grab something there. I'll make us something, okay?"

Jeremy kissed the top of her head, leading Harper out of the diner after placing a few big bills on the table to cover all the trouble they had caused to Ma and Pa Forrester. He was more than ready to go. He felt (and rightly so) that he had done more than his part tonight to just Shut Up.

Chapter Twenty-Four:
Lydia's Preoccupations

Lydia frowned, looking outside the window of her office at Eco as Cal's puppy legs sprawled over her bare feet. The weekly roses from Xavier were fragrant and lovely on her desk. Today's bouquet was dressed all in pink and looked as fragile as she felt at that moment. She had asked Xavier as nicely as possible (trying desperately hard to not sound rude or ungrateful) to stop sending flowers, but he had ignored her quiet protests, overruling her with a big smile, generous heart, and fragrant bouquets that arrived on Monday morning with the precision of a Swiss clock.

Xavier's inquiry into Lance's persistent deafness worried her. He was right. It had been well over two months since Lance's parents' death and it was starting to become more of a worry that the young man's hearing had failed to return. The lively chatter of Lydia and the twins at breakfast and dinner seemed to go over Lance's head like windborne party balloons. Sometimes, on rare occasions, he would look up from his plate (food did seem to have a remarkably strong hold over him) glance at each of them in turn, and smile a beautiful smile with flashing dimples. This encouraged Lydia that even if he couldn't hear anything, he still liked being there. Liked being part of their family. These feelings were as fleeting as Lance's smile, but it helped to reassure Lydia that things were still going according to plan: Lance was on track to graduate from high school, go to college, and start a fresh, happy, new life Very Soon.

Lydia had ensured that Lance's mundane needs were all met: food (plenty of it), shelter, clothing, friendship, and the minor incidental needs of most young men (electronic games and portable PDAs, subscriptions to magazines on how to stay fit and active, and a first-rate home computer system). Having had daughters and no sons, she had tried to figure out what more he might need and was growing more and more impatient with her own (and Harper's) inability to properly communicate efficiently with Lance using American Sign Language. She was beginning to think it might be better to hire a special tutor just for that purpose alone. It might be nice for him to have someone at the house who could make him feel more comfortable with his temporary infirmity, and to help him discuss what was truly on his mind. The problem was that even if Harper grew in her proficiency, Lance's own inability to understand American Sign Language would continue to make the whole process of communication awkward, strained, and ultimately useless.

Lydia was at a loss over where to turn next. Xavier had visited her last week at Eco with his own suggestion that had not gone over very well. He had wanted Lance to move into the boarding quarters at Prep. After thinking it over for a few days, Lydia had quietly broached the subject to the girls. The twins had resisted that recommendation as misguided and inappropriate, citing numerous reasons of social isolation, hazing, and all other kinds of BAD things that Could Go Wrong if Lance were to take up residence at Prep. Discussing the matter at dinner, two nights ago, had proven to be disastrous. Jeremy, seated across from Lance (and in his usual spot next to Harper) had listened to the argument, saying very little. Against her own better judgment, Lydia had asked Jeremy for his opinion and had received little more than a sullen shrug and a "Harp is right – for a change" response after tossing a rather sharp glance in Lance's direction.

Harper was right about what? The fact was not lost on Lydia that Lance would be one of only two boarders – the other young man, Julio Garcia (uncharitably known as "Who-Thanks" at Prep – a deliberate perversion of his name from WHOlio Garcia to WHO-GRACIAS), was the son of the Ambassador of a tiny Central American country whose father's conservative social outlook had compelled his admittance to Prep. The ambassador had heard all about the all-male private schools in Washington, D.C. that were known for partying, drugs, and ruined girls whose salacious pictures always seemed to end up on the Internet. He did not want such pictures to also end up in the college application files of his son, so it was with great eagerness that the ambassador had selected Lakeshore Prep. He did not want young Julio caught up in scandal and had considered Prep to be a safe haven from the level of debauchery witnessed at some of the more prominent D.C. academic enclaves.

Lydia wondered briefly what types of hazing activities poor little Who-Thanks had to suffer through each day, and if Lance would be forced to endure the same treatment if he were to become a boarder. Lydia considered the possibilities. Maybe Lance, unlike Julio, would escape the brunt of Prep cruelty. Unlike Who-Thanks, who hailed from foreign shores and had a thick Latin accent, Lance was not from another country – he was from D.C. and spoke like everyone else at Prep. It also helped tremendously that Lance was a good athlete, attractive, and already in attendance at Prep. It also didn't hurt that Lance was smart and had attended a D.C. school where hazing was as natural a rite of passage as a bloody nose.

Lydia hadn't asked Lance, but if she had, she would have discovered that he was more than prepared to handle anything dished out by Prep students. The fact of the matter was that Lance enjoyed living with Lydia, Cal, and the twins, and didn't see any reason why that should change. He had followed some of the debate by reading lips, but the twins spoke too fast and finished each other's sentences without speaking, making it hard to track conversations with them.

Looking across the table that day, Lance knew that despite his rather comfortable existence with the Reynolds family, Jeremy was a lot less than enthusiastic about his presence at Idislewilde. But Jeremy's discomfort didn't really worry him all that much because Lance understood the reason for it and didn't take it personally. Jeremy did everything except put his leg up and publicly squirt on Harper to make it clear to everyone over the age of two that she, Harper Leigh Reynolds, belonged to him, Jeremy Alexander Fletcher.

A year older, and a lifetime wiser because of Life's recent tragic events, Lance was only mildly annoyed with Jeremy's antics. He could have told Jeremy not to fret so much – and that he, Lance, had other things going on – but he figured it was none of Jeremy's business as to what he did with his free time. And he certainly did not want Lydia or the twins to get involved in his private life more than what was absolutely necessary. Lydia would be too maternal and the girls possessed skills he wasn't sure could always be counted on to be used to everyone's good – including his own.

The Big Thing that Lance was keeping secret was that like Chester many years before, Lance had found his way to Emerson Pond and was spending quality time each day after school with its fascinating inhabitants: Kayla, Mona, Aura, and Electra.

And loving every minute of it.

An awesome discovery had been made by Lance – a discovery

that was as unexpected as it was fortuitous. As soon as Lance would enter the property line of Emerson Cottage his hearing would return as if it had never disappeared. Couple that strange (but wonderful) occurrence with the fact that all four pet birds (no matter how fickle and erratic their temperament) absolutely, positively adored him, and he was a seventeen-year-old in heaven!

It was Kayla – or was it Aura? – who had said that "All Lost Things Get Found at Emerson Cottage." He couldn't remember exactly when it was because being in that Cottage with those four women created so much mystery that losing track of time was the least of it. Lance was completely baffled and awed by their Powers, their Magic, and their ability to transform the sublimely Ordinary into the supremely Extraordinary without much fuss or fanfare.

He couldn't remember precise details, but he knew that it had definitely been Mona who had announced one afternoon that Lance was to be renamed (at least at Emerson Pond) "Master of the Keep" for his effective handling of their four noble birds. He liked that title: Master of the Keep. And was considering having a tee-shirt made with that name and the picture of all four birds soaring in the background. He knew he deserved that title as he was the only one (other than the women) with whom the birds were that friendly and trusting. They loved Lance dearly and became fretful each Thursday afternoon - a day that pulled Lance closer to the weekend that meant that he would be spending precious time away from them. They understood, but failed to accept, that he had to spend time elsewhere on Saturdays and Sundays, doing things with the Reynolds or at school. Unknown to the women (or Lance) the birds had begun to deeply resent these lost days and were devising a plan to change things around to what they most wanted. They wanted Lance seven days a week and they were willing to do what it took to make that happen!

Mirroring the feelings of the birds, Spectra had teased Lance one day, inviting him to move to the Pond to permanently regain those things that had been lost to him: his hearing and his family. But Lance had passed on that offer, knowing in his heart that when the time was right his hearing would one day be restored outside of Emerson Cottage. He also knew that his parents, now gone, could not – and should not - be returned no matter how hard the four women tried. Unlike Chester, they had not gotten lost. They had been killed. A tragedy, but a fact. And nothing he was prepared to battle God against. To try anything less than acceptance, at least from his perspective, was sacrilegious and should not be attempted. Sixty minutes of hearing each day from Monday through Friday with no strings attached was like having a five-hour holiday each week and he cherished the time spent with the women and their winged, endothermic vertebrates.

"They'll trade two of us for one of you, Lance." That had been Mona, laughing one day as he had played with the birds in the Cottage's backyard. A favorite new game was for Lance to perch two on his shoulders with the other two settled gently on each forearm while Lance would pretend to be a plane, swooping and howling through the grass like an eight-year-old with the birds squawking in delight. They would hang on, ecstatic with hilarious joy, cawing for MORE, MORE, MORE!

Lance had smiled at the memory of that outing that had taken place just last week, thinking of how even that sporting game could be improved.

But Lydia knew nothing of Lance's sojourns to Emerson Pond. Coming home at five o'clock each day, Lance would recover Cal from wherever he was playing in the house (if Lydia had not taken him to Eco), go to his room, and study until dinner. These seemed to be scripted and solitary pursuits that Lydia thought might be too lonely for a boy of his age.

This was the reason why she had, with great reluctance, called for a private meeting with Jeremy. She had asked him to meet her at The Owl Bistro, away from Eco and away from the house. She resisted the idea of inviting another Fletcher into her business, no matter how harmless that Fletcher seemed to be, but she knew that she had to do something about Lance, and Jeremy seemed like the best solution.

Or at least a good start.

The Owl Bistro has been the local hangout for the teachers and faculty in Oceania since the day the last brick was placed in the building's façade over thirty years ago. Dark cherry wood, overstuffed upholstered chairs, and a large marble owl wearing spectacles, clasping a thick-paged book to his chest, adorn the middle of the foyer. A sign from the base of the marble owl announces rather unpoetically: Welcome to The Owl: The Place Where Wisdom Meets Wine and People Make Friends!

On Thursday nights, the youngest Sisters of Sacred Names meet in the private dining hall for an opportunity to escape their cloistered grounds and discuss more worldly pursuits; movies, music, and the occasional town gossip. One of their favorite new topics was the latest Incident at Shut involving the women of Emerson Pond. It was all over Oceania about the Sighting of the Fletcher's deceased little girl, Ophelia, and the even more spectacular Sightings of Eloise and J.L. Winthrop. The youngest of the youthful nuns, Sisters Antonia and Theresa were like drug addicts on an urban street corner – they couldn't get enough! Under twenty-five, the two nuns had been trying (with prayer and confession) to replace their ravenous appetites for gossip with The Owl's delicious deep dish pizzas and other specialties, but they couldn't resist questioning their young servers about Everything Going On. They tried to cloak it in spiritual terms "We will pray for little Mary and her Problem with Alcohol", but it was clear that their prurient interests went far beyond their Calling to the Cloth.

Tonight, the two Sisters were happily eating alone, without the companionship of the older nuns, and because of that fact they were not given the private dining room (as was customary), but were seated directly across from the table reserved for Lydia and Jeremy. It was fortunate for Sisters Antonia and Theresa that they were placed where they were (a type of random divine intervention?) as new information regarding Things Going Wrong in Oceania was about to be rather openly and publicly revealed.

Lydia was running late. It wasn't like her to be late, but she had had to stop to check on an order she had placed with Plants R Us! in the little town of Marbury, thirty miles northeast of Oceania. She had been going there for years and she was anxious to consider which plants to grow around the house before the onset of spring which was months away but never too far for serious gardeners like Lydia.

She checked her cell phone. Two messages. One from Harper. The other from Leigh. Timed one minute apart. That meant they were not together and that each had a different question. That was especially unfortunate because of her tight schedule, but she called them back in the order that their calls had been received.

"Harper? Mother. What's up?"

"Are you meeting with Jeremy?"

"Yes." Lydia pulled over to The Owl's parking lot and was pleased to see that there was plenty of room. That meant fewer people and a shorter wait time for service.

"Am I in trouble?"

"No."

"Is Jeremy in trouble?"

Lydia paused, reflecting briefly on how to answer that. She decided that the truth, in all cases, was best.

"I have no idea. What do you think he has done?"

Harper sighed heavily.

"Mother, what I mean is – is Jeremy in trouble with YOU?"

Lydia smiled.

"No, Pumpkin. He is not."

Harper smiled back, relieved.

"Okay. So why do you want to talk to him? And, by the way, he just tweeted me. He's already in The Owl. Where are you?"

"Parking. So are you going to let me go in or not?"

"Go. Have fun." There was a pause. "Can you bring back leftovers?

Leigh's cooking is not all it should be, if you know what I mean, and tonight is her night to FC (Family Cook) and..."

Lydia laughed.

"I'll bring back something. Now let me go please so that I can finally get inside!"

Lydia disconnected the call and hit the "L" button where Leigh's number was programmed. The call went straight into voice mail.

"Hello, Leigh. It's mother. I'm returning your call. Having dinner with Jeremy at The Owl. I'm bringing something back for everyone as a treat, so stay out of the Danger Zone (their code for kitchen). See you soon."

Lydia put away her phone, thinking that this would end, for at least an hour, all communication with the people she loved (and who frustrated her) more than anyone else on the planet.

But, as Lydia was about to learn, expectations are, like hitting the lottery or finding true love, usually just wishful thinking.

Lydia's long legs moved her quickly from curb to the front door of The Owl in almost record time. There was no doorman, but a man standing close to the door held it wide open for her. Lydia was too tall to duck under his arm, so he was forced to drop his arm to let her pass. He stared hard at her, as if he were trying to place her from somewhere – somewhere Not Good At All. Lydia smiled graciously, her mind already on what she was going to say to

Jeremy, and eyeing the hostess desk up ahead, she failed to notice the hate-filled expression on the man's face as he stared after her. Moving too quickly, she failed to see that he was holding a small photograph of a pretty young girl. It was the ninth grade school photograph of Leigh Harper Reynolds. But, she was too busy to stop and striding purposefully toward the desk, Lydia was ready to bark out her reservation and head to her table. Before she could reach the reservationist, someone grabbed her from behind.

"Who DARES!?," she began sharply, and then recognizing Xavier, she broke into a smile. "Xavier, what a lovely surprise! How nice to see you here!" They had dined at The Owl where Xavier had pointedly shared a dislike for dining alone.

"Are you with someone?" Lydia was not being coy or curious, just courteous, but she saw from the delight in Xavier's eyes that her intentions had been willfully misconstrued.

"All alone, my dear," Xavier gave a little bow, taking Lydia's hands into his own. "And you?"

"I'm having dinner with Jeremy. You know Jeremy Fletcher?"

"Of course I know young Jeremy. He's been at Prep since he was four years old. Exceptional athlete. He's the most popular boy at Prep. Dating your daughter is he not?"

"Yes, you're quite right on all counts, Xavier."

"Zee, Lydee. Call me 'Zee.' How many times –"

Lydia took a quick breath. There was no time for this! She didn't want to put him off (after all he was helping her to locate her lost husband), but she had to keep the clock moving and she was already late.

"Okay, 'Zee' it is. Gotta run. I'm already late for dinner with Jeremy so I must dash. Let's talk later, okay?"

Xavier released Lydia's hands and she made good on her words and dashed up to the front desk.

Lydia panted out her name and Jeremy's description. The young hostess smiled patiently, gesturing for Lydia to follow her. For some inexplicable reason, Lydia suddenly felt nervous.

"Mrs. Reynolds." Jeremy half-stood as Lydia was seated in her chair by a weathered old gentleman, who appeared by her side out of thin air, and who looked more like he was in need of a good seat of his own and perhaps a late afternoon nap.

"Thank you so very much, James." James Marshall had been the Official Seater at The Owl since it was built and Lydia knew that tipping him was unwise as he considered his job to be almost akin to community service. It was enough for James, at eighty, to still be able to be of some use and giving him money for something he enjoyed so very much was considered by him to be offensive and tasteless.

Jeremy shifted in his seat, straightening his tie. Lydia smiled at the effort.

"Jeremy, you are probably wondering why I asked you here for dinner."

Jeremy nodded, saying nothing. Lydia could see his mind racing with possibilities, but at least he had the good sense and maturity to say nothing.

"It's about Lance."

There was an almost imperceptible tightening of Jeremy's lips and dimming of the expression in his eyes, but still, he said nothing.

"I have been asked to care for Lance, Jeremy, and I know so little about boys – I mean young men, so I was hoping that you could give me a little advice."

Jeremy remained stiff, but his lips relaxed ever so slightly to allow him to speak.

"Advice on what, Mrs. Reynolds?"

"On what you think Lance likes, Jeremy."

Jeremy's thoughts ran as wild as red ants in summer. Harper. He likes Harper and you're trying to tell me in a gentle way outside of your house and away from Harper (so I don't just grab her and RUN!!) that Lance is going to take Harper away from me. That's what this is all about, isn't it, Mrs. Reynolds? It's all about –

"Harper says he likes putting together model planes. She's watched him make two already."

That fact was enough to add fuel to his rambling thoughts,

making him feel even more nauseous than just a few seconds ago. Why was Harper watching something as tedious as the making of a model airplane? And to do it twice?

"Well, that's good." Lydia pulled out a pad and pen and wrote quickly. "What else?"

Jeremy had a sudden epiphany.

"That's what I'd like to ask you, Mrs. Reynolds. Does Lance seem to have any romantic attachments?"

Lydia blinked at Jeremy. For some reason, girls and Lance had not crossed her mind.

"I don't think so. He hangs out at the house with the twins. Especially Harper. She's trying to help him with Sign Language."

Jeremy looked hard at Lydia, without blinking.

"Did you know that Harp doesn't know Sign Language? Did you know that?"

"She's learning," Lydia found herself in defense of Harper's limited skill in this area, "And I think she's made remarkable progress."

Jeremy continued to stare at Lydia, his expression hardening.

"But he doesn't speak it either. So what exactly are they communicating about?"

This time, Lydia got it. She finally understood why Jeremy seemed so standoffish when he was usually so eager to please.

"I see. You think Lance has designs on Harper. Well -"

Jeremy held his breath, waiting.

"- nothing could be further from the truth! Lance is busy with Cal, his school work, and processing the death of his parents. Jeremy! I expect more from you."

Jeremy was stung by Lydia's slight, but not enough to completely discredit his own feelings of jealousy and insecurity.

"You have no idea what's been going on, Mrs. Reynolds."

Lydia reflected on that. She realized that between Eco, looking for Chester, Xavier Montague, and Lance, she had probably not paid enough attention to the twins.

"So fill me in." Lydia was humble. She loved those two girls more than anything in the world.

Jeremy felt somewhat vindicated.

"Harp wants Lance to marry Leigh. She thinks we should have a double wedding."

Lydia smiled.

"Oh, Jeremy, really. Harper is just overly romantic – which is really your fault. There's no way that Leigh is interested in Lance and he has expressed no interest whatsoever in either Harper or Leigh. This is just a figment of Harper's unusually active imagination."

"Oh, really?"

Jeremy reached into his shirt pocket and pulled out a small piece of paper. He shoved it over to Lydia.

"L and L 4EVER!" the paper read.

Lydia folded it over and handed it back to Jeremy.

"Harper's imagination, Jeremy. That's all it is."

Jeremy unfolded the paper and pointed.

"Harper didn't write this. Neither did Leigh."

Lydia looked quizzically at Jeremy before the light dawned.

"Harper says it's Lance's handwriting. She should know with all the notes they scribble to each other back and forth and back and forth."

Lydia frowned.

"Can I keep this? At least for a day or two?"

Jeremy nodded, delighted that he was finally, and at long last, making the kind of headway about the Situation with Lance that he had been striving for since the first day of Lance's arrival to Harper's home.

"Of course."

Lydia put the paper in her purse, her interest in finding out more information about how to make Lance happier deflated by the news she had just been given.

"So, you think that Lance is in love with Leigh?"

Jeremy shrugged.

"You need to ask him, Mrs. Reynolds. You need to know what's going on – and soon. Before it's too late."

Lydia rose at this. The suggestion of impropriety was a like a slap in the face.

"I just –," Jeremy stammered, realizing that he was starting to step over the line.

"I hope you don't mind if I order carry out from here, Jeremy. You are more than welcome to join me at home with the girls and Lance. I need to talk to everyone and all at once."

Jeremy stood as well, his tall frame inching out Lydia's by more than a few inches.

"I'd like that very much, Mrs. Reynolds. And I apologize if I've said anything to upset you. About Lance and Leigh being in a relationship..."

Lydia shook her head.

"You've only helped me to pay attention to what I've been thinking for sometime, Jeremy. No worries. I will figure out what to do and do it. It is my responsibility."

Jeremy thought that Lydia couldn't have said it any better.

Neither Lydia nor Jeremy noticed the two Sisters from Sacred Names who had stopped talking to each other in order to better hear every word at the table with a now agitated Lydia Reynolds and slightly defused Jeremy Fletcher. The fact that Leigh Reynolds (a girl who had – at least until recently – been considered a model Sacred Names student) might be having a romantic interest in the new boy in town was thrilling enough, but the possibility that the two might be actually having an affair (after all, the Lance fellow lives in the same house, under the same roof!) was even more scintillating.

Pretending to be interested in eating when Lydia and Jeremy passed by, Sisters Antonia and Theresa simply Could Not Wait to return to school and like the Gospel of Paul, spread the news.

Chapter Twenty-Five:
Change of Plans

The house was filled with a chill that Lydia failed to eliminate – no matter how high she turned up the thermostat. When the dial reached eighty degrees Farenheit and nothing had changed, Lydia realized that Something Was Wrong and there was nothing more that she, with only the most rudimentary knowledge of home heating (things like where the heating unit was kept, when it was time to call for maintenance work, and things of that nature), could do. The ultramodern (and ultra-expensive) heating and air-conditioning system was usually such a reliable dispenser of warm and cool air that Lydia often took it for granted in their big, Queen Anne Idislewilde home. Chester had named their private residence and its surrounding gardens, Idislewilde (pronounced I-dissle-wild) – a whimsical name that was suggestive of elves, fairies, and lovely sounding flutes. Most people got it wrong and called it "Idle-wilde," but Lydia didn't mind. It used to bother Chester tremendously before he got lost, but now it was pretty much a non-issue – at least until the time (which Lydia fervently hoped was soon) that he got himself found. The controversy over the proper nomenclature and pronunciation of their home could resume at that time, if considered still necessary and appropriate. Right now they had bigger controversies with which to contend – that she had put off – at least temporarily.

Shivering with cold, Lydia remembered last night's Owl Bistro's take-out dinner (as a time in which Idislewilde had been warm and cheerful) with more than a pang of regret and shame. She had had every intention of talking to Lance and the twins about whatever was going on between Leigh and Lance, but she had lost her nerve. She was a coward and she was sorry that she had to see the truth of that reflected in Jeremy's disappointed eyes, but he had honored her right to Do What She Felt Was Best by biting his tongue and keeping quiet. She did notice that he made certain to put his hand as close to Harper's as possible without actually picking it up and feeding her. And even though he never looked directly at Lance, the frost in his sky-blue eyes never melted for one second unless they were explicitly directed at Harper. And then they softened and shone with genuine warmth.

No question. She was craven. Cowardly. A big, old scaredy-cat – a hundred times worse than Tibby who ran from her own shadow. She was all of that and more.

But today was not the day for calling names – at least not regarding an ill-conceived (and not yet verified) adolescent romance or badly pronounced name of their picturesque estate. Today was a day to solve mundane household problems like finding and providing heat for her family.

Lydia was completely disgruntled that Idislewilde was being less than cooperative with respect to managing a comfortable living temperature on a day that promised to be full of its own problems. Even after she had opened all windows to circulate slightly warmer air from outside, there was still no relief from the intense cold. The late autumn wind from the garden and grasses that co-mingled with the frigid inside air stopped in place as soon as it entered the airspace of Idislewilde. As if paralyzed, any warmth surrendered without much of a fight, retreating in the face of its frigid counterpart. There was something dense and impenetrable about the cold in the house that stubbornly refused to give way to heat, no matter how hard Lydia tried, and it was starting to seem more than a bit unnatural. Maybe it was a type of spiritual residue from Jeremy's discontentment?

At a loss, Lydia finally gave up with an admonishment to the girls to not touch the gas heater itself or use electrical or manual appliances unintended for service as heating devices (things such as candles, blow dryers, and microwave ovens) to warm themselves as "That's how foolish people die every year from preventable heating-related injuries. Foolish people die doing foolish things! So don't."

Harper and Leigh were wearing warm, woolen sweaters, ski

tights, and mittens and appeared to be surviving just fine in the cold climes. It was Lance who seemed to be suffering most.

Before leaving for an early, unexpected, and unwelcome Saturday morning budget meeting at Eco, Lydia had advised him to layer his clothes and get under the covers of his bed if things did not improve. In the meantime, she would be calling a plumber to come over and take a look at things. She wanted all three children at home to greet the plumber and ensure that he focused exclusively on the work at hand. The last plumber (a greedy man with out-of-date tools) had tried to give advice on developing new architecture and plumbing that Lydia had not requested, was not interested in, and was not willing to approve or pay for. Having learned that lesson the hard way, this time around she wanted the twins and Lance to keep this particular plumber on track and on time with an estimate and scope of work that only involved the given assignment. Nothing else.

If she knew who the plumbing company was going to send, she would have suggested that everyone leave the plumber to his solitary task at Idislewilde while they all rode their bikes over to the Oceania Public Library (a place always chocked full of fun things to do on Saturdays) or an interesting outing with friends. But since she had never met this new plumber, she didn't feel safe leaving him alone at Idislewilde without some supervision no matter how cursory or fleeting.

With final instructions regarding what they were supposed to do with the plumber, Lydia left the house. Cal had retreated to Lance's room, leaving the twins and Tubby Tibby (Tabitha Samantha Elizabeth) to themselves downstairs in the large Great Room to contemplate Project C and whether or not there should be a modification to that designation. Should it become Project C-O as Harper was considering, or was that simply too much?

Tubby Tibby yawned widely, relaxed and unconcerned in the face of what was becoming a rather heated discussion about Jeremy, Ophelia, and the sacred purpose of Blood Oaths. Suddenly, the cat sat up, tense and watchful, her haunches rising and her eyes widening. Jumping down from the sofa, she began walking in circles, sniffing like a bloodhound after quarry.

Tabitha looked up at Leigh and mewed plaintively. Leigh held out her arms for Tabitha to jump on her lap.

"Come on, Tibby. You can do it. Come to Mama!"

Harper sighed.

"That big, fat cat is not going to jump up on anything if she can help it, Leigh. Let her stay where she is before she hurts herself."

Tabitha narrowed her eyes at Harper, as if understanding the slight, and jumped happily into Leigh's waiting arms. Glaring at Harper, she turned her head and hissed into the air, pawing infront of her as if to ward off something.

"Harp, I don't think she's fussy because of just you. I think she's letting us know that..." she dropped her voice. "...Those - those women are here."

"You think?" Harper didn't mean to be snarky, but she was a little put off by Leigh's less than enthusiastic support of her idea to expand their search for their father to include Jeremy's little sister, Ophelia. Less than enthusiastic was being kind. Leigh had said "NO. NO. And in case you missed it - NO!" If she had been any more emphatic, it would have been downright rude.

Leigh's reasoning, however unwanted, was not off-base:

"Harp, that little girl is as dead as good manners are in our school cafeteria! I mean, c'mon! I've heard that our own Mother held her in her arms at the scene of the accident. As horrible as it is, she was killed on impact and she died. Simple story. But the truth is that Father is not dead. He's just LOST. How many times do I have to explain it before you get it? We don't have time to search for every lost soul on the planet! And Ophelia – Rest Her Little Soul – is not lost. She's DEAD!"

For her part, Leigh was no longer trying to avoid snarky. She was knee-deep in it. And jumping around. In thigh-high waders.

"You broke a crystal." Harper stared with angry eyes at her sister, seeking her own irritated retort. "And now we have EIGHT escaped souls. We need to get them all back where they belong before we can do anything. Can you – the person who caused this ginormous mess with all these crazy souls roaming around Eco and now here – here in our own home!! - think of just exactly how we're supposed to do that?"

Leigh grinned broadly.

"The Book! You use The Book and say whatever it says to say and do whatever it tells us to do. That's how."

Harper studied Leigh quietly.

"When did you think of all that? Before or after the breakfast I didn't get to have today? You ate the last bagel and last egg. All I got was a moldy piece of stale wheat toast. I wanted more of something better!" Harper glared at Leigh, who shrugged, aware that fighting over food was usually not ranked high on their list of things to fight about.

Leigh was at a loss, not making a connection between Harper's rumbling stomach and simmering temper. In her mind, she saw no reason why food would have anything to do with accomplishing the tasks they had set aside for Project C.

The cold intensified as two shimmery figures appeared. One in front of Harper. One in front of Leigh.

"Didn't I say we should do something after we get The Book? Why on earth is this happening now?," Leigh hissed.

Harper shrugged.

"As if I gave them a special invitation?! Please stop blaming me for stuff I have no control over –"

"But you do. Have control. Both of you. And you will both PAY. And pay dearly."

Leigh felt ill. The spirit seemed to be speaking in her head and the harder she tried to rid herself of its taunting voice, it remained with her, echoing its voice through her head like a bad wind tunnel. Pay sounded more like PAAAAYYYY!

"I'm not scared!" Harper announced bravely (meaning at least half of what she was saying). "That little talking-inside-my-head business is no different from what we do when we twin, Leigh! Stop letting them get to you. I say bring it on! I mean, enough is enough! We are not trying to hurt any of you and according to The Book, no one will get hurt if you would all stop fighting us and just cooperate!"

As if in answer, the two women materialized fully, looking like they had just stepped out of a painting or an expensive art book. They looked as if they had always been standing right there, as if they belonged at Idislewilde.

"What do you want from us?," Leigh asked in a small voice, aware that she sounded as frightened and as guilty as she felt.

"We want to be returned."

Simple answer to a simple question.

"That's all any of you ever say! We want to be returned. Returned to what? A picture on a wall? A page in a stupid art history book? Who wants to go back to that? Oh, to heck with it! I need to move Project C along because I have to focus on Prep Princess and this is all getting to be WAY TOO MUCH!" Harper jumped up from the sofa, suddenly ferocious – whether it was from an empty stomach, frustration with the spirits, or determination to become the next Prep Princess, it was hard to say.

"I'm getting The Book. We'll figure this out right now! I'm tired of everyone telling me what to do and what NOT to do!" Harper rushed upstairs to her room, leaving a terrified Leigh, who was too frightened to move, downstairs with the women and Tabitha the cat.

The two women looked at each other and then back to the girl who was holding the rather rotund feline. Tubby Tibby's paws were tucked under, her eyes large, and her lips pressed together. It was certain she did not feel that what was transpiring was necessarily Very Good, it was just that she had not quite made up her mind to determine that it was Very Bad.

One of the women, who seemed to be the elder of the two, spoke first:

"Allow me to introduce myself. My name is Mary Elizabeth Stewart, Sacred Names, Class of 1962. I'm not sure you care what my name is as my unnecessary appropriation had less to do with me as a person and more to do with your careless and inhumane assumption of my soul for your own purposes."

Leigh smiled. There was something winning about Mary Elizabeth. She didn't feel afraid of her at all.

"You talk just like our mother. She was born about ten years after you attended our school. You should still be alive. You're really not that old. You must've had some kind of illness. Why are you dead?"

Harper bounded down the stairs.

"Who sounds like Mother and why are you asking how they died? That's none of our business and it's not something suggested that we should discuss with them! Have you lost your mind?!"

Leigh rolled her eyes.

"The least we can do, HARPER, is to be civil! These are all perfectly nice people!"

"We don't know that for sure. Not all of them are one hundred percent good!" Harper flashed angrily. "I grabbed some of them out of books on classical art. I didn't have all the time in the world to consider who was good or bad. I put those eyeglasses on like The Book said and then I just LOOKED. Wherever I looked, they got captured. I could've been on a page with vampires and witches for all I know!"

"Art books at Sacred Names do NOT have pictures of witches and vampires, Harper, and you are perfectly aware of that! Mary

Elizabeth is hardly a witch – much less a vampire. She's from the Class of '62. And, she's from our school."

"MY POINT EXACTLY!" Harper raised an eyebrow, signaling her perpetual, never-ever-ending disdain of her academic institution. "Like some of those nuns don't fly to town on broomsticks! Please."

Harper looked suspiciously at the two women, as she scanned through The Book.

"Listen, Leigh, All I'm saying is that I think it's a really Bad Idea to get too close or friendly with these folks -if you know what I mean."

Leigh placed Tibby gently down on the floor. She watched as Tabitha looked up at the women, unafraid.

"They must be nice," Leigh offered. "Tibby likes them. See? She's just looking at them. They're perfectly harmless."

"And you really think you're qualified to make a decision like that based on our cat?! You would really do well to listen to ME on these matters – given the fact that I'm the one that started this whole thing. The only thing Tubby Tibby knows for sure is that she gets fed on time. Can we please move on? Okay," Harper looked up at the two spirits. "This shouldn't hurt you two, but you will feel weird, okay? Bear with me."

Alarmed, the women shook their heads. The second woman spoke:

"My name is Kara Vivian Vanderhoff and I say strongly that it is not okay that you do anything more to us. I rebuke you! And my sisters and I will do everything in our power to stop you from your heinous activities!"

Another Kara? Leigh gasped in surprise. Harper looked up from The Book.

"Kara? Another Kara? Do you know J.L.? Is it YOU he's looking for? Are you HIS Kara?"

The woman refused to answer. She eyed Harper with deep dislike, mistrust, and suspicion.

Harper and Leigh sighed in unison.

Another Kara?

"Okay. Here goes. I don't know about you, but I've had enough hate, cold, and confusion for one day," Harper inhaled as if about to submerge herself in deep water: "RETURN TO THE PLACE THAT I SET FOR THEE. RETURN TO THE CRYSTAL IN OBEDIENCE TO ME."

There was a rush of cold wind, stirring the fur on Tabitha's back and face. The two women screamed out their protests, their mouths elongating until it seemed that their chins would reach the floor. Their eyes turned crimson and their skin became as pale as blown glass. Furious, their shrieks and protests were loud but largely lost (Leigh covered her ears as Tabitha cringed in terror by her feet).

The muffle of stormy air drowned out the worst of their shrieks (to Leigh's relief).

It lasted less than ten seconds (but felt to Leigh and Tibby more like thirty) and then they were gone.

"I thought," Harper said with the quiet calm of someone on attack, still harboring a grudge about Leigh's refusal to add Ophelia to the search for their father, "that you only broke one crystal."

"I did!" Leigh's defense was vigorous.

"But there were two. One whose name I didn't catch and our brand new Kara. Unknown ghostie plus new Kara. That makes TWO." Harper's logic was irrefutable.

Leigh shrugged, defeated.

"I was too scared to look in the bag when it all happened. I guess it was two if two of them showed up. Listen, HARPER, I did the very best I could ALL BY MYSELF while you were off being crowned Miss Stupid Chair!"

Harper rolled her eyes heavenward, forgiving Leigh in that moment. Without being told, she understood that this was about more than Ophelia, more even than about her ongoing relationship with Jeremy. It was about Harper's potential ascent into the socially popular world of Miss Prep. A seductive world of parties, picnics, sports events, and proms that could (if she allowed it) take her away from Leigh.

"For your information," Harper announced softly, "I have no intentions of being Miss Prep if you don't become Miss Sacred Names first. And I have a strategy to get us both what we need – using THIS."

Leigh stared at The Book with a mixture of confusion, dread, and hope. Not certain which emotion could – or should – prevail.

"But we have to focus on Project C, Harp. We have to do this for Mother."

Harper grinned.

"Listen, Leigh. If there's nothing else, there's one thing I do and do well and you should know that."

Leigh blinked, shaking her head in confusion.

Harper laughed.

"Multitask!"

There was a chime and then a hard knock on the door.

"Must be the plumber," Leigh remembered, hastily jumping off the sofa. "Mother said to let him in and then watch him like a hawk!"

"Oh, right! But it's starting to feel warmer already. It was the women who made everything so cold. We don't really need a plumber now, do we?" Harper shook her head, the thought of Mother paying something for nothing rubbed her the wrong way.

"We'll just get rid of him," Leigh suggested practically, thinking it could be something easily managed.

As the twins made their way from the expansive Great Room and its creature comforts, they were surprised to see Lance, already at the door, deep in an embrace, with a man who, at least at first glance, looked very much like Lance himself in height, coloring, and age.

"Do you think that's his brother?" Harper whispered.

Leigh shrugged.

"He's an only child."

"Then who?" Leigh followed up her answer with a question of her own, her eyes growing bigger with each second as she stared at what could easily pass for Lance's twin.

Harper folded her arms and quickly concluded that since it did not seem to involve Project C it was probably really None Of Their Business and something better left for Mother to manage.

"I'm actually more interested in how he heard the bell! Isn't he DEAF?" Harper pondered over that for a second or two. "It's not his father who is deceased, his brother who never existed, or the plumber - who would be in some kind of uniform – but he also doesn't seem like a threat so let's just go back upstairs for awhile and let him have his space, okay?" Harper resorted to commonsensical advice, not wanting to take on more than what they had already committed to doing. The fact that Jeremy was giving her the blues about Lance made her wary of getting too personally involved in his private life. If Leigh wanted to know more, she could ask him herself. In fact, that might be a Good Thing – Leigh getting more involved and Harper that much less.

"You should ask him – I mean, not right now – but later?" Harper threw out the suggestion casually, her mind and heart racing with the possibility of Lance and Leigh finally becoming romantically involved. The thought of who this new young man might be was incidental. Hopefully he was a distant relative who was dropping by on his way to D.C. and this drop-by would be over in a friendly hour. It was practically irrelevant and Harper dismissed it quickly from her thoughts, her mind already returning to what they needed to do next for Project C and her date with Jeremy that evening at The Shut.

Leigh nodded, satisfied with Harper's answer. And, like Harper, not quite ready just yet for anything new.

Chapter Twenty-Six:
Family Affairs

Today would be Monday. I understand that Monday always comes after Sunday, but it seems to me like every once in awhile the world could mix things up and have Monday follow Tuesday. Would that really be so hard? I mean, why not? It beats having that sinking feeling at the beginning of every week that two days of fun have been replaced by five days of terror and torture in that awful place that some people call school, and I get to specifically call the Academy of Sacred Names.

My phone is buzzing. It's Jeremy. We've been in discussion since Saturday about Lance's cousin, Arthur. It's obvious that Lance and Arthur are super close by the way they practically twin when they do everything. Eat, talk, play ball, you name it. Barely a word has to pass between them, but they still seem to understand each other. Mother grins all the time now because Lance's hearing has finally popped back for good AND he has someone to hang out with other than Cal. I'm ready to float on air because now I don't have to try to learn one more word of American Sign Language from that smug, superior-acting Hannah who was actually trying to lord it over me with her daffy self because she knew at least one thing better than me. I can not wait to tell her the good news that her services are no longer needed. That should deflate her little balloon ego. Can NOT wait! If it wasn't for the fact that I'm already headed for school, I would find a way to get to her house. As I think through my schedule of when I might see her, I realize that YES! I will see Mademoiselle in third period French. Ooh-la-la!

I finally pick up the phone before you-know-who gets a you-know-what. Jeremy with an attitude is definitely not a good way to start the week.

"Hey, Germ. Yeah. Yeah. I honestly don't know." He is asking me for the twentieth time if Arthur's appearance could be linked in the very near future to a possible *DIS*-appearance for Lance?

"Okay." I hang up. Jeremy has bought a gift for Lance under the pretext of joy that a family member has come forward to claim him. Not-so-secretly, he's fervently hoping that this Arthur person will return soon back to D.C. with Lance in tow. I am actually a little embarrassed that Jeremy is acting so mean-spirited about Lance's dilemma. After all, Jeremy still has both parents and even though his sister is gone, he could barely even remember her so how close could they have possibly been? And how old was he when that happened to Ophelia? Three? Four? Lance is seventeen. A huge difference! A whole lifetime different.

My phone buzzes again. This time it's Linda Applegate. She has what she likes to call "new information." It's nothing but gossip, but she prides herself on being different from Elaine Henderson – or as Elaine is more commonly called - Stupid Big Mouth or SBM because she (Linda), as a staunch defender of All Things Good, detests the idea of being linked to low-minded, petty "gossip."

"Oh, yeah?"

I don't want Mother or Leigh, who probably couldn't hear my conversation even if she tried with her headphones blasting the latest hit by Goffes and Grant – a crazy part-Rasta, part-British, part-no-talent-if-you-ask-me group that has everyone running out like crazy people spending their hard-earned allowance money. I refuse to spend ninety-nine cents to even download one of their songs. The guy with dreads to the floor can't sing and his lead guitarist plays like some of Jeremy's friends who not only do not have record contracts, they play in people's basements. For good reason.

I mean, really.

Linda is babbling in my ear about some REVENGE plan that Leila has out for me and Leigh because of what has become known at school as "Locker Gate." Please. She thinks I'm scared of her idle baby threats when I have GHOSTS after me??? If only my problems were so small!

"So," I have to interrupt Linda because she loves telling what she calls "back story" to her long-winded "Tell All" discussions and right now she's back to when Leila was in second grade and set a rival's strawberry-blonde hair on fire. Sounds like good old-fashioned detention material to me, but Leila escaped that particular punishment by avoiding Sacred Names until fourth grade.

Smart girl.

"SO," I yawn. "What is she planning to do?" I try to keep my words and tone neutral as I know that Mother, who pretends not to listen to our conversations, is hanging onto every word that will be used later, if necessary, in our monthly Family Court – held periodically to address grievances large and small, such as a failure to clean properly (we have impossibly different definitions of clean so I'm never in the right with Mother on that!) ; a large number of detentions in a month (for me that's over thirty); unruly behavior at the dinner table (laughing on purpose with a mouth full of food, throwing food, hiding food you don't like in napkins) – all the usual you're-no-good-so-we-must-talk-about-it-as-a-family stuff.

I'm lucky though. A couple of kids I know still get spankings. From their FATHERS. Which, I've heard, is monumentally harder than when mothers do it. Not that Leigh and I would really know.

We've only been spanked once or twice and it was just a swat on the bottom. Mother was really undecided which one of us was which (although she was well aware that it was usually something done wrong by me), so her attempts to spank us were just as unenthusiastic and charitable.

Linda, still in my ear, as usual, had no facts. Just speculation laced with memory. She remembers how Leila had done this to such and such person so THEREFORE she is likely to do the same to me and Leigh. She recalls how Leila had tried to poison this one girl, Primrose (who would name their child something that SCREAMS out "please poison me"?) back in sixth grade and how no one could prove it, but that she, Linda, knew for a fact that it was Leila because she saw her do it! By the time that particularly story was retold over and over (creating its own sick urban legend), Linda had knocked the poisoned cup from the victim's hand (just like something out a movie) and had rushed her to the hospital on the handlebars of her bike. Yes, the handlebars. But my question has always been why all the hospital drama would have even been necessary if Primrose had not taken one sip. For me, that was always a big loophole in the story, but now as Linda gears up to recite it again for the nine hundredth time, I decide I had heard enough – even if she changes the ending and Primrose dies. From stupidity. Enough is enough.

"O-KAY! SO," I try to repeat the "So" for emphasis, "What's the plan now?"

Silence.

Translation: Ignorance.

"Okay, well tell me when you know something, Linda, okay?"

I hang up gently – or as gently as you can by pressing a button.

Mother looks over at me. Leigh is in the back, her head bopping to that foolish beat from the G&G album that is making those idiots a FORTUNE (I should throw together a band tomorrow)! Alone, I'm trying to figure out what feeble attempt Leila might try to undermine me and Leigh.

"Is everything okay, Harp?"

That is a loaded question. If you answer "yes" to Mother then an explanation is requested. "No" and an answer is demanded.

I plant my feet firmly on Swiss ground.

I shrug.

Mother keeps her eyes on the road. Her short nod means she knows that I'm being evasive, but she's willing to let things go. Which typically means that she has bigger problems of her own.

I'm not sure if that's good or if that's bad. Mother's problems often involve us and I'm wondering – hoping against hope – that she is still completely clueless about Project C.

The phone buzzes again.

"Hi, Germ." Jeremy is already at Prep and he says that he is watching as Lance introduces Arthur to Dr. Montague. He wants to know why Lance is doing this. What possible reason would ARTHUR have for meeting with Montague? I have no answers.

"Let me call you back."

"Mother?"

"Yes?"

"Why is Arthur at Lance's school? Doesn't he have to go to school back in D.C.? Did he take a day off or something?"

Mother sighs.

This is definitely not a good sign.

"Arthur is going to remain at Idislewilde for the remainder of the term — just a few more weeks are left anyway so where's the harm? Apparently, he finished up his college classes early to do this and we both think it might be a good idea for him to stay through the spring. Help Lance get over things."

I feel my stomach do little flip-flops. I simply cannot call Jeremy back and deliver that "wonderful" news to him on Monday morning. Not after he has gone out and bought a really expensive mitt and bat for Lance. His hearty "Hail and Farewell, Lance!" presents have just become "Hail and Welcome to Arthur!" presents.

I push "J" for Jeremy on my phone and wait.

"Let's talk our usual time?" That is our code for ten o'clock when we both have breaks scheduled.

"Tell me."

The hard thing about keeping stuff from Jeremy was keeping stuff from Jeremy.

"Okay? Sounds great. Tell you all about it then. Mother and I are almost to school." I chatter like an idiot to cover my tracks. There is no way I'm going to have a frank conversation about Lance and Arthur in front of Mother.

I hang up, knowing I'm taking a really big chance because being hung up on is high on Jeremy's list of things I Am Not Supposed To Do. But throwing in Mother's name means that I am not free to talk and he completely understands that. He tries as hard as he can to stay on her good side and I can tell that she (most of the time) actually appreciates the effort.

"Have a good day." Mother always says it like a blessing of some sort – which is precisely what's needed for any day at Sacred Names, but especially one that falls on a Monday with a vengeful Leila waiting in the shadows to exact foolish revenge for something as completely stupid as a fight over locker space.

I say my own prayer.

Deliver me from STUPID. Especially today.

I guess God is not listening to me this morning, or He is

particularly busy, because who is the first person I see as soon as my feet touch the sacred ground of Sacred Names?

Meredith Ford.

What a bowl of jelly beans!

Leigh sends me a text.

"MEET AT DUD'S. 10AM."

I want to go back to that place like I want another big old hole in my head. I know I have to go back in the afternoon anyway as part of my continued community service (I did not finish dusting those awful paintings) and the afternoon is more than soon enough for me. Besides, I have to talk to Jeremy about Arthur – I can't dodge him forever. It's just too bad that it's at the same time as Leigh wants to meet. As much as I hate disappointing my sister, I think that it's more important right now for me to tell Jeremy the bad news about Lance and Arthur. Besides, I'd much rather do that than steal more chandelier crystals to capture more souls. Doing all this from the top of a very high ladder in a room that's practically pitch-black while angry spirits are whirling around your head trying to make you fall and BREAK YOUR NECK so you'll end up dead like them is not fun at all.

Easy choice.

"CANT. GOT 2 DO SMTNG ELC." I text back.

I wait for a response. Nothing is forthcoming and I can feel Leigh's disappointment in the silence.

I understand that we have a plan, a goal, and a mission. But I have a life outside of Project C and I have to talk to Jeremy! It is still my month to be squired around town to fancy restaurants and I see no reason why I should end up at McDonald's over -

"C U AT 10."

I look at the text and sigh. That means that I have to talk to Jeremy on my way to the Art Center. Which also means I have to risk being overheard by people like SBM and Linda. Not ideal. The TMZ Hotline for Oceania.

"FINE."

She can tell from my hostile, one-word response that I am less than pleased. But she also knows that I'll be there. The last thing we do to each other is let each other down.

I put away the phone to concentrate more completely on what Sister Mary Ellen is saying about the artwork in the million pound books that are circulating through the room like a twenty-four hour virus.

I raise my hand. I have a flash of inspiration.

"Sister, do you have any books from this period? Like now?"

Sister Mary Ellen considers that question.

"I do have a few contemporary books, Harper, but I'm not sure if you'd be that interested. I can check into that for you. Bring them next time for you to see."

A hand shoots up. It's Cynthia McIntyre. Vicious girl. Word is that she's even meaner to her little brother, Casey, who is six years old in first grade at Eco. She calls him – her own baby brother! – 'a stupid little warlock weirdo'!

Talk about HATEFUL.

"I think Harper has just the book she needs. It's the perfect book for her, Sister. It's going around the room now. There!" Cynthia points – as if she really cares about what I read. Miss Hate Everyone. I track with my eyes on whose desk the book has landed.

Of course.

Meredith Ford.

Meredith shoots a grin to Cynthia, who returns it with a wink. Sister Mary Ellen is not oblivious to their shenanigans, but she just ignores them to keep the class moving, and I don't really blame her. They are such amateurs! Walking over to Meredith's desk, she picks up the book and then walks over to me.

She places it on my desk. It is a very thick volume with gilt-edged pages. A gold-colored cover depicts a stern-faced representation of St. Michael holding a blazing sword. The book is called "A Pictorial of Saints." I look up at Sister. She gives me a quick wink of her own and returns to the front of the room.

Do I dare? A SAINT??!!! Can I do this? I know I absolutely shouldn't, but the bigger question is can I do it at all?

I take the glasses out of my backpack. I put them on.

And I slowly open the book.

Chapter Twenty-Seven:
Valley of the Dead

I am not as afraid of them as most people. Even the teachers avoid meeting their eyes, but not me. At least not now. I've hit on what I consider to be a perfectly brilliant plan and I think it's worth executing. I want to try it right away and Harp had just better be at the art center at ten o'clock like I said or she will be in very big trouble with me. I need for her to at least try to do this. It could fail, but it could succeed. Even beyond our own expectations. I know she's going to glare at me and try to make me feel ridiculous, but I honestly think this plan could really work!

We deserve a little good luck with Project C after everything that's been going so wrong. Besides, I feel guilty about breaking the crystals and causing havoc at Idislewilde. It was all unintentional and I'm trying as hard as I can now to make up for it, but Harp just looks at me like I'm a big baby or a loser and I'm neither! She's only forty-five seconds ahead of me – not even a minute more – so I hardly think that qualifies her to be the boss of me! What can a baby do in forty-five seconds? Write a sonnet? Solve a criminal case? Win a Nobel Prize?

Daphne O'Hare was seated alone today in the cafeteria. It was unusual to find one of the Dead alone. They usually travel in packs of three or four – whether for company or protection it's hard to say. No one bothers to pick on them anymore – not since sixth grade - because everyone is too filled with either pity, revulsion, or both. Four years is a long time to belong to the Valley of the Dead, but most of them have had that unenviable membership for at least that long.

I sit next to Daphne, gently sliding beside her on the glazed wooden bench.

She is wearing a blonde wig to match what would have been her true hair color – almost all of the Dead do that to cover the fact they have no hair left. Not even wisps of hair at this point. And no eyelashes, eyebrows or anything that would take up too much protein from the heart, lungs, and brain. Their stick arms and legs resemble bone-white pencils and thin blue veins appear like bulk muscle in skin that is so stretched and transparent that it's painful to see. They sit way in the back on the most secluded side of a cafeteria that is, for them, a private purgatory. They have been haughtily told to remain in what has become known as the "Valley of the Dead" because their appearance is (to quote from one of the more intellectual Royals) "so antithetical to the purposes of a cafeteria – a place whose primary function is to create an environment for NORMAL people to EAT what is necessary to LIVE."

It is sad but true that all eight girls have varying stages of anorexia or bulimia. Two have died already, but one of the two was brought back to life through the prayers of her desperate mother. Last year, at aged thirteen, their courageous but emaciated little hearts had given up – deciding that nourishment was not to be had in this life so it was better to go into the next. Daphne was one of those girls whose soul had seen the Other Side and I was determined to capture what she had seen – what she knows – for Project C. The other girl, Laura Flynn, whose parents had tried everything, was lost forever. Her mother had prayed, but perhaps she had prayed more for Laura to find peace than anything else.

Daphne and I had once been very good friends. We had played together in and out of Idislewilde like skipping butterflies. Her mother had always been kind to me and to Harper, telling us with serious eyes that not having a father at home was not always such a bad thing. Daphne had two older brothers and a little sister – none of whom are afflicted with what she suffers from and that's why I have always secretly thought that her main problem was that she wanted to be too much like the Dead's ringleader, Jordana Powell, a once-beautiful girl whose only ambition since we were all in second grade was to Marry Well and Stay Thin. Her large brown eyes in her chocolate brown face were like bulbous chestnuts in a flesh-starved face. Her once-lovely smile was deformed by worn gums and loose teeth. It was whispered by SBM (and Linda) that Jordana's father, a wealthy dentist, was prepared to fit her for dentures if her mental and physical health failed to improve this year.

Given what I'd seen of her in the last couple of weeks, I'd tell him to get his denture molds ready.

It was a running joke by meaner girls that Jordana would win hands down at the Staying Thin part but that only someone who had no eyes and no arms would ever marry a walking stick. Nothing to see and even less to touch. However, unlike the Royals and the others who are habitually cruel and unkind to the Dead, I refrain from taunts and jeers. These are all kids we've grown up with since we were in kindergarten. If they had cancer would we be so unkind?

I think again. Reflecting on the people involved.

Sorry to consider that even that might not even make much of a difference to some of the meanest of the mean.

"Diddley?"

I used our childhood nickname. Her father had loved old Bo Diddley records and used to play them when I'd come over and ask us to dance with him. He would put Daphne on his feet and twirl her around and around, calling her his 'blonde beauty queen' and 'shining star.' She used to look at me with almost frightened eyes whenever he would do this, but I loved it – not having my own father around to twirl me. I would feel his rough, unshaven face against my own as he would hold me close and twirl me faster and faster and faster! His hand would form a seat under my bottom and I felt secure and safe as he would dance that way with me, calling me his "pretty brown sugar pie." Over and over and over. "Pretty brown sugar pie."

And then one day, Daphne had come up to me at school and asked me to stop coming over. We were eight by then and in third grade. I asked her why and she would never say and refused to speak to me or play with me anymore. My feelings were crushed. Harper was not-so-secretly glad because she had always said that the O'Hares are not very nice people. She used to repeat things she had overheard from snobs in our school like "small houses can often breed small minds" and I would ask what was meant by that, and she would just give me that poor-born-forty-five-seconds-too-late-so can't-figure-things-out-by-yourself look. But she had never answered me directly, just mumbled something about how Mother had decided that it was BEST for me to play with others because of Things I Didn't Need to Know Right Now that worried Mother about the O'Hares. I never agreed with the "small minds" stuff because Daphne's family was super smart and super sweet. As usual, Harper was just being Harper. She was protective of me, but clueless about anything other than sports (this was pre-Jeremy). When it was all said and done,

Mother's caution didn't matter at all because by aged twelve, Daphne was hanging out faithfully with the Dead and included herself in their number as well as in the body count of last year's tragedy that almost lost her to us forever.

"Please don't call me that, Leigh. I've hated it for years."

Daphne's voice (like all of the Dead's) barely rose above a whisper.

"Okay." I wanted to take her hand and hold it, but I was afraid. Her ill-health looked not just contagious, but dangerous. As if to touch her would cause irreparable harm. I didn't want to make things any worse than they already were, so I just sat quietly by her side.

"I miss you, Daphne." I didn't know that I was going to say it, but there it was.

And, regardless of how much it hurt her (or me), I took her hand and held it in my own.

All of a sudden we weren't teenagers anymore, we were five years old and laughing hysterically in her backyard about nothing at all. We were free! We were so happpppyyyy!

And then I knew what I must do. I must take her to the art center with me at ten o'clock. Not to capture her soul, but to free it. Once and for all!

My heart was pounding so fast I was glad that I had skipped

breakfast. I would have definitely thrown up. What I had in mind just now was beyond sane. It was crazy. Utterly and completely insane!

What was I thinking?

I drop Daphne's hand and stand up quickly, spit filling my mouth.

"I gotta go, Daph. I'll come back tomorrow," I promise quickly, almost running away to the other side of the room.

Away from my thoughts.

Away from myself before I do something that I will not only regret, but can't repair, restore, or redeem.

Chapter Twenty-Eight:
Marbury County

On maps of the areas surrounding Oceania, it can be fairly stated that there are few pockets of unattractive or unappealing parklands or neighborhoods. Everything within a fifty mile square radius of Oceania is considered by visitors and residents alike to be quite lovely and beautiful. You can rarely go wrong if you are anywhere on that corridor of Interstate 30 that wound its way from land to shore, but the little town of Marbury is always thought to be most particularly picturesque and charming for its lush flowering landscapes and well-kept homes.

The biggest difference between Marbury and Oceania is size and composition. Marbury is much smaller in dimension than Oceania. Where Oceania boasts a robust ten thousand in population, Marbury has one-tenth of that number. Oceanians, though democratic in the ways in which they express their sense of community, still have pockets of class elitism that are inescapable and fairly obvious: Lakeshore Prep, Sacred Names, and even Eco are considered exclusive private training grounds for the sons and daughters of the wealthier classes. Although there is a public elementary, middle and high school in Oceania, there isn't quite as much attention paid to the students, faculty, or staff who attend those institutions. The focus of Oceania's newspapers and less official rumor mills is almost centered completely around the "high society" goings-on at those three academic institutions, particularly the first two (as the Reynolds have implemented severe gag orders at the opening of Eco years before and have threatened all manner of lawsuits as a means of enforcement).

Nevertheless, despite (or perhaps because of) its egalitarian nature, there is a quiet peacefulness that settles over the open spaces and community enclaves in Marbury. Unlike Prep and Sacred Names in Oceania, the proms, cotillions and other private dances of the local Marbury High and Middle School are rather pedestrian affairs. Proud mothers in Marbury compete in baking contests for their pies, cookies, cakes, and even fancy fruit tarts and tiramusus to be used at middle and high school events. Mildly competitive fathers compete on room designs and party trimmings for the local community center or gymnasium that are used for the larger events. No one ever considers their labor to be a hardship and everyone always has fun. Naturally, however nice Marbury is, it is still not Shangri-la - meaning that conflict does occasionally arise if two vain girls wear the same gown; a foolish boy unwittingly invites two different girls to the same dance; and two mothers make the exact same cake right down to pink and green-colored coconut sprinkles - the sort of silliness that is found in Anytown USA (or the world for that matter) and is not specific to Marbury, Oceania, or anywhere else.

Similar to its much wealthier Oceania counterpart thirty miles away, Marbury has a Main Street that hosts boutiques, hardware, and other sundry stores that manage the more mundane needs of the townspeople. If people want something Very Special, they either drive into Oceania or all the way to D.C. - a little over sixty miles (an hour's ride) away. Rarely is there ever considered a need so great (unless it is medical) to go that far away for anything – especially not if the desire is to simply be grand or to show off for one's friends. Every once in a very great while a young bride, whose heart is set on fashionable things, will brave the trip (and peer ridicule) to the Vera Wang boutique at the Watergate, or Saks in Chevy Chase, or Meeps (a vintage shop) in Adams Morgan, but that is probably the case only once every ten years as most young brides in Marbury are neither unduly brave nor particularly fashion-conscious.

The Marbury flower shop (really more of a flower warehouse if one is to consider its size) is called "Plants R Us" by Oceanians (and some Marburites) as a nickname. The actual name is "Flor Roja" (or Red Flower), underscoring its Latino owners, the Medinas, fascination and love for plants that are of red or of reddish origin.

In celebration of its name, each customer is given one red rose (if it's a lady) or a one-dollar-off coupon (if it's a man), but only if that customer has spent more than twenty dollars that visit and said the magic words: "Love's Power is in which Red Flower?" There is an ongoing guessing game as to which red flower currently grown in the Medina's nursery is meant in the riddle, but to this date, no one has discovered the answer because the species of plants are so widely varied and their pots and locations in the nursery change faster than the seasons. The first person to guess the answer wins a five-hundred-dollar gift certificate and a year's worth of free fertilizer and weed treatments. These offers make it difficult to ignore the question and at least once a week it can be said that someone in Marbury dutifully tries. This quirky little tradition has attracted repeat visitors to the shop for over twenty years – since the Medina family started its flower business in Marbury.

Still considered young (at least by geriatric standards), the adult Medinas are in their late 40s and are busy, smart, attractive entrepreneurs that want nothing more than to continue to place Marbury in the "Top 100 Prettiest Places to Live" in America, and keep their two children, fifteen-year-old Rosita "Rosie" Medina Gomez and seventeen-year-old Adelio "Leo" (Adelio means 'father of the noble prince') healthy and happy. Rosie and Leo have helped their parents, Rose and Oscar, catapult the little town of Marbury to a distinguished number twenty and Oceania to number forty-five in the entire country – that is the entire U.S. of A. that now recognizes the sumptuous beauty of Marbury and Oceania! This rapid ascent up the surprisingly cut-throat competitive ladder of horticultural success has been mainly due to Lydia's voluminous, creative, and expensive purchases at Flor Roja for Eco and Idislewilde, but owes most of its success to the greenest thumbs on this side of the Atlantic belonging to Oscar and Rose. Leveraging this success, Oscar and Rose next plan to break into the top ten this year for Marbury and the top twenty for Oceania, and are confident they will be successful. Only then will they feel vindicated that they have started to attain the goals they had set for themselves when they first met in college over twenty years ago.

The Medinas' values of family, working hard, and love of the outdoors is shared by one of Rosie's best friends, Isadora "Izzy" Giordano's family, who does business with the Medinas and whose thriving landscape and construction company is the crowning centerpiece of the Marbury business community. The saying in Marbury is: "No one builds success like a Giordano!" Being a so-called typical Italian-American family means the Giordanos have produced more than fine flowerbeds and azalea bushes for their landscaping company, Giordano's Gateway. There are plenty of little Giordanos whose helpful hands have helped to mulch, weed, and prune the Giordano's blossoming shrubbery. Those same hands (usually male) have also lifted the heavy sandbags to the massive trucks that have carried them to building projects all over Interstate 30. Very pretty children with long dark hair, olive-tanned skin, and gray-green eyes, one only-child Giordano, fourteen-year-old Isadora (Izzy), stands out even among the most popular Giordano children as the one "Most Likely to Succeed" and "Most Likely to Marry a Prince." Izzy herself is torn between the two options, but being an only child and abandoned by her mother, decides that banking on success is more likely to last than banking on marriage. She puts her two cents in that camp, having decided that marriage (at least for her) is something that can possibly wait until the very last minute. She thinks it better to not repeat her mother's mistakes and rush headlong into marriage and motherhood as an impulsive and over-excited nineteen-year-old (which is a scary FIVE years away!), but wait until she is almost forty, with commonsense, her own bank account, and practically too old to hatch anything more than one perfect egg.

She has it all planned out. It will be a boy. Named Angelo after her dad. And she will raise "Little A" (as he will be called) all by herself – just as her dad is raising her. That way, Little A's dad won't be able to tell her what to do or when to do it. She will take Little A to the Orioles games in Baltimore, Maryland and to the Nationals in Washington, D.C. She will tell him that mermaids DO exist and that sometimes dwarves and trolls can be just as friendly as fairies and elves depending on how they are treated. She has had first-hand, direct-experience-in-the-grassy-knolls-of-Marbury of such things and will show him captivating pictures from her cell phone as certifiable, verifiable one-hundred-percent proof of her close ties to that Secret and Sensational World! She will also show him that the little waves that splash at the edges of Marbury's ragged inlet coastline are not strong enough to hold him back from the much bigger Atlantic that is just over the horizon and his for the taking.

She will do all of this with Little A after returning to Marbury from having an adventurous and rapturous life Out In the Real World. A life spent designing beautiful sets on Broadway (and with any luck – Hollywood!!!) with one of her best friends, Rosie, who also attends Marbury High (called the "Big M"). The Big M stands out from the "Little M" for Marbury Elementary or "M&M" for Marbury Middle School. Big Ms love their little brothers and sisters, but every chance they get they do tend to 'lord' it over them in lots of fun and good-spirited ways. Last year, enterprising Big M freshmen staged a circus for the littlest of the Little Ms, using their pet dogs, cats, and hamsters in a string of tricks that captured the attention of parents and teachers alike. Izzy had designed the little costumes and Rosie had created the sets. All in all it was a magnificent success and word of it reached all the way to Oceania and, to the surprise and delight of all involved, made the Front Page of the Oceania News!

Where Izzy's forte is interior and exterior design, Rosie's passions are fashion and costuming and they decided that like their parents, they would form their own partnership called Marbury's Masterpieces. Unlike her dear friend, Rosie is one of the handful of people in Marbury who thinks that D.C. is more important for its clothing stores and chi-chi malls than its politics on Capitol Hill. She would move to D.C. tomorrow if it weren't for two things – close friends and her family, whom she loves with great affection. In teen fashion, some of her other friends in Marbury make fun of their parents and ridicule close friendships, Rosie's family is extremely close and supportive of each other's hopes and dreams. Although her mother, Rose, would secretly like to see Rosie happily married and settled down after completing a year or two of college, her father, Oscar, wants to see Rosie go all the way through business school with an MBA to help him run Flor Roja one day. His not-so-secret desire is to make it into a multinational business with ties back to his and Rose's native Peru where magical things happen at five o'clock every morning and old people tell stories that seem to come true. If all goes According To Plan, he and Rose will retire to Peru and experience that magic once again.

Unlike their parents whose minds were drifting to thoughts of things that are old, Izzy, Rosie, and another best friend, Minnie, have a standing appointment to Discuss Everything New on Friday nights at the Big M students' favorite hangout named Munchies (which everyone – for no apparent reason – calls The Munch). Every once in awhile an adventurous Big M would take his girlfriend all the way to Oceania to eat at The Shut, but in Marbury, The Munch was THEIR place and the most popular kids wore tee-shirts and jackets in celebration of it. Everyone knows that big red "M" insignia on the middle of the back of a jacket means two things: you went (or had attended) the Big M and you had been (or still were) a regular at The Munch. Only after your one-hundredth visit to The Munch (that information is kept in a computer, but is actually first stored in Kai, rhymes with "sky", Claussen's amazing memory) is a person "allowed" to purchase the $29.99 faux-leather jacket. The Claussens who run The Munch are originally from Oceania, but left in a snow-blinding blizzard after their fourteen-month-old died of pnuemonia in one of Oceania's worst winter seasons. Needing a change of scenery, and hearing how lovely Marbury is in spring, they packed hopeful bags after that brutal winter of losing little Johnnie and made their way to the little town that has now been their home for well-over twenty years. They were melancholy and depressed (even in the splendid beauty of Marbury) for nearly four years until the day that an international adoption agency secured for them a beautiful, round-faced, plump-cheeked baby from China.

It was a stroke of good luck for everyone involved as this child had been dangerously close to becoming another statistic of China's unfortunate "One Child Per Family" Law. The young twenty-year-old mother, who had already had a son, was happy to help the childless American family and had hidden away with Mormon missionaries during her secret, second pregnancy. To the young mother, saving a life and creating a family Somewhere Else meant that she would spend the rest of her own young life having Very Good Luck indeed, and she had seized upon the opportunity with youthful fervor.

Knowing that this child would look very different from their own very blond Norse antecedents, Mr. and Mrs. Claussen, were nevertheless delighted to once again have a baby to hold, spoil, and love. They didn't care if her eyes were shaped like half moons and were dark as midnight. Nor did they care if her hair grew into flowing ebony silk. They loved that baby as if Kai Claussen had carried her for nine months and had delivered her from her womb at Marbury Morningside Hospital.

Everyone in Marbury loves the Claussens, and practically everyone calls them Mr. and Mrs. Claus because of the remarkable resemblance to that more famous couple. But eclipsing that fondness is the delight the people of Marbury feel for the owners' brilliant and lovely fifteen-year-old adopted daughter, Minnie "Min" (which when translated from Chinese means "quick"). Minnie Claussen opens the diner each morning before going to the Big M. She counts the money from the night before, checks it off in a ledger that is kept by the cash register, opens the blinds, and dusts off the tables and counters. After doing this, she is ready to leave for school and is usually joined on the sidewalk infront of the store by her two best friends: Izzy and Rosie. Together, they form a triumphant trio known at the Big M (and all over town), as the "Three Ms" for the Three Mouseketeers!

No one would see Izzy without seeing Rosie without seeing Minnie. If they aren't together it is only because they are busy helping their parents at their respective businesses. Izzy with Giordano Gateway (where she serves as a cashier and price checker); Rosie at Flor Roja selling flowers behind the counter and serving as adjunct wipe-up tech (for clumsy patrons who knock over pots or track dirt into the tiled indoor nursery); and Minnie, who is typically helping to serve tuna melts, chocolate sundaes, and sunshine smiles behind the counter at The Munch.

All in all, the three girls would agree that they have led pretty normal, fun, but uneventful lives. Until that fateful November evening when Lydia Reynolds from Idislewilde, Oceania, Maryland showed up to Flor Roja with Harper, Leigh, Lance, and Arthur to buy flowers from Rosie's parents for Idislewilde's planetarium; talk to Luciano Giordano (the CEO of Gateway) to consider the possibility of building an all-glass annex to the left of Eco (pending the issue of the proper building permits still being negotiated with Oceania's

City Council); and to eat, with her family, a hearty dinner at The Munch. That Friday was the day that Izzy, Rosie, and Minnie call D-Day as the day that everything, from that day forward, became quite different. And their standing Friday evening discussion at The Munch was fraught with more lively giggling and blushing conversation than in the ten years since they had first met at Baby M Nursery School and had become triple best friends!

And nothing in Marbury – at least as far as the three girls were concerned – was ever going to be the same again.

Chapter Twenty-Nine:
Rules of Engagement

The ONLY reason I'm sitting in Sister Dominguez's office right now next to Leigh is because Stupid Big Mouth and Linda have not figured out yet how to Mind Their Own Business. I have reached the unhappy conclusion – and it's taken me awhile – to understand that People Without Boyfriends are like a tribe – a lost tribe – but a tribe nevertheless. I call them "The Wandering Tribe in Search of a Teepee to Call 'Home'." The problem is that this lost tribe is really NOT that innocent no matter how homeless and harmless they may seem to be. I should know. This band of conniving renegades always manage to pitch their tents square in the middle of my space – for no reason (at least that I can figure out)- and proceed to very deliberately start a raging, out-of-control campfire.

That burns everything down.

Sister Dominguez has called Leigh in because no one is absolutely certain which of us is which and she wants to make sure that "The One Called Harper" hears what she has to say.

And, unfortunately, there's plenty of that.

"I have not contacted your mother just yet because I wanted to discuss this information with you first."

Translation: Your no-good-mother has threatened us before with lawsuits so I would prefer to avoid a public trial and court fees. She is a hard-nosed, aggressive, wretch of a woman, and we prefer to deal with smaller, younger (more manageable) versions of her whenever possible.

But having done nothing to incur the wrath of any Sister that day – much less the headmistress! – I don't quite know what to expect so I just sit and wait.

Leigh says nothing either. I know what she's up to, but she doesn't have to bother trying to pretend to be me. I'm not afraid because for one of the few times in my miscreant life – I've actually done nothing wrong.

"I understand that you are engaged." The Sister glares at Leigh (and then at me) over her glasses.

Leigh gasps, slapping both hands over her mouth and completely blowing her cover. She stares at me with eyes as big as – as – well, the LIE itself.

If I had the skin color of Meredith Ford, I'd turn blood-red. As it is, steam rises from my smoldering brown head and I feel almost dizzy. So THIS is what this is all about?!!!

"No. I'm not. I am not engaged." This is more to Leigh than the

Sister, who as far as I'm concerned, can just go spin around in circles on Oceania Park's merry-go-round. "I. Am. Not. Engaged."

I figured that for a lie that stupendous, I have to say it twice. Slowly. Distinctly. As if talking to someone whose first language is not English. Who might actually be from another planet. MARS.

The Sister fixes her eyes on me as if her gaze could burn the truth out of me.

"I was friended, Sister. Something we're allowed to do. It's even in our Handbook under the section on "Proper Deportment with Men of Young Ladies Who Have Accepted a Ring of Promise.""

Leigh gasps again – much quieter this time but enough for it to register to Sister Dominguez that she has no knowledge of what had transpired between me and Jeremy last night at dinner.

The Sister rises from her chair and comes from around her desk to stand closer to us.

"Leigh, you are free to go."

Leigh clenches her jaw.

"There is nowhere I'd rather be, Sister, than right here. If I may?"

Polite to the end. That's Leigh. Asking permission to be stubborn.

"Of course, Leigh. I can see this comes as a shock to you as well."

The two stare at me as if they wished I would burst into flames (or tears), but I do neither. I don't feel bad about the fact that Jeremy gave me an absolutely beautiful Promise Ring from Tiffany's and I don't feel bad for not telling Leigh. I had tried a million times last night (well – maybe not a million, but I did send her THREE texts on my way home from dinner telling her that I wanted to talk to her as soon as I got home about something IMPORTANT!!!), but she kept sending back MEAN texts making me feel bad for going out and leaving her alone with Lance and Arthur who couldn't stop talking about those three stupid girls we'd met in Marbury. Who cares? She can have Lance all to herself if she wants to – I mean, really. Are any of those girls going to travel thirty miles to Oceania when they have homegrown guys right in their own backyard? Really? I know that if I were them – I wouldn't. I really wouldn't. That Leo guy was cute and I'm sure he has cute friends. No need to drive all the way to Oceania. Unless they're just plain STUPID.

But Leigh was nervous and uspet – even though she's not even sure she really likes Lance and she kept calling me (WHILE I WAS AT DINNER WITH JEREMY) to tell me that I need to help her to understand this and I need to help her to figure out that – all of this conversation going on in my ear as Jeremy is trying to give me a Promise Ring. From Tiffany's. That actually has diamond clusters. OMG. OMG. Ohmigod!!!!!

Of COURSE I hung up on her. I couldn't throw my arms around Jeremy, squeal, squeal some more, and put on my perfectly beautiful ring (that's a little too big which is why I'm wearing it around my neck on a gold necklace – also given to me by Jeremy) while talking on the phone to Leigh about a boy she thinks she MAY like – or may NOT – and girls that she thinks she MAY like – or may NOT – and these last three people are people we don't even know! I can't even remember their names!! I just couldn't do it. I had to make a decision as to what was more important to me at that moment in time and I made it. Madder than mad dog Cujo, she didn't say one word to me when I came home and I let it go – we do sleep in separate rooms even if we share one mind. It was late for a school night and I went straight to bed, cradling my ring in the palm of the hand that Jeremy had kissed. It was all so romantic. It was at the Crystal Inn and everything was beautiful. Me. Jeremy. Candles on the table. The Inn. The only spot of ugliness was seeing Linda and SBM (what are the odds on that??) dining with their families. But after my initial I-won't-be-rude-so-I-will-wave to them, I ignored (and forgot) about them for the rest of the evening. I had better things to think about.

Until now.

Leigh is looking at me as if I've grown an extra head – like we're now triplets – and Sister Dominguez is looking at me as if I am an alien life form. From the same Martian planet she's from.

I pull out the ring from under my uniform blouse. Leigh gasps again. I mean, if she keeps it up she'll fall out from lack of oxygen. It's really NOT that big of a deal. I mean it is. But it's not that much of a surprise. Is it?

Sister Domingues pushes her glasses up, studies it. Determines that her information from unreliable sources is just that – unreliable and inaccurate - and pulls her glasses back down.

"You are dismissed."

Leigh jumps up first and runs out before I have a chance to say anything to her. Which is perfectly fine because I have PLENTY to say to two other people.

Stupid Big Mouth and Linda.

PLENTY.

Shouldn't they be forced to report to Detention and write five million word essays on "How to Mind My Own Business?"

Well, I personally don't care if I get detention for the rest of the year. At this point, I don't care if I even have to spend the night in the Oceania Jail!!!

Those two nosy know-nothings have gotten me in trouble for the last time if I have anything to say about it.

They are toast. And not the kind with jam.

Chapter Thirty:
Heaven and Hell

I'm not mad at Harper. It was almost inevitable that Jeremy would give her a Promise Ring. He's like a floating pink cloud in Harper's blue sky. They're inseparable. I get that. I've known for the last two years that Jeremy was not ever going to leave Harper, but I guess that stupid ring makes it official. One day – not right now – but One Day in the Future - Jeremy and Harper are going to be married.

Harp is going to leave me.

I go into the bathroom and sit quietly, not caring if I'm supposed to be in class or not. I don't even care if someone I don't like sees me going in because I'm so filled with dread and anxiety. What if they run off and get married tomorrow? What would happen to Project C? Mother?

Me??!!!

I put down so much toilet paper that the seat is invisible and I sit. I have no plans to go anywhere else anytime soon.

My mouth fills with tears.

There's a knock on the stall. I recognize her shoes right away.

Even though we all wear pretty much the same mandatory style of shoe (Ugly in Sizes 6, 7, 8, or 9), I know that it's Harper.

I lean forward and open the stall and she squeezes in. She smiles at me, her eyes full of concern. I frown back, my own eyes full of betrayed rage.

"For Heaven's sake, Leigh. It's just a Promise Ring." She flashes it to me from under her blouse. Harper is contrite but belligerent. Her usual emotional contradiction. I flinch. How in the world can a person be sorry and mad at the same time? Although, in truth, that's exactly how I'm feeling right now.

"And you never break a promise, Harp." I am relentless in my attack. "I know you better than you know yourself. You NEVER break a promise!" I know I'm repeating myself but I want to underscore my panic.

I feel like an idiot, but I can't help myself. The tears that are in my mouth are suddenly in my eyes and I begin to cry. Big, splashy tears. Harper looks so distressed I think she might join in, but she squinches up her face and takes deep breaths and clenches and unclenches her fists to calm down.

"Stop it, Leigh. You gotta stop all this! I'm not going anywhere anytime soon. Germy and I aren't getting married for years and years! We won't get married until you get married, too. And that's a promise!"

The magic words. Harper would rather endure Chinese water torture than break a promise.

"You won't get married before me?" I know I sound pitiful – pathetic really, but I can't help myself.

Harper grins.

"We're having a double wedding, remember? We've been planning it since we were four."

We hear people come in and we get quiet. Too late.

There's hushed whispering and we can tell that whoever they are have stopped close to the stall, trying to figure out what to do next. If we had had time I would've asked Harp to stand on the toilet seat so only one pair of shoes would be seen, but we weren't thinking – too busy and too caught up in my unfortunate, unnecessary breakdown over nothing.

Next, we hear giggling. Harper looks at me, her eyes signaling to me that she's heard (and had) quite enough. She unlocks the stall and swings the door open so hard it bangs against the stall wall. As if reverting back to a much younger age, the girls hold hands, scream, and run – out of the bathroom and all the way down the hall. Harper stares after them and comes back laughing, holding her sides.

"What a bunch of Looney Tunes!" That's her favorite description for people she feels are supremely unworthy of attention and who act more like cartoon characters than real people. People like SBM and Meredith Ford top that list.

I hate having to touch the toilet paper mountain I have created, but I do believe in cleaning up my own messes, so I flush down the paper in the proper way – bit by bit - while Harper serves as sentinel, look-out by the door.

"You know," she comes back over after she hears me washing my hands. "You know that Lance likes you. You just have to show him that you like him back."

I think about that for a minute.

"All he could talk about last night were those three girls. And they both kept saying how they thought they were all so pretty!"

Harper sighs and I can feel her impatience. In her mind, out of sight is really out of mind and she thinks that WE are more than pretty enough and (judging from Mother's looks) will one day be downright beautiful. As far as she is concerned, she is more than a match for anyone and deserves the absolute best as a result. I don't disagree with her assumptions, it is just that it seems easier for her to feel that way with one boyfriend than me with none. Her confidence is almost as alluring as her smile and for the first time it occurs to me that maybe that's why Jeremy makes sure to be around all the time. So that he is not only in sight but constantly on her mind.

"They are like thirty miles away, Leigh. Thirty. Not three. Who is going to drive thirty whole miles for someone they just met?"

"Mother bought Lance a car, remember?" I explain the reason for my concern. "I heard them planning how to go back."

Harper takes in a breath, nodding.

"Okay. Theoretically he could go to Marbury, but why would he go? Besides, guys say stuff all the time and then they forget about it. Why don't you ask Lance to take you to Shut this weekend? That'll make him forget all about those daffy Marbury girls."

I shake my head, feeling in my gut that it is not as simple as Harper thinks.

"They really liked them, Harp."

Harper sighs and shrugs.

She turns to face me and her eyes are sparkling with her usual mischief.

"Do you like Lance?"

I shrug in return.

"I don't know." My last crush was in fifth grade and it was a boy who moved so far away with his parents that you need a flight pattern, a passport, and a visa to see him.

"I think you should find out before you get all wrecked (one of her favorite words) over him. I say that a double date is in order!"

She said it like it was some sort of proclamation or something.

"I can't ask him out, Harp. That would seem desperate! And he doesn't even seem to notice me except as a little sister. I mean –"

Harper clasps her hands together, her eyes shining.

"Leave it to me and Germ. We'll fix this. Only my idea is a little different from you and Lance going to The Shut for dinner. Jeremy and I had planned to go to the Gregorian Manse this weekend. As Lady of the Chair, I have just made a royal decision that you and Lance will be our invited guests. Not as my sister, but as one of the Lady of the Chair's royal court. And Lance HAS to honor a request from the Pirate Captain. It's tradition at Prep! He'll be shunned if he doesn't accept!"

I like it. It sounds manipulative, controlling, and not one-hundred-percent on the level, but I like it. The Gregorian Manse is like a first date dream come true. Very few Sacred Names girls can boast a date there until their senior year. It's usually reserved for the date that Tells The World that the couple is serious. That dinner means that her guy is giving her a Promise Ring or even something more substantial – his class ring. Every girl knows that the guy's class ring (that she wears faithfully around her neck – even in the shower and to bed) - is only to be replaced around her neck by an engagement ring on her left fourth finger. That's why the Promise Ring (that gets worn on the right hand ring finger) – as important as it is - is only the first leg of the marriage race for most Sacred Names girls. The real prize is the class ring and dinner at the Gregorian Manse. Sacred Names girls who have passed through the Trifecta of Love (Promise Ring, Class Ring, Engagement Ring) are the senior girls most admired and adored on campus. Only twenty girls have managed to win the Trifecta before graduation. Of that twenty, all married right after college and have stayed happily married after. All twenty also ate dinner with their intended beaux at the Gregorian Manse. Talk about a winning combination!! At fourteen, Harper already has a Promise Ring and we're going to be eating at the Gregorian Manse. All this and we're only SOPHOMORES! I am elated. I can only imagine the pure-almost-demonic envy of our classmates. It's thrilling!

I am picturing ME at the Gregorian Manse in a fabulously elegant dress. I am picturing ME savoring every splendid drop of taste and charm afforded guests of the Manse. A butler opens the door and I was told that each guest has their own private server. EACH GUEST. I am picturing absolute heaven on earth. And then I remember.

"This Saturday?" I am called back to reality, remembering something I had forgotten in my anxiety over Lance and the girls of Marbury County.

Harper has her back to me now, staring at herself in the mirror, making faces. Pouty lips, sultry eyes. Batting her eyes, and then finally pushing her nose up with one finger while wagging the rest of her fingers from her ears.

"Sure. Why not this Saturday? This Saturday is just as good as any."

I hate to put a damper on things – especially things that I SO want to do, but...

"Project C, Harp. I saw some stuff we can use at Gateway. While Mother was talking last week about adding the glass wing on to Eco, I was looking around and they have some really nice crystal containers. And cheap." I explain things and watch as Harper stops playing in the mirror and her expression shifts to one more serious and decidedly unhappy.

"Listen, Leigh. We can pick those things up on Friday. Why does that have to be a Saturday activity? Plants R Us and all the other stores in Marbury are open on Friday nights until eleven at night. I've been there enough times with Mother when you were pretending to study. Hmph!"

I can breathe again. I had thought it was not possible. I know that the football team practices on Friday for their Saturday games and that would mean that Jeremy and Lance would be too busy to take us to Marbury on Friday and I really wanted to get it all over with and was hoping that it would happen sooner rather than later so Project C can really take off and –

"Arthur can drive us over. Germ and Lance have practice."

I hold my breath. Again. Arthur with those girls??

"Doesn't that defeat the purpose? Arthur will see those girls again and remind Lance of how pretty they are!"

Harper laughs at me.

"Please. This way you can see what they're really like – that is if they're working on a Friday night. I really do hope they are at the store because you get to see your competition up close and personal. Compare notes. Check things out. Come on, Leigh!! We're Oceania. Marbury doesn't stand a chance against us!"

I swallow. My competition. Not fair. Three against one. The Gregorian Manse was sounding better and better. Maybe that's all I need to focus on and leave Project C alone.

"Gotta go." Harper announces suddenly. "I have two people to see: Linda and SBM. I say we ask Artie tonight about taking us to Marbury on Friday right after school. It's all going to work out. TRUST ME."

The door opens and closes behind her in one motion and she's gone.

I know it's past time for me to get back to class without needing an explanation, but I need to take at least one more minute to digest what has just occurred.

Me at the Gregorian Manse. Me back in Marbury to check

out my competition. And, at the end of it all - ME with a possible boyfriend??

It was too much. I hastily check my face for tear steaks and rush out of the bathroom to return gratefully to the sane world of science, math, and history.

It's hard to say WHY you know that something is Not Good, but you can always tell. I can tell when my head feels all fizzy. Harp says she gets the same feeling except it feels more like steam is rising from hers and mine feels more like someone just popped the air out of a balloon.

I feel like an air-popped balloon.

Everything looks normal. The kitchen with all its shiny, expensive fixtures, appliance, and gadgets. The heated enclosed patio where Jeremy, Lance, and Arthur are flipping burgers and hot dogs on the grill while grilling each other on the latest NFL playoff news. It's almost Christmas. It's freezing cold but I'm so happy. I am all tingly with the anticipation of gifts from "Mother Santa." Two days away from the Big Day and I'm like a six-year-old this year. I'm not sure why but I can't wait to see what's under the tree for Harp and me.

Inside, Harp and I have been designated as the salad fixers and table-setters. I start to object but decide that maybe it's better this way so that Harper and I can Talk About Things without fear of being overheard. Mother is at Eco for a long meeting on the new expansion so it's just five adolescents (Arthur is only eighteen), a kitchen and a grill left to fend for ourselves.

Jeremy comes into the kitchen and stands in the doorway watching as Harper cleans the vegetables to go on the grill. He is smiling and his eyes are happy. Why, I take that happy moment and turn it into something its complete opposite is a mystery to me (at least until I figure it out later), but I proceed to do just that.

"You look happy, Jeremy."

"I am. Very." His smile lingers in his eyes, still watching Harper at her wifely-type tasks, her back to him and the running water drowning out his voice.

"Speaking of Happy – have you seen him lately?"

I may as well have slapped Jeremy. The contented look he had didn't just fade from his eyes and lips, it wipes away clean like a dry eraser.

He gives me a stunned look and walks back out to the patio without saying a word.

Harper turns around. Her expression is serious, slightly irritated.

"I finished my part. It's your turn now and you'd better get crackin' because you haven't done very much, Miss I-Want-Lance-

To-See-I-Can-Cook. You haven't even chopped an onion or a carrot -- what?? What's wrong now?"

"Have you heard anything about Happy?"

Harper makes a face.

"Germ is NOT happy with Happy." She grimaces. "In fact Germy is so mad at him, I don't mention his name anymore. It's too bad that Happy weirded out after his break up with Leila. He was even acting loopy at The Shut with Germy's folks. I know for a fact that it has to do with Leila. When she broke it off, he fell apart. Went nuts."

She gives me a knowing look as if to say – "like you – going nuts...?"

"I am not going nuts because of Lance or anyone else. I don't even know if I like him or not, for your information!"

Harper laughs.

"Well, for YOUR 4-1-1, you need to get over here and peel these apples for the fruit salad. Whether you like Lance or not. ME want some fruit salad!" She laughs again and I find myself relaxing. When Harp is in a good mood it is as if everything turns pink and yellow. Happy colors.

Happy.

"You think Leila cheated on him?"

Harper's face drops and she looks around to ensure that no one is around.

"You gotta promise not to tell anyone this –"

I feel my head tingle.

"Sure."

"Okay." Harper nods as if in agreement with herself on something. "I told Germy that I would only tell you. I wasn't going to even bring it up, but since you want to know...Happy and Leila had to end their relationship because he was – he was acting really uncool. He hit her. I think he gave her a black eye or busted lip, but Germy wouldn't really talk about it."

I feel funny. As if what I am hearing and what Harper is saying are not in sync. As if the words are coming out of her mouth, but garbled somehow.

"He acted like a real creep, Leigh. I didn't know until the day before yesterday. Happy wanted to go back with Leila and she said 'no' – and who could blame her - and it got really bad. I mean he hit her! Not with his fists like when guys fight each other, but he still hit her. Real uncool stuff."

That's why Leila wasn't in history class! Her absences from school were so rare that it had raised quiet speculation. Her best friends had all looked very strange at school – not meeting anyone's eyes – not taunting the Dead - and now I understood why. Their queen had been brutalized by her former prince. Talk about royal intrigue. Talk about dangerous liaisons! Talk about Me saying "Never Mind To Dating Anyone!" Including Lance.

"What happened?!"

Harper shrugs.

"Happy called Germ two days ago to pick him up from Leila's parents' cottage by the lake. Apparently, they used to sneak there from time to time on weekends and Germy knew about it. Happy claimed his car wouldn't work and he and Leila would need a ride back to town. So, Germy drove out there and when Happy got in the car, he was breathing like he had swum the length of the lake. Germy asked about Leila and Happy claimed he didn't know where she was, but that it didn't matter because they had fought and she had run off. He said she had all kinds of friends at the lake that would be happy to bring her back to Oceania. Germy didn't believe him – not for one second – and he got out of the car and went into the lake house to see about her and found Leila crying and saying she would fix Happy if it took her the rest of her life. Can you blame her? Before Germy could get back to the car to bring Happy back to explain himself the rat took off, leaving Germy alone out there with Leila. Leila's car was there but he couldn't find her keys and he couldn't find the keys to Happy's car either. It was like Happy set him up to be the only one there with Leila. Germy called 9-1-1 and when they got there, the ambulance people gave him a lift back home. They took Happy in for questioning right away and told Germy to stay away from him. They had to take Germy's car in as part of the investigation – and you know how much he loves that car – so you know exactly how he's feeling about Happy! He can't get it out for weeks – maybe months – depending on how long this investigation takes. This is now an Official Police Matter. It's a simple case of assault and battery or is it simple assault and battery? At any rate, it's gone legal and Happy's in Big Trouble."

I am speechless.

This makes me want to RUN from Lance. Stay as far away from the opposite sex as is humanly possible. I thought this stuff only happened on T.V. or to really poor people or people on drugs. I consider this as the most likely answer.

"Is Happy on drugs?"

"Only if you count Leila. Hap doesn't even like taking aspirin! He's addicted to Leila. Crazy stuff, huh?"

I am silent, accepting the apple from Harper's hand. I go over to the sink, aware that my whole world has changed in those few moments. My holiday spirit melts away like the snow is starting to do outside.

Lance comes in, grinning. With a heated porch, he seems oblivious to the cold.

"Ladies, your meats await you. Are you ready?" He leaves the kitchen without waiting for an answer.

Without turning around, without looking into his handsome, winsome face, I decide that No I Am Not. Not ready for Lance. Not ready for love. Not ready for Simple (or Complicated) Assault and Battery. Not ready for anything except pursuing Project C. Maybe with Father at home I could feel safe enough to pursue a boyfriend, but right now, it was hard to keep my hands from shaking.

Harper came from behind and hugs me around the waist, leaning her head into the crook of my neck like we used to do when we were very little girls.

"Don't be scared, Leigh. Germy and I won't let anyone hurt you. Not ever. And that's a promise."

I feel better, but Not Good. Not like when Santa drops off a new bag of goodies or anything remotely like it.

And I feel even worse when I look over in the corner and there is Eloise Winthrop – glaring at us with barely contained fury.

Harper's arms fall to their sides and I drop the apple into the sink.

My appetite for everything drains as clear as the running water.

"Leila won't be the only one living in fear, you little fiends!" Her voice is shrill, but we know that we are the only ones who can hear her. "There will be more dastardly deeds perpetrated in Oceania until you stop your own nefarious plot. And as each tragedy falls – your guilt shall grow!!!"

She vanishes. Just in time because my legs give out and I slump to the floor, landing in an unceremonious heap at Harper's feet.

So much for Merry Christmas, I think as the room fades to black, *and jolly good luck for a Happy New Year!*

Chapter Thirty-One

Oliver Wendell Thomlinson of Marbury County

The day started out bright and sunny as most May days in Marbury and Oceania are apt to do. There was a sprightly feeling in the air as if the winter gloom with snow, sleet, and hail had finally, and at long last, been washed away until next year.

The annual MOMMY! march-a-thon was about to launch and promised to involve most of Oceania, Marbury. Even residents from places as far away as Philadelphia, Richmond, and D.C. have been known to drive into either Marbury or Oceania to participate. The "Mothers Organized March Means Yes!" (MOMMY!) organization hosts an annual march-a-thon every May from Main Street in Oceania to Main Street in Marbury – a directed thirty-mile trek that lasts all day and involves men, women, children, and even pets (at least those that can be faithfully maintained on a leash). Last year over one hundred D.C. residents drove into Oceania and walked the thirty miles to Marbury side-by-side with Oceanians in a show of spirited solidarity to end preventable and catastrophic infant and childhood injuries. At last tally, this year promised to be bigger than ever. The event sometimes falls on the first weekend and sometimes the second weekend of May as the Walk's planners strive to find the most perfect weather date a year in advance. This particular year it fell on the first weekend of May and organizers felt (as unreasonable as it was) personally and happily responsible for the beautiful run of days for their walk to celebrate those who found that particular activity to be more difficult than most.

No humidity and a temperature in the high seventies!

Tall and as gangly as an awkward octopus, Oliver "Ollie" Wendell Thomlinson's long waving arms, freckles and red hair were signature statements in Marbury, and this year he was the Master of Ceremonies for the MOMMY! march. His inability since his difficult birth to walk unassisted rankled the active young man, and upon reaching his sixteenth birthday, Ollie responded like a miner in the California Gold Rush – he struck fast and hard at Life – not willing to settle for seconds or second best.

Ollie was promised a car by his father if he kept up his grades and if he tried as hard as he could to endure (without too much complaint), the rigor of some of his more painful physical therapies. This last fatherly request was more for the mother's benefit than Oliver's, but the young man diligently kept his side of the bargain and his responsible father kept his. A specialized car arrived just in time - two days after mind-numbing finals in his favorite subjects (math, physics, and chemistry) – subjects that even his most brainiac classmates found to be as intimidating (if not MORE intimidating) as fifteen and sixteen-year-old GIRLS.

Ollie could not believe that he was able to go from leg braces to car brakes so quickly and with such little fuss. After "acing" all exams (both academic and driving), his parents proudly awarded Ollie with the keys to his first car. Thrilled that he would no longer have to rely on the kindness of strangers as he navigated the walking world on his slower and more socially awkward crutches and leg braces, Ollie was over the moon over his good fortune and wanted to celebrate with another friend, Karalyn Tatewin "Tate" Waters who had childhood leukemia that still allowed her the ability to move about with some assistance. His parents had nixed that idea, feeling that Oceania was still too far for him to drive unaccompanied. Ollie didn't fight it too hard because he didn't want to make it too obvious that Tate was more than just a friend – she was his Most Special Friend and she lived not just in Oceania, but at Eco – something of which his parents were completely unaware and would have felt to be completely unacceptable.

Being savvy as well as smart, Ollie had figured out that a trip to Eco could be postponed until the day that he was able to Do The Thing that would change his life, and Tate's life, forever. Tate had told him about Eco's mysterious Room of Clocks, and being a gifted physics scholar, Ollie had started to figure out that the Room of Clocks matched his own assumptions about the flexibility of time, space, and distance. He wanted nothing more than to see Tate and visit Eco's Room of Clocks. But like everything else in his life, Ollie knew that patience was the answer and he was willing to wait because they only had one shot at Doing The Thing and he wanted it to work more than anything he had ever wanted in life – other than Tate.

For the time being, Ollie conceded his own desires to meet the demands of his parents, not wanting to have his driving privileges revoked in the first week of sweet, sweet freedom. However, he was determined to see Tate again – and soon – and knew that it was simply a matter of time.

In his new car, he was able to fly by the pedestrians of Marbury whose legs, even on their bad days of arthritis or joint inflammation, worked better than his at their best. But his new four rubber wheels acted as a kind of equalizer and he loved every second of whizzing by the world through glass, chrome, and steel, waving merrily to the people of Marbury, who always waved back with the same hearty fervor.

But as much as he loved his car, the MOMMY! march meant that Oliver would be forced to walk the path with all the others who would be traveling on foot. Some of his peers were in motorized and colorful wheelchairs to help make the journey more tolerable. Different wheelchair leagues had formed: The Bluebird League (in which blue balloons hung gallantly from the backs of the mobile chairs); the Redbird League (red feathers festooned the sides and back of those chairs, causing them to look like animated roosters); and the Canarybird League (yellow streamers and balloons gaily waved from the back of those chairs – some with pictures of Tweety Bird and Sylvester)! Ollie belonged to none of the Leagues, preferring to use his crutches and brace as his only assistance. He had been warned by his parents and friends that nearly thirty miles is a Very Long Walk, but he was a hearty young man, whose upper arms were as thick as tree trunks from pushing off for sixteen years on steel braces and heavy wood crutches. Ollie tended to disregard words of caution or danger unless he had absolute, incontrovertible proof that he should pay attention and he had found nothing to that effect. Just well-meant advice from loved ones.

But the proof was there, lurking in the shadows of Ollie's backyard tree, but no one knew about it and no one (not even Ollie) saw it. A man, once known to a certain young lady of Oceania as Poem Boy, lurked stealthily in the quiet shade of Ollie's family's backyard tree that was so close to his own home. Watching. And Waiting. No one spotted him. No one noticed him. No one knew that Poem Boy, who was really a disgustingly ancient fifty-year-old Poem MAN, had plans of his own for the MOMMY! march. Plans that had nothing to do with charity, helping the community, or participating in a very good cause.

No, Poem Man's plans had to do with one purpose only. A purpose who was on her way from Idislewilde Oceania to Marbury County. A purpose whose innocent and childlike mind was variously fixated on thoughts of three Marbury girls and one Oceania boy and something called Project C. A girl whose radiant and youthful teen beauty was matched only by her Gifts – Gifts that made Poem Man HUNGRY as a wolf to claim her and her Gifts as his own.

A young girl who goes by the name of Leigh Harper Reynolds, but will answer to "Leeds" if so called by her Mother and her best-friend, Harper. A twin sister who was unknown to Poem Man as he thought them to be one and the same, never having the opportunity to see them together. To figure things out more completely.

Poem Man pondered his good fortune. The MOMMY! march was less than three days away.

Like any professional he was prepared. In fact, he could hardly wait.

Chapter Thirty-Two:
Day One – No Turning Back

Lt. Col. Mortimer Blaine examined the empty barrel of his rifle. It was an old habit that died as hard as his other habit of looking for trapped submarines in Emerson Pond.

The knock on his front door startled him as he was unaccustomed to having visitors at this time of morning. It was barely six o'clock and he had yet to have his favorite breakfast of brandied coffee and two smoky cigars.

Who on earth could it be?

The knocking continued and was more insistent than before.

"COMING!" Mortimer bellowed, wrapping the terry cloth robe tighter around his still military-straight-as-a-ramrod physique. For a man of eighty-five, he was still considered quite a catch in the little town of Marbury and he knew that. Just as he knew that he would never marry again no matter how many widows or divorcees baked him pies, cakes, and casseroles. It was not just that he was too old. It was more that he was still in love with his departed wife, Lisbeth.

And time was on his side now. He didn't have as long to wait for their reunion.

Pulling the door wide open, Mortimer was pleasantly surprised to see his grandson, Oliver, standing before him.

"Well, come in, Oliver. Come right in!" Mortimer hugged the young man hard, and then standing aside to allow Oliver to enter, stared after him with a puzzled, quizzical frown. Why was Oliver up so early? It must be important to get a boy that age up before school.

"Grandfather!" Oliver shouted in youthful excitement, "I just had to talk to you! You're the only Pelican I know and you know everything about adventure and Things That Are Odd, so I figured that you of all people would know how to help me to Do The Thing that will change everything."

To anyone else, Oliver would have sounded like a crazy adolescent or someone who spoke only in indecipherable riddles. But Mortimer knew exactly what his grandson meant, but he wasn't ready to do anything about it. Just like he wasn't going to help that woman, Lydia Reynolds, who had disturbed him several months ago. On so many levels. The fact that for some inexplicable reason she felt the need to "Do Something About Emerson Pond" was troubling to Mortimer who preferred to maintain the sanctity of the Pond for the sake of his precious submarines that lay beached on its sandy depths.

He had two subs perched there and he didn't want Mrs. Reynolds unwittingly interrupting what was Very Important Research just to explore the Pond's depths, on some woman's intuition, for her husband who was lost. Mortimer had indeed known Chester and had been Most Impressed by the newly minted member of The Pelican Club in every way. His intellect had soared like an eagle and his love for his wife, Lydia, and Harper Leigh and Leigh Harper (those names were always a source of amusement to the members) was unsurpassed. But, despite these shining qualities, Mortimer was more in the business of jealously guarding his own project that had nothing to do with Chester, Lydia, or their twin girls. And he was determined to preserve and protect it No Matter What.

It was possible that he had the means and method to help Lydia Reynolds find her lost Chester. But it was unlikely. Not when it would involve disturbing fifty years of careful calculation – careful preparation - for an event that he was certain could change the whole world! One life, one family – no matter how special they were - could jeopardize his work. And as lovely as Mrs. Reynolds had been that day at breakfast with his old friend, Xavier Montague, he could not meet her tearful request for help. In his heart, he knew that her cause was just and that Pelican owed her some understanding of precisely what Chester had been working on that had caused him to go missing, but he owed more to his membership than to her. It was that simple. And that hard.

"Grandfather, I plan to go to Eco the day of the Walk."

Mortimer studied Oliver. He was always surprised at how healthy the boy looked despite a rather difficult start to life. His energetic glow seemed to render his braces almost invisible as the focus was drawn to the sparkle in his eyes rather than the limpness so apparent in his legs.

"Well, my boy. Sit down and tell me all about it. I suspect this has something to do with Tate." It was a statement, not a question.

Oliver turned red, his grandfather getting right to the point of things was a bit unnerving. His parents always danced around issues with him. Not wanting to be too intrusive, but wanting so much for him – hoping that he was enjoying the same kind of carefree adolescence as the other children of Marbury.

But not Grandfather. He never stared at Oliver's braces, nor looked away. To his grandfather, they were as much a part of him as his arms, his hands, or his winning smile.

"Tate has something to do with it. And the rest has to do with the Room of Clocks." Oliver acknowledged truthfully, somewhat embarrassed about the fact that his grandfather (unlike his parents) was aware of his true feelings for the young and beautiful American Indian girl, Karalyn Tatewin ('Wind Woman') Waters.

Mortimer gestured for Oliver to sit. Oliver remained standing, too excited to be contained.

"I am going to Do The Thing in the Room of Clocks, Grandather! No one can stop me! Not even you. Not this time!"

Mortimer frowned.

The Room of Clocks was a tricky proposition and he and the others at Pelican had warned Chester to be very careful in its construction. Chester, acting brash as well as thinking brilliant, had only pretended to listen to his elders' advice and had gone ahead with his plans like a bumblebee buzzing to golden nectar. The Pelicans had been all in a flutter about the development of a room that would be able to manipulate time as easily as turning the dial on a wristwatch, and had asked, in writing, for some type of barrier containment device to be built that could control what could become a relatively dangerous property. Chester had received the letter from the Pelican Council on a Wednesday and had gone missing the following day. No one knew if any containments had been erected in the Room of Clocks and Mortimer was inclined to say "no" just as he was inclined to tell his only grandchild that he could definitely not go to Eco, and most specifically, not go into the Room of Clocks.

"That is a dangerous place, Ollie."

Oliver's bright smile faded. His grandfather rarely called him by his parents' pet name, Ollie. Grandfather was more formal and preferred to address people as he liked to be addressed. Lt. Col. Mortimer Blaine. He had earned the distinction and liked hearing it. He had killed twenty men in Vietnam and thirty in Korea before that. Fifty fighting soldiers were felled by his ferocious hand. That was what he would tell himself (and Oliver) whenever thoughts of regret would torture him. Felled by his ferocious hand!!

Mortimer shrugged off the memories of those dying men. No time for that now when his grandson needed him. Oliver. Mortimer preferred 'Oliver' to 'Ollie' - except when he was worried about Oliver, or bringing something up that required conciliation (typically on Oliver's part). He knew that it was a type of emotional blackmail, but there it was. Also, he felt that the name 'Ollie' sounded a lot like 'Ali' and as Mohammad Ali was one of his all-time favorite heroes, he liked calling his grandson 'Ollie' once in awhile in deference to a once-great boxer and a perennial great man.

"You told me to be afraid two years ago, Grandfather, and I listened to you then. But I'm not fourteen anymore. I'm sixteen and I am not afraid. Not at sixteen! You said you pretended to be eighteen when you were only sixteen - and you joined the Army and fought in Korea! You killed thirty people before you turned twenty! You're the bravest man I know! And now it's my turn!"

Mortimer couldn't resist a smile. Oliver did sound a lot like the courageous lion, Ali. And himself. Much, much younger.

"No one really understands that room, Ollie. I don't think that Mrs. Reynolds can fully appreciate what her husband has wrought and I don't want you to get hurt. You're all I have. You and your mother."

Oliver smiled.

To be such a warrior, Grandfather was sometimes little more than the gentlest lamb.

"I'll be fine, Grandfather. I have to save Tate."

Mortimer sighed. Nothing ever changes, he thought wryly, shaking his head. Young men trying to rescue young damsels in distress. Dragons. And dragonslayers.

"And why does Tate need rescuing, Oliver?"

Oliver's eyes turned dark.

"Her parents want to take her somewhere else. Somewhere out of the country for some kind of experimental treatments. But, I can't lose her, Grandfather! If they take her away, when will I be able to see her again?"

Mortimer smiled softly.

"In about two years or so, Ollie. When you finish the Big M and go off to college. You two have your whole lives ahead of you. Maybe Tate's parents are on to something. Maybe this treatment will help her. The Room of Clocks may only make things much, much worse."

Oliver pressed his lips together. His red hair and blue-green eyes both seemed to shimmer with suppressed emotion.

"Nothing can be worse than me losing Tate, Grandfather. And not Doing The Thing. Will you please help me? PLEASE?"

Mortimer was torn between his concern for his project that might certainly be jeopardized by the Room of Clocks and his love for his only grandchild.

This decision was one of the most difficult he had been forced to make in a very long time.

"Okay, Ollie. I'll help you."

Of all the regrets that Lt. Col. Mortimer Blaine had ever had, this agreement with his grandson to help him go into the Room of Clocks would prove to be the one action that would cause him the greatest and most lasting pain.

I watch as Leigh paces my room, back and forth. Back and forth. She's like a pendulum or a crazed trapped rat in a maze and there's nothing I can say to calm her down. She has it all stuck in her head that Eloise Winthrop is going to kill us – or kill somebody. Granted, that ghost scared me when she suddenly appeared in our kitchen at Christmas. I mean, really, Eloise? You had to show up out of nowhere and make threats? I felt like I was back at Scary Names with Meredith Ford. Same difference. Frightening face. Nasty mouth.

My giggles grow into a belly laugh as I consider the possibility that Eloise and Meredith could actually be related! It's not really that far-fetched. Transgenerational evil.

Leigh stops pacing.

"I don't see how you can find anything remotely funny with what is going on, Harper!" Her eyes are all scrunched up like she can't see and her hands are knotted into fists. If I didn't love her so much, I'd really burst out laughing. She looks like a raging teddy bear hamster. Cute but deadly.

I can see her anger is mounting. I stop laughing. It's true. There is so much to be upset about that laughter is not really all that appropriate. But this is me you're talking about and since when do I care about appropriate?

My phone buzzes.

"Don't answer that."

Now I know she's gone completely crazy-out-of-her-mind! She really has allowed Eloise to snatch her brain. I stare at her pointedly as I answer. I make a "you really need to calm down" face that she knows only too well.

"Hi, Germy! What's up?"

I watch Leigh out of the corner of my eye because she seems

desperate enough to do something rash. What that would be - beat herself over the head with my hairbrush? Drink my Christmas perfume from Germy? Rip up her clothes like a zealot? Come at me with scissors? It is not known, but I do want to keep her in my line of vision. Just In Case.

"Okay. Okay. Okay." I hang up.

"Jeremy says it's been decided that Foster Bellows will be walking with us to Marbury for the MOMMY! march. Apparently Lance isn't going to play on Saturday. Germy says it's something about the coach putting someone else in his place as a favor to that guy's dad. Whatever. I doubt Lance cares and this is good for us. With Lance and Arthur with us, that makes for a three-man escort!"

Leigh begins pacing again.

"I bet they're just going to the march to see those three girls again. They don't strike me as being all that concerned about causes!"

I watch her leap on to that idea like a frog on a lily pad. I decide to leap with her.

"Alright, let's just say that's true. Let's suppose that it's true that good old King Arthur and loyal Sir Lancelot have the idea that they will cross the Marania Bridge (named for Marbury and Oceania as it was approximately the halfway point between the two counties) to see whatever their names are..."

"Izzy, Rosie, and Minnie."

I digest that for a second. Too many 'ees'. For me. But who am I to judge what guys find cute? As a girl, I think it's pretty daffy for everyone to have names like that which is why my closest girlfriends (since Kindergarten) have names that have nothing to do with cutesie. Rachel. Gretchen. Logan (and yes, that's a girl who likes boys, ballet, and a fierce game of field hockey)! She could probably beat Prep guys if they ever played her on field. I would sell tickets and run side bets on her. She's that good.

"Okay. Those three. So, let's say that's what they have in mind. They have to walk thirty miles to get there! Thirty! With us by their side the whole way there. People get married and start their honeymoons in the time it will take us to reach Marbury. Think about that. Five Oceania babies will be born in the time it will take us to get there! One whole day, Leeds. Come on! There's no way that given ten hours you can't have Lance completely in love with you! You can do this!"

I watch as Leigh sinks into the nearest chair. And in my room that means she's sinking into shared space. I usually have clothes, books, electronics, and other paraphernalia strewn on every surface that will allow it. My two days of reprieve from my sloppy self are when the maid service comes to Idislewilde (on Tuesdays and Fridays) to rescue me. On those days, I love, love, LOVE Miss M (that's what we call Marigold Littlejohn) with a passion I usually reserve for

Jeremy. She allows me to see my room for the potential it can become right before I massacre it with clothes and trash for another round of messiness that I can't seem to control. I really can't help myself. I mean, I could if I tried really hard, but I'm better off paying attention to things that matter.

Like Jeremy.

Like Project C.

"Okay. Let's leave Eloise and her threats out of it for now. What are we going to do about the eight escaped souls? It's been months and we've made practically no progress at all!"

Leigh sighs heavily.

"What happened when you looked into the Saints book?"

I shiver at the memory. I remember opening it in class with the Special Glasses I had put on for a quick capture, and then I remember the book being closed. I seem to remember Sister Mary Ellen standing over my desk and looking down at me with a stern but loving look (two things that co-exist on the rarest of occasions in my life), but not much else. There was a momentary flash of blinding light that I saw more in my mind's eye than in the actual classroom (because no one seemed to notice anything but me) and then nothing. Sister Mary Ellen carried the book away and I was sitting in my seat feeling like someone had punched the wind out of me. If I hadn't known better, I would swear that Meredith Ford (or one of her henchwomen) had hit me or poisoned me or something else that would be considered Not Nice.

"It doesn't work on saints, I guess." That is the simplest way to describe what had happened.

"I didn't think it would." Leigh rolls her eyes. "We'll probably be punished for the attempt. It was SACRILIGEOUS! I just hope that my soul is not doomed to hell!"

I sigh. Leigh has always been far more susceptible to religious beliefs and rituals than me. I think a lot of that wine business is for the Sisters and priests to get tipsy and all that incense is to hide other odors just like Betty Leonard who always comes back from lunch smelling suspiciously like rosewood and jasmine incense after hanging out with her pothead friends. Please.

"I would imagine that God has better things to do than yell at fourteen-year-old girls for trying to do something wrong when there are people a whole lot older actually more successful at it."

Leigh stares at me, and I stare back. I know she is trying to make a point – that I am No Good – but that's already been agreed to so many times and so long ago that it's not worth her effort. I mean, really?

"Fine. So, no saint is going to be captured or come to our rescue."

Agreed. No saint with a flaming sword, pitchfork, or even a fork and spoon is coming to save us.

"What about Kara Victoria Pennington? She seems nice." I offer a bone.

Leigh is not biting. At least not at semi-good ideas.

"She didn't even show up the last time we called her."

True. Too true. Nothing and no one seems dependable at this point. At least nothing related to Project C.

My phone buzzes again.

Linda.

I hit speakerphone and her excited voice comes across too loud and too clear.

"Leila's just been spotted in Marbury with her new boyfriend, Leo. She was at The Munch and let's just say that lunch wasn't the only thing on the menu! There's some sort of fight going on Right Now between Leila and some girls named Izzy and Rosie!"

I frown. Not that I care. At all. Happy doesn't deserve even a popsicle date with Cruella deVille the way he's been acting, but it seems a little odd that Leila would feel ready to bounce back into the dating world so soon after her fight with him. Unless this boyfriend was around longer than we all suspected?

As much as I hate to gossip and mind other people's business, I have no choice but to ask this question because it is the question that everyone else has been wondering since Leila and Happy broke up. And it might make Germy feel less mad at everybody, including me. Or maybe not.

"Is Leo the guy that Leila was seeing behind Happy's back?"

Linda gurgles.

"Of course, Silly! Why on earth would someone bother to go all the way to Marbury otherwise? Everyone knows about Leila and Leo! Even a two-year-old!"

Well, that answers that. Jeremy (who reluctantly but finally) told me about the note he had been so fired up about – that STUPID note that has that STUPID "L&L 4EVER!" message on it that he gave to Mother. He needs to know Once and For All that the note must've been written by Leo for Leila and somehow it must've slipped out of someone's pocket – maybe Happy's?? - and Lance got hold of it. Happy must have stolen it from Leila somehow – sneaked in her purse or something. Nothing could be easier to figure out at this point. It's Leila and LEO - not Leigh and Lance.

God.

What a stupid mess. It would be downright funny if Leigh wasn't involved at all.

So, Leila got a smash-up from Happy over a boy from Marbury? Someone at the Big M? When she had Happy at Prep? I have to wonder if she had her priorities straight. Didn't being Prep Princess for the second year in a row matter to her at all? What could she possibly get from a guy from the Big M that would compare? I know it sounds superficial and petty, but being Prep Princess is a Really Big Deal. At least to most people. To ME.

I guess I'm too proud or too something, but I would NEVER give up Germy, Captain of the Prep Pirates, for a guy at the Big M. Even if he was class president!

I mean, really? If I did that, how would I ever be Prep Princess? Nothing in my fourteen-year-old head is more important to me except for Mother, Leigh, and Germy. Project C is way high on that list, too, but Prep Princess is near the tippy top.

And Prep Princess is what I will be in less than six weeks or Oceania will never be the same again!

Izzy and Rosie were out of breath in Izzy's room. Minnie had called to say that she would be coming, but she was running late.

Izzy was sprawled out on her bed, spent. She had not had an altercation that bad since nursery school when someone had taunted Minnie about the shape of her eyes.

Although her home was not as capacious as some homes in Marbury, Izzy loved the way her room and the rest of the house reflected her personality. Being an only child with just a father had its advantages sometimes as her dad tended to spoil rather than criticize her tastes in decorating, clothes, and even music. The one thing they disagreed on was boys. One boy in particular, whom Izzy had liked – well, to be truthful – LOVED – since first grade (despite her adolescent desire to be a single mother with her future son). The boy in question was seventeen-year-old Thornton "Thor" Bartholomew Sinclair, who also happened to be the oldest son of the wealthiest family in Marbury. He and Izzy served together at the Big M on all sorts of committees that had bred a certain comfortable feeling that they could do more than run the holiday bake sale or spring car wash festival – but that they had all the right ingredients to make it as a real grown-up couple someday. Sometimes Thor would hold Izzy's hand for too long for a particular project they were working on, or his gaze would linger on her face (or sometimes her legs or other places of interest to teen-aged boys) and Izzy would find herself blushing uncontrollably.

Angelo's reasons for not liking Thor had little to do with Thor himself. It had a lot more to do with the fact that Thor's father, John Lewis Sinclair, had property rights to all the best land in Marbury and was refusing to sell to the Giordanos for reasons that were inexplicable and had nothing to do with business. Angelo's secret guess was that it had to do with Izzy and Thor, but he had no concrete proof. He had tried to ask John Lewis (who always used both names – never Jack, Johnny, Louie, or J.L.) if this lack of cooperation had anything at all to do with their children and the poor man had looked as embarrassed as a nine year-old caught playing video games after bed-time. He had muttered some vague references to his wife, Veronica, and some girl named Priscilla from Oceania who his wife thought was the perfect little girl ever and it was All Decided and something else that Angelo couldn't quite make out because John Lewis had ended the confession in a pitiful splutter of incomprehensible sounds.

If it had been for any reason other than Izzy, Angelo would have felt sorry for the man, but as he got the distinct impression that Izzy's own happiness was at stake, this confusion was only not endearing – it was downright unendurable.

In defense of his darling Izzy, Angelo had demanded more information and a clarification of John Lewis' own feelings on the matter. At that request, the man, a tall, handsome figure with dark chiseled features like Cary Grant, had almost run off. But even the charm of John Lewis did nothing to defuse Angelo's paternal fury and from that second forward the Sinclairs (particularly father, mother, and eldest son) were considered anathema to Papa Angelo. With that incoherent confession, regardless of Izzy's protests and Thor's feeble attempts to get in Angelo's good graces, the boy's proverbial goose was cooked.

That was one year ago. In that one year, a lot had happened – dinners at The Munch, boat rides, cookouts, and all sorts of teen activities that had brought the two young people ever closer together despite Veronica and Angelo. Things had gone off without a hitch until six months ago and the imposition of a certain Priscilla Halston from Oceania who had been showing up with disconcerting frequency for many Big M events typically reserved for Big M'ers only. Princess Priscilla (second to Queen Leila of Oceania) was seen at all Big M events that included Thor, particularly those events in which Thor was considered the star, such as his prowess on the varsity lacrosse team – a game at which Thor excelled and had led the Big M to victory over their rival peer school, Winthrop Memorial High (known as Oshee High), Oceania's premiere public high school. Some of Izzy's friends thought it was a little odd that Priscilla showed up for everything that involved Thor and they went out of their way to stop Priscilla in her tracks. Spreading rumors. Last minute party cancellations or moving parties to new places that would admit invitees by code word only. They did their very best, but Izzy did little to help, feeling that their efforts were for nothing as Thor was not interested in Priscilla. Minnie and Rosie especially tried to get Izzy to see that it wasn't Thor they were worried about and that his affections for Izzy, though genuine, were not without their own challenges given the way that Mrs. John Lewis Sinclair felt about

Thornton Sinclair's choice in girlfriends. Everyone in Marbury knew how snobbish Veronica Sinclair was about her standing in town and how she felt towards Izzy. Although they sided with Izzy, they also could secretly understand why Veronica would choose a girl like Priscilla for a boy like Thornton because they were as beautiful together as two glamorous Hollywood movie stars. Thor's dark looks and Priscilla's bright, blonde beauty made them a rare and lovely commodity in Marbury. There was a certain natural symmetry to them. Like closing a loop or crossing a 'T.' Their relationship finished things off nicely and seemed to make sense in an intuitive kind of way. It would have been perfect. Except for one thing.

Izzy. One of Marbury's most beloved teens.

As a result of their deep affection for the Three Mouseketeers, the people of Marbury circled the wagons and decided to take no prisoners. The more Veronica and Priscilla pushed, the harder the rest of Marbury pulled. Looking back on those days of innocent, romantic rivalry, the residents of Marbury feel a heavy guilt that the events of the last week of Everything Normal in Marbury were transformed by one Marbury resident into something twisted and evil that changed their lives, and the lives of the people of their fair town and Oceania, forever.

But at the moment, the only thing Izzy and Rosie could focus on was the unusually bellicose fight at The Munch. There was nothing like this in their young memories and they couldn't wait for Minnie to arrive with the latest news of what had happened since everyone had been rather unceremoniously ejected from The Munch with very loud 'GET OUT RIGHT NOW!!' shrieks (Mrs. Claussen) - coupled with flourishes of a broom and mop – (Mr. Claussen). The Claussens were a friendly couple who had never been forced to display that level of violence before to their favorite clients, many of whom were also their daughter's friends.

Rosie was sucking on her hair. Something she only did when she was particularly nervous.

"I feel bad that I picked on Leila at The Munch and caused a fight over nothing. I guess it's really none of our business if she drives all the way into Marbury, but –"

Izzy held up a hand.

"Stop it, Rosie. I know you did it for me. It wasn't really about Leila and your brother, Leo, as much as it was about Priscilla. Leila made it sound like that stupid girl was about to date my Thor. You didn't get really nasty with her until she made that comment about Priscilla inviting Thor to some Sacred Names dance next week and then everything went south – including the soda you accidentally on purpose spilled in her lap. And, of course things got even worse when you called her the unrepeatable name."

Rosie rolled her eyes and sighed.

"Tell me this, Iz. Did Oceania get blown up by nuclear weapons or something? I mean, don't they have enough guys there? Why must all these Oceania girls keep coming here for excitement?"

The two girls fell silent at that open question, each remembering with sudden transparency that Oceania produced more than just girls, and the fact that Oceania boys were every bit as attractive as their female counterparts. Izzy remembered with great clarity the way Lance had smiled at her with a beauty she thought reserved for girls only; and Rosie remembered the fact that Arthur's eyes had held hers for much longer than any other boy had ever done. Each blushed deeply at their private recollections.

"Well," Izzy offered timidly, knowing that her mind had wandered down a forbidden path – a winding way that did not lead directly to Thor but seemed to suggest an alternate, dangerous future. "I guess we brought some of this on ourselves with those two guys - Lance and Arthur? Maybe they went back to Oceania and talked about us and those girls got jealous? This is just awful. We just gotta apologize to Minnie's parents for being such dodo birds. As bad as this is, I just have to wonder what can happen next?"

As if hearing the question from beyond the door, Minnie burst into Izzy's room like a spray of sunshine, her pretty round face aglow with youthful exuberance.

"Boy oh boy!," she exclaimed, "Do I have news for YOU!"

Chapter Thirty-Three:
Day Two: One Step Forward

The room in his brain was finally silent. Not the sound of a television, radio, or car horn penetrated its empty isolation. It was as if that part of his mind had been put into some sort of suspended animation, away from all the cares of the world. Save one.

There was one care that was not put in solitary confinement. It was the careful concern of a man who had inhabited a sullen, solitary room (at least in his mind) for the last fifty years. A half century that had witnessed a woebegone childhood that had turned into a troubled adolescence that had eventually transformed into the final metamorphosis of a malevolent, twisted, and vicious adulthood. No interventions by caring family members or friends. Just a nightly reminder that abuse is not always perpetrated by men nor is it the exclusive domain of female victims. Sometimes women are the perpetrators of violent acts. And sometimes little boys are their victims.

Poem Man was known to the quiet people of Marbury as Dr. Eugene Flint Caldwell. The town's veterinarian. He was known as

Dr. Domuch (as opposed to Do-LITTLE) because of his steady and sure touch with the cats, dogs, and other family pets that had come to his office for over twenty-five years. No one knew that he was known on TeenVillage as Poem Man. No one knew that he had been privately stalking young girls like Leigh Reynolds for the last thirty years. Who would ever suspect it? Dr. Caldwell was the town's well-respected professional who had a reputable family and practice that was above suspicion for anything remotely deviant – especially anything associated with child endangerment. Could the same man who treated the town's pets harm its children? Of course not! No one in his or her right mind would ever consider Eugene to be a problem in need of a solution.

Nor would anyone ever suspect his forty year-old wife, Jennifer Caldwell, who was a school teacher at the Big M. Jennifer taught literature and art to bored teens who barely contained their yawns in a class that everyone knew was popular only because the prettiest girls at the Big M took her classes. To feign interest was to curry favor. Despite their lack of academic enthusiasm, Eugene was always delighted when some of her comeliest students would follow Jennifer home to hear more pearls of art and literary wisdom. Too popular to pay proper attention in class, but desperate to get good grades, these students would try flattery and anything else to get more information on what to expect on pop quizzes and upcoming exams, and they were often successful as Jennifer wanted more than anything to help all of her students do well. Jennifer, who was expecting their first child, was so distracted by a triumphantly late motherhood that she was completely unaware that her favorite students were false and that the man she had married had a penchant for cheap poetry, online chats, and pubescent girls. If she had known these things, she would have never agreed to help construct the Grand Surprise her so-called Husband-of-the-Year and Father-to-be-of-Next-Year was plotting for Marbury – a surprise that she had thought would be full of innocent, exciting, creative fun. Not particularly prescient, but in a rush of maternal hormones, Jennifer nursed a hard-to-shake feeling that things were all wrong. About the Grand Surprise. About the integrity of her students. About the trustworthiness of Eugene. About everything. Trying to dismiss it as first pregnancy-related paranoia, Jennifer breathed in and out, practicing the meditative state she had been advised would be useful in delivery.

Caught up in the swoon of impending motherhood and unable to think of little else, what Jennifer didn't know was that by the end of the next day, she would realize just how very much her misjudgment would cost everyone and everything she held most dear. Misdirected actions that would one day force the town to acknowledge a father-to-be once known to the world as Dr. Caldwell, who would later become known by a more infamous (and unfortunately – more permanent nomenclature). The Poem Man of Marbury County.

Harp is really starting to drive me crazy with all her Big Ideas on how for me to snag Lance on the way to Marbury for the MOMMY!march. The more she talks the less interested I am in being anyone's girlfriend – especially when we are being interrupted every two seconds by Jeremy. He seems to want her to listen to so many random things that I am losing track of it all. Good thing he is dating Harper because I would have lost patience a long time ago with all the nonsense I am hearing from my end. Harp has to promise to tell him where she is, what time she plans to get home, who she is with, blahblahblah for every minute of the day tomorrow. He growls that he is extremely worried about the fact that she is going on the march without him tomorrow and he Doesn't Like It. Not one single bit. And that maybe she should cancel – never mind that one of the primary responsibilities of the Lady of the Chair every year is to be Oceania's La Grande Dame of the MOMMY!march.

I have to laugh to myself at the thought that unfortunately for Jeromeo, the Prep Pirates have an away game on the day of the march and poor little Germy can't escort his Lady of the Chair across the Marania Bridge with all the hoopla that follows this kind of occasion for the Pirate Captain and his Lady. He is going to be way out in Somerset County, Maryland and unable to even consider returning to Oceania in time to do anything more than call Harp and ask her to tell him about her day. Jeremy is positively and completely beside himself that his coaches have not paid attention to any schedules beyond the dates and time of their games. Nothing else at Prep (or Oceania County for that matter) is of concern to them and it shows. I can hear him ranting in Harper's ear regarding the failure of his favorite coach to remember that the Lady of the Chair has to serve as the march's Grande Dame – and where else was HE, as Pirate Captain, supposed to be except right by his Lady's side???!! I do feel a little sorry for him – his anger and fear pounds in Harper's ears, hurting my own. He reminds Harp that he is going to get one of his friends, Foster Bellows, to watch over her. Ever since he and Happy have been on the outs he has been forced to rely on Foster to act as his best buddy. Foster's a perfectly nice guy, but everyone knows that he's someone whom Jeremy doesn't trust nearly as much as he had trusted Happy and it has made Jeremy even more anxious than usual. Harper insists that she'll be fine with Lance and Arthur, but that seems to make him more upset. The thought that she might actually be with Lance alone (as if I were a dust ball or piece of dirt-stomped grass) makes him ballistic! Harper tries to get him to Calm Down and assures him that Foster will be right by her side every inch of the walk. I'm confused and frustrated listening to all of this, but there's not much I can say. He's not talking to me. He's talking to Harp. If he wasn't screeching so loudly, I wouldn't even know what he was saying because Harper is trying as hard as she can to shush him with her quietest inside voice. But I'm not deaf, and I'm not stupid so I can hear and understand where he's going with all of this. But he seems to forget that Lance is supposed to be for ME. Even if I'm on the fence about whether or not I want a relationship with Lance does not mean that Harper is willing (or interested) in dumping Jeremy for Lance. It is not only doubtful that this is likely to ever happen, it is about as possible as Harper becoming best friends with Meredith Ford or capturing new souls for Project C during the march tomorrow morning.

Jeremy, I think in exasperation, you really need to give this a rest! My appeal is in my head but as if he has heard me finally, and at long last, Harper hangs up the phone as Jeremy gets out his last splutter.

When Harper turns to me, her eyes are more troubled than I would have expected. She usually laughs off Jeremy's tantrums and ignores his concerns as being over-the-top and just plain silly. But for some reason, his concerns for her safety seem to get under her skin this time and she looks at me as if I should share a concern that has now become her own.

"Germy seems scared, Leigh."

I stare at her. He sounds the way he always sounds to me. Like an absolute nut.

"Scared of what? You and Lance? He's scared of you running off together? Like Romeo and Juliet or somethin'?"

Harper bites her lip and shakes her head.

"No. That's what he pretends it's all about, but it's not. He tried to hide it just now, but he's scared that something bad is going to happen on the march. I don't know what he thinks might happen, but with J.L., Eloise, and all these other souls floating in and out of crystals – stuff he still doesn't even know about - it's hard to say what could go wrong at the march to Marbury. But whatever we do tomorrow, let's do it together, okay? We gotta stick together, okay?!" The fact that Harper is so insistent and keeps repeating herself tells me that she is really unnerved by Jeremy's anxieties.

I nod. I agree completely. Between those three crazy girls in Marbury and Project C, I think we can't be too safe and sticking together sounds like the way to go.

"Like glue on the bottom of my shoe." I say and mean each and every word.

Lydia stared out the window at the full moon.

She knew that there was a lot to consider with all that was at stake with the proposed expansion of Eco and the fact that the end of May meant the beginning of the graduation season for Echoes who were advancing to middle school, upper school, college, and the Big, Wide, World Beyond. It was this latter group of young adults that caused Lydia the most heartache. She had so wanted to start a graduate program for older Echoes who were apprehensive (and rightly so!) about going out into Life unprepared for whole groups of people whose unfamiliarity with their particular Gifts created difficulties – both real and imagined.

But, she could not convince Graydon Fletcher to sell the necessary tracts of land that were needed. And she refused to involve Harper and Jeremy in their parents' adult struggle. This was her fight and she was determined to win it. Not simply because she was in the right, but because it was right. For the Echoes, for Oceania, and even for the Fletcher family.

Especially Penelope.

Even if Graydon didn't know it.

The phone rang. Lydia glanced at the clock. It was almost midnight. The Caller ID indicated who it was and Lydia ignored it. The light across the lawn in Leigh's room was still on and it was time for her to go to them and tell them "Lights Out!" in her firmest parental voice, but Lydia resisted leaving the guest house for now. Fatigue, worry, stress were starting to overcome even her strong maternal instincts.

All good reasons not to rush out and make demands on the girls, who were always so happy in each other's company. What was the harm in letting them stay up longer? Tomorrow was the MOMMY!march and Lydia was delighted for Harper, who was serving as Oceania's La Grande Dame. She worried that Leigh might feel a little left out, but those fears had been put to rest by Leigh's seeming industry in other areas of her life that were kept private from Lydia, but seemed to be productive and satisfying to Leigh. Lydia's gauge on this so-called contentment was Leigh's ever-bright smile and abundant enthusiasm whenever Lydia would see her at home or out and about in town with her friends or Harper.

Those examples and the rather loud whisper around Oceania that Leigh was now in the running for the post of Miss Sacred Names calmed some of her anxieties over Leigh. Lydia wasn't quite sure what that particular honor entailed, but she was willing to support Leigh in whatever she needed. Despite her own personal feelings for that august institution, being a Mother outweighed any other considerations and Lydia stood ready to assist Leigh in whatever manner possible.

Leigh as Miss Sacred Names was not something as unbelievable as Harper as Miss Sacred Names, but it was still a bit much to digest. Doing anything with that school beyond the required academics was going above and beyond the call to duty (at least as far as Lydia was concerned), but she still felt a rush of maternal pride.

A slight breeze ruffled the curtains and Lydia settled back against the floral upholstered sofa with a smile. It seemed like the end to a stressful day might be unwinding.

There was a knock at the door. Cal stood up, a small growl alerting Lydia that whoever was at the door was not a family member, but was someone known, and trusted, to Lydia and Cal.

Lydia opened the door after checking to see who the visitor was at this time of evening. It was late, but not too late for this caller. Not for this guest, the original purveyor of Excalibur, who probably felt it was just in time. She regretted ignoring the phone call as she realized that the visitor (who was also the earlier caller) was well aware that she had been deliberately ignoring the call.

"Zee. Please come in." Lydia stepped aside to allow Xavier Montague the opportunity to visit.

"For you to be in your private sanctuary is an indication that you have a lot on your mind, Lydia. Do you care to share any of it with me? I am here – a willing shoulder on which you can lean."

Lydia was surprised on two accounts. First: How did Xavier know that she retreated to Idislewilde's guest house when she needed to think? She knew for a fact that she had never once shared that with him. Not to mention the fact that she was curious how he had so deftly evaded the guard at the gate. Two: Why did Xavier think he could help her with anything other than finding Chester – or is that what he assumed – that she was thinking about Chester? Somehow she knew that it was inadvisable to ask him either question as there was no immediate remedy at hand. If she was under some kind of intrusive surveillance executed by Xavier Montague, or if he wanted to give her unsolicited advice about matters not pertaining to Chester, there was little she felt emotionally prepared to handle.

"I'm fine, Zee," Lydia told a small untruth, aware that the man's eyes seemed to bore holes into hers. He pierced her in ways that she found to be distinctly uncomfortable. It was as if he had a million unanswered questions for her of which he was determined to find the truth. Her truth.

Xavier shook his head, unconvinced, but deciding to play it straight.

"Lydia, I've been behind the scenes trying to help you find Chester. I've been working with members of the Pelican Club. I know that Mortimer Blaine has been most unhelpful and as unfortunate as that may be – given his close proximity in Marbury – there are other people who can be of service. My question to you is how would you like for me to proceed? This effort will take time and I am determined to spare no expense -"

"I will pay you, Zee!," Lydia shot back, with a clenched jaw. She did not want to be beholden to Xavier beyond what was reasonable.

Xavier's jaw jutted out in turn.

"I forbid it."

Lydia choked down her gasp. It was insane for Xavier to use such determined language. How on earth did he feel that he was in a position to forbid her anything? Especially in this regard.

"Chester would insist, Xavier."

There. Using Xavier's given (rather than pet) name forced his hand. Xavier's healthy tanned skin flushed red.

"I will let you know if I need anything, Lydia, but I prefer to do this my way. If you will allow it. Please."

This last bit of acquiescence was forced and they both felt it. Xavier was obviously a very take-charge kind of man and this inability to do things completely his way did not suit him.

"Can you give me the names of these people in Pelican, Zee?" Lydia tried to soften the anger between them and get information she needed to move forward with her search for Chester.

Xavier shook his head.

"Absolutely not. I'm sorry, Lydee."

Lydia winced at the use of the endearment. She understood that to get the things she needed from Xavier, she would have to use more than just her considerable intellect. She would also have to use her womanly charm. It was just difficult because she knew that Xavier liked her more than he should like a woman who was married with two young daughters and one semi-adopted son, but their conflicted feelings stood between them in an uneasy truce. He would make no romantic moves that could be construed as overt advances, and she would make no countermoves or strikes that would do anything to explicitly reject him.

"I understand you must maintain your privacy, Zee, but I worry that this is going on for too long. I have a gut feeling that something must be done soon. Done NOW."

Lydia tried to keep the desperation from her voice, but the attempt was futile. It was actually the presence of another adult that allowed her to release her true emotions. To not always be strong when she wanted to be weak.

"I'm here, Lydee. Just reach out." Xavier moved in closer to Lydia on the sofa. He gestured for her to come into his arms that were ready to encircle and welcome her into an embrace.

Lydia resisted, fighting back her emotions of sorrow, anger, and fear. She saw the trap for what it was and deftly evaded it.

Shining her brightest smile, Lydia met Xavier's gaze with her own, but held her ground exactly where she was.

"I'm fine, Zee. I really do appreciate your efforts on our behalf, and I thank you for coming all the way to Idislewilde to check on us like this."

Xavier noted the plural use of language. Lydia was letting him know that this visit would be translated only as a measure of his concern for everyone at Idislewilde: herself, the girls, Lance, Arthur, even Cal.

"There is nothing I will not do for you, Lydia. I hope you understand that."

Lydia felt like she was breathing underwater.

"I do."

"Good. That is very important to me." Xavier's unspoken intentions hovered between them like charged telephone wire. He couldn't have communicated his desires any better than if he had spoken them or put them in writing.

Lydia needed Xavier's help to find Chester. What she wondered (and not for the first time) was what Xavier planned to do once Chester was found.

In other words, what did Xavier Montague expect from her once her husband was returned? Lydia's mind raced. None of it made much sense unless...?

Unless Xavier had no expectation of Chester's return.

Lydia took in a quick breath.

Nothing else made much sense. There would be no other reason for Xavier's imprudent interest in returning Chester to the woman who loved him. Not when Xavier was, himself, so very obviously interested in that same woman.

"Do you think that you can return Chester?" Lydia posed the question that she dreaded asking but didn't want to put off another second.

Xavier studied her face thoughtfully. His lips curved into a smile that didn't quite reach his guarded eyes.

"Can you make us a cup of tea, Lydee? I'd really appreciate it."

Lydia knew not to pressure him. There was no reason to push Xavier to do what she needed from him. It was clear that his desire (and methods) of helping her were as complicated as the man himself.

"Of course, Zee. Earl Grey or Ginger?" She knew his two favorites by heart.

"I think a little bit of the Earl might be good, my dear. If you don't mind."

Lydia sensed that Xavier had decided that an emotional retreat was in order and she was more than willing to play along. It was easier on her already frayed nerves.

"No trouble at all, Zee. I'll just be a few minutes. Please make yourself comfortable. Turn on the T.V. if you want."

Lydia left Xavier in the comfortable sitting room that had a direct view of the main house. Rising, he went to stare out of the window, and wondered (not for the first time) just how much Idislewilde was worth on the market.

His thoughts wandered down an emotional path he had tried to avoid, but found himself traversing more and more of late – almost against his will. The question was whether or not Lydia would mind terribly if one day soon she and the children came to live at his plush estate? His grand house and surrounding gardens didn't have a whimsical name or stir the emotions quite like Idislewilde, but they most certainly did have two things that most people would consider possibly even more important.

History. And a mature and quite capable Man of the House.

I can't sleep. I see the light on in the guest house and watch as Dr. Montague gets in his car and drives away. Leigh and I are not stupid and we know that he doesn't buy flowers all the time just because he likes flowers or because he wants to share his love of flowers with random people and Mother just happens (like rain hitting an umbrella) to be on some short flower charity list of his. He's as obvious as the fact that my daily trig homework problems are still not on my list of Things To Do When A Favorite T.V. Show Is On.

The head of Lakeshore Preparatory likes Mother. Too much.

I watch him all the time now because he (even more than those malicious souls) has the potential to mess up Project C beyond control. What if Mother starts thinking that those flowers actually mean something or worse - that HE smells as good as they do?

When was the last time she laid eyes on our Father – much less received luscious bouquets of very expensive and very beautiful roses from him? It's been like a hundred million years and there's no doubt that Mother is like everyone else (including me – and especially prissy Leigh) - she likes nice things and special attention from handsome, rich men.

I haven't said anything yet to anyone, but I'm really starting to panic. Dr. Montague has the same look on his face that Jeremy gets when he talks about us getting married. Can Dr. Montague's thoughts be that much different from Germy's? Are boys that different from men? Somehow, I don't think so. I think that Dr. Montague is like auditioning or something for Dad's job. I can tell. He's got the hungry look of a ravenous vampire or werewolf. I'd call him a monster, but who can blame him? Mother is still so beautiful and Father is still so lost.

I close the drape. I am glad he's leaving and didn't stay very long. I don't hate him. How could I? He gave Cal to Lance and took him into Prep without making any noise about it. Once he got his hearing back, Lance happily fell in love with Prep – practically more than

Germy! If everything works out the way it should and it will work out if Leigh just learns how to CALM DOWN and try a little harder to outsmart those three girls from Marbury – MARBURY???!! - I mean, really? Marbury! If Leigh would just focus on being precisely what she is – Beautiful and Interesting - like ME! – she'll be fine. If she plays her cards right (and she will do that because I plan to stack the deck with my best and most wonderful ideas), I can almost guarantee that good-old Lance will be my future and permanent brother-in-law.

I cross my fingers, my toes, and my eyes at the same time – my own personal ritual for good luck. I whisper over and over under my breath – just like the HeeBees (Sacred Names' Holy Bible loony tunes sect). Those six crazy HeeBees march up and down the halls in two lines against the walls muttering and chanting to themselves. No one bothers them – not even the meanest nuns. I think that even THEY are scared of them! Their super-zealous religious club (called the Sacristy) prays for Namers to pass tests, find new boyfriends, get into the colleges of their choice, just about everything short of military coups or political assassinations. In some ways they have almost as much clout at Sacred Names as the Royals. I think (and not for the first time) that maybe I'll just give in and pay them the requisite one hundred dollars for a prayer request to go up for Lance to marry Leigh. And then I think of better uses for that money. A new skate board. Donations to charity. A cute new sundress. Besides, just because the Sacristy pray doesn't mean they don't talk and there have already been enough rumors circulating through school about Leigh and Lance. I don't know who started them, but part of me is mad that it happened sooner than it should have because it makes Leigh feel all nervous and jittery. I really wish I knew who had started the gossip because I would give them as good as they gave – these no-good Perez Hilton wannabes! Mother always says that "what goes around, comes around" and I guess that's true. Capturing souls is Not Nice so I guess Bad Things can happen (or should happen) as a result.

I take a deep breath – leaving the mystery of the Sacred Names gossip mill to later thoughts. I need to focus on the matter at hand. With my whole body practically twisted like a pretzel, I pray my own (FREE of charge!!!) prayer with the urgency of a Sacristy convert at a candlelight vigil.

And that's pretty desperate.

But that's exactly how I feel.

Chapter Thirty-Four:
Day Three – The Edge of Forever

Jennifer felt her anxiety growing as rapidly as her protruding abdomen. Normally, she was proud of the fact that she had beaten the odds and gotten pregnant at forty. Sure, there were plenty of rich movie star moms at forty – even fifty! – but ordinary women like herself were lucky if they could spawn at thirty-five.

Jennifer paused. Spawn?

Her mouth flooded with the taste of unwrapped aluminum and she realized that her fear levels were rising faster than anticipated. The late-term mother-to-be knew that Something Was Not Right. The question was what to do about it. Or more to the point, what to do about him. The man she had married.

The father of her unborn child.

Since the night before, as she had quietly watched as her husband frantically constructed the Grand Surprise, she had found herself feeling more and more like the lead role in *Rosemary's Baby*. She was at the same point that Mia Farrow was in the scene where Rosemary, looking almost doll-like in her sailor dress, is lugging a too-large suitcase filled with hospital delivery and newborn baby clothes to an outside phone booth to call a *STUPID, IDIOTIC, PAID-TO-BE-DUMB* doctor who would later turn sweet, gullible Rosemary over to her fiendish no-good husband. That movie was always too scary for words and now it was too scary for thought. She was so Rosemary right now. With her very own husband as Rosemary's lunatic spouse. Granted, instead of the devil it was something a little less sinister, but who in their right mind ever EXPECTS Lucifer to show up??? Jennifer couldn't quite figure it all out because her raging hormones clouded her usually meticulously logical mind, making substantive thought more and more difficult. She taught literature, but her brain typically processed information like a mathematician. When she wasn't pregnant. But, even as cloudy as her judgment had been lately, as far as she was concerned there was real reason to be afraid and for at least One Very Good Reason she wanted more than anything to call for help. Three little numbers on her cell. 9-1-1. Run. Hide! And not necessarily in that order!

The expectant mother looked down at her hands that were now trembling. One was holding the cell phone and the other was resting nervously on top of her almost nine-month pregnant stomach. Her fingers seemed to strum mindlessly on their own – playing a song on her rising mound that she could neither truly appreciate nor fathom. With her other hand she had speed-dialed her mother, but as usual

That Woman – that thoughtless, pleasure-seeking woman - was unreachable. The one time that she really wanted to talk to her – really NEEDED to talk to her, and she was unavailable. Figured. Probably hanging out with one of her new boyfriends. At fifty-five, her mother still Had It – whatever IT is.

But none of the foolishness between her and her mom mattered right now. What mattered most was the fact that she needed her more than she had ever needed her in her entire forty years of life. Yes, Jennifer had been her mother's fourteen-year-old teenage mistake, but as a current forty-year old mother-to-be, she needed the woman she had called "Mother" more than ever before. And that reason had started last night at eight o'clock.

In a spurt of nesting, Jennifer had decided to try to clean Genie's private room – the one he usually barred her from as his male sanctuary. Normally, she let him have his way as he made so few demands on her. But this time, she did it – as she did all things now – FOR THE BABY. She knew where he kept the key. She had always known. It was just that she had never cared before. Until now. She wanted their home to be spic and span from top to bottom.

Jennifer shivered. Genie's room – no, EUGENE's room – was a horror film that seemed to move through her mind in relentless slow motion. Eugene. The thought of calling him "Genie" ever again made her physically sick. They had once been Jenny and Genie and

365

everyone had thought that was so cute, so winning. So sweet. He was the doctor and she was the school teacher. What could be more quaint?

What would they call them now? Jennifer wanted to vomit. Bonnie and Clyde? The Monster and the Bride?

She had discovered Eugene's private collection of secret photos. And more than anything in her life (except this baby), she wished she had done something else. Anything else. Cleaned the windows. Dusted on top of the ROOF.

Anything.

In that room - that secret, dusty little room - she had discovered a wall of photos – a shrine of sorts. All of one young, African American girl. The child looked like she was no more than twelve, but Jennifer knew that she was actually a bit older. She knew that statistic because she knew the girl – having taught for a year at the infamous Eco in Oceania and having seen both girls flitter in and out of Echo like young moonbeams. The only thing was that she knew (unlike her insane husband) that there were really two of those girls. Harper. And Leigh. From the e-mails posted on the wall, she could tell that for some strange reason Eugene was unaware of the existence of the other girl. The one named Harper. It was pretty obvious because the words "Leigh Harper Reynolds" were repeated over and over. Apparently tiring of so much effort, the initials "LHR" were scratched under several of the photos.

She knew she had to tell someone. By rights, she should tell Lydia Reynolds, but she was terrified of what that woman might do to her. Or to her unborn baby. Everyone knew those Reynolds people were magical! Hadn't Chester Reynolds gotten himself lost into thin air? Lydia was well-known in Marbury. She drove in for garden tools and plants for her fabulous estate, Idislewilde. Not to mention Eco. And she spent lavishly and always had a kind word for the people of Marbury.

Jennifer shivered again and it was not from cold. She tried calling her mother again. Still nothing.

With a pounding heart, she did the unthinkable. Searching through her phone for the directory, she reached the alphabet "E" and then paused. She remembered how she had worked at Eco for a time and had fallen in love with the children, the ethos of the school, and even some of the gruffiest faculty. There were faculty at Eco who possessed odd Gifts that Jennifer (being a completely lay teacher and secular in all thing magical) had found hard to understand or accept. As a result, she had mastered the art of looking away or feigning disinterest in something she considered to be disquieting or hurtful. When she was actually anything but disinterested. But she could always trust Morgan Newton, Eco's Deputy Head and 24-hour guardian.

Everyone knew that this child (whichever one of the twins Eugene had designated as worthy of his compulsive fixations) was one of the most treasured figures in their two counties. Given these facts, Jennifer was sure that she was completely incapable of Just Looking The Other Way. Not this time.

There it was. Her fingers hovered above the phone's touch screen. The words seemed to scream something to her. Asking her to do more than just stare at them with a numbness she was starting to feel.

The Enchanted College of Oceania.

Dear God. Jennifer chewed her lip. Calling Lydia Reynolds might be premature. Maybe she didn't see anything at all in that room. Maybe it was just like she had heard about where pregnant women sometimes lose touch with reality. Go crazy. Pre-partum insanity. Maybe that's all it was.

And then she remembered what she would rather forget. A picture of Eugene from their wedding book nestled in the coterie of photos. He was standing stiffly in the standard groom uniform (a black tuxedo and black bowtie) and looked every bit as frightened as he had felt that day over twenty years ago. She was what then? Twenty-one? Twenty-two? Barely out of college. This unprepossessing picture was taped next to a beautiful color picture of Leigh (or was it Harper?)

and demonstrated the loveliness of the Reynolds family in its purest form. Leigh looked to be about ten in that picture, so Jennifer guessed that it was taken a few years ago. Back at a time when she thought that nothing could go wrong when two people like Jenny and Genie were really and truly in love. Miracles can happen – even to ordinary people. Pregnant at forty. Married for almost twenty years when most of her friends had never married or their marriages had ended in costly, ugly divorces. She had thought herself to be one of the lucky ones. THEY were lucky. They were happy and still in love. She had believed so much back then.

Back when she was a fool.

Not for the first time, Jennifer realized that in some strange fashion, over the last ten years she had isolated herself from most of her friends, leaving her with virtually no one to help her. No one to reason with her – talk her out of her unfortunate (and hopefully inaccurate) conclusions. That her husband liked small girls. That her husband was a good man who just happened to be fascinated with young girls like Leigh.

Going over to the wall, Jennifer studied the handwriting on some of the pictures. It looked like childish, untutored scrawling rather than the penmanship taught to Sacred Name girls, Prep boys, or Eco children (as Jennifer would know having worked as a substitute teacher at two of the three institutions). Even Big M students, who hated to write essays from scratch in class, had better handwriting.

Bur she recognized it for what it was. Or more importantly, WHOSE it was.

Eugene's.

She tried her mother again, glancing nervously at her watch. Eugene had gone to the hardware store to get more things for the Grand Surprise and she knew that it took him at least twenty minutes to get there, pick out the stuff, and return, so she had a little time. She wasn't sure why she had come back to this room. Did she think the pictures had magically disappeared? Did she really think that she had imagined the whole thing? Was she going crazy?

This time, Merciful God, her mother picked up.

"Mother!"

Jennifer listened for two seconds as her mother drawled out (obviously still tipsy from a late evening cocktail) that she had Been Out and About with her latest flame named Roger – Roger Lambert. Jennifer interrupted. She could barely listen to that kind of drivel for two seconds, much less ten.

"Mother – I have something to tell you. Something about Eugene. Something that's very bad."

The door opened wider and in the man in question walked. Jennifer thought she would faint.

He held out his hand for the phone, his eyes as dead as she knew she would be in a matter of seconds. In his other hand, her husband wielded the largest knife she had ever seen. She looked at it in wonder, feeling that everything happening was just part of a very bad dream brought on by too little sleep and too many anxious thoughts. She focused more clearly at the instrument. It looked like the kind of knife that professional butchers must use to cut fresh slabs of beef or pork. Jennifer thought about this cooly as if she were watching a documentary on the Discovery Channel. And then something inside of her frozen heart, mind, and tummy moved. THE BABY! Oh, no, God. NO!

For the first and last time in her forty-year life, Jennifer used a term of filial endearment previously shunned (not uttered even on birthdays or Christmas): "MO-MMYYYY!" Frantic, she took in a breath and screamed in a feverish rush: "I NEED YOU TO CALL THE PO-" Before she could finish her sentence, Eugene snatched the phone with one smooth motion and turned it off. With a silent, deadly CLICK. His eyes fastened to hers like a button, closing off all hope.

The room went to silence and husband and wife stared at each other, breathing in each other's air, for what seemed like an eternity. One awaiting death and the other a freedom to finish the task he had set for himself long ago in a TeenVillage chat room with a lovely young girl named Leigh.

"It won't hurt," he promised, his eyes as empty as his thoughts as he leaned closer into his wife's space as if to meet her in a passionate embrace. "Just don't move, Jenny dear, and I'll be quick and then it will all be over. Once and for all. Just like it was always supposed to be."

Dr. Eugene Flint Caldwell, who had been trained to heal sick animals, also knew the tools and methods to end their suffering and misery when it was their time. And it was this latter practice of his training that he fully exercised at that moment with his wife and unborn child. True to his word, he made it as painless and as quick as possible.

After all, he was, if nothing else, a professional.

What a skunk. Now I understand perfectly why Harper is not overly fond of Foster Bellows. He told us (like we need another boss besides Mother, Lance, and now Arthur!) that we are to dress alike for this ridiculous Lady of the Chair MOMMY!march event to Marbury. If Foster didn't look almost exactly like the younger brother of Orlando Bloom, I would let him know that he was not now or ever the boss of me, but he's saved from a once certain doom by the flash of deep-dish dimples. He has no idea what was in store for him otherwise, so I recommend strongly (which he completely ignores) that he should probably speak less and smile more as a way to distract me from the fact that he is starting to really get on my last nerve. He says (in this annoying Big Boss way) that Jeremy says that if we dress just alike no one – not even our own mother - will be able to tell us apart. The scary part about that is that he's right. We've done it enough times since we were three years old to know. It's funny and a little intimidating. No one ever thinks about this, but it's a responsibility being yourself and someone else all at the same time. Twinning is harder than it looks. People don't understand that.

I ask Harp what the real purpose is for us to dress alike and she says that she doesn't really know except that Germy thinks it is a good idea. A good idea for what? It doesn't make much sense to me or to her, but Harper is instructed –INSTRUCTED??? - what does he think we are? Little kids?? We are instructed to please do as he asks as He Knows Best About These Things.

What things?

Harper is as unconvinced as I am that any of this is really necessary. Foster Bellows standing guard over us like Secret Service. As if he knows what he's doing! But, she has decided (if you want to call the way she processes information these days as 'decisions') that it's much easier to just do what Jeremy says and avoid a lot of problems down the road.

I ask her what road that is – the road to insanity or the road to becoming Prep Princess and she just rolls her eyes at me. But she seems to not clearly understand the difference between right, wrong, and Just Plain Stupid when it comes to Germy and becoming Prep Princess. Sometimes I wonder if she would be willing to forsake everything – even me – in pursuit of a stupid diamond tiara and purple satin sash with the initials "PP" (Prep Princess) on it.

I figure that if I'm not careful, I just might be swapped for a purple sash.

And, as far as I'm concerned, that is Not Good.

Lydia frowned at herself in the mirror. It was bad enough that the MOMMY!march was starting later that day, but it was the fact that Eco's security could be compromised that had her most on edge. Xavier had already called her – just as she was having her morning cup of green tea. He had told her that she could use his services, and the strong arms of his best athletes, to protect Eco if she had any lingering fears. Against her better judgment, she had reluctantly agreed to use them as stand-by guards if the need arose and Xavier had sighed in contented pleasure – glad to finally be of service (beyond the delivery of weekly roses) to the woman he most wanted to demonstrate his feelings of abject loyalty and service.

The tea stirred uncomfortably in her empty stomach, reminding Lydia that she had eaten nothing last night and had had the same incomplete fare for breakfast. For some unknown reason her nerves were completely on edge and it didn't make sense beyond her usual frustration over not yet finding her lost husband or figuring out what to do about expanding Eco.

From her window, Lydia watched as Harper and Leigh prepared to leave out early with Lance and Arthur. The twins were dressed in the same kind of pink, frilly puffy dresses that Lydia thought looked like something out of *The Wizard of Oz*. The girls looked more like fanciful munchkins than modern-day princesses, Lydia acknowledged. Harper and Leigh sported tiaras that shimmered and sparkled in the early spring sun, matching their bright smiles, and Lydia had smiled at their youthful innocence and playfulness. Lance and Arthur were flanked by Foster Bellows, who seemed more intense than seemed necessary for a local fundraising walk-a-thon. There was something about the set of his jaw and the stiffness of his demeanor that seemed skewed from the more celebratory mood of the other revelers from Sacred Names and Prep who had shown up to Idislewilde to escort the Lady of the Chair to the opening ceremony. Lydia had wanted to join in with the day's festivities, but protecting

Eco from the annual mock invasion of the curious, the detractors, and the mischievous meant that she had little choice but to remain behind in Oceania. Every year there was an attempt made to breach the gates of Eco and she didn't dare take the chance.

"Good luck, girls!" Lydia called from her window, waving madly.

The twins turned to stare back at their mother's face framed in the window, like a cinnamon-colored, lovely Rapunzel. Her hair was loose about her face and tumbled to her shoulders, adding to that imagery. The girls grinned and waved back with equal enthusiasm.

"See you tonight, Mother!" they called out in unison. Unafraid of being called sissies (as are most boys of that age), they finished it off with a sing-songy: "We Love You!"

Lydia felt her heart lurch and tears begin to burn in her eyes. She had no idea why she was so emotional these days, but she had been feeling almost out of control lately. Losing Chester to the bell tower had never been easy on her, but why was it so especially hard these days? Was it that Xavier Montague was finally starting to get to her? Were those twelve roses sent with the precision of Time itself finally starting to make an impact on how she felt about Xavier? About Chester?

The thought of betraying herself to Xavier made Lydia physically sick and she pulled her head in from the window to retreat to the quiet darkness of her room in which the heavy drapes served to block out the morning sun.

The house phone rang. Lydia sighed. It was probably Xavier. Again. Making sure that she didn't want a lift to Eco (she didn't) or that she would change her mind about having lunch (she wouldn't) and if she would reconsider opening up Eco to a select few VIP visitors who were his private friends (she absolutely couldn't!!). Who these VIPs were was not explained and any attempt to get more information from Xavier only resulted in more evasion and double-talk. It was pretty obvious that Xavier was the VIP in question and it was HIS curiosity about Eco that needed to be satisfied.

The phone rang with an insistence that Lydia found as annoying as Xavier's request, so she picked it up.

Nothing.

"Hello?"

Nothing.

"HELLO?!" Lydia allowed her impatience to show.

"Lido (Leedo)?"

Lydia felt her heart stop. Only one person in the world called her 'Lido.' Chester.

"Chester?"

"Lido – you gotta go to –" Static covered the rest. Lydia pressed the receiver so close to her ear it left indentations in her skin.

"Chester? CHESTER???!!"

The phone went dead and there was only a fast busy tone. Lydia hung up slowly. Chester? It was unmistakably his voice, but what did it all mean? And what was he trying to tell her? She had to go to where? Eco? Was Eco in danger? Lydia shook her head, trying to feel her way through the jumble of emotions that grabbed her stomach, twisting it into knots. The bad feeling she had been having all morning roared into full-blown panic at the thought that Something Bad was about to happen to the institution that she and Chester had so carefully nurtured and loved.

Lydia made up her mind as she prepared to leave Idislewilde. She would let no one and no thing stand in her way if it looked like Eco was in danger.

No one.

She picked up the phone again.

"Zee? I would definitely appreciate your help. Six young men should probably be enough. Ten? I hardly think –", Lydia paused, remembering the call from Chester. "Yes, ten. And the sooner the better. I'm headed there now. Will let them into the gates myself."

Lydia hung up, feeling more fretful than ever as if taking this action had put her in the wrong direction of Chester's warning. But what else could he possibly mean? Lydia took a few deep, calming breaths. It was Eco. It had to be a potential assault against Eco.

What else could it be?

Her eyes rested on a recent picture of the twins with Arthur, Lance, and Cal. It was such a sweet family picture and had quickly become one of Lydia's favorites.

Hurrying out of the room, Lydia wondered briefly if the kids were all starting to have fun at the march. Tomorrow she would have something very special for the four young people at Idislewilde to celebrate Harper's triumphant march as Lakeshore Prep's Lady of the Chair and Leigh in her coveted role as the Lady's First Maid-in-Waiting. It was silly, frivolous nonsense, yes. But it was good, harmless fun and the Prep tradition would serve as an entertaining memory for both girls well into their dotage.

Lydia thought quickly. A barbeque or fish fry would be fun. Something outdoors. She was already looking forward to it. But as happy as the prospect of that kind of family fun was, she couldn't quite shake the nagging feeling that Something Was Not Right. Not At All.

Rushing out of the house and into her car, Lydia refused to succumb to the angst that threatened to engulf her. She would handle whatever (or whoever) came her way. Today, more than ever, she would be absolutely fearless. After all, she had heard from Chester, who might be lost, but had still managed to somehow find a way to whisper a five word message to his beloved wife. It wasn't absolutely certain what he meant, or what was said, but it was clear that it was Chester who had come calling and that he still cared Very Much for Lydia and their girls.

And if nothing else, as far as Lydia was concerned, that was Very Good News indeed!

The wind blew gently, rustling balloons and streamers from wheelchairs and other modes of easy transport for the Bluebird, Redbird, and Canarybird Leagues of Marbury County. Having forsaken these jerry-rigged vehicles, Oliver was content to walk under his own steam to Oceania, convinced that his passionate mission to rescue Tate and Do The Thing would be enough to carry him full speed ahead to his destination. His leg and arm braces were enough to get him where he needed to go to Do The Thing that would, he hoped, solve everything.

Oliver watched as some of his friends from the Big M assembled on the lawn outside of the school grounds. The band was ready to blast out rousing anthems to participants, who still bleary-eyed from the early call to action, were doing their best to appear as energetic as they could without keeling over from the unusual strain of standing upright just after sunrise on a Saturday morning.

The Munch contributed to the festivities with the Claussens

serving as de facto hosts, handing out steaming cups of coffee and doughnuts. Mr. and Mrs. Claussen were like bright rays of sunshine as they zipped in and out of the crowd, dispensing their own brand of liquid light from white styrofoam cups.

Oliver decided to forego food and drink. Nothing that would cause him to slow down or break his stride for bathroom breaks.

Mortimer Blaine walked beside his grandson, using his own thick staff as a way to guide his steps faithfully along the twenty-five mile path. He was, after all, eighty-five years old and a little assistance was more than just nice – it was necessary.

"Grandfather?" Oliver looked over at Mortimer, who was resting easily on his cane, watching the crowd start to form an impromptu, and slightly ragged, line of four abreast. "As Master of Ceremonies, I have to start things off. I have my horn. Are you ready?"

Mortimer beamed. Was he, Lt. Colonel Mortimer Blaine, an honors West Point graduate, decorated war hero from Vietnam and Korea, ready? Of course he was ready. He had stood salute at the beginning of many military honor parades overseas and in Washington, D.C. infront of generals and admirals and other military men who had served with great distinction in some of the nation's most infamous wars. This was really no different. There was another kind of serious war at hand – a battle against preventable birth defects and other childhood illnesses that needed all the warriors that could be mustered. Mortimer was intensely proud that his grandson was leading a fundraising parade that championed research and political activism that could potentially undermine and destroy diseases that attacked unsuspecting infants and children. This was a war he could understand. It was simple. Good versus evil.

He was more than ready.

Oliver took the golden horn and held it to his lips and blew. The pure sound filled the air and sent a shockwave through the drowsy crowd. The battle call had been sounded and everyone stood up straighter and focused their attention on the young Oliver who made his way to the front of the line after blowing his horn with all of his heart. He played Taps and the melancholy notes hovered in the air reminding everyone of their soulful, deliberate purpose.

Mortimer, arrayed in full army dress, walked in gallant splendor next to his grandson.

"Fair citizens of Marbury, are we ready?!," Oliver bellowed, in a deep, mature voice that surprised even his grandfather. Mortimer tried to hide it, but a tinge of fear coursed through his aging frame. Oliver was more than just the little boy who confided his deepest secrets to his grandfather from time to time. Oliver was now a young man and more than capable of reaching Eco, finding the Room of Clocks, and Doing The Thing. Mortimer wondered, for the first time, if he could really stop this newly discovered Oliver. Did he have what it takes?

Not waiting for Mortimer to gather his thoughts, a rowdy cheer went up and the MOMMY!march on the Marbury side was officially underway.

You've got to be kidding! I have to wear this frumpy, pumpkin shaped nonsense and pretend to be happy all at the same time? As much as I love Harp, the idea that I have to wave, wave, wave and blow kisses to people I hardly know (and some of whom positively get on my nerves) is not what I call a fun Saturday morning! My idea of fun on Saturday is waking up early, painting a scene of the garden from my window at Idislewilde or watching my favorite old T.V. show with really cute guys who always fall in love with the girl no one likes because she's not super popular, but she is pretty and smart and can play the piano.

"You have to keep up, Leigh. This is my third warning. Please make it my last."

That was Foster. I wonder for the hundredth time if he has lost his mind, too, for coming along as an unpaid bodyguard – chaperone – or whatever he is supposed to be for Harper. I know I'm perfectly crazy for doing this, but at least I have a good excuse called family. What's his?

"Jeremy said that you two are to stay together. So, either keep up or I'll have to hold your hand. Okay?"

No. It. Was. Not. Okay.

I just glare at him. So, he's doing this for Jeremy - and because why exactly? Everyone knows that Jeremy's best friend has always been Happy, so what's this whole Jeremy-Foster thing all about? I mean, there has to be something other than the fact they go to the same school. I know for a fact that I wouldn't do it just because some girl from Sacred Names asked me to do it. Not unless it was a really good friend. And even then I'd have to consider it as carefully as I think about what new toy to buy for Tibby or what my next A-plus bonus essay should be on for my AP American History class. We would have to have been friends going all the way back to first grade. All the way back to freeze tag and hide-and-go-seek. That kind of way back. And not like those criminal ex-friends that abandoned me to go worship in Queen Leila's court! Not like those phonies. It would have to be someone as true as I am to Harp and she is to me. Not people that trade you in like a used car.

"Look, you." Foster's tone is as harsh as my current thoughts. "Jeremy Fletcher tutors me in chemistry and I don't want to lose out on a good thing, you hear? I gotta ace my next exam or I'm off all varsity teams for good. I'm not at the game today because I'm already on academic suspension. Jeremy asked me to do this favor – watch his girl and her sister - and I'm doing it. Whether you like it or not. If I have to drag you all the way to Marbury by the hand or carry you in my arms, you will get there. Got it?"

Got it. And that explains that.

I pick up my pace, certainly not wanting to be held by the hand like some errant three-year-old because it was clear that Mr. Baseball would most definitely do what he promised.

Harper seems oblivious to what we're up to – she's too busy waving and grinning and grinning and waving. She calls it her Prep Princess royal salutation. Never mind what I call it. I swear that if I did not love her so much, I would completely lose my mind with all of this foolishness!

Unfortunately for at least one or two Prep boys, The Lady of the Chair is not just a title. There is a fairly large ceremonial chair decorated with purple and white streamers that is being pulled along in a wagon by Prep boys, who take turns with the assignment. The idea is that when we reach a certain point, Harper is supposed to assume her throne and declare the march officially. The Master of Ceremonies, some boy named Oliver, is supposed to wave the Lady's wand on the Bridge, declaring the march to be officially over for Marbury and Harp is supposed to blow the Master's horn. The tricky part is getting Marbury's Master and Oceania's Lady to meet at the same time to make the treasure swap (wand for horn) on the Marania Bridge without either having to wait too long in the boiling sun in the middle of the Bridge for the other. At over fifteen miles from Oceania, that bridge is the almost halfway point for the march and the thinking is that it all starts to go really fast to the end after that. The walk is timed, and there are about equal numbers of physically challenged people on both sides so it should work out if everyone keeps pace. Including me. So I scoot up.

Foster keeps an eye on Harp and me, but I can see that he is starting to get more caught up in the athletic banter going back and forth between Lance and Arthur over batting stats for some guy on the Washington Nationals or Baltimore Orioles or WHATEVER, so I (and even Harper) have become less and less of a real concern for the time being.

Which is perfectly fine with me.

"Leeds, isn't this fun?"

Harper hasn't called me Leeds in ages. It is shorthand for "follow the leader" – my all-time favorite game when we were little. I usually won because Harper could never concentrate long enough to do the exact thing I was doing. Being four was wicked fun when I would win at that game (among many others), but fast forward ten years and there is no question about who is now the leader and who is the reluctant, unhappy follower. Not with the leader's shining tiara sparkling like cut diamonds on the roof of her swollen, big head.

"If you ask me – and you did - a chocolate sundae is way better. Way more fun." I can't resist being just a little snarly. I'm only human. And I can feel beads of perspiration starting to prickle my neck and the middle of my back.

Harper casts me a baleful glare and then turns her back to me, continuing to wave as if it comes as natural to her as breathing. As if I am being the nicest little sister (by forty-five seconds) in the world and she's in some private air-conditioned bubble without a care or trickle of sweat to be felt anywhere.

This last bit of nonchalance stops me in my tracks. Tired already from being under surveillance by General Foster Bellows, and tired of the act of being cheerful when all I want to do is find the nearest tree and sit under its big, long, cool branches – I find that I am unable to move. Even in the morning it is steaming hot and miserable. I can only imagine the bake fest I have in store for me in the afternoon. And I can't stand it. I can't walk into a fate almost as bad as a timed pop quiz from Sister Mary Agnes who would have just spent three hours grading English Composition papers from (in her own words): "Girls who are functionally, emphatically illiterate!" I just can't.

'Fun' is definitely not a word I'd use today to describe anything.

Foster suddenly notices that everyone in the royal procession is not moving in one fluid motion and he turns back to me, gesturing angrily for me to move forward. I want to walk up because being hot AND embarrassed are not on my List of Things To Do today, but I seem to be stuck in my tracks. It's like I'm paralyzed. Rendered immobile. Stubbornly resolute. Unwilling to give an inch.

Until I realize – too late - that mortification is infinitely worse than capitulation. Foster waits ten seconds for me to obey and when he sees that I'm rooted like a hundred year oak in the place where I'm standing, he comes galloping (yes, galloping) back to me and picks me up in his arms as effortlessly as if I were made of feathers and deposits me (no, DUMPS me!!!) in an empty wagon that is being pulled by a Prep lackey named Spencer Gordon. The spare wagon is being dragged along in case the "authentic" Lady's Chair Wagon has a flat or some other technical problem. Thankfully, fluffy cushions are already in place so the metal doesn't burn or feel scratchy – not that Foster cares one hoot about that when he slams my round rear end down into its hard flat exterior. Despite the small comforts of the pillows, I am completely and utterly lacking my usual composure, fully aware that being "treated" to this ride is hardly to be considered A Good Thing. I fight back raging, fierce tears, hoping that no one (at least no one I care about) has witnessed my final humiliation. I promise that I won't cry because that would let that odious little ogre know how much he has hurt me. I refuse to let on how absolutely obliterated I feel. Because I can tell from the ridges of their indifferent backs that Mr. Baseball and Lady Harper simply couldn't care less. They are too busy being popular and exciting to be interested in me.

I know that without any effort at all, I will soon hate this day more than any other day for as long as I live.

I just don't know just how true that will be. In just under two hours that will be the truest statement I would have ever made in my almost fifteen years. And if I could take back the day, the morning, the event, I would. Every minute. Every second.

But, I can't. I wish – more than anything – that I could.

But I just can't.

There are two schools of thought where evil is concerned. Some people will argue that people are born bad. That evil is in the hearts of certain people from the time they are formed like jelly beans in the safe clutches of their mothers' wombs. Others will declare that evil is learned – much like children learn their alphabets. That someone must teach it to them, carefully and with great persistence at the earliest of ages.

And then there are people in a third group, who fall (like most people) somewhere in-between. They feel that the seed once planted must find fertile ground or it will wither and die. For these people, an evil predisposition not cultivated in sin will invariably turn away from the bad in favor of the delights of the good.

Unfortunately for Poem Man, the tilling of his childhood soil in abuse, neglect, and hardship reaped a violent harvest that established an almost inevitable life of evil that could not be avoided or denied. By giving into the anger and hatred that had dominated the way he had looked at life from the time he could walk (thanks to derelict, hateful parents who had often lit matches on the soles of their two-year-old's feet to "Train you to walk FASTER, Buster!!"), Poem Man would commit one of Marbury's most heinous and cowardly acts on historical record. An act rooted in sick, twisted thoughts about Bad Things involving a Young Girl that had consumed him, obsessed him, for nearly a year. Thoughts of all the Things He Could Do to a beautiful fourteen-year-old named Leigh Harper Reynolds. Thoughts that had nothing whatsoever to do with the good qualities of the girl, but only what his wicked and vile imaginations could conjure.

By the time the sun had started to crest in the sky towards noon, Poem Man's diabolical plot was fully underway.

With a disloyal wife securely out of the way, there was no one who knew, suspected, or considered that Dr. DoMUCH was anything other than Dr. DoGood. The kindly handsome veterinarian whom everyone loved. Not in their wildest dreams would anyone have ever considered him capable of the crimes he was about to commit. He reveled in the anonymity and secrecy.

Not one person in Marbury suspected anything. Not the Claussens. Not Minnie, Izzy, Rosie or Leo. Not Oliver or even Grandfather Mortimer, who had fought in wars and stared death in the eye.

No one, least of all Harper and Leigh, who were from Oceania, and who were not at all prepared for what was to come on the Marania Bridge at noon.

No one - except for Dr. Eugene Flint Caldwell – knew what to expect. Leigh's uncertain fate was known only to one person.

A man to be hated, avoided, and feared.

Poem Man. Marbury's very first Monster.

Chapter Thirty-Five:
The Bridge to Tomorrow

The sun was high and hot in the spring sky. Leigh had been given the same lavender colored parasol as Harper, and the twins had reconnected once more – as twins are apt to do – in a willing spirit of friendly compromise. Leigh had agreed with Foster to behave and was allowed to exit the wagon on a temporary reprieve with the stern provision that she keep pace with the rest of the group.

Leigh had raised her hand, as if being sworn in by a magistrate, solemnly pledging to stick to Harper like butter on bread. Foster had ignored her playful tone, taking his security role as seriously as an FBI agent or U.S. marshal.

Harper finally tired of waving to a crowd that had long grown bored with the novel and courageous emotions that had overflowed at the beginning of the march. She was now willing to walk quietly alongside the wagon bearing the Lady's Chair. She made no more generously overt gestures that signaled her role as Oceania's leader in the march. Rather, she looked increasingly, at mile ten, like someone who was starting to regret wearing a poofy dress and cutsie low-heeled sandals as one was starting to itch and the other offered inadequate arch support.

"Why don't you hop on your chair?," Leigh suggested casually, eyeing Harper with some concern. "You look like you're ready to fall out. At least use the wagon for a lift."

Leigh tried to turn her forced confinement into something more positive for Harper.

"I think I'm supposed to wait at least until we get past the Bridge. I'll make it." Harper sounded as doubtful as she felt.

Listening to the exchange, Foster jumped in, providing his own recommendations.

"You need to hop in the spare wagon, Harper. You know – where Leigh was stylin' earlier." Foster tried to sound light-hearted, jovial. Completely unlike the tone he adopted when speaking to Leigh. He must really need Jeremy, Leigh thought uncharitably. What a toad. As far as Leigh was concerned, he deserved a D-minus in chemistry for the treatment she had received. Jeremy or no Jeremy.

Leigh resisted the urge to openly counter that throwaway statement of "where Leigh was stylin'" with her own, more accurate, version of "where Leigh was tossed like a sack of potatoes," but as Harper looked extremely exhausted, Leigh figured that Harp probably didn't need to add bickering to a growing list of things to think about.

"Let's go home right after this, okay?" Leigh whispered in Harper's ear as the elder twin slowly accepted a gentle push from Leigh into the wagon's comfortable, pillowy interior.

Harper considered that her level of exhaustion was not anticipated given her love of long walks and sports in general. But something was tiring her out. Wearing her down. She had a newly found respect for long distance runners or anyone with the kind of stamina that could bear the heat, the sun, the noise, and the clamor of long range marches. She had never considered how much energy it took to stay cheerful and upbeat in the heat and monotony of a march – even for one as well-intentioned as this.

"A nice long bubble bath is what I need," Harper yawned slightly at just the thought of a heavenly soak. "I can't wait, Leigh. I cannot wait to go home!"

Leigh said nothing, but her feelings of unease were every bit as intense as Harper's feelings of physical discomfort.

As Lydia drove towards Eco, and away from Idislewilde, she saw an amazing sight from her rear view window. Tabitha, the family's cat, was running at full speed, her forepaws stretched out like a mountain lion and her face as set and determined as a person on a life or death mission. Watching as the cat veered away from the road and into the woods, Lydia wondered what would make such a housebound pet suddenly take off like a feral wild animal. But there simply wasn't time. She had to get to Eco and fast. Everything in her mind and heart told her that danger was at hand and the appearance of Chester had underscored that feeling.

A call came through the car's phone system.

"Hello?"

There was no doubt who it was as soon as the deep, sonorous voice came through.

"Lydia. We are here at Eco. I have everything under control."

That carefree assurance actually bothered Lydia more than her own unconfirmed apprehension and trepidation.

"You are a saint," she tried to fight against her anxiety, trying to sound as appreciative as she felt was warranted for a man who had willingly given up his Saturday morning to protect her from harm.

"No problem, Lydee. Anything for you. I'll see you when you get here. Explain the lay of the land."

Lydia frowned slightly at that. Explain the lay of the land? What in the world did that mean?

Rather than ask or probe further, she simply hit the red disconnect button and settled into an uneasy state of mind, driving as quickly and as safely as she could to the school that she and Chester had built from the skeletal frame of an abandoned estate to the world's most celebrated safe haven for children and young adults with Special Gifts.

A woman's figure suddenly appeared in the middle of the road and Lydia slammed on brakes. Her seat belts locked against her chest, bracing for what the flexible mind of the car's engineering system thought was an imminent crash. Lydia bit back a scream and struggled to get out of the seatbelt to help the woman who, though unhurt, must be frightened out of her mind. Lydia could only imagine how she would be feeling with such a close call!

Scrambling to her feet, Lydia reached the front of the car and approached the woman slowly, carefully. Suddenly, Lydia felt as if she had entered a time warp in which there was no here, now, tomorrow, yesterday. But as oddly as she felt in the awkward space between herself and the woman, the almost-accident victim appeared to be vaguely familiar.

"I'm Eloise Winthrop, Lydia. Do you remember me now?"

Lydia felt a chill run through her like a bad 'flu. How could she forget the woman that had haunted them for so many years at Eco?

"I do. Thank you for allowing us to use your home for Eco."

Eloise laughed a short, bitter laugh.

"Thank me? I hardly think you understand the wickedness that has gone on as a result of your misguided attempt to bring order to chaos. Do you even know what your villainous twin girls do with their free time? Do you? What kind of mother are you? Do you even CARE about those girls at all?"

Lydia took in a deep breath. Enough was enough.

"I have to go, Eloise. You take care of yourself. I mean – I hope you find peace." Lydia burned inwardly at the chastisement, but she said nothing to reveal her true feelings.

Lydia hurried back to her car, no longer concerned about the safety of a woman who had been dead for a very long time. She had to get to Eco and protect the living. She wasn't sure what Eloise knew about Harper and Leigh, but it was enough to know that as far as today was concerned, they were both safe in a wave of Oceanians who would protect and care for them.

Lydia gunned the engine, like a bull pawing at the ground. Eloise vanished and Lydia continued on her way to Eco, more anxious than ever.

Upon reaching the gates of Eco, Lydia was astonished to see Xavier at the outside of the gates with ten grown MEN – not Prep boys – and at least half as many dogs. And not just any dogs, but Dobermans, Rottweilers, and German Shepherds. Lydia could tell from the bulges on the sides of the men's jackets, that their pockets were stuffed with more than just sweet treats.

Rather than opening the gate, Lydia jumped out of the car and made her way over to Xavier, who separated himself from the pack at her arrival.

"Lydia, I was hoping that you would tell someone inside to let us in, but I'm glad to see that you are finally here, my dear."

Lydia felt like her heart was in her throat and she was ready to choke.

"I did not ask for an army, Xavier. You said you were bringing a few of your Prep boys. I hardly call these men with guns and dogs a few harmless boys."

Xavier blinked. It had not occurred to him that Lydia was going to be angry. He had painted himself as her rescuer, her savior and to have this reaction was something completely unexpected.

"That's unfair, Lydia! I'm here to help you. We are at your disposal. Nothing more."

Lydia glared openly at Xavier. It was one thing for him to persist in sending flowers, or calling, or even insisting on providing unsolicited advice on how to most effectively run a school – something she heard at least once a week from him, but this? This was WAY too much.

"Please ask the men to leave, Zee." Lydia softened it a little. "But you may stay."

Lydia returned to her car and watched as Xavier instructed the men to take their leave. She sat in the car waiting until they were a safe distance away before moving forward to release the gate. As her car began to enter the gates, the men (who had walked away) turned and ran into the gates, with their dogs, guns, and whatever other malicious intent had prompted their arrival in the first place.

Stricken, Lydia jumped out of the car, racing to Xavier, who rushed to her side, his arms out in a beseeching "Please forgive me!!!" gesture.

"It's for your own good, Lydee. You must trust me!" Xavier tried to placate her, his eyes moist and his voice calm and steady. "I only want to help you."

Lydia tried to understand Xavier's position. With all her strength, and with every fibre of her being, she understood that Xavier meant well, but she couldn't let anyone take control of Eco. Eco belonged to her! To Chester! Putting her full weight into it, Lydia shoved Xavier as hard as she could. Watching him stumble was not satisfaction enough, but it was going to have to do because she knew what had to be done.

Lydia flew into Eco, up the stairs, and to the bell tower. Eco's gate slammed closed behind her. She rang the bell ferociously, its pealing sounds reverberating throughout the school and across the lawn. The clamor from the bell seemed to dim all other sounds on the campus. As far away as the town square, the bell could be heard. No one had rung that bell since Chester's disappearance, but everyone from the youngest to the oldest Echo knew that it meant trouble and danger.

The sound of sirens, police and fire, could be heard starting up, drawing closer and closer. Lydia ran back downstairs to greet the First Responders, grateful for their rescue. Upon reaching the lawn, she was proud to see the children had all lined themselves up according to the drills that were rehearsed four times a year. The oldest children, the college-aged Floor Monitors, had their list of names and were going through their assigned lines in methodical order. Xavier's men had vanished, but Lydia didn't trust that they were really gone and she would ask the policemen to help her search every room in Eco (except for a few that were off-limits - like the Room of Clocks - and a few others that had properties best left unexplained and unexplored by Outsiders).

Xavier suddenly appeared, working his way through the organized crowd of children.

"I am so sorry that you didn't trust me to do this the right way, Lydee."

Lydia drew herself up to her full height and looked Xavier square in the eye.

"Men with guns and dogs are not permitted on MY property, Xavier. Not now. Not ever. Do we understand each other?"

Xavier looked at Lydia, trying to fight back his growing admiration for her strength when he so wanted her to be weak and needy, but it was hard to not respect her. She was magnificent!

"We do."

Lydia reached in her pocket, pulling out the device that allowed the gate to swing open and allow the police and firemen to enter.

"Would you like for me to stay, Lydia, and explain things?"

Lydia shook her head.

"I think it's better, Xavier, that you go."

Defeated, Xavier walked away. Giving up ground – this time.

Lydia watched him leave, feeling more alone and anxious than ever. What had possessed Xavier to try to take over Eco? Wasn't Lakeshore Prep enough for him to manage without trying to instigate a coup d'etat of Eco? And where were those ten dishonorable men and their weapons?

The captain of the police force strode purposefully over to Lydia, his own canine flanking his side. Lydia smiled. Good will flush out evil, she thought as a peaceful feeling replaced the raging emotions from just seconds before. Lydia watched as the gates closed, putting bars of steel between herself and Xavier. Only then did she feel completely safe and secure. With Xavier on one side of Eco, and she on the other.

"Captain Daniels? Please. Let me show you the way and explain what has happened. Our security has been breached and we need your help and the help of your men. There are ten intruders in Eco with guns and dogs. They came uninvited and I'm afraid for the safety of our children."

The captain shook Lydia's hand and followed her wordlessly, aware that this was the first time that he had set foot into a building that was reputed to house some of the biggest mysteries in Oceania. But as a trained officer of the law, he was more than ready to apprehend a band of renegades. It was the other unknown spectacles at Eco that made him nervous, but there was something soothing in Lydia's manner that put his mind at ease. He knew that she might not be able to fight men with guns (that's why he was there, right?), but she was more than capable of handling all the rest, and between the two of them, order would be restored to Eco. She could count on that.

Spectra looked out at the sunny sky. She and the other three inhabitants of Emerson Pond were unofficially in hiding from the town's gaiety associated with the march. No one knew that they were hiding because few ventured out to visit. There had been Chester – but that was before he got himself lost. And the Lt. Colonel from Marbury, who had parked submarines that had not been removed (out of respect for him) at the Lake's bottom. Those submarines were there for heaven knows what purpose, but they chose to tolerate them as long as the inhabitants remained inside the submarines and not out.

And then there was Lance. A quiet, but most observant young man who had captured their hearts and imaginations like none other. It was as if they had spontaneously produced a favorite son, nephew, godson, and little brother. All at once.

"Today is the march!" Spectra announced, as if a question or concern had been posed by one of the foursome.

Kayla laughed.

"I honestly don't know why they keep at it. Something always happens during that march. Every year. Remember the child that fell off the Marania Bridge one year?"

Mona shuddered.

"At least it didn't drown."

Aura nodded gravely.

"But it did drown. It just came back. And has had visions and premonitions ever since. That's why it's at Eco. The parents are now terrified of it."

"Stupid parents," Mona observed, looking down at the piece of knitting she was making. "I think you should have to pass a Stupidity Test or something before you're allowed to have children."

"I often think we should join the march," Spectra offered. Kayla scoffed. Her snort said it all.

"It's for a good cause!," Spectra continued defensively.

"We know that, Spectra, but we also know that it is dangerous for us to leave Emerson Pond unattended for longer than an hour. Going to The Shut the other day was precarious enough."

The four fell silent at that memory. It had been quite a moment, their entrance into a place that had held fond memories for them. Things had gone well until the sighting of Eloise and J.L. Winthrop. What a spectacle that had caused!

"What a terrible way to go through eternity," Aura shivered. "Chasing each other like demons."

Kayla shrugged.

"Where there's that much passion, there's still that much love. I don't think J.L. is even aware of it – much less Eloise. No one chases after someone for that long that they barely like. Not even the dead."

The room fell silent at this observation.

"So, what do you think? Do you think the Colonel will visit us?" This was Mona, who had always had a small crush on Mortimer Blaine. She much preferred to focus on the living.

Mona's question hovered in the quiet space. No one ventured a response and Mona retreated to her own thoughts. Kayla smiled sympathetically at Mona's rather obvious feelings for the Colonel, but not sharing them (not even in the slightest), she kept her own counsel and said nothing.

Aura was the first to break the silence.

"I say we cook something special for tonight. In case Lance comes – and perhaps the Colonel?"

Mona blushed deeply and tried to hide the evidence by rubbing her cheeks vigorously in a pretend show of random energy. It was really to hide the excitement she was beginning to feel over the mere possibility – the mere PROSPECT – of seeing the Colonel again.

"That would be lovely," Mona ventured. "Let me know if you need my help."

Aura nodded, her eyes meeting Kayla's in a quick understanding gesture of Mona's latent affections.

"Sure. I'm sure there will be plenty for us to do together."

Mona beamed, happy at the thought of doing something that might contribute to a lovely evening with two of her favorite people: Lance and Mortimer.

"Where do you think they are now?," Kayla queried. "Are they nearing the Bridge?"

Aura fell silent, holding her hands to her temples.

"They are. About ten yards from the Bridge. The march is almost over."

"Do you sense anything bad?", Mona ventured, her heart and mind on the Colonel.

Aura touched her temples again. Her face lost its smooth composure.

"Dear God."

The other three women froze at her tone.

"Something awful is about to happen on that Bridge, my sisters. Something Perfectly Awful."

"Is it the Colonel?," Mona blurted out, worry for the aging man's health at the top of her list of fears.

"It involves the children of Chester. The twins."

The room fell silent.

"We MUST save them!," Kayla demanded. "For Chester's sake!"

The silence deepened after that outburst and fear could be smelled in the room, like a musty, dank scent.

"But HOW?," Mona wailed. "We have no car and they're practically on the bridge! What can we do? How can we warn them?"

Aura gritted her teeth.

"We go down to the bottom of the Pond and ask the – ask THEM for help. If we don't, we'll never forgive ourselves."

That was a true statement and there was nothing more that could be said in retraction. The four women rose as one body, making sure that nothing was left cooking on the stove or oven, and made their way out of the familiar, safe cottage to the unknown territory of the bottom of their Pond.

Courageous, yes, but more than that. Loyal. To the friend that had visited them when all others in Oceania had been too afraid. Bravery didn't prepare them to go to the bottom-most depths of Emerson Pond. Nor did a misguided sense of duty to just do what was right. They went from the strength of memories of a friend who had taken the time to make them feel safe, loved, and protected.

This they did for Manchester Stuart Reynolds.

I am SOOOO glad to see that the bridge is finally in sight because I know for a fact that Leigh is more than ready for all the hoopla to be over, and to be perfectly honest, if this was not one of the things I just absolutely have to do as Lady of the Chair to pave the way to be Prep Princess, I would be in Somerset at Germy's game cheering him on. Or teasing Leigh about the prospect of snagging Lance - within the safety of our bedrooms. He's mad as dry spit that I couldn't bring my cell on the march to talk to him, but those are the rules – as stupid as they are. The Lady can't be seen doing anything other than attending to her court and the people of Oceania and

Marbury blahblahblah. No phone chats. After that really unfortunate conversation with Leigh at the Prep's home football game, I am not allowed to even send telepathic messages to anyone while I'm in Lady regalia. I have to pretend that the only people I care about are Preppers, Namers, and townies that matter. My sister and I will be like toxic waste on the social scale if I mess this up.

Sometimes I wonder if being Prep Princess is really worth it.

As we near the bridge I see the guy named Oliver. He looks just like his picture he sent to me online. He's walking with an older man in a soldier's uniform. If it wasn't for the fact that the old guy looks really good in it, I'd wonder if he isn't more than slightly bonkers. It feels like it's a hundred degrees out here! You couldn't pay me – even with the thought of being Prep Princess – to be in all that hot stuff with collars and jackets and long pants. No way. The weather man was wrong. It's almost eighty-five degrees in bright, stifling sunshine. I honest to goodness feel like ripping this dress off down to my pink camisole.

"Okay. Here's the deal, Harper," Lance turns to look at me, his face torn between amusement and seriousness. "You need to go to the front of the line now to get into position to meet the Marbury guy with the horn – what's his name? Oliver? – and then you climb back in the wagon so we can move as fast as possible to Marbury and get this all over with, okay?"

Lance says it all in a rush like it is almost all one word. I wonder if he's had a chance to talk to Leigh. They are supposed to be getting to know each other better in a romantic sort of boy-discovers-he-loves-girl kind of way, but the last time I saw Leigh she looks just as hot as me and the idea of gazing at some boy – even our own gorgeous Lance – is not the answer for her right now and I really can't blame her. Even the thought of being touched by anyone leaves a scorch mark in my brain.

"Sure. I can do it." I smile back at Lance, looking over my shoulder to see where Leigh is hiding because she is all the way in the back and she's supposed to be up front with me. I want to call out a loud warning to her, but I know that Foster would be all over her like a swarm of ants on honey, so I keep quiet. If she wants to hang back, play incognito, that's fine with me.

"Where's Leigh?"

That was scary-ready-to-turn-Nazi-at-any-minute Foster.

"She's trying to catch up, but the crowds are so huge…" I start trying to cover for her, but it's too late. The only thing that will calm Foster is seeing us together. If he could sew us together like Siamese twins, he would. I'm convinced that he would. I know better than Leigh or anybody except for Germy how much Foster wants to go to the Majors one day and a school like Prep can make that happen for him. Get him into the best baseball college that will shoot him straight to Yankee stadium – or wherever. That's his dream and he needs Germy to get him there and he's not going to let two stupid (in his opinion) girls in poofy dresses mess that all up.

I watch as Foster races back to find Leigh who, at least for the moment, is lost. At least to us. But if Foster has his way, not for very long.

Six-year-old Kara Boardman, who had sneaked away from Eco, was not pleased to see that everyone seemed to rush away so very far ahead of her. Her only consolation was that Miss Lydia's daughter, Leigh, was willing to walk with her and stay behind the others. That made her feel special and it helped her to forget the awful animal faces that seemed to fill her dreams. The bloody bunny in her classroom was no longer the talk of the Lower School (thanks to the Room of Clocks), but for some odd reason Kara remembered every detail and tried as hard as possible to pretend that she had nothing to do with that terrible day. If anyone brought up the fact that they had not seen her presentation she would say that it was that other Kara that presented it and the other children would get confused and walk away, shaking their heads, wondering what other Karas were at Eco and if this Kara herself wasn't just plain old cuckoo.

But Kara was telling the truth about seeing another Kara. It was Kara Victoria Pennington who had befriended the little Kara immediately after the bunny incident. "Miss Penny" – that's what Kara Pennington had asked to be called - had told little Kara not to be afraid. Miss Penny told Kara that they shared the Gift of Animal Telepathy that made them capable of sensing when animals were in pain or afraid or when evil was near.

Thinking about what Miss Penny had shared with her, Kara clutched Leigh's hand tightly because those feelings were starting to come over her. Stronger than ever.

Kara tugged on Leigh's hand. Leigh looked down at the little girl.

"Tubby Tibby is on her way. She says you are to wait. Not walk too fast because she's getting tired from running so hard."

Leigh felt her mouth go dry. How would this girl know anything about her nickname for Tabitha? And even more to the point – why was Tibby RUNNING?

Leigh felt sick. Her head felt light and she knew that between the heat and the ramblings of this little girl, she was one step away from falling forward into a dead faint.

"Look!" The little girl whirled around, twisting Leigh with her, her index finger pointing like a dagger. "There's Tibby!"

At that point, Leigh was really ready to just fall out but she turned instead. And just in time!

Like a miniature lioness, Tabitha stretched out into a straight leap into Leigh's arms. Panting, tongue hanging out of her mouth at a sharp right angle, Tabitha recovered slightly as Leigh pushed her face down into the cat's fluffy exterior. Tabitha seemed to finally catch her breath and as Leigh bent over her face, the cat touched Leigh's nose in a show of endearment and uttered a soft, "DANGER, Mommy, RUN!" If Leigh had not loved that cat with all her heart, she would have dropped her (and herself) directly to the ground, and closed her eyes – anything but consider the fact that Tabitha was TALKING. As it was, she could only stare, open-mouthed, in terrified bemusement.

Kara looked up at Leigh.

"She said to run. I think we should run."

At those words, Foster showed up.

"The only running you will be doing is at the FRONT of the line, Leigh. Do you hear me? And put that crazy cat down!"

Foster grabbed Tabitha from Leigh's arms and then held her away from himself in disgust.

"This cat is practically dead, Leigh. Did you know that?"

Leigh snatched Tabitha from his unsympathetic hands and cradled her in her arms. The cat's breaths were low and faint, but she was purring deep inside as if to comfort Leigh, who was almost beside herself with grief.

"She said to tell you good-bye. She said it doesn't hurt at all and that she's going to play with a little girl named Ophelia who was lost because of an accident a long time ago."

Leigh looked at the little girl, whose pretty face was serious with purpose.

"She said not to worry about her." The little girl hesitated. "She said good-bye Mommy. I'll love you forever."

Leigh let out a wail that seemed to rip apart the air around them. All gaiety stopped in place, as if snuffed out like an extinguished candlewick. Leigh screamed out Tabitha's name over and over like a mantra.

Harper turned to see what had caused Leigh's distress because she knew without a doubt that it was Leigh who was shouting. It was what she was shouting about that was so confusing. What was going on with Tabitha?

"Come, Miss Lady!"

A clown came over to her. To act as her escort? Harper felt a quick thrill of fear and dismissed it. Obviously, the clown was sent by the Master of Ceremonies to escort her to the bridge. He even had one of those little clown cars. It was adorable and as tired as Harper felt, it looked like a Rolls Royce. The bridge was really less than five minutes away, but that five minutes would go like sixty seconds in a car and Harper had no twinges of regret or shame as she hoisted herself and her long dress into the car.

The clown honked his nose that lit up in playful introduction.

"I think we know each other, Miss Lady."

Harper decided to play along.

"Sure we do, Mr. Clown."

The clown didn't say anything, but his manner appeared less eager, more cautious.

"I'm ready to capture My Lady and take her away!"

Harper was starting to feel uncomfortable and wondered if walking wasn't perhaps a better idea.

"To the bridge, My Clown!" Harper felt the forced laugher come out as she internally grappled with growing feelings of fear and revulsion.

The clown stepped down on the accelerator and sped away at an angle away from the bridge.

Harper closed her eyes. Dear God. No. Kidnapped by a Marbury clown? What was next? A fire-breathing giant?

"I'm taking you somewhere special," the clown shrieked over the roar of the engine. "Poem Man has something very special planned for his little Leigh."

LEIGH? POEM MAN??? Oh my God! Harper was desperate to get out of the little car, but was too afraid jump out as the car seemed to be doing a hundred miles an hour. To turn around and face the fact that the marchers were growing more and more distant would be even worse. Despite Foster's frantic surge towards the jeep (he was handicapped by being so far in the back of the crowd with Leigh), the lunatic clown had gotten too much of a headstart and there was nothing anyone could do but watch in horror.

Leigh stared in disbelief as Harper disappeared in a clown car with a clown man. She watched as Foster chased the car as fast as he could, but it was clear that the car had been revved up to go much faster than the cars in the circus and Foster was outgunned. Like a dark streak of lightning, Cal raced passed Foster, rushing towards the errant car. Holding the now deceased Tabitha, who lay limp in her arms, Leigh watched as Cal chased the car until he was just a black dot in the distance. Unable to see anymore of Harper or the clown, car, or Cal, Leigh finally sank to the ground and did the only thing left to do.

She wept.

The sun was as hot in Somerset as it was on the Marania Bridge, but around noon it felt like the yellow ball of fire had moved closer to the earth and Jeremy was literally baking. If it wasn't against the rules, he would have stripped to his boxers to play the rest of the game. Suddenly, he felt as if someone had punched him HARDER than hard in the gut and he bent over, his head hanging down to his knees. He knew that everyone was waiting for him to throw out the next pitch, but it was all he could do to not THROW UP. He felt dizzy, sick, scared.

And crazy.

The only thing he could think of was one thing and he screamed out her name as if his life (or hers) depended on it.

"HAAARRPEERRRR!!!!"

The four women of Emerson Pond realized that they were too late when they saw the chaos and empty eyes of the marchers, who seemed disoriented and out of sorts.

Leigh, still in shock from her double tragedy (a newly departed Tibby and kidnapped Harper), was sitting on the ground unable to move, talk, or think. No one dared to touch her. Everyone knew that Leigh and Harper were closer than close and this abduction represented a second kind of death for the teen whose huddled frame resembled the pose of a small and helpless child.

Aura knelt beside Leigh. Retrieving a vial from her cloak, she poured some liquid out in the palm of her hand and gently pushed Leigh's face down into the wetness. Leigh lapped it up gently, like

Tabitha, who had always taken Leigh's special treats from her soft palm.

"I am too late for the kitty, Leigh. I hope you understand and are able to allow the peace from the elixir to soothe you."

Leigh felt better than she had felt since she was about three years old and Mother and Father were still happily together and Everything Was Good. She had forgotten what that felt like and she realized that it was better than she had remembered. She understood about Tabitha. It was time for her to go and she had died a hero. She had tried to warn Leigh to run. And she had called her Mommy – MOMMY!! The sting of emotion brought tears to Leigh's eyes, but something in that sweet drink took away the bitterness and she felt only the warm glow of Tabitha's love.

"We were too late to save the girl." That was Kayla.

Leigh felt hollow inside. The thought that Harper might be no more was too much to take in at once.

"She is alive," Mona whispered soothingly, kneeling down on the other side of Leigh. "But she is with a very bad man."

"A dangerous man." This was Electra's observation and she said it with a contempt that matched her expression.

Foster looked at the surreal scene. The four women of Emerson Pond, a frozen Leigh, and a dead cat. The end of his career in Major League Baseball.

First things first. Foster gently extricated Tabitha from Leigh's arms. Handling dead cats was not on his To Do List, but he knew that Jeremy was going to lose his mind over what had just happened to Harper and the least he could do was help Leigh regain herself. If he had been less strong, he would have wanted to sink down beside her and cry. But, he was not weak and he would do what was necessary to take care of what had become an unbelievably awful situation. He carried Tabitha over to a bush and covered her gently with leaves. A proper burial would have to wait until they were back at Idislewilde with shovels and a box.

Finally, the sirens. Someone had had the presence of mind to call the police and they had finally arrived. The four women gathered themselves up and seemed to melt into the day as if they were wisps of cloud. Just in time as the police officers jumped out of their cars, walkie-talkies crackling with communication from their dispatch officers back at the Oceania station.

"We have this under control, people," the senior officer began authoritatively. "We need statements."

"You need to find my sister," Leigh said evenly, and her quiet intensity was unmistakable. Nothing short of finding Harper – and finding her Right Away – was going to be satisfactory to the young girl. It was clear that as far as she was concerned, giving eyewitness reports were worthless wastes of time. Her glare said it all. Even five-year-olds know that most people don't remember anything correctly. She had seen a clown drive off in a clown car, but who's to say that it wasn't just some lunatic red-headed banker whose getaway car was a tiny European import?

The younger officer knelt down and stared Leigh in the eye. He recognized correctly that she was in shock, but he needed her.

"We'll get her back, Miss Reynolds. That's why we're here. Now, we need your help. Are you ready to help?"

Leigh nodded. If nothing else, she could do that.

"I'd do anything to get Harper back. So, yes, of course I'm ready. What are you waiting for?"

�

The building seemed to hum. It was a sign that something was off, amiss. Not that Lydia needed a hum, song, or any kind of music to remind her that things at Eco were out of control. First, Xavier. And now an infiltration. She was convinced that those henchmen had somehow made their way into Eco and were up to some shenanigans. What were they about? Why were they at Eco?

Lydia headed for the steps that led to the library. She didn't really think that the men were there, but it was worth a shot to see if they had managed to make it this far through Eco. Where were the dogs?

Speaking of dogs. Where was Cal? She had seen him at Idislewilde earlier that day. She had overheard Lance saying that he was taking him on the march, but it had seemed that Cal had hung back, stayed close to home when it was time for the children to leave.

She could definitely use him now, Lydia thought wistfully. Cal had a heart of gold and a mouth of very sharp teeth. A lethal (and welcomed) combination in a building this size with ten grown men hanging about with ill-intentions. Turning a corner, she took in a sudden breath of fear before realizing it was one of the police officers.

"Thank God."

The officer smiled.

"It might be better if you stay outside with the children, Mrs. Reynolds, and let us handle this."

The walkie-talkie crackled and the officer turned his head to listen. His face turned pale and he averted his eyes.

The sick feeling in Lydia's stomach got worse. Much worse.

The officer turned back to look at her. It was plain that his news was Not Good.

"Ma'am, I think you'd better sit down."

For Lydia, those were the worst seven words she had ever heard.

She was in the hallway with no chair in sight, so she quietly knelt to the floor like a novice in supplication to the altar, her eyes fixed on the officer's face.

"Tell me." Her demand was quietly made, but the passion in her eyes was unmistakable. This had something to do with the children. She could feel it. It was Harper. She felt the warmth of her first-born's cheek against hers – something Harper still did when she was feeling particularly babyish. At night, or whenever she was feeling afraid for some reason, Harper would creep into Lydia's room and rub her cheek against her mother's before wrapping her arms around Lydia's neck, and climbing into the expansive bed.

Harper was her oldest child and the pain in her heart was as wrenching as if someone had taken a knife and stabbed her straight through.

"It's one of your girls. A man dressed like a clown has kidnapped her. They tried to catch them –"

Lydia held up her hand.

"And Leigh?"

The officer shrugged slightly.

"There was only news about the one who was kidnapped, ma'am. Would you like for me to inquire?"

Lydia nodded weakly, feeling like all breath was leaving her body. Just the feeling she needed because all she wanted to do was put her head down and rest.

And so she did as she listened to the young officer ask about her baby. Leigh.

"She's fine, Mrs. Reynolds. Would you like for me to bring her home?"

Lydia looked up from the floor, wondering for a split second if this was all just a terrible, stupid dream when suddenly the room started spinning and the officer's mouth fell open and got stuck in an inane position that showed all canines and molars in perfect exposure.

Holding her hands to her temple, Lydia let out a scream and pulled herself off the floor, pushing past the officer who seemed to be paralyzed in one place. Making her way down the corridor, Lydia reached the Room of Clocks where Tatewin was standing guard.

"Tate? Did someone get in to this room?," Lydia gasped, out of breath from the struggle against time that was seeping away millisecond by nanosecond.

"He tried to open the door and it did crack for a split second," Tate confided, her eyes staring straight ahead, not looking directly at Lydia. "But then it got taken care of."

The man in question, one of Xavier's crew, lay prone on the ground, knocked unconscious.

Suddenly the room righted itself and Lydia felt her breathing return to normal. All feelings of vertigo were gone.

"Thank you, Tate. You're a brave girl."

"But it wasn't me, Lydia."

Lydia looked confused.

"It was J.L. Winthrop. He said that no one would ever harm a girl named Kara. Not ever. And then he did something and the man flipped in the air and fell over there."

Feelings of light-headedness returned to Lydia and she wanted nothing more than to lie down with a cool cloth on her forehead, but she had Things To Do.

Finding Harper was at the top of the list. And bringing Leigh home. If J.L. Winthrop terminated the intruders, so be it.

"I guess Oliver won't be coming to Eco today afterall." Tate spoke aloud, but it was obvious that she was directing that statement to no one in particular as Lydia had already walked away from the young girl and was headed for the stairs. Tate followed behind, slowly.

Lydia's cell phone rang.

She snatched it off the waistband and held it to her ear.

"LEIGH?" Her voice was raw with emotion.

It wasn't Leigh. It was a man. A man with a very nasty voice. A voice that sounded like it had slithered up the sewers of life into a world of bright sunlight and its eyes hurt.

"I have Leigh." It was all he said before hanging up.

Lydia dropped the phone, sickened to her core.

There must be some mistake! That lunatic said that he had Leigh, but Leigh was still at the march. Isn't that what the officer said? Why would he think he had Leigh when he had Harper?

Lydia caught herself. How many times had she, their own MOTHER, mistaken one for the other? They played that game to perfection.

Lydia turned to the officer, who had regained his composure and had made his way over to her.

"The man who took Harper? He was aiming for Leigh." She said it all matter-of-factly, despite the fact that her heart was thudding as loudly as a ticking time bomb and the idea to collapse into a dead heap seemed like a pretty good option at that moment.

The officer frowned.

"He took the wrong girl?"

Lydia shook her head, considering the fact that the clown had actually selected the more likely twin to escape. Harper was a tomboy still and was not above getting dirty or putting a tight fist in someone's face. Lydia smiled. Maybe this was actually a reason for cheer. Not that Leigh was incapable of fending for herself, but Harper was so much more likely to construct a daredevil stunt to effect her own release. Yes, she would be afraid, but she would do it because she would consider it worth doing – like some crazy Hollywood stunt. Unlike Leigh, who was far more patient and pragmatic, Harper would use the abduction as A Legitimate Excuse to do something dangerous and foolhardy.

For the first time in her life, Lydia actually hoped she would. She hoped against hope that Harper would do the thing to save her life. And the sanity of her Mother. If she did not get both girls back in one piece, Lydia decided that she would not be able to guarantee her ability to bounce back from this day.

The officer's walkie talkie crackled again. The static was so loud and the voice so faint, it could barely be heard.

"You must go to Marbury, Lido! Save Harper!"

Not again. Chester's repeat appearance was both wonderful and unsettling. He was instructing her to leave Eco and go to Marbury? To save Harper. Nothing made more sense than saving Harper from what was an apparent maniac. If Chester thought she could do it, then she could do it. She WOULD do it.

"That was my husband, Officer. Could you please take me to Marbury? I need to save my daughter - Harper."

The officer looked dazed. He had heard how odd Eco was, but now he knew first-hand that all speculation was – True.

"And the other one? Leigh?"

"We will pick her up on our way to Marbury. That is if we ever get out of here."

The Officer flinched a little at this rebuke.

"At your service, ma'am. Please follow me."

Lydia embraced Tate quickly.

"You've been a very good girl, Tate. You can rest back in your room for now. The danger – at least from those bad men - is all past. Am I right, Officer?"

The young man smiled. Lydia Reynolds was certainly magical. She had no way of knowing that the other nine and their animals had been apprehended. He had just found that out in the text sent to him by his superior officer.

Lydia swished past the officer and made her way downstairs. She was anxious to get to his squad car with the siren blaring to reach Marbury, Leigh, and Harper. Her girls. Her world.

The Officer rushed to keep up with her long strides.

As he reached her side, barking information into the walkie talkie, Lydia blinked rapidly to hold back the flood of tears that threatened to erupt. There was no time for weakness. No time for anything except rescuing her children from what had turned into one of the worst days of her life.

Near the beginning of the ride, Dr. Does-WAY-too-MUCH had jabbed Harper quickly with a needle loaded with sedatives. He was used to dealing with skittish pets and knew how to do it with a smooth, fast, professional motion that brooked no argument or defense.

When Harper awakened, she was in a room filled with pictures of herself that weren't herself. Unlike everyone else in the world (except for Leigh), she knew who she was and she knew that the girl on the wall was Leigh.

"Ahhh...my little Leigh does arise. And I am once again permitted to look into her dazzling eyes."

Right. Poem Man. Writes poems. Badly.

Harper took a deep breath not sure if it was safer to continue to pretend to be Leigh or be herself and KICK BUTT.

"Where am I, Mr. Clown?"

"I prefer you call me Dewey, Leigh. Don't you remember our little pet names from TeenVillage? I was Dewey for 'Do We love each other?' Remember?"

Harper was so grossed out, she thought she would gag. Dewey was a joke and Leigh had been perfectly out of her mind to spend more than one second with such a loser. Even online!

Harper gritted her teeth, trying to figure out from the dank basement, just where they were.

"Dewey," she almost choked on the word, "Can I have some water, please?"

Poem Man looked as pleased as if she had offered him a winning lottery ticket.

"You're making yourself at home!" He beamed at her, the clown make-up seeming to glow with delight. "I'll get the water now."

Harper said nothing. Just watched as Poem Man climbed the mountain of stairs to reach the top of the basement. The door opened and closed. Harper looked around the basement, seeking a means of escape. She noticed a window that was too high up for her to reach and then she saw a shadow move and then move again. She recognized those movements for what they were and felt a surge of elation. The shadow stopped, sitting in place.

It was Cal. Good old faithful Excalibur! He had followed her to this wretched place, and if she knew her Cal (and she did), it wouldn't take him long to help her escape. He hadn't followed her this far for nothing.

Hearing Poem Man's fiddling with the latch to return back downstairs, Harper moved to the center of the room, not wanting to give away the fact that Cal was outside or that Poem Man's goose would soon be cooked. Or, more accurately, BITTEN.

"I have your water, my darling girl!," Poem Man called out gaily, making his way carefully down the rickety steps.

Harper said nothing in return. Like Cal, she was content to simply wait. If all else failed, there was at least one person (other than Leigh or Mother) who would save her and of that she had no doubt.

Mr. Jeremy Alexander Fletcher.

The End of The Enchanted Cottage of Oceania

Book One

June 30, 2010

Illustrator, Nicole Brown

CPSIA information can be obtained at www.ICGtesting.com
Printed in the USA
BVOW031605050612

291828BV00001B/4/P